Plain *Jayne*

HILLARY MANTON LODGE

HARVEST HOUSE PUBLISHERS

EUGENE, OREGON

The author is represented by MacGregor Literary.

Cover by Left Coast Design, Portland, Oregon

Cover photos © Pascal Genest / iStockphoto; AVTG / iStockphoto; Susie Prentice / Shutterstock; Sigrid Olsson / PhotoAlto Agency RF Collections / Getty Images

Author photo by Danny Lodge

PLAIN JAYNE
Copyright © 2010 by Hillary Manton Lodge
Published by Harvest House Publishers
Eugene, Oregon 97402
www.harvesthousepublishers.com

Library of Congress Cataloging-in-Publication Data
   Lodge, Hillary Manton.
   Plain Jayne / Hillary Manton Lodge.
      p. cm. — (Plain and simple)
   ISBN 978-0-7369-2698-0 (pbk.)
   1. Women journalists—Fiction. 2. Amish—Oregon—Fiction. 3. Oregon—Fiction. I. Title.
PS3612.O335P53 2010
813'.6—dc22

                                    2009018880

Printed in the United States of America

      10 11 12 13 14 15 16 17 18 / RDM-SK / 10 9 8 7 6 5 4 3 2 1

For Danny

I couldn't have done it without you.

While Amish believers do reside in western states such as Washington and Montana, the Amish community in this novel is purely a work of fiction. However, several Mennonite congregations make their home throughout Oregon and the Pacific Northwest.

Chapter 1

Sol called me at ten. Wanted to see me in five.

I couldn't tell if I was jittery with espresso or excitement.

"So, Brian." I propped my chin on the edge of our cubicle wall. "Who do you think he's gonna send to Miami?"

Brian sighed and didn't look up. "I have no idea."

"You don't want that story, do you?"

"Marisa would change the locks if I left that long."

"Are you talking about Cuba?" Laura stopped midstride as she nearly passed us. "Did Sol say anything?"

I masked a smirk. "I'll find out in five minutes."

Laura tapped her pencil on the ridge of Brian's cubicle. "*Such* a great story. Cuba, post-Fidel—"

"Miami, in April—" Brian drawled.

There was a moment of silence, out of respect for sunshine. Portland, Oregon, isn't known for its sunny springs.

Miami in April, a shot at an above-fold feature...

I wanted it. I wanted it bad.

⁓⁓⁓

"Have a seat, Tate," Sol said, stretching out in his chair, his cocoa brown arms tucked behind his head. All he needed was a stogie to top off his newspaper editor image, and a year ago that might have been the case. After twenty-five years of marriage, the missus finally got to him.

That, and the building's nonsmoking policy. Instead, Sol's arms lowered and he reached for his stress ball. A copy of yesterday's newspaper covered the immediately visible part of his desk. He tossed the ball from one hand to another.

I sat and crossed my legs.

"How's life?" he asked?

"Um…" Where was this going? "Life is good."

"Any major stresses going on?"

"Not really, no."

"Huh." He set aside the stress ball, adjusted his reading glasses, and leaned over his newspaper. "'Henry Paul Tate of Lincoln City, OR, passed away Monday, March 20, of a heart attack,'" Sol looked up. "I'll skip a bit. 'Tate is survived by his wife, Kathy, daughters Beth Thompson, of Neotsu, OR, and Jayne Tate, of Portland, OR, and granddaughter Emilee Thompson, of Neotsu.'" He folded his hands. "I don't think I need to read the rest. There aren't any other Jayne Tates in Portland who grew up in Lincoln City, much less with a father named Henry."

"Are public records that amusing?"

"Were you going to tell me your father passed away?"

"That's my personal life." Such as it was. "I didn't think it mattered here."

And I didn't. Mom held the service on a Saturday, I drove to Lincoln City long enough to hear my uncle's very long eulogy, sing all three verses of "Blessed Redeemer," and hand wash the punch bowl set.

I did my duty. It wasn't as though I showed up in jeans and a Good Charlotte T-shirt and explained to everyone how my father could suck the joy out of a five-year-old. How he smiled about once a month, and usually to people other than his younger daughter. How my sister Beth married at eighteen to get out of the house, though I explained at the time how leaving for college accomplished the same goal.

No. I wore a nice black pantsuit with sensible heels, played the good daughter, drove home, and vacuumed my apartment.

Sol didn't say anything.

"Really, we weren't close."

He shrugged. "Whether you were close or not makes no difference to me, but I'll tell you this—your work is slipping."

"I'm your best features reporter!"

"Lanahan's my best features reporter. I keep you around for the day he digs too deep and they find him at the bottom of the Columbia River."

"Thanks." I was better than Lanahan and we both knew it, but Lanahan had staff seniority I couldn't accomplish without a fake ID.

"You're welcome. But you're not bad, your sources love you, and you can write your way out of a wet paper bag. That's why it's easy to tell when your work is slipping. Your leads are flabby and your descriptions are clichéd." He picked up a piece of paper and read from it. "'Rain-soaked highway'?" He snorted in disgust. "Are you kidding me? What, you think you're writing for your college paper again?"

"I'll edit anything. You know that."

"But you've never had to edit this much. Look. You've always been the wonder kid around here, but times haven't been kind to this business. We're laying off good reporters left and right and printing more AP celebrity fluff. If Bernstein and Woodward were trying to expose a presidency in this day and age…well, let's just say they wouldn't have gotten that far. Papers around the country are cutting their foreign correspondents and satellite offices or, worse, resorting to online editions only. People don't read newspapers anymore. Can you believe that? I'd be suicidal if my wife didn't have me doing tai chi. Does wonders for my nerves." He set his reading glasses on his desk and massaged the bridge of his nose. "Basically, the way things are going, you need to get yourself back together or look for a job elsewhere. Except, there really aren't jobs elsewhere. When was the last time you took some time off?"

"Aside from weekends…" Not that I ever really relaxed, per se, even on weekends. Either way, my relaxation techniques or lack thereof weren't Sol's business.

"According to your file, you have a lot of PTO time built up. I think you should use it."

Every muscle in my body tightened up. "How long? Is this a forced leave?"

"It's you getting a chance to save your job. I'm doing society a favor—you'd make a lousy waitress. You've got three weeks saved. Use a week and a half, and I'll make up the rest."

"Sol—"

"You might think about some tai chi while you're out."

"What about…Miami?"

Sol sighed. "I'm sending Laura."

The words hit like a blow to my stomach. I could barely breathe. "She can't write a lead."

"Right now, neither can you."

My trip to Miami. My shot at an above-fold feature, all gone because I'd probably slipped too many passive verbs into first lines of my articles.

"It's for the best," he said. "There will be other big stories, Jayne."

I agreed with him out loud, but in my head I was shouting like mad.

* * *

I finished up my last projects and left work early. No sense in sticking around if anything I turned in was going to be thrown right back at me.

I wrestled into my motorcycle gear and hopped on my bike, thinking I might calm my nerves with a ride.

I didn't get past Powell's Books. I guess that's the curse of being bookish. I got lost inside every time I visited, but there are worse places to be lost. Each of the rooms is color coded, but I always got the red room and the rose room mixed up. Not that it mattered—I was still surrounded by hundreds of volumes.

Even as I fingered through shelves of books promising to teach me about fine paper folding, I couldn't get the scene with Sol out of my mind. Ever since I'd started work at the paper, I'd continued to work at ninety miles an hour. I couldn't slow down. I didn't know how to slow down. At this particular moment, I felt as though my insides were tearing me in forty different directions.

What would I do if I had to take a vacation? I didn't want to see my family. My sister would show me which wall she had just painted and what item she had ordered from the Pottery Barn catalogue.

Maybe I'd be okay with that life at some later date, but at twenty-six I wasn't there yet. I didn't know how I'd fit a car seat onto my motorcycle.

Probably couldn't.

One magazine cover caught my eye. A long line of laundry fluttered in the breeze, and a little girl in a dark dress was either hanging it up or taking it down. She faced away from the camera.

I flipped through the pages until I found the article. The journalist—who wasn't half bad—wrote a portrait of a people apart. They forgave when faced with searing hatred. They often provided for other members of the community. They called themselves Amish after Jacob Amman, a man who set his group of followers into motion before fading into obscurity.

My mind starting ticking, even as my insides seemed to quiet down. I couldn't take my eyes off the picture of the girl hanging laundry. What would cause people to live like that, when there are electric dryers with de-wrinkle cycles?

I bought the magazine and started home.

A little internet research revealed an Amish community just outside of Albany. Yet more research reminded me of Harrison Ford's role in *Witness*, Jodi Picoult's *Plain Truth*, and a small army of other books about the Amish. They certainly didn't lack media representation.

I wondered how they felt about that representation. Nothing I'd read made this group seem as if they particularly enjoyed the limelight. I wondered how accurate that representation really was. The idea of a utopian society, working off the land and truly caring for each other—frankly, I had a hard time buying into it. Even if it did work, what was their secret?

I read a little more and learned that the Amish were similar to the Mennonites in their pursuit of a simpler lifestyle. Both were pacifists and against infant baptism, but the Mennonites connected to city electricity and drove cars. The Amish who left the community often became Mennonite.

My mind started whirring again. A column the paper occasionally picked up was written by a Mennonite woman—could she have connections to the Amish? Probably. I chewed my lip as I considered the possibilities.

A story was in here, and I had three weeks all to myself.

⁓⁓⁓

Shane frowned at me. "You're going to do what?"

I suddenly regretted my need to share the plan with my boyfriend. "I've got it all worked out," I said, a little defensive. "I'm off work for three weeks. There's an Amish community outside Albany. I'll stay in Albany for the first week or so. I'm hoping I can board at one of the farms after that."

Shane leveled his serious brown eyes on me. "You're going to knock on doors and ask if anyone has room in the hayloft?"

I straightened my shoulders. "We occasionally print the column of a Mennonite woman—"

"What?"

"Don't interrupt. Ethel Beiler's the name of the columnist. I already talked to her. She knows a couple families in that area, and she's going to talk to them about me staying with them."

"That's crazy."

"That's journalism."

"Jayne." Shane released a frustrated breath. "Your dad just died."

"We weren't close. I told you that."

"But he was your dad. It doesn't matter if you were close or not."

We weren't getting anywhere. "Do you have anything interesting in your fridge? And when I say interesting, I don't mean, 'it's changed color since last month.'"

"There's some Mongolian chicken. Tell me again how long you're planning on being gone."

"About three weeks."

"Are you…" he hesitated. "Are you still serious about us?"

My eyes widened. "Of course I am! Are you?"

"We've been together six months. You've met my parents, my brothers, everybody."

I sat down beside him. "And I think they're great, really."

"But you don't want me to meet your family."

"You don't want to."

"Yes, I do."

"No, really, you don't. I'm trying to save you the mind games, the guilt trips—you don't need that. *We* don't need that."

"Your sister? Your sister's like that?"

"My sister is brainwashed, and anything we say gets parroted back to the parents."

"Parent. Your dad's dead."

I cupped his face with my hands and planted a kiss on his unresponsive lips. "Trust me? Please?"

He sighed. "Three weeks?"

"Three tiny, little baby weeks. I'll be back before you know it. I do have a favor to ask…"

"Yeah?"

"Pick up my mail?"

"For you? Anything. Just make sure you come back."

≈≈≍⁄ℐ⁄ℼ≈

I knew I couldn't head out of town without clearing it with Joely, Kim, and Gemma, so I called them all and set up lunch for the following day.

Joely Davis, Kim Keiser, and Gemma DiGrassi were, for all intents and purposes, my best friends in the world. Kim and Gemma I knew through the paper. Kim was on city beat—and the only writer I knew who can make a highway construction piece read like an acetic social commentary.

Gemma worked in food, which meant she ate at fabulous restaurants and criticized the staff. Despite her job, she was one of the sweetest people I knew. And she made amazing *pots de crème*.

Joely and I met when I was on the crime beat—she was usually the only cop on scene with a sense of humor. I introduced her to Kim and Gemma, and we've all lived in each other's pockets ever since.

Joely shook her head as I approached the table. "Such a sweet bike. It's a Triumph, right?"

"We saw you through the window," Kim added. "Sit. Order. I'm hungry."

I glanced over the menu and picked everything I might not be able to eat while I was gone.

Kim lifted an eyebrow after the waitress left. "Giving up food for Lent and eating while you can?"

I shook my head. "I'm headed to Amish country for a couple weeks."

"As punishment for what?" Joely asked.

Gemma swatted her arm. "Shut up. You'll have fun, Jayne. My aunt did that—went on a buggy ride and everything."

"Where did your aunt go?"

"Ohio."

"I'm actually heading to a community near Albany."

"What about the Miami story?" Kim asked, swishing the ice around in her water glass.

"Laura got it. I'm actually on leave for a bit."

Gemma nodded. "Because of your dad? That's probably a good idea."

"Laura can't write a lead to save her life," Kim said. "What are you going to do?"

"I'm using the time to get a story on my own."

I received three blank looks.

"Freelance," I clarified.

"Let me get this straight." Kim leaned forward. "You're taking leave to get this story? Did Sol not want it?"

"Sol doesn't know anything about it. The break was his idea."

"He wants you to take time off, and you're using it to get a story in Amish country?"

"Yes." I looked down and unrolled my napkin, setting my utensils aside and placing the napkin in my lap.

I could feel the exchange of looks crisscrossing the table.

"Look," I said, "I don't do vacations. I'm a reporter—so I'm reporting. It's what I do."

Joely shrugged. "Hey, if you want to spend your time off writing about riding in a buggy, knock yourself out."

"Wow. Three weeks," Kim said with a chuckle. "You'll love that. The simple life, no BlackBerry—"

"Who said I had to give up my BlackBerry?"

"Are you positive you'll have reception?" Gemma asked.

"Then I'll drive to town."

"Tell me how it all goes," Joely said, leaning forward. "My cousin—the one in Pennsylvania—says he busts Amish kids all the time."

Somehow, that didn't seem to jive with my mental image from what I'd read. "Busts? Use your civilian words, please."

"Do you have any family members who aren't cops?" Kim asked.

"Just my grandmother—on my mom's side."

I snorted. "So what do these kids do? Use unkind words when cow tipping?"

Joely shrugged. "The teen boys drive like they're not aware they're mortal, they throw huge parties with kids coming in from several other states... Tim says they hand out MIPs like candy canes at Christmas."

"Minor in Possession," Kim translated before anyone asked.

"Amish kids will do that?"

"With enthusiasm. Hey, it's the conservative kids who can rebel the hardest. Last month, my brother arrested two homeschool kids for dealing meth. It can happen anywhere."

"So." Kim grabbed my hand. "What are you doing with your bike while you're gone?"

"I've got to get there somehow."

"You're going to drive a bike to an Amish community?" Kim laughed. "What about your car?"

"In the shop. If I leave a key with one of you guys, can you pick it up?"

They all nodded. "No problem," Kim assured me. "So…what does Shane think about all this?"

"He thinks I'm crazy. Nothing new."

"I still think it's weird that you guys have rhyming names," Joely said.

The waitress came with a tray full of food. Joely, Kim, and Gemma received their respective plates…

And I got my four.

"Have enough to eat there?" Kim asked, poking at my sushi with her fork.

"I think it'd be clever," said Joely, "if you freeze-dried your leftovers."

Gemma nodded. "Then you could reconstitute them at your leisure. You know…a little water, some sleight of hand with a camp stove…"

"I hope you're all enjoying this. Maybe I'll learn to cook while I'm there."

"You're afraid of ovens," Kim lifted an eyebrow. "Remember?"

"It's not a fear, per se. It's apprehension," I shot back. "Over a heat source. Joely's afraid of clowns."

Joely crossed her arms. "Lots of people hate clowns. Fear of ovens—that's odd."

"You'll have to tell me what the food's like," Gemma said before taking a bite and chewing thoughtfully. "I've heard it's mainly German. A lot of carbs, a lot of meat…" Her voice turned thoughtful. "You know what I think? I think this trip will surprise you."

"I wanted Miami to surprise me."

"You hate flying," Kim pointed out.

I shrugged. "You may have a point there."

Chapter 2

After packing for five minutes that evening, I realized that maybe taking my bike wasn't the best idea. I had no idea what to bring with me.

Normally, I'm the girl who could travel the world with a shoulder bag. I wad, I roll, and when necessary I do without.

But this time I had no idea if I was dressing to fit in with a church service or a barn raising.

I'm not like most girls. I'm not given to fits of indecision over what to wear on a Saturday night. My sister, Beth, was always the pretty one—I never felt the need to dress up. Jeans and a T-shirt, slacks and a blouse—my wardrobe pretty much ended there. If it was cold, I'd throw on a hoodie or a blazer.

How did the Amish feel about pants, though? None of the women wore pants. Would they be offended if I did? Would I be exempt?

I sighed and dug through my closet. Somewhere at the back I had a skirt my mom made me wear to band concerts in high school.

It was in the back, clipped on a skirt hanger to a cloth I used as a photography drape. I held it up and sighed again.

My hips had grown a bit since I was seventeen.

Defeated, I picked up my phone and called Gemma.

I skipped the preliminary greetings. "I need clothes," I said in lieu of hello.

"Are you ill?"

"Really, I need at least one skirt or something if I have to—"

"You have to be running a fever if the word 'skirt' came out of your mouth."

"Do you want me to call Kim?"

"I'll be there in twenty-five minutes."

Sure enough, she was, with a garment bag in tow. "You weren't specific, so I brought a selection," she said, giving me an awkward one-armed hug that ended with a hand on my forehead. "You don't feel warm."

I rolled my eyes. "I wore a dress to my sister's wedding."

"Right," she said, heading down the hall. "But, see, I wasn't there to see it. And if I didn't see it—did it really happen?"

I didn't honor that with a comeback. Gemma's lips settled into a smile. "Okay, then. I know you've got a lot of black, and frankly, you can wear black slacks with a black blouse and a colored scarf. You'll be dressed like an average Frenchwoman."

"Dressed like your mother, you mean."

Gemma pointed a finger in the air. "And her friends!"

"I need something skirt-ish. I don't know how they feel about women in pants."

She laid the bag on the bed and tugged on the zipper. "You didn't say what length you wanted, so I brought all of them. What size are you, anyway?"

"Larger than I was in high school."

"Helpful. Try this one," she said, giving me a handful of black skirt. "We're about the same size."

I didn't even have the skirt zipped when Gemma began shaking her head. "Nope, not that one. Here—"

"What's wrong with it?"

"It doesn't hit your hips right. Try this." She handed me another.

"It looks just the same."

"It's not."

"But—"

"Kim's on speed dial."

I yanked the second skirt out of her hands and then shimmied until the first fell to my ankles.

"Now..." Gemma's brow furrowed, "remind me why you're gong to investigate the Amish?"

"Look at them. They can't be that perfect."

"I don't think anyone believes they're perfect. If I remember right, the kids are only educated to the eighth grade level."

I shrugged. "It's an instinct thing. I always know when I'll find something."

Gemma opened her mouth, closed it, and turned her attention to skirt number two. "That's the skirt."

We studied my reflection in the mirror. Gemma tilted her head. "I think you're ready to be Amish."

~~~

With Gemma's help, I managed to pack up the panniers and fit my electronic equipment into my laptop backpack. I didn't pack everything, figuring I could always go home if I wanted my extra memory card for my camera. Either way, I needed room for my copy of John Hostetler's *Amish Society*.

I left early the next morning.

The cold April air whispered around my collar as I rode south on I-5. The busyness of Portland disappeared, office buildings giving way to hills and trees.

I missed the buildings. A part of me never felt comfortable outside the city. I forced myself to brush off the feeling and ride on. I was a reporter. I had work to do.

After what felt like forever, I finally parked my bike outside Albany's Comfort Inn on the south end of town.

The room was nice enough, not that I was paying attention. I unloaded the panniers, stuck my digital recorder in my jacket pocket, and headed back out.

~~~

The whirring of saws and other limb-severing equipment could be heard from the street. I parked my bike and proceeded with caution.

More internet research had revealed an abundance of Amish carpentry businesses. And while I did not close my eyes and point to one in the phonebook, I did pick the one whose owner's name sounded the nicest.

Levi Burkholder. Good man name.

The scent of sawdust filled my nose. The door I'd chosen led directly into the shop. Men fed pieces of wood through huge saws; others sanded assembled pieces with electric sanders. Strains of the Blue Man Group melded with the din of the machinery.

One of the workers noticed me. "The customer area is through those doors," he said, pointing.

"I'm looking for Levi Burkholder. I'm a reporter."

"A what?"

"A reporter!" I yelled.

"Reporter. Right. I'll tell Levi. I'll have him meet you in the customer service area."

"The what?"

"Customer service area!" he shouted before turning around. I hoped he was going to look for Levi, but shop culture wasn't my realm of expertise.

As instructed, I waited in the customer service area, where I found outdated copies of *American Woodworking, Modern Woodworking,* and a *Woodcraft* catalogue. I flipped through one and read about wood garage doors making a comeback.

Fascinating stuff.

The door opened and a man stepped in. He was about my height and broad shouldered, although younger than I'd pictured. I put the garage doors down. "Are you Levi?"

"Hmm," he said, seeming to consider the idea. "What if I were to tell you that I was?"

Then I would ask to see ID. "Then I would have a couple questions for you."

He leaned against the counter. "Really."

"If you really were Levi."

"What makes you think I'm not?" His expression turned injured.

I wasn't born yesterday. "We'll call it gut instinct."

"Yes, let's."

"Let's what?"

"Call it gut instinct. You have a very interesting gut, what with its instincts and all. I always thought guts were for digesting. Glad yours can multitask."

I suddenly remembered why I hated small towns; weird people lived there. "It's a gift."

"A very special gift," he said, and probably would have continued if the door hadn't opened. "Hi, Levi. You're just in time. We were talking about her multitasking gut."

The real Levi stood a head taller than the first guy, his wiry body and ruffled dark hair covered in sawdust. He rolled his eyes and looked to me. "Is he bothering you?"

"Not yet," I answered. Close, though.

"I apologize, really. Spencer was just getting back to work."

"I was?"

Levi didn't break his gaze. "He distracts easily. Spence? Go file something."

"Right, boss," Spence answered with a salute.

"Sorry about that." Levi stuck out a callused hand. "Levi Burkholder."

I shook it. "Jayne Tate."

"You're a reporter?"

"Yes. I'm writing a piece on the Amish community, and I was wondering if I could interview you at some point."

"Come on back to my office." He gestured down the hallway, and I followed.

Levi opened the door; I could see Spencer beside the desk.

"Are you trying to be in the way?" Levi asked.

"You told me to file. I'm filing."

"Go help Grady."

"She looks nice. You should ask her out."

"Spence!"

Spencer hustled out the door. "Finding Grady."

Levi turned back to me. "Have a seat. Did I already apologize for him?"

"Yes, you did."

"Well, I apologize again." He tented his fingers. "Have you ever had your own business?"

"No, I haven't."

"If you do, don't hire your friends."

"Point taken."

"They are very hard to fire. I've tried several times. It doesn't help that Spencer is one of the best carpenters in town. And his mother would skin me alive." He shook his head. "What were we talking about?"

"The Amish."

"Why did you want to talk to me?"

"You run an Amish furniture business."

"What do you want to know?"

"How many Amish workers are in your employ? Do you come from an Amish background? How does the Amish lifestyle and work ethic affect your business, if at all?"

He nodded and glanced at his watch. "Those are a lot of questions. Unfortunately, I don't have much time today. I can tell you that I have eight Amish teenagers under my employ. Six of them are carpenters, the young men. Two young ladies come after hours to clean up the shop."

I raised an eyebrow.

"Not that they couldn't make a chair as well as their brothers," he added. "Their families prefer for them to have more...domestic jobs."

I held up a finger. "Do you mind if I record this?"

He shook his head. "Not at all."

I retrieved my digital recorder from my bag, pressed the record button, and set it on his desk. "Thanks."

"No problem. So that's eight Amish teens. I pay all of them what they're worth—a lot of businesses who hire them don't."

"Why don't they?"

"These kids are raised to work hard and expect little in return. It doesn't occur to them to complain."

"Why not?" When I was a teen, it had occurred to me all the time, to my parents' chagrin.

"Their group culture centers around a strong work ethic, and their personal identities center around that group culture."

"What's your personal connection to the Amish?"

"Pardon?"

"You sound like you have more than a passing knowledge of them."

He checked his watch. "An interesting question for another day. What's your schedule like tomorrow?"

I made the pretense of pulling my date book out of my bag.

Tomorrow's page was blank.

"I have time in the morning and later in the afternoon," I said.

"Do you want to come back by in the morning, then?"

"That works." I began to pencil it in. *Levi, woodshop.* "What time?"

"Ten thirty?"

"Ten thirty." I wrote it in before looking up. "Thanks for your time today."

He smiled. "You're welcome. I'll walk you out."

"That's all right. I'm sure I can find my way."

"I don't know where Spencer is."

I hoisted my bag over my shoulder. "Lead the way."

Spencer was indeed lying in wait at the front counter. "Very nice to meet you. Come back again."

I waved a goodbye.

Levi followed me out the door. "He's stupid but harmless."

"I'll take your word for it."

"That your bike?"

I allowed myself a smile. "It is."

"2007 Triumph Bonneville?"

"2008."

"What's the capacity?"

"About 865 ccs."

Levi let out a low whistle. "She's pretty."

I smiled. "I think so." I reached for my helmet.

"Drive safe."

"I will," I said, before turning the ignition switch and revving the motor. When I turned the corner, I noticed Levi still stood near the curb.

I stopped for lunch, picked up some groceries, and took a long ride through the back roads of Albany before returning to the hotel that afternoon. Once I was settled in there, I checked my messages.

Joely wanted to know if I'd been run over by a horse yet.

Gemma left a voice mail with care instructions for the black skirt.

Kim let me know that Laura emailed the paper, informing them that, in less than twenty-four hours in Miami, she'd managed to wind up in the ER with sunstroke.

Nothing from Shane.

And nothing from Ethel the Mennonite columnist, who had sounded optimistic about finding an Amish host family for me.

I thought about calling Shane but then changed my mind. With me gone, he was probably stationed in front of the TV, and a conversation punctuated with "How could he miss that shot?" wasn't my idea of fun.

Instead, I typed out my notes from my interview with Levi and settled in for an evening watching *Little House on the Prairie* reruns.

I parked my bike in front of Levi's shop at ten thirty the next morning. I entered through the customer service office, a little electronic *ding* signaling my presence. Footsteps sounded down the hall. As they approached, they seemed to slow until the person stepped cautiously around the corner.

"Are you the, um, the reporter?" the man asked, his face turning brick red.

"Yes, I am," I said slowly, not wanting to scare him.

His head bobbed a couple times. "Okay. Okay, good, that's good. Um, Levi told me if you came that he'd be back in just five, maybe six minutes."

"Oh. That's fine."

"I'm Grady," he said, holding out his hand like a peace offering.

"Nice to meet you, Grady."

"Did you, um, go to high school in Lincoln City?"

Oh, no. His face did look a little familiar. "Taft?"

A tentative smile touched his lips. "Yeah. Are you Beth's sister?"

I sighed on the inside. More than sixty miles away, and I still couldn't run incognito. "Yes. My older sister."

"We graduated the same year. I moved here a couple years ago," he said, giving a sheepish smile. "Too many carpenters in Lincoln City."

"True, very true." As in, you could throw a rock in any direction and hit a contractor.

"I was sorry to hear about your dad," he added. "My mom told me."

My inward sigh deepened. I hugged my arms to myself. "Thanks," I said, not knowing what else to say.

Levi chose that moment to step through the shop door. "Good, you're here." He closed the door behind him. "Hope you haven't been waiting long, Jayne."

I shook my head. "Grady and I have been catching up."

"We went to the same high school," Grady told Levi.

Levi's eyebrows lifted. "Really? In Lincoln City?"

"Her dad was an elder in the church I grew up in."

Ah. No wonder he knew. "He passed away recently," I blurted out, wanting to get that in the open before Grady could.

Levi's face softened. "I'm sorry to hear that."

I hiked my bag higher up my shoulder and nodded.

"I'm ready to go when you are," he said.

"Go?" I'd anticipated another interview in his office.

"I'm desperate for coffee."

"There's coffee in the kitchen..." Grady offered.

"Spencer made it."

Grady winced. "Oh."

Levi turned back to me. "Are you game? There's a coffee shop within walking distance."

"Ah...sure. That sounds fine."

"Excellent." He brushed off the few remaining wood shavings from his shirt. "If Mrs. Van Gerbig calls, tell her the walnut came in and she'll be very pleased."

Grady nodded and then Levi and I set off.

"Tell me how you decided to write about the Amish," Levi said about six steps into our walk. "I gather you're not on assignment."

"I'm a staff reporter for the *Oregonian*," I answered, fighting the indignation welling inside me. "But I also write freelance on the side."

"No offense to your professionalism. I just figured there's no breaking story around here—didn't think a newspaper would pay for you to come down unless someone was dead. You're at the *Oregonian*? I think I've read some of the pieces you've written."

I must have heard him wrong. "Really?"

"Didn't you write that article on children in foster care?"

Officially impressed. The indignation died down. "Yes, that was me."

Granted, he very well could have googled my name. Most of my stories live on in online archives.

"I remember reading that story. You made the children and their foster parents seem so…real."

"They are real."

"A lot of people don't like to observe the reality. They record the surface and pat themselves on the back. You didn't." He shot me a look. "A lot of writers do that with the Amish."

"I noticed that."

"Will you be different?"

"I'll try. From what I've read, the Amish hold the rest of the world at arm's length. I can only observe so much from the outside."

"That piece you wrote about the gubernatorial scandal—that wasn't bad either."

I suppressed a grin. "That was actually a whole series. I was the one who discovered the diverted funds."

"I'll bet you're popular in Salem."

"I'm fairly certain there's a picture of me with some darts in the middle. I had good sources, though. Something I need for this story too."

He seemed to process that thought for the rest of the walk.

The café featured small, uncomfortable-looking booths, cranky baristas, and coffee so strong I felt my tooth enamel cringe.

"Much better," Levi said after a sip. "Spencer makes the office coffee much too strong."

"Spencer's is too strong?" Stronger than the cup o' joe eating away at my stomach lining? "Does he brew it to float a horseshoe?"

"Hand planer."

"Ah." How appropriate.

"Are you going to answer my question?"

I furrowed my brow. "What question?"

"Why are you interested in the Amish?"

Cute. "Maybe. But yesterday I asked you about your personal involvement with them. I asked first. I win."

"Touché." He shrugged. "My best friends growing up were Amish. We played a lot of volleyball, spent all of our time together."

"Amish kids play volleyball?"

"Like there's no tomorrow. Baseball and soccer too. And they can be very competitive."

"Huh." I fished my digital recorder from my bag again. "Do you mind?"

"Go ahead."

"Why an Amish-style carpentry shop? What made you want to start a business?"

"I have an economics degree from the University of Oregon. Worked in corporate land for a few years, made money. At the end of the day, I wanted to be closer to my family."

"Why?"

"You like the tough questions, don't you? My parents are getting older, and I'm the oldest. I suppose I feel a certain amount of responsibility. I have different...resources, I guess, than they do. As for the shop...well, like I said, I wanted to move closer and I'd always liked working with my hands. There's a market for the Amish woodcraft, as well as a steady supply of labor."

"How many siblings?"

"A lot."

"'A lot' being code for..."

"Seven," he answered, before downing the last of his coffee. "Okay, your turn. Why the Amish?"

I thought about turning off the recorder but decided against it. I never knew when he might say something interesting.

"Hard to say," I told him truthfully. "There's something very simple and beautiful about the Amish, yet also very confusing."

I watched Levi's expression but couldn't read the emotions behind his eyes. "Confusing?" he asked.

"It seems like such a difficult lifestyle. The rest of America is so driven by technology and information that the fact the Amish aren't in school after eighth grade astounds me."

"Technology and the Amish aren't necessarily mutually exclusive."

"No?"

He checked his watch. "I know an Amish family in the community outside town. They'll serve lunch soon, and I'm sure we could invite ourselves over."

"Really?"

"You can observe firsthand."

"My goal is to spend some time in an Amish household," I admitted. "In fact, I'm waiting to hear back from one of the columnists I know from the paper. She promised to look into that for me."

Again, the face I couldn't read. "I may be able to help you with that," he answered after a moment. "But lunch first. If you walk with me back to the shop, we can take my truck."

I hesitated. Driving to a place I'd never been with a man I didn't know to a location with spotty cell phone reception did not rank high on the list of good ideas.

"Or you can follow on your bike," he added. "I have four younger sisters. I wouldn't want any of them riding with strange men."

That was the thing; Levi wasn't strange. There was something about him that was completely trustworthy.

And I had pepper spray in my bag. Just in case.

I watched the landscape change as we drove by. Once we were out of town, we passed neighborhoods with houses perforated by a dozen wires. Satellite dishes served as lawn ornaments.

I hated small towns.

And I grew up in one, so I was allowed to say so with experience.

After a while, the neighborhoods thinned out and cattle ruled the open spaces. A few sheep.

I remembered my earlier conversation with Joely. "Do Amish kids cow tip?"

Levi laughed, an easy laugh that made me remind myself I had a boyfriend. "None of the kids I knew did—they were busy dating. Can't say about some of the Pennsylvania kids."

Twenty minutes later occasional clusters of homes came into view. They sat in a small valley, homes surrounded by pastures and farmland. There were no wires, but if I wasn't mistaken, a sprinkling of wind-power generators.

Interesting.

It started to rain as Levi turned the truck down a long gravel road. A large white farmhouse sat at the end, with a barnlike building on either side for moral support. A woman hurriedly removed several pairs of pants from the laundry line as the raindrops grew larger. Levi raised a hand in greeting.

She waved back, yanking the last pair of trousers off and carrying the basket inside. By the time we made it to the covered porch, she was waiting for us at the door.

"Levi!" she said, standing on her tiptoes to cup his face and kiss his cheek. "What are you doing here?"

"Do you have extra for lunch?"

"I always have extra for lunch," she answered, her eyes on me.

"This is Jayne Tate. Jayne, this is Martha."

Martha looked from me to Levi, her eyes searching but guarded. "You are welcome in our home."

I tried not to stare. She was dressed as I'd seen Amish women in photos—a long dark blue dress, black apron, and white kapp. Her feet were encased in black, lace-up shoes. Dark, itchy-looking stockings covered the visible part of her legs.

A small storm of footfalls thundered from the upper floor, and two little girls, an almost adolescent boy, and a teen girl descended the stairs. The youngest girls squealed Levi's name and ran for his legs. He hugged them both, calling them by name. The older two followed at a more dignified pace. That they knew him well was obvious.

"Jayne," Levi said, continuing the introductions. "This is Sara—" he started with the teenager, "Samuel, Leah, and," he picked up the littlest girl, "this is the oldest, Elizabeth."

"I'm not the oldest!" Elizabeth squealed, revealing a missing front tooth. "I'm only five!"

"And they're all playing hooky from school today."

Another round of giggles and disagreement. "It's grading day," Leah said. "No school."

"Oh, right," he said. "They're all out of school and they're all having lunch with us."

"You're staying for lunch!" Elizabeth wrapped her arms around his shoulders, preventing him from putting her down.

But she had to get down anyway, because Martha ordered a group hand washing. Each child, except Sara, had a surprising amount of grime coating their fingers.

Lunch consisted of chicken potpies, cooked cabbage, rolls, stewed tomatoes, and sliced apples hidden under layers of brown sugar and oatmeal.

I enjoyed the potpie and decided that if I didn't think about the calories, they didn't count.

I ate a sparing amount of cabbage.

And avoided the tomatoes.

The rolls and apple dessert were divine—I knew Gemma would want the recipes.

I asked some questions about the farm and how the family spent their day. Martha gave simple, short answers. They began working at dawn and retired for the day around nine. The younger children attended school during the day while the older ones worked. Amos helped his father on the farm while Elam worked as a bricklayer in town. Sara made most of the family's clothes and mended on demand.

I tried to scribble down notes as I ate.

After the plates were cleared away, Martha showed me around the farm with the children following like ducklings. They ignored the rain and I tried to follow suit, even as the raindrops seeped into my clothing.

Once inside the barn, Samuel, Leah, and Elizabeth showed me the animals they took care of. Samuel had a pig, while Leah and Elizabeth watched over a pair of lambs. I could hear Levi mentioning something to Martha, but I couldn't make out the words.

We trudged back a few moments later. Levi hugged them all around. I shook Martha's hand and waved at the kids. Then Levi opened the truck door for me, and I climbed in. Samuel and Leah ran after the truck for a little while, feet bare in the mud. Levi relaxed when they turned back to the farmhouse.

"I hate it when they do that," he said with a sigh. "I don't think they really understand how dangerous cars can be."

"Your truck is probably one of the only motorized vehicles that comes on their property."

"Buggy accidents happen every year. They should know better."

"How many accidents? I remember seeing reflectors and lights on the buggy in the..." Buggy barn? Garage? What did they call the buggy-storing shelter?

Levi didn't seem to notice my terminological confusion. "Lights and reflectors don't negate the fact that they're still unprotected on the road. Even motorcyclists wear helmets, and the wood buggies leave the Amish every bit as exposed as a biker. They may as well be walking down the highways."

I didn't know what to say. "They seem to like you."

Levi's hands began to fidget on the steering wheel. "I've known them for a long time."

"Through your business?"

"No, before that. They're...my family."

As Levi's words sank in, I felt myself stiffen. "Wow. Okay. Your family. Right. You see, in journalism school they teach us to begin with the most important information."

"I know I should have explained earlier—"

"I don't know. Do you think that would have been helpful?"

I replayed scenes from lunch over and over in my head. Everything made sense now. I couldn't believe I hadn't picked up on it before now.

"I don't know why I didn't say anything."

"Hey, your call. By the way, I'm actually a European royal. Sorry I didn't mention it earlier."

"It took me years to get over the stigma of being 'the Amish boy.'"

"I was the elder's daughter. Didn't slow me down."

I looked into his eyes. Levi had very nice eyes; I tried to remember if I'd noticed his eyes before. I caught myself before I continued down that mental road. He had lied to me. Well, he hadn't exactly lied to me, but he had deceived me, and I didn't much appreciate it.

Frankly, being a reporter, it was fairly embarrassing. That's what I got for not asking the right questions.

***

At Levi's suggestion, he and Grady grabbed some wood for a ramp and rolled my bike into the back of the pickup. I sat and waited for them, teeth chattering. My clothes had refused to dry, despite the fact that Levi turned the heat on until it felt like inner Qatar inside the cab.

Levi never complained.

He dropped me off at my hotel and helped me unload my bike. "I could arrange a time for you to interview my parents, if you're interested."

I chewed on my lip. "I'll let you know." Frankly, I was feeling pretty forgiving at the moment and I couldn't trust myself to be rational.

Inside my hotel room, I stripped off my work clothes and wished I'd brought my sweatpants. Instead, I made do with the softer clothes that I had, rolled up my pant legs and soaked my feet in the bathtub.

I called Shane while my toes turned lobster red.

"Jayne?" He sounded surprised. "Where are you?"

I was surprised to hear the amount of noise surrounding him. "In my hotel room. Where are you? It sounds like you're at a club."

"Something like that. How's the story coming?"

I'm spending a lot of time with a guy you probably wouldn't like. "Fine. Taking some interesting turns. I miss you."

"Yeah. Good. Good for you."

Okay… "Can you hear me?"

"It's pretty loud in here. Can I call you back later tonight?"

"Okay," I said, trying not to feel blown off.

He never called back.

⚬⚬⚬

I considered my options the next morning.

First, my absence from the paper was limited. I really did need to manage my time well, which meant I needed to use the resources I had instead of wasting time finding new ones.

And second, if I was going to use my existing resources, I needed to forgive Levi.

What a pain.

I took a shower and checked my phone afterward. Still no call from Shane. Where had he been the previous afternoon, anyway? He'd never been that much into the club scene…and usually when I called, I very nearly had his complete attention.

Unless he was watching a game. At that point, my only chances for conversation came at commercial breaks. Maybe.

Shane aside, I put away my pride and called Levi's shop.

Spencer answered the phone. "Albany Amish Woodcraft, how may I direct your call?"

"May I speak with Mr. Burkholder?" I asked, trying not to sound like myself.

"I can see if he's available," Spencer replied. "May I tell him who's calling?"

I sighed on the inside. There was no avoiding it. "Jayne Tate."

"Jayne?" The tone of his voice switched from phone automaton to best buddy. "When are you coming down here?"

"If you transfer me to Levi I'll be able to find out."

"I can ask him for you. Wouldn't want to add to your stress level."

"I'll live."

Spencer gave a dramatic sigh and I heard a click before being transported into harpsichord land.

When Levi picked up, I heaved a sigh of relief. "I hate harpsichord."

"Who is this?"

"This is Jayne. Tate. Sorry—you have harpsichord music playing while your listener is on hold. I hate harpsichord. Makes me want to jump off of things. Tall things. I'm rambling. I didn't mean to call and ramble."

"Why did you call?" He didn't sound annoyed, only curious.

"I had a couple more questions for you. For the story."

"Oh. Does that mean you accept my apology?"

I wanted to find a way to skirt around answering that and came up blank. "Yes."

"Thank you," he said, his voice softening. "In that case, I can tell you that my mother called me this morning. Said she and my dad talked it over, and they've agreed to let you stay with them while you're working on your story."

"Really?"

"I assured them that you wouldn't be bringing drugs or alcohol into their home. They're prepared to keep your bike in their shed, and when you need to charge your laptop—I'm assuming you have a laptop—you can bring it here."

"I don't know what to say."

"'Thank you' should do it."

"How much should I pay them? I mean, I'm not expecting free room and board."

"My mom said something along the lines of thirty dollars a day."

"I'm sorry…thirty?"

"Yes. They're very thrifty."

I shrugged, not that he could tell over the phone. "Could I pad that a little more?"

"If you want. I wouldn't worry too much about it."

My mind reeled. I'd never thought this trip would be saving me money. "Thirty?"

He chuckled. "Do you want me to tell them you'll come?"

"Yes, before they change their mind!" I said, and then I caught myself. I never meant to be so relaxed around Levi. It just happened.

"How soon do you want to go down? I'll drive. We can load your bike in the truck again."

Was I ready? A part of me balked at leaving civilization behind. I knew journalists who had survived the difficulties of the Afghan desert, but while I stayed within American borders I expected a certain standard of living.

Electrical outlets. Wireless connections. That sort of thing.

"Do they have indoor plumbing?"

Levi laughed. "Some Amish families don't, but my parents do."

"You think I'm a wuss."

"I think you're normal."

"I guess I should pack and check out…"

"Do you want me to drive you down?"

"Probably better that way."

"Meet me at the shop?"

"Okay."

"What time should I expect you?"

I checked my watch. "Half an hour? An hour? Something like that."

"Looking forward to it," he said.

And I believed him.

❦

My hands shook with nervous excitement as Levi drove me toward the farmhouse for the second time. I was going behind the closed doors of one of America's most introverted societies.

And I couldn't stop worrying about the fact that Shane hadn't called me back. The concern kept me quiet through most of the drive until Levi commented on it. "You seem distracted," he said.

Understatement.

I tried to remember if I'd mentioned the presence of Shane to him or not, and then I berated myself for caring.

It's not as though I were *interested* in Levi. I was with Shane, right?

"I tried to call my boyfriend last night," I said, and found myself watching Levi's reaction.

His grip on the steering wheel shifted. "Unsuccessful?"

I shrugged. "I don't know. It sounded like he was out. At a bar or something...who knows. He said he'd call me back, but he didn't."

"Does he usually?"

"Usually what?"

"Call you back."

"I think so. It's not something that's been a problem before."

"How long have you been together?"

"Six months."

His grip shifted again. "Is he a social guy?"

"Not really. We are more of a coffeehouse couple, I guess. It's nothing."

"Hmm."

"Hmm?"

"I don't know what to tell you."

"Oh."

Yet another change in grip. "I suppose you could call him."

I scratched my neck. "I suppose."

"You don't want to?"

"I want him to call me back. I don't want to be the girlfriend who has to call constantly to get her boyfriend to return a call."

"I don't think two calls equals *constantly.*"

"You know what I mean."

"It's up to you."

"Is there much cell service at your parents' place?"

"Sometimes. Sometimes not."

"Serves him right."

As we pulled into the long drive toward the farmhouse, Levi pointed ahead. "Look."

I squinted. "What is that?"

"Your welcoming committee."

As we approached the house, I could see what he'd been pointing at. A row of children stood like sentries outside, facing us. "Those aren't all your siblings, are they?"

He laughed. "No. Some neighbor kids are mixed in there. They're all going to be very curious about you."

"Hence the lineup and the stare down?"

"Exactly."

I smiled at the kids as Levi pulled the truck around to the side. Martha came around to meet us, a cautious smile on her lips.

"Thanks for doing this, Mom," Levi said after he climbed down from the cab.

"Your father believes this will be a good experience for everybody."

"Is he home yet?"

"Soon." She turned to me. "Come along inside, Jayne. I will show you around the house."

"Go ahead," Levi said. "I'll put your bike in the shed and bring in your bags."

"Are you sure you don't need a hand?" I asked.

"If I do I'll find Samuel or Amos. Don't worry. I'll catch up."

I followed Martha into the house and tried not to pay attention to the small herd of children who followed us.

The farmhouse smelled like baking bread and cedar, with a faint tinge of body odor. Martha led me through the dining room to the kitchen and front rooms, down the hallway to my bedroom.

A brightly patterned Amish quilt covered the bed. There was a small flashlight on the bedside table, and a large armoire rested against the opposite wall. I smiled. "It looks very nice."

Martha brushed aside the compliment. "The toilet and shower are across the hall."

I heard Levi's heavy footfalls a second before he came around the corner with my bags.

Martha frowned. "Your father will be home at any moment."

Levi hoisted the bags over his shoulder. "I'll be gone in seconds."

"Your father…" my voice trailed off as I followed him.

"Isn't all that happy with me." He set my bags on the bed. "There, I'm done." He kissed Martha on the cheek. "I'm out."

I looked from Levi to Martha, trying to read their faces. "Can I walk out with you?" I asked, stalling. I wasn't quite ready to be left behind, deposited into another family's personal drama.

If I'd really wanted drama, I would have gone home.

But then, my family's not Amish, and therefore not newsworthy.

"Absolutely," Levi said, even as he patted heads and said goodbyes to the younger children.

I waited until we were well into the yard. "Why doesn't your mom want you home when your dad gets back?"

Levi reached for his car keys. "I left the community. My father doesn't talk to me."

"You mean, you're...shunned?"

Levi shrugged. "Not formally. I never joined the church," he said, sighing. "Come by the shop tomorrow or give me a call. Sorry to dump you here like this, but I really should leave. Don't mention my name to him, okay?"

"Okay," I agreed as he climbed into the truck. "Bye!"

He paused and threw me a smile. "I'll see you later."

I watched him drive away.

Chapter 5

Martha found me upon my return to the house and finished the tour. Afterward I asked about the possibility of borrowing some clothes. In my jeans and sweater, I felt like a visiting alien.

I also hoped that the children might stare at me less if I looked like them.

Martha considered my idea, eyed me up and down, and called for Sara.

Sara and I are, apparently, about the same size.

She caught the vision, enthusiastically going through her own clothing collection and creating a pile of garments for me to try. She gave me two dresses of varying dark blue, a black apron, long black socks, a white kapp, and a black bonnet for outdoor wear. "If these don't fit," she said, "I'll make you new ones."

"I don't know that I'll be here that long…"

"I sew fast." It wasn't a boast, just a statement.

"Let me try these first," I said, carrying the pile back to my room.

There were no mirrors inside, but I had a small compact mirror stuffed into one of my bags. When I'd finished dressing, I held my arm as far from my body as I could. The glimpse I caught caused me to physically flinch.

Breathe, I told myself. *Clothes don't change who you are. While you might appear to the casual passerby to be a cautious, conservative farmwife, you know that underneath you are a liberated, talented, tough biker babe.*

I did not recognize the woman in the mirror. I'd known Jayne Tate for a while, and Jayne Tate didn't wear dark dresses—or any dresses at all, for that matter. And yet, when I moved, so did the simply-clad woman.

There was something oddly Marx Brothers about the whole thing.

I found Martha in the kitchen. She didn't say anything about my change of attire. Instead, she handed me a sack of potatoes and a paring knife. "If you would like to help with dinner," she said, "you may peel these."

Gideon walked through the door when I was halfway through my first potato.

After my conversation with Levi, I expected Gideon to resemble a haggard, ugly old miser.

He looked more like a moustache-less Santa Claus, his beard to his chest, cheeks rosy from outdoor work. His eyes lit up when he saw me. "You are Jayne?" he asked, his voice tinged with a Germanic accent.

"Yes, I am." I offered my hand, which he studied for a moment before shaking.

He turned abruptly from me toward Martha. "Is dinner ready? I'm starved."

"Almost. I'll call the children in—" she started to say, but the sound of children's feet on wood floors drowned her out.

"Grandma!" they cried in unison, joy marking every face.

I peered out the window to see a tiny old woman emerge from a car. A dress like Martha's hung on her thin frame, although the older woman's had a floral print.

Martha removed her kitchen apron and joined her children outside.

"That is Martha's mother, Ida Gingerich," Gideon said, but he offered no further explanation.

Martha and her children led Ida into the house. "This is my mother, Jayne. She's staying for dinner," Martha said as she entered. "Mother, this is Jayne Tate. She is our guest for the time being."

I wanted to ask what Martha's mother was doing with a car, but I refrained. "Pleased to meet you, Mrs. Gingerich."

"Very nice to meet you, Jayne," she said, casting a shrewd glance over my person. I got the feeling she knew something I didn't. "Call me Ida."

Martha and I finished preparing dinner while Ida sat in the kitchen. They spoke in Pennsylvania Dutch, as far as I could tell, and I really didn't mind. Their world made no sense to me, and my brain had had about all it could take. Trying to decipher a conversation might push me over the brink.

Me and the potatoes, we were good.

"Let us give thanks," Gideon said, his voice soft with a rumble. Nine heads bowed in unison.

I used the moment to stare without being noticed. The men sat on one side of the table, the women on the other. We were surrounded by bowls and platters filled with food, tall glasses of thick, white milk, and a conspicuous lack of fresh vegetables.

After the moment of silence, I watched in fascination as this large family calmly, methodically downed huge quantities of food, with the men serving themselves first. Dinner conversation revolved around household chores and retellings of the workday. Samuel, Leah, and Elizabeth still attended school, while Amos, Elam, and Sara worked.

Gideon discussed with his sons which cattle needed to be moved, when to butcher the pigs, and the fact that some of the fence needed repair. Martha commented to Sara which garments were wearing out beyond use and which could be mended. Sara promised to start work on a new pair of pants for Samuel.

Not what I was doing at seventeen. My teen years consisted less of housework and family than of daydreaming about faraway colleges.

"Tell us about yourself," Ida said, interrupting my thoughts. "Where are you from?"

I shoved my hair out of my face. "I live in Portland, but I grew up on the coast."

Squeals of delight erupted around the table. "Where on the coast?" Sara asked.

"Lincoln City."

Leah leaned forward. "Did you go to the beach every day?"

"No…not every day. The weather's pretty nasty."

"Jayne, would you like more potatoes?" Martha interrupted.

I declined.

Ida pressed forward. "What is your family like?"

I told them about my married sister, Beth, and her little girl. How my mother still lived in Lincoln City. Alluded to the fact that we didn't talk often. Work, you know.

"Only one sister?" Elizabeth's brow furrowed.

I smiled, realizing how strange that must sound to her. "Only one sister. Sometimes it got lonely."

I offered to do the dishes after dinner. Nine faces looked at me, aghast, but Gideon said yes.

After I'd finished scrubbing the last baking dish, albeit with Sara and Leah's help, Gideon offered to give me a tour of the farm.

"Whatever I can help with, put me to work," I said as we stepped out of the house. "Milking, whatever."

Gideon howled in laughter, but when we got into the stalls I saw why. The milking machinery towered over us both. "Many people think we Amish are against technology," he said, "and that's not true. We believe in three things." He held up three fingers. "We believe in serving God by being Plain. We believe in living outside the world. And we believe in hard work. Life should never be too easy for us. Milking equipment—" he gestured at the stainless steel tanks—"makes the milking easy, but it also makes it so we can work at other things even harder. We run the machinery on diesel and wind generators. We do not bring in outside electricity."

"I stand corrected."

Gideon led me to the corral next. "Our horses are not for riding, they are for pulling. Sugar and Shoe pull the buggy—"

"Shoe?"

He gave a rueful smile. "Elizabeth named him when she was tiny."

"Good choice."

"Balsam pulls the tractor."

"What do you grow?"

"Mainly sorghum and oats. Maybe next year, though, I will take out the sorghum and put in solar panels." He shrugged. "Maybe. The families living here in Oregon came because we wanted to follow the old ways *and* use technology. Many groups in Ohio use the technology, but their children run wild and the *Ordnung* became less important. There was too much compromise."

I tried to look as if I understood.

~~∙≫∕∣∖≪∙~~

Ida drove herself home shortly after dinner. Even before the sky quite darkened, the children quieted, and before I knew it, everyone headed for bed.

At nine thirty.

Hadn't gone to bed so early since middle school.

After an unsuccessful attempt at sleep, I booted up my laptop. A message bubble informed me that no wireless networks were in range.

Somehow, I was not surprised.

I transcribed a few of the day's conversations and events for use in the future article. Played a couple hands of solitaire. Moved on to Minesweeper when it was time to relax, and then powered down the machine.

I burrowed under layers of quilts. Wished I had an electric blanket.

Sat up straight when a light flashed into my room.

Several irrational explanations fought for first place.

Maybe Ida had left something, and the lights were her car's headlights.

Maybe Levi was coming to tell me something. I dismissed that idea as soon as I'd thought of it—for Pete's sake, I wasn't fifteen anymore.

There could be robbers of some sort, but unless they were after the giant milking equipment or Martha's cast-iron cookware, I couldn't think of anything worth stealing.

And I doubted the resale value on cast-iron cookware made the effort financially viable. Cattle? Were cattle rustlers outside my window?

The light flashed again. I rolled out of bed, staying close to the ground. Glad I was a brunette and not a light-reflective blonde, I raised my head until I could just see out.

A man was outside with a flashlight. Okay, an Amish man, but an Amish man hanging around outside with a flashlight didn't seem that safe, either.

My heart stopped when I saw him reach toward the window next to mine.

Sara's window.

I pulled a quilt around my shoulders and whipped out to the hallway, the protective moves I'd learned in Joely's self-defense class playing through my mind.

I could have at least brought a heavy shoe as a weapon, I thought before turning the knob on Sara's door.

The opening door revealed the young woman, sitting at the window. "Get down!" I ordered, all but tackling her to the ground. "There's a man outside!"

"No," Sara said, her voice hushed but firm. "There's none but David Zook outside."

I tilted my head to see David Zook peering at us through the window.

The "male lurker" was about seventeen, confused, frightened, and in need of a good haircut.

"What's he doing skulking around?" I asked, gesturing wildly at the window while vaguely aware of my fleeting dignity. "And pointing his flashlights at people's windows in the dead of night?"

Oh yeah, and never mind that this particular "dead of night" landed two hours before I usually went to bed.

"David is my..." Sara's eyes darted to the window and back at me. "He's my, um..."

"Gentleman caller?"

"Boyfriend," she spat the word out. "He's picking me up for a date."

I felt a headache coming on. "You knew he was coming?"

She nodded.

"Okay, whatever." I turned around and walked to the door. "Just remember," I said before making it out the room, "ninety-two percent of female murder victims were killed by men they knew."

I doubted this kind of thing ever happened to Seymour Hersh.

I dreamed about aliens that night. They landed in front of the farmhouse, their flashing saucer lights causing everyone concern. Shane captained the ship, although the aliens had trouble communicating with him. Instead of the helm, Shane stayed in the party area of the ship, where the aliens served orange fizzy drinks and made *Star Wars* references.

They clapped to an odd kind of rhythm with their webbed alien hands. At some point, I realized I wasn't listening to the clapping of extraterrestrials but someone knocking at my door. I sat up and reevaluated my surroundings. The tiniest hint of morning light was peeking through the windows.

The knock sounded at my door again. I shook my head to clear it. "Come in."

Sara poked her head in. "Could I come sit?"

I waved her in. "Sit." My mouth tasted awful. I yearned for an orange Tic Tac. "What's up?"

"I told David to be more careful with his flashlight," she said, pulling lint off her apron. "The boys always come to the girls' windows after everyone goes to bed. That's how we have dates. That's how my parents had dates."

"Your parents are perfectly fine with you crawling out of windows with boys they don't know?" My parents would have had joint hernias, and before this conversation I would have considered them *less* conservative than Gideon and Martha.

"Oh, they know David."

"Do they know you're together?"

"No."

"How many girls come home pregnant?"

Sara's eyes widened. "None that I know."

I wondered how many she didn't know about, but I kept that question to myself. "I'm sorry if I startled you last night."

She giggled. "David might not come back."

"I'm truly sorry," I repeated.

"There are other boys," she said, with a shrug that was almost coy.

I played along. "Oh?"

"There is Milo Stutzman. And Henry Mullet."

I pressed my lips together to ensure a serious response. "You have choices."

"Yes."

"Tell me about your grandmother," I said, swinging my feet around. The floor was freezing. "Why does she have a car?"

"Grandma is Mennonite."

"Oh."

"She joined the Mennonite church when I was little, she and my grandfather."

"And your family still has contact with them?" I didn't say, "unlike Levi," but she caught my meaning.

"They joined a Mennonite church. Because they did that, we could still see them. Not Grandpa anymore, though. He passed on. But Levi joined a Baptist church. Our bishop didn't accept it."

"But the Mennonite church is acceptable?"

She nodded.

"Do you miss your brother?"

Sara nodded again. "Very much. Everyone thought he would marry Rachel Yoder. I heard that she wouldn't leave with him. Levi wouldn't talk about it."

"How often do you see him?"

She shrugged. "When my dad's not home, he'll come visit. Sometimes…" she leaned in closer, "I visit him in town."

"Really?" I couldn't hide my surprise. "At the shop?"

Sara gave a secret smile. "Grandma takes me."

Ida was more of a rebel than I'd given her credit for. "So he's stayed in touch with your grandmother too?"

"Oh, yes. Everyone but Dad."

"Your dad's angry?"

"Hurt, I think. But it's not my place to question."

At that moment my stomach gave a long, loud commentary on the state of its condition.

Empty.

"I think I'm ready for breakfast. You?"

Sara grinned, and the rest of the day began.

Chapter 6

I called Levi after breakfast, using the cell number he'd given me earlier. "Your grandmother drives a car and your sister sneaks out at night," I said. "There's so much you didn't tell me."

"Is everything okay? Are they treating you well?"

"They're fine so far. Why didn't you warn me that things between you and your dad were weird?"

"If I tried to warn you about every family struggle, we'd be talking for a very long time."

"Oh. Well, then. Anything else you want to fill me in on while you've got me on the phone?"

He sighed. "My mother is wary of outsiders. Amos and Elam rarely speak to me if they have a choice."

"Why the tension between you and your dad?"

"It's complicated."

"Try."

"Cutting me off is the Amish version of tough love. The reasoning is that if I'm separated from everybody, I'll eventually relent and return."

"But you aren't separated from everybody. Your mom and your sisters talk to you. Ida too."

"They figured out I had no intention of returning, ever. I think my mom decided she still wanted me as a son."

"That's good, I suppose."

"And as for Sara sneaking out, that's how they date."

"She told me. Still doesn't make sense to me."

"Imagine having seven or more siblings teasing you about the guy you're dating."

I winced. "Good point."

After breakfast, the younger children went to school, the men went to work, and I shadowed Sara with her chores. The Burkholder household attained a level of clean I doubted I could ever aspire to. We scrubbed the floors before moving on to the laundry.

Never again would I take washing clothes for granted—Sara and I had to start their washer using the gas generator. To dry the clothes, we pinned them to a line of twine strung across the washroom. "If we hang them outside in the wet, they'll turn colors and smell bad."

"I'll bet," I said, pinning the shoulder of one of the boys' shirts. "Mildew is gross."

"Mildew?"

"They get greenish-grayish patches?"

"Yes."

"That's mildew."

"What is it?"

A part of me wondered how on earth she didn't know about mildew, and then I reminded myself that she'd stopped attending school at fourteen. "Like mold. It's a fungus—it starts out with spores and it likes to grow in warm, damp environments."

"Spores?"

I bit my lip, thinking of how to phrase it in a way she'd understand. "Fungus seeds."

"Fungus seeds," she repeated, mulling over the concept. "I understand."

"And they're nasty to get out of clothes. I lost a load of towels that way— left them in the washer. Stank so bad."

She pinned up a dark dress. "You talk like Levi."

"How so?"

"You both seem to understand the world better. You've learned things. Gone to school."

I wanted to tell her she could go to school too. I mean, there had to be some sort of program that would help her catch up, wouldn't there?

But I didn't think today was a good day to make waves in the family. "You can learn things outside of school."

"I've learned everything I can here," she said.

The bitterness in her voice took me aback. "Do you want to learn more?"

She seemed to catch herself. "I want to learn how to be a better person. To serve my community, to serve God."

I shrugged. "I'm probably not the best person to talk to when it comes to God, but my guess is that it's possible to learn and serve at the same time."

"Maybe in the English world," Sara said, pinning the last pair of pants to the line with a kind of sad finality. "In the Amish world, there is only serving."

⋙⋘

"We're going to Grandma's," Sara told me that afternoon. "There is room for you to come if you like."

"I'd love to." I put down the laundry I'd been folding. "What's going on at Ida's?"

Martha secured a bolt of purple cloth beneath her arm. "Quilting."

I almost froze in place. "Quilting? You mean, like actually making quilts?"

The women gave me twin blank looks.

"Yes," Sara said. "Don't some English women quilt?"

"They do, some of them. Just not any of the women I know."

I dropped my cell phone into my apron pocket, on the off chance that Shane got through. Reception had been spotty during the day.

Martha hitched the horse to the buggy, and then we set off bumpily down the road. People waved at us as we drove by; Martha nodded, Sara waved back. I probably looked as though I had missed my calling as homecoming queen.

Along the way, Sara told me about the quilts. Friends and family members often gave quilts as wedding gifts, but the market for Amish-made quilts in the last ten years had skyrocketed to the point where the women felt no qualms about meeting during planting season and working on quilts to supplement the family income.

I fingered the bolts of cloth as I listened. There was the purple cloth Martha had carried, which reminded me of a Sunday school lesson about Lydia. I couldn't remember who Lydia was or what she did, only that she dealt in purple textiles. She was probably a believer—most of the women in the Bible were.

A second bolt shimmered yellow in the pale afternoon sun. "You don't wear yellow, do you?" I asked Sara.

She shrugged. "Sometimes the younger children do. Why?"

I pointed to the fabric.

"Oh," she said. "English women like light colors in their quilts. The lighter quilts sell faster than the darker ones."

"Makes sense." That also accounted for the pale blue fabric that reminded me of the last robin's egg I'd found as a child. "How far is it to Ida's?"

"She lives on the outside of town, on the other side."

"So...we have to drive through town?"

Sara nodded.

Martha remained stoic.

As we neared town, the other drivers' stress levels rose. Some passed us in a swoosh of metal and air, honking as though they were auditioning to be New York cabbies. The buggy shuddered each time.

Others just sat behind us as if we were leading a procession. I suppressed the urge to repeat my homecoming wave.

Once we got into town, people stared. Some stared openly, others used techniques usually reserved for checking out members of the opposite sex. A few people whipped out their cell phones to take pictures. Sara ducked her head. Martha's gaze remained fixed on the road ahead of her.

Suddenly it occurred to me that people were also taking *my* picture. A giggle started deep inside and grew to a laugh. Sara turned around. "What?"

"They're taking pictures of us," I said, another peal of laughter threatening to break loose.

Sara's expressions darkened. "It's hard to stop them."

"But they're taking pictures of me too! Me! And I'm not even Amish!" Another cackle escaped. "The joke's on them!"

She smiled. "I suppose so. But you're giving them something to photograph: a laughing Amish woman."

"Sorry." I sobered. "I'm just not used to dealing with the paparazzi."

<hr />

Except for the cars in the driveway, Ida's house and the Burkholder home could have been one and the same. A couple other buggies were parked in an adjoining field, attended by bored-looking horses. Martha pulled up next to them.

I saw that hitching posts were actually in the field and watched as Martha tied up the horse.

It answered my question about how one parked a buggy without an emergency brake.

The sound of women's voices met us on the porch before we even made it into the house. Once we were inside, I paused.

How did so many women fit in here? It was like the circus Volkswagen with the clowns. And not only were the women packed in like sardines, they had quilts pulled taut in giant frames.

Crazy. I assumed the fire marshall had no idea what went on in normally quiet Mennonite homes.

I watched from a safe spot near the wall as Martha and Sara moved into the crowd. They greeted, they hugged, they commented on fabric. After a few moments, Sara stopped, her eyes searching. When she found me, she wove through the masses toward me and grabbed my hand. "Come and sit with us! You can cut squares."

"You don't want me cutting squares," I said, shaking my head and trying to free myself.

But Sara had a farm girl's grip. "Anyone can cut squares."

"I tried making a nine-patch in fourth grade. I was the only kid whose project looked less like a quilt and more like Jackson Pollock. And I really mean Jackson Pollock—not one of his paintings."

"You're not in fourth grade anymore," Sara retorted, all but shoving me into a chair. I received a few calm smiles, as if reporters got harnessed into sweatshop labor all the time. "Here are your scissors," she said, giving them to me handles first, "a template, and fabric." She set the purple bolt in my lap. "Make sure the corners are nice and crisp."

And with that she left.

I struggled through the first few squares. I couldn't get the fabric to cut without it folding oddly on the scissors, resulting in a less-than-straight edge of the square.

Or rectangle. I began to think that maybe Sara needed to be more open minded when it came to the desired shape of the quilt pieces. What was the template but a constraint against creativity? She might think she wanted squares, but had she really considered rectangles? Rectangles opened up so many possibilities. They were easier on the eyes, visually.

At least, that's what the guy at Video Only said when he wanted me to spend the money on a widescreen TV.

"You need to use the edges of the scissors," a voice said to my right.

I jumped and turned. With the complete commotion all around me, I hadn't noticed Ida taking a seat next to me. "Sorry…"

She waved a hand. "Didn't mean to startle you. You might try moving the fabric down so it's closer to the tip of the scissors. I think that pair has a dull spot in the middle."

I obeyed, moving the fabric down the blade before making the snip. A clean-cut piece dropped into my lap. "Thank you!" I said, picking up the fabric and eyeing its perfection. "That's much better."

"You've never sewn before," she observed.

"Never."

"It's useful. Even in your world, there's wisdom in knowing how to sew a button back on."

I couldn't tell her I usually chucked clothes once they began to shed their buttons or grow holes.

I cut another square. This time it actually looked like a square. "This is fun, though. And I enjoy learning new things."

"How is my grandson doing?"

Okay, that was a serious change in subject, although I suspected this line of questioning to be her original intention. "Fine, I guess. I talked to him this morning."

"He's a good boy, Levi. He had a lot of opportunities to do other things, but he chose to stay near the family that rejected him."

I hid my surprise that she would discuss such a personal subject in such a crowded room. Although you could barely hear your own thoughts, much less another conversation. "Why did he leave the community?"

"I don't know how he stayed so long. He was so curious, so smart. He wanted to know how the world worked, and he couldn't understand why no one else did. The teacher at the school used corporal punishment, at the time, and Levi was strapped for asking too many questions. He read better than many adults, and he would read the family Bible. He asked the bishop once if King David got into heaven even though he led armies."

"What happened?"

"The bishop told Gideon, and Gideon had to discipline Levi, or else the community would have looked down on him for being a lax father."

"Is the community that involved?"

"Everyone has to keep up appearances. Watch the squares—you don't want them too small. There needs to be seam allowances."

"Seam allowances?"

"About half an inch, since they'll be sewn together."

"I get it." No, I didn't.

"After Levi left he went to school and got himself a fancy education on scholarship money. Worked for a big company in California before he came back here and opened his shop. He's been here ever since."

"Why do you think he came back?"

Ida arched an eyebrow. "To be close. To be available."

"Available in case…" I followed Ida's gaze to where Sara stood, overseeing one of the frames and examining the seams.

Of course.

He wanted to be close to help his siblings get out, if they wanted.

I looked around at the Amish women filling the room. They weren't highly educated, but these women appeared happy. Industrious. Savvy in their craft. Aside from the overzealous watchdog community, why would anyone ever leave?

I asked Ida as much.

"I left because my husband left, and I didn't want to be apart from him. Not everyone is cut out to be Amish. Still…"

I waited.

"Well, I was a little surprised about Levi's leaving, at least concerning Rachel."

Rachel?

Ida pointed to another woman.

This woman looked around my age, and resembled what the rest of the world would consider the ideal paragon of Amish beauty.

There wasn't a trace of makeup on her face, but she didn't need it. Her skin was clear, her cheeks, rosy. Her teeth were white and straight, her hair a rich chestnut. She looked like the sort of woman who followed the rules and always did the right thing.

"Were she and Levi…"

"They were never engaged, though everyone thought they would be." Ida shook her head. "But I don't know that Rachel would have been able to leave."

My chest tightened as I looked at Rachel and realized she was everything I wasn't.

The buzz of my phone interrupted my jealousy of Rachel. "Excuse me," I said to Ida. I disentangled myself from the pile of squares before picking up the phone.

The caller ID read "Shane Colvin."

About time. I snapped the phone open, even though I couldn't hear a thing. "Let me get outside," I said, hoping he could at least hear me, even if I couldn't hear him.

Come to think of it, the last time we talked he couldn't hear me because he was in some kind of club. This time, I couldn't hear him because I was off quilting.

Oh, the irony.

"Hi," I said, then stalled. "Um, how are you?" Why haven't you called me? What have you been doing?

"Fine," he answered, as if he hadn't been putting off calling me at all. "How's the story?"

"Interesting, very interesting."

"Did you find someone to stay with?"

"I did, actually."

"Yeah?"

"Yeah."

Ladies and Gentlemen, the world's stupidest conversation.

"Who with?"

I sighed. "An Amish family outside of town. I found them through a contact."

"The Mennonite lady?"

"You know, call me old-fashioned, but I always thought that 'I'll call you back tonight' meant that the caller would call back that same night. Maybe it's supposed to be a different night. Maybe that's what all the cool kids are doing now. Or is it code? Because I left my secret agent decoder ring back at my apartment, thank you."

"I'm sorry I didn't call you back…"

"You're calling me back now, and it's not even sunset. Not at all nighttime, so now I'm really confused."

"Jayne…"

"The cool kids must really hate you."

"I'm sorry. I went to a talk at the university with my brother; you caught me just as it let out. Then Jordan wanted to go out for a drink, and I got distracted."

"You got drunk?"

"I was the designated driver. Jordan was singing sea shanties by the time I took him back to his dorm."

I winced. "He can't sing."

"No, and his pitch gets worse after a couple brewskies. And he forgot words…I don't know why I'm telling you all this."

"Is it true?"

"Why wouldn't it be?"

I wrapped my nonphone arm around myself. "Sorry. I'm feeling very vulnerable right now. Must be the bonnet."

"You're dressed like one of them?"

"Down to the kneesocks."

"I bet you look cute."

"Shut up," I told him, but in truth a smile sneaked out. He always had that effect on me.

"You're doing okay?" he asked.

"I'm doing okay. What's going on in the world out there?"

"Oh, you know. Death, destruction, political upheaval. The usual."

"There's something comforting about not getting a newspaper." I paused. "Don't tell anyone I work with I said that."

He chuckled. "Don't worry, I won't. I don't think Kim would ever talk to you again."

"She wouldn't. Ever." Kim. I missed Kim. And Joely and Gemma… "I miss you."

"I miss you too."

I met Shane when I covered the construction of the new Civic Center. Shane, being near the bottom of his architecture firm's food chain, was the most accessible source. I asked him about the design process and inspiration; he asked me to dinner.

Being with Shane excited me. For the first time I was in a grown-up relationship involving dinners at nice restaurants and intellectual conversation.

There wasn't a beach bonfire to be found, no sad high-school dances with wilted helium balloons, no furtive make out sessions in dorm hallways. I felt as though I'd finally broken free of my past.

Shane took me home to meet his parents and two younger brothers. I think a part of him waited for me to return the gesture.

Scratch that. I *knew* he wanted me to. But I just couldn't do it.

How could I explain that he represented my separation from home? I liked Shane for a lot of reasons, one of which was that he knew nothing about my life before I came to Portland. If I took him home, it could ruin everything.

But another part of me wondered how long I could continue to run.

⋯≈⋗⋗⋯

After I hung up with Shane, I brushed Rachel from my mind.

Jealous? I wasn't jealous. I had handsome, urbane Shane waiting for me at home.

Urbane Shane. That was funny. I would have to call him that in passing some time.

Levi was just a guy. A complicated guy, but a guy nonetheless. I was, perhaps, a bit attracted to him, mainly because he was here and Shane wasn't.

I was bigger than that, stronger than that. Levi certainly had his own baggage as well, and I didn't need to go near that with a ten-foot pole.

Although professionally, it could help with the story.

Being a journalist was complicated sometimes.

⋯≈⋗⋗⋯

I cut a total of fifty squares that afternoon. Sara examined my work on the way back. "Good," she said. "I should be able to use these."

Don't know how she could tell, with the buggy bouncing the way it was.

Martha made a beeline for the kitchen when we returned. A pot of stew bubbled on the stove. Baking sheets of yeasty dinner rolls rose in the oven. "Is there anything I can help with?" I asked.

She wiped her hands on her apron. "I don't think so. All that needs doing is baking the rolls. Why don't you see if Sara needs help with the mending?"

They were awfully eager to arm me with a needle, first with the quilting and then with the mending.

I didn't mention my concerns. Sara sat in the family room beside the glow of a propane lantern. "Your mother told me to help you if you needed it."

She cocked an eyebrow. "You can sew?"

"No."

"Okay." She took a critical look of my Amish ensemble. "If you would like," she said, "I can make you a new dress."

I sat down next to her. "I'm not going to be here that long..."

"I'm quick. I could have a dress for you in a couple of days."

"Only if you want to..."

"May I measure you?" She didn't stop for an answer. "I'll get my tape."

"Shouldn't we..." Was it proper to be fitted in the family room? But then, I didn't suppose the Amish were all that concerned with the finer points of tailoring. I waited. If she wanted to make me a dress, who was I to stop her?

I started writing in my head—*Within a few days, Sara wanted to sew for me. But why?*

She returned a moment later, arms laden with fabric, a tape measure, and a pincushion shaped like a cupcake. "I ain't opposed to taking in the dress you're wearing."

"Do whatever you want. Do you enjoy sewing?"

"I do."

"When did you learn?"

"I started when I was eight," she answered, pinning my dress along the sides. "This dress was made for someone larger than you. You're also wearing a real bra."

As opposed to fake ones?

Sara must have read my expression. "We usually make undergarments to hold and...flatten." She began to blush.

"Oh." No lift and separate here, then. I stuck my hands on my hips. "Well, what do you need me to do?"

She regained her composure. "To start, I need the length of your torso, arms, and legs from the waist."

I held out my arms. "Should I stand like this?"

"You could, but I left my notepad in the kitchen."

"Ah." I put my arms down.

For all of her quiet Amishness, Sara possessed a surprisingly acerbic wit. There was a real teenager struggling to get out.

Heaven help us.

She came back from retrieving her notepad and started with measuring my arm. I stood very still. "Do you sew all the family clothes?"

Sara scribbled a number. "Most of them. Sometimes Mother and Leah help with the hemming."

"Leah sews?"

"Elizabeth is learning. All Amish women sew."

But Leah and Elizabeth were so young. I couldn't imagine wielding a needle and thread at that age.

Nor could I imagine feeding cows, but the children took care of the livestock on a regular basis.

"You're going to be here tomorrow?" Sara asked, after measuring my torso.

"Yes."

Sara looked over her shoulder toward the kitchen. "Could you take me to town?"

"What?"

"I need to take mending back to Levi."

"You do Levi's mending?"

"Shh!" She waved her hand at me. "Not so loud."

I lowered my voice. "Why are we whispering?"

"Normally Grandma takes me to town, but she can't for a week and suggested you take me."

"Why are we whispering?"

Sara glanced again at the kitchen. "I don't want my mother to hear and tell anything to Father."

"Doesn't your father wonder why you have normal clothes in your mending pile?"

"I mend them in my room. Can we take your motorcycle?"

"What?" I forgot to whisper.

"Shh!"

"Sorry," I spoke in a hush again. "I don't have a second helmet."

"That's okay."

"No, it's not okay. It's illegal, and even if you had a helmet, I don't think you could ride and keep your skirt free."

"What if you borrowed Grandma's car?"

"I thought she was busy."

"She might not need her car."

"Well, let me know."

Truth be told, being jarred by the buggy all the way to Levi's didn't appeal to me.

⁂

Apparently Sara was a skilled negotiator, because I found myself driving Ida's Buick to town the following afternoon.

Ida held my bike as collateral.

"Remind me what you told your mother?" I said as we zipped down the highway at fifty-five beautiful miles per hour.

"I told her Grandma needed us to take some things to a neighbor, and they were too heavy for her to lift, so she asked us to help."

"And then didn't come along?"

"She's busy today."

"With what?"

Sara shrugged.

If there was anything I remembered from my teen days, it was the necessity of details in a good parental lie. Not that Sara needed to know that... although she seemed a bit proud of her subterfuge.

She had also insisted that I stay in my Amish clothes, lest anyone suspect we were headed to the outside world. But being a reporter, and a darn good one, I didn't mind the fact that I was driving a Buick older than my older sister and wearing a bonnet.

The Buick? The bonnet? All prime material.

As was Spencer's face when we walked in.

"Ms. Tate!" he said, and that was all.

Nothing makes a man speechless faster than a grown woman in a pinafore.

"I have mended clothes for Levi," Sara said, full of noble purpose.

Spencer nodded, still silent, before retreating down the hall toward Levi's office.

Sara frowned. "He's usually more talkative than that."

I restrained a smirk. "It's been a tough day for him."

"Jayne! Sara!" Levi grinned like a boy receiving a dirt bike. "What are you ladies doing?"

Sara pulled the bundle out from under her arm. "I have your clothes."

"Oh. Good. Come back to my office."

Sara all but skipped after him. I lagged behind, watching.

They belonged with one another, brother and sister. Seeing them together, studying their faces, I could see the family resemblance. Granted, Levi's hair was dark and Sara's blond, but the slight upturn of the nose and the shape of the eyes identified them as siblings. The way they both seemed to smile with their whole face. Not that I'd seen Sara smile very often. Was she simply more serious in disposition, or unhappy? I'd had friends in high school with permanent rain clouds over their heads. Somehow, Sara didn't strike me as being one of them.

Levi turned at the threshold of his office door. "Coming?"

I nodded and quickened my steps.

"You know," Levi said, closing the door after I'd stepped through, "I haven't seen Spencer speechless since his mother announced that she was 'down with new bling.'"

I winced. "I hate the word 'bling.' It came and went and yet it's still printed in the media."

"And uttered by mothers."

"I'm sure Spencer was glad to know how hip his mother was."

"He couldn't talk for five minutes."

"That must be a record."

"Levi!" Sara tugged on his sleeve. I quieted and let her have a moment with her brother.

With painstaking care, she pulled out each garment and showed him how she had tended to each piece of fabric.

"They all look perfect," Levi told her.

Sara smiled and tried on the humble-Amish expression, but she didn't quite make it. They chatted for a few minutes before she excused herself to the ladies' room.

Leaving Levi and me alone together.

"She's starting to talk like you," he said.

"What?"

"Your mannerisms, your patterns of speech. She admires you."

I snorted. "You wouldn't think it."

"She's seventeen," he said with a laugh. "It's her prerogative."

"I met Ida."

"How is she?"

"Fine, although I have no previous experience to compare it with. I can't tell you if she looks worn or has lost weight, but I can say she likes personal questions."

"She is fine then."

"And she likes to talk about you."

Was it my imagination, or was that a blush forming near his collar?

"She has always been very good to me."

"That's nice."

"She's also sad I'm single."

"Most grandmothers are, I guess. Mine passed away a long time ago, but that seems right."

"Have you heard anything from your boyfriend?"

I ducked my head. "Yeah. He called yesterday."

The expression on his face turned plastic. "Glad to hear that."

I flushed. My heart raced. My mouth grew dry—all in all, my body is very good at impersonating a high school crush.

And if I didn't know better, I'd think he was looking at my lips.

Or was I looking at his?

I had to get out of that office. Without any sort of verbal warning, I stood, turned, and headed toward the door.

At least that was my intention. Next thing I knew, my foot caught, the world spun, and I had carpet lint between my teeth.

Chapter 8

In an instant Levi crouched next to me on his hands and knees. "Jayne? Are you okay?"

I blinked from my position on the floor. "How did that happen?"

"I think it was the garbage can."

I lifted my body enough to look. Sure enough, there was an ankle-biter garbage can, overturned and looking guilty.

Sara peered over me, having returned in time to see my appointment with gravity. "What happened?"

"I'm a moron, that's what happened." I put my wrist down to push myself up, and then I yelped in pain.

"What's wrong?" Levi's gaze focused on my hand. "Did you break something?"

Was it me, or did my left wrist look larger than it used to be?

———※———

The X-ray tech squinted at me. "Looks bad."

I stopped myself from rolling my eyes. My wrist, by now, was three times its normal size.

The woman positioned me on the table, laying a lead apron over my torso. "So, are you Amish?"

I winced. Levi had driven us straight to the hospital ER, no matter how many times I begged for him to take me back to the farm so I could change clothes. I mean I wasn't going to die. Really, just the quickest of clothing changes…

But he didn't, and here I was on the X-ray table feeling like a kid who got caught playing dress-up.

"Sure, yeah, I'm Amish," I said. I was embarrassed enough without having to explain that I was undercover reporter Amish.

I mean, really.

—⊰≫⋇≪⊱—

The glow of the streetlights reflected on the bright white compression brace. "It's just a sprain," I groused as we drove back to the shop. "Don't know why I need this thing. It's not very Amish."

"I could make a black sleeve for it," Sara suggested.

"More punk rock than Amish." I sighed. "And I can't ride my bike with this."

Levi shot me a quick glance as he drove. "What did the doctor say about you riding?"

"The swelling should be down in a week or two, but I shouldn't ride until I get my full range of movement back." I sighed again. "That part may be a while."

"At least the sling's navy!" Sara chirped.

"Yes, the sling is appropriately Amish looking."

"Don't worry about your bike," Levi said. "I can take it back to the farm if you can drive the truck."

"That's all well and good, but that leaves me with only a buggy."

"Buggies are good enough for a lot of people."

"Hmm, yes, but I need to have a motor of some sort around." I looked him in the eye. "And the tractor doesn't count."

His mouth snapped shut. "Fine. I won't suggest that, then."

"Don't." I thought out loud, "My car's probably out of the shop by now..."

"Do you want me to pick it up for you?"

"No. Kim probably has by now."

"I could drive it down."

"It's in southeast Portland."

"I need to make a delivery in Portland anyway."

"How are you going to get there if you're driving the car back?"

"I could take your bike."

Like that was going to happen. "Nobody rides my bike but me."

"Really?"

I would have crossed my arms if the action hadn't shot sparks of pain to my shoulder. "Yes. Really."

"You're getting cranky. Do you need another pain pill?"

"No, I don't need another pain pill. And how would you make a delivery using my bike?"

"It's a box. I could easily put it into a well-padded backpack."

"You own a furniture store."

"Yes."

"And you're delivering a box?"

"If there's one thing they teach you in business, it's diversification."

"Do you even have your motorcycle endorsement?"

"I do. I've got my own helmet and everything."

"Good, 'cause you're not wearing mine."

"Why not?"

"You'd get man cooties on it."

Sara giggled from the backseat.

"That's enough from you, young lady," I said. "Man cooties are very serious. They cause all kinds of problems."

The girlish giggling continued, and I couldn't help but join in. I sobered when I looked at Levi's earnest face.

Yes, man cooties could do all sorts of things. They could make you forget about your boyfriend.

"So," Sara said, interrupting the moment, "what are we going to tell my parents?"

I shrugged my right shoulder. "I don't know. What are you going to tell them?"

"You're not going to help me?"

"I'm not going to lie to them."

Sara opened her mouth, shut it, and then crossed her arms.

"She's right, Sara," Levi said. "Mom can smell a lie twenty feet away. Lies and rock music."

"She's got a good nose, your mother."

"Woman's got eight kids," Levi said. "By now I think she's telepathic. Don't worry about it. I'll come in with you—that'll be distraction enough."

"How are you going to get back?" I asked. "I mean, after you take Ida's car back to her."

"I can take your bike, or Ida can drive me home."

Sara snorted. "And send you with two loaves of bread and a batch of cookies."

"Oh," I said with a nod. "Such sacrifice."

⁓⁓⁓

In the end, my wrist brace stole the show. Gideon roundly ignored Levi, Martha hovered around my arm, asking if the brace came off so she could put a poultice on it, but then suggesting maybe putting it on my fingers might help.

Sara all but ducked away to her room.

Smart kid.

I sent Levi out with the keys to the bike, telling him I'd call him about it later. Then I headed to my room to see if the magical phenomenon of cell service happened to be functioning.

For once it was. I dialed Kim's number. "Do you know if anyone's picked up my car yet?"

Kim snorted. "You leave for Amish country, and you're worried about your car?"

"I sprained my wrist—"

"And here I am being a jerk. Bet you can't ride like that. Sorry. Do you need me to drive your car to you?"

"Actually, a friend of mine is going to pick it up."

"Someone Amish? That's original. I thought they didn't drive."

"They don't, and no, he's not Amish."

"*He*? Who is he? How did you meet him? Have you told Shane about him?"

There are disadvantages to being friends with investigative journalists.

"He is the owner of a local Amish-style woodcraft store. It's complicated. His family is Amish and they're the ones I'm staying with."

"Interesting. And Shane?"

"No."

"Even more interesting. Why haven't you told Shane?"

"Haven't really had the opportunity," I hedged. As in, Shane hadn't directly asked about him.

Not that Shane had a reason to, but never mind.

"Anyway, he's going to drive my bike up and I need someone to give him the car. Who picked it up?"

"Joely was going to, but she got called out. It's sitting in my driveway."

"Can I send him to your place, then?"

"What's his name?"

"Levi Burkholder."

"Nice strong man name."

"Whatever. Flirt with him all you like—just let him take the car."

"So you're not interested?"

"I'm with Shane."

"Right. Are you leaving the bike here?"

"Hmm." I thought for a moment. "Would it put you out too much to meet him at my place with my car? That way he could leave the bike there."

"Good enough for me. Is he cute?"

"I'm not answering that."

"He is, then."

"Kim—"

"I know, I know. You're with Shane. I can flirt all I want, and I'm looking forward to it."

⁂

I called Levi moments after, using my window of airtime before the airwaves shifted and I lost reception.

"So she's expecting me?" he asked after I gave him directions to my apartment.

"Expecting" seemed so...subtle. "Yes."

Next thing I knew, the call dropped. No service.

Part of me wondered if I should have warned him. I mean, if we were golfing, and there was a golf ball headed for his cranium, I would yell "fore" or "heads" or whatever you're supposed to say to warn people on a golf course.

But on the other hand, Kim was single, Levi was single, and they'd probably have lovely sandy-haired children. Bully for them. I had Shane.

⁂

There's something about sleeping in an Amish house. Aside from the sound of teenagers skulking in the night, it's silent. I couldn't even hear the traffic from the highway. And the stars? Impossibly bright. I'd forgotten how bright stars could be.

When I was a teen, I'd hike to Cascade Head at night just to look at the stars. They reminded me how little I was, and how big the rest of the world was. Sometimes I would pray, back when I did such things. I thought I could hear God better when I was under the stars.

Is that why the Amish lived so far from the city lights? Could they hear God better?

⚶

After the demise of my arm, I found myself in strictly observation mode. When the children were home, I followed them around with my notepad in hand.

I had avoided children in my old life. But the children I had interacted with, including my niece, were nothing like the youngest Burkholder children.

There were moments when they laughed like normal children. When Levi appeared, you'd think they were promised a trip to the circus.

Were children still into the circus? Or did they prefer to stay home with their Wii? I wouldn't know.

Either way, these children spent the bulk of their time in a state of soberness I'd never observed in any other American children. They attended to their chores without Martha harping on them.

And yet they still had very individual personalities. Samuel had a penchant for practical jokes; I'd actually heard some of the family members refer to him as "Joker Sam." Permanent nickname? I hoped not for his sake. But when he wasn't tending to the cows or doing his homework, he seemed to enjoy removing key items and putting them somewhere else. Martha found half of her kitchen pots on the seat of the tractor once. Elizabeth's faceless doll was in the pantry, next to the flour.

Samuel at least had sense enough to leave Gideon's things alone, though I wondered if in the past he had tried something and paid the consequences.

Leah, by contrast, was shy and reserved. She probably paid the most attention to her schoolwork, and she seemed to be constantly cataloging information.

Elizabeth was the dreamer. If I was sitting in the living room with my notepad, she would occasionally curl up next to me with her doll, telling me what "Mary" had done that day while she was away at school.

The older boys remained a mystery to me. I knew Amos helped his father with the heavy manual labor around the farm. I asked Sara once if he were planning on marrying soon; she answered that marrying season wasn't till November. Whether there would be a family wedding in the autumn or not remained anyone's guess.

Elam worked in town, often coming home covered in concrete dust. At least, I guessed it was concrete. He resembled Levi in face but not expression. Whereas Levi's face was usually open and friendly, Elam's was wary and often creased in a frown.

Then there was Sara.

Sara tired of my brace within days. "You're going to have to learn to sew a button sometime," she said. "Your left hand doesn't do *that* much. Don't you think you could try?"

So I did.

If I held my injured left arm just right, I could manage to hang onto the fabric while my uninjured right arm maneuvered the needle. Sara helped with the threading for humanitarian reasons. A needle through my finger didn't help anyone.

"You insert the needle here," she said, pointing at a spot in the fabric scrap.

"Why there?"

"Because that's where the button's going."

"What if I wanted to put the button somewhere else?"

"You don't."

"I don't?"

"No."

"Okay." I followed her directions. "Like that?"

"Yes."

"Shouldn't I have a thimble or something?"

"For just sewing a button, you'll do."

Five minutes and two thread knots later, I held up my button-laden fabric scrap with pride. "There!"

Sara nodded. "That will do."

"Are you ever proud of your work?" I asked.

"No. It is not Amish to be proud. To be prideful, arrogant—*hochmut*—is a sin."

"You're not rubbing your work in other people's noses, though. It's pride of a job well done."

"It can become arrogance."

"But what if it doesn't?"

Sara opened her mouth to answer when Gideon stomped in the door, fresh from the fields.

And I do mean fresh. I could smell him eight feet away.

"The Colblentzes' barn caught fire," he announced with a wheeze.

Martha left the kitchen. "Is anyone hurt? Did the fire spread?"

"None's hurt. Jacob's Billy got the animals out. Titus said bad wiring's to blame."

"And the Colblentzes' house?"

"Fit and fine."

By this time Samuel, Leah, and Elizabeth were down the stairs and full of questions.

"Billy's barn? Did he get burned?" Samuel asked.

Leah tugged on Gideon's shirt. "Is Susie okay?"

Martha held a hand to her chest. "Was there damage to the house or fields?"

Gideon shook his head. "They said it was the wires, so it burned from the inside. The fields are fine, the house is fine. We'll have the barn raisin' on Friday."

I stifled an excited gasp. A real, live Amish barn raising? How lucky could I get!

couldn't have planned for a barn raising better myself, unless I'd personally set fire to the Colblentzes' barn.

Which, of course, I didn't. I'm afraid of matches. And it's unethical journalism.

The day before, Martha's baking and cooking kicked into a gear I'd never seen. With impossible speed she produced three pies, a baked custard, a side of roasted pork, and four loaves of bread.

The woman's a machine.

I worked in the garden that day, as best I could. Without using my left arm, I sat on the ground in the dirt, pulling weeds and neatening rows of beans and vegetables that the family would can for the next year. Leah kept me company, commenting on the state of the plants and the likelihood of rain.

We'd counted our third water droplet when my phone rang in my apron pocket. "I'll be right back," I told Leah.

She watched as I walked back toward the house. It occurred to me that she didn't watch people answer cell phones very often.

Shane's name flashed on the caller ID. "The rain must help the reception. How are you?"

He exhaled hard into the phone. "Feeling pretty stupid."

"Why?"

"I went to pick up your mail like you asked. Who was the guy at your apartment with your bike?"

Uh-oh. "I sprained my wrist pretty bad. Levi's a friend of mine, and he offered to take my bike back and get my car."

"He did."

"Yes."

"Why didn't you call me? I would have taken care of everything."

I sighed. "Shane, you're up to your eyebrows in work, and it's not like your office is anywhere near the repair place or my apartment. You would have been driving all day."

"I wish you'd asked."

"Service cut out. Aside from smoke signals, there was nothing I could do. And you don't really have any south-facing windows."

"Glad this is all a joke to you. Is your wrist okay?"

"It's fine, and I'm joking because you're overreacting. There's nothing for you to worry about."

"Sorry. You're a beautiful woman—"

"Yeah, well, so is Kim, and she sounded single and motivated when I talked to her."

"The guy looked like a real rube."

I bristled. "That was uncalled for."

"He does!"

"He worked hard to catch up with his peers and is the first member of his family to attend, much less graduate from, college. He left a corporate job to be near his family. I think you can cut him some slack."

I guessed it was a corporate job. Ida had said "big company." Either way, Levi had achieved more in his lifetime than most of us, Shane included.

"I just don't like him," Shane said, his voice weighted with resentment.

"Couldn't tell."

"Look, if you say it was nothing, I'll believe you."

"Nothing," I said, hoping the slight shake to my voice didn't travel over the cellular frequency.

"Sorry I got upset. You said your arm's fine?"

"It is."

"Tell me if you break a leg?"

"If I have cell service, you'll be the first to know."

⁂

When Leah and I finished in the garden, I took my notepad and sat in the kitchen while Martha toiled away. I didn't think that many pies existed outside of a Shari's.

She worked uninterrupted until Elizabeth ran in squealing that the pig was in the garden.

"Jayne?" she said.

I looked up from my notes.

"Could you remove the pie from the oven if I'm not back in five minutes?"

"Of course," I heard myself agree.

Maybe she'd be back in five minutes and be able to remove the pie herself. I mean, how hard is it to chase a pig?

Five minutes rolled by. No Martha.

I set my notes down and approached the oven. The familiar coil of discomfort tightened in my stomach. I hated ovens. Always had.

Martha had left a hot pad by the stove. I used it to open the heavy door. I peered in—a lemon meringue number sat inside, looking lightly browned, innocuous, and yet menacing at the same time. It *knew* I had to deal with it. And it might be lightly browned now, but if I just left it there, that nice golden color would be a thing of the past.

Gingerly, I reached in, greeted by waves of oppressive heat. Were there any other hot pads? I backed away, looked around, and eventually located a few more in a drawer.

Two per hand. Except that my left arm ached. Armed with two pads in my right hand I reached in again toward the lemon meringue with its caramel-tinted peaks. I grasped each side of the pie and lifted it from the rack. The contents swished; I froze.

Seriously, it was a pig in the garden, not a yeti. What was taking so long? It seemed safer to leave the pie in the oven than risk coating the floor with it, but I heard no sound of approaching footsteps.

Breathe, I told myself. *You're an adult. Adults remove things from ovens. They seldom die from the experience.*

My hands were growing warm, even through the double layer of protection. Now or never. With careful movements, I raised the pie in my grasp and placed it on the stovetop. Finally. I closed the oven door and backed away with a jump.

Done. I had survived. No burns. The pie looked beautiful, and a part of me felt proud that I had had a hand in it. Maybe I could try baking.

Then I smelled it. The tiniest whiff of smoke. I looked at the pie— not a burnt or charred spot on the thing. Where else could it be coming from?

The scent grew stronger. "Sara!" I called, hopeful. Nothing.

Logically, it had to be coming from the oven. Now that I thought about it, it should probably be turned off, right?

I turned the knob all the way to the left. Maybe the smell came from something that fell to the bottom of the oven. Martha *had* been cooking all day, so I supposed that something dropping or dripping wasn't a stretch of the imagination.

I opened the door to the oven; at the sight of flames, I jumped back. But even as I saw the flames, I saw the source.

Hot pad one of two.

Probably should have counted when I was done.

With the new influx of air, the flames experienced a growth spurt. I yelped and made a mad grab for the water faucet in the kitchen sink.

Martha had to have tongs somewhere… When I found them (located oddly near the canned goods), I snatched the blazing hot pad from the oven and flicked it to the sink.

It landed with a satisfying hiss. I poured more water over the smoldering ruins before closing the now flameless oven. As I closed it I saw a figure in the kitchen entryway.

I'd come through the pie and the following emergency with a certain grace, but seeing Levi caused my heart to pound.

"How long have you been there?" I demanded.

"Long enough," he said, his smirk answering my question.

"Do you make a habit of sneaking up on people?"

"I didn't want to startle you while you were firefighting."

"Thanks."

"Where's my mom?"

"Chasing a pig and taking too long."

"She likes you," he said, replacing the smirk with a smile.

"How can you tell?"

"She trusts you with pie."

"Good to know. So you came down to give me a hard time?"

"Yes. And I have your car."

"As long as you've done something useful."

"Keys?" He held out a familiar-looking set of car keys.

I took them and dropped them in my apron pocket. "Thanks. Everything go okay with Kim?"

"Yes," he said, but another answer flashed in his eyes.

"What happened?"

"Your boyfriend is Shane?"

I chewed my lip. "Yes…"

"He came for your mail. That's what he told Kim."

"Okay."

"I don't think he was happy to see me."

Not really, no. "I wouldn't take it personally. How's Kim?"

He shrugged. "Fine, I guess."

Huh. "She's one of my best friends," I said. "She's brilliant. Great instincts."

"Good for her."

"And she's pretty. Don't you think she's pretty?"

Levi sighed and leaned against the wall. "I'm not interested in Kim, if that's what you're hinting at."

"Well, you should be. She's a catch."

"I'm sure she is."

"You should be so lucky."

"Jayne—" He opened his mouth as if to say something, but he must have changed his mind. "Never mind."

"Thanks for getting my car. It was a huge help."

He gave a small smile. "You're welcome. Anytime."

⁓⁓⁓

There are buffet restaurants with less food than at an Amish barn raising. Tables had been set up thirty feet from the charred barn. Pies upon pies stretched nearly as far as the eye could see. The sky threatened rain, but this group seemed to hold back the emptying of the heavens out of sheer will.

"How often do you guys do this?" I asked Sara as we carried food items to the tables.

She shrugged. "As often as we need to. Usually not till summer. We don't get many fires this time of year."

"Makes sense. Thanks for my dress, by the way."

Her face lit up. "Do you like it?"

"I do. It seems like it hangs really well."

"It's because I cut it on a bias. That's why there's a seam down the middle—if you look at the weave, it forms a V-shape when it's sewn together."

"Clever." I set the pork down on the table. "How's that?"

"Fine."

"Do we have to carve it?"

"The men will."

"You really like sewing, don't you."

Her face grew still, and she looked as though she chose her words carefully. "I understand fabric and the way it covers people. I understand it the way Levi understands wood."

"Do you think you would ever want to work with fabric outside the community, the way Levi does?"

"I think there's another pie in the buggy—I'll go get it," she said, her words coming out in a panicked jumble.

She all but ran back to the field of parked buggies.

⚜

I felt like Kelly McGillis in *Witness*, walking around and watching men sweat, move beams, and pound nails.

Except there was no Harrison Ford or that other blond guy vying for my attention. And that was okay with me, because I'd come to the conclusion that there were too many men in my life right now.

Personal life aside, I focused my attention on the structure taking shape before my eyes. What would it be like to live in a community where everyone took care of each other? When my dad died, my mom had the reception catered. I had the feeling that here, she would have been swimming in custard and cobbler.

One year a coastal storm blew a tree into our kitchen. We had to leave it until the insurance man came out; contractors arrived two weeks later. What would it have been like if the neighbors had come over with their tools and gotten the job done?

On the other hand, the din was incredible. Aside from the gaggle of men constructing the new barn, another group tore the old one down, piling the burnt and damaged wood near the road. The scene looked and sounded like a battle, builders versus breakers.

I tracked down Leah and Elizabeth, who were playing with the other children mercifully far away from the noise. Two sets of sticks had been driven into the ground, turning an otherwise ordinary field into a soccer stadium for the kids. Leah and Samuel, in particular, could boast of FIFA-worthy feet. I'd never seen kids move like that.

Not that I was a soccer aficionado of any kind, but I'd watched enough with Shane to know what did and didn't constitute ability. If these were any other kids, they'd be recruited out of high school to play nationally. Not these children, though. At some point, they would put down the soccer ball and turn to adult responsibilities full-time. But wasn't it better that way? I'd known scores of people from school who dreamt of the rock star or pro-baseball player life, but whose careers never made it further than the video rental store. These kids were realistic, or at least their parents were.

Were they losing anything by having fewer opportunities? Or did their lessened options serve their purpose?

I mulled the thought in my head as I watched the ball travel up and down the field.

⁂

"Jayne?"

I jumped, nearly dropping my laptop. I looked up at Sara. "You have very quiet feet."

"Can I show you something?"

"Of course."

"In my room?"

"Okay." I closed the lid to my laptop and followed her.

When we were inside her room, she shut the door and spent another moment with her ear pressed to the doorframe. Once she decided the coast was clear, she walked across the room and stamped her heel.

At least it looked like a heel stamp, but her foot went right through the floor, revealing a loose board. She got on her hands and knees before retrieving what looked like a stack of magazines.

"Yes," she said, laying the pile on the bed.

I took a closer look. There were catalogs for JCrew and Anthropologie, as well as copies of *InStyle* and *Vogue*.

"Yes to what?" I asked.

"Your question."

"Which one?"

"The one about me and Levi being the same."

lowered my voice, not wanting my questions or Sara's revelations to be overheard. "You would leave?"

Sara clasped her hands around her knees. "I would think about it."

"What would you do?"

"Go to school. Become a clothing designer."

"Really." I sat back on the bed. "Where do you get these?"

She looked down. "Sometimes I get them when I go to town. Sometimes Levi gets them for me."

I tried to picture builder Levi, motorcycle-riding Levi, purchasing a copy of *Vogue*.

Nope. Couldn't get there.

But Sara as a fashion designer? Couldn't get there, either. "When did you start getting interested in—"

"We would go into town, and the women would be wearing such beautiful colors. Not just blues and greens and purples, but reds and pinks and yellows. I could tell by the cut of their clothes which ones were more flattering and why. And," she said, reaching to the bottom of the stack, "I have these."

She held a sketchpad.

"May I look?"

She nodded.

The sketches were very well done. Even I could tell that. Sara's designs showed a creative use of lines and a good eye for color. I would have expected an Amish girl to design dresses with high necklines and low hemlines, but these weren't. "I can see Gemma in this one."

"Gemma?"

I lowered the sketchbook. "Friend of mine, back home."

Sara pulled her legs up and hugged her knees to herself. "What's it like choosing what to wear from a hundred options every day?"

"I don't have a hundred, although Gemma probably does. I don't know. It's hard sometimes to choose."

Sara looked skeptical. "Really?"

"Usually I throw things on and don't think about them much, but I've known Gemma to be twenty minutes late because she couldn't decide on an outfit."

"But you don't?"

"Well, most of my clothes are black. Matching isn't hard at that point. Gemma has shoes that match sweaters, and bags that match pants, and skirts that match earrings. Dressing like Gemma is complicated."

"I want to meet her."

I smiled. "Maybe I can get her to come down."

"I hate wearing black. I don't like blue, either."

"What do you like?"

"Yellow. Purple. Orange. Bright green. Pink."

"Hopefully not together."

She laughed at that. "No, not together. I like white too. Everything looks cleaner with white."

"How would you leave?"

Sara bit her lip. "Levi would help me. I'd live with him for a while. Get my GED. Try to get into design school." She shrugged. "I don't know. Maybe I'll stay and be baptized here. My parents stayed."

"Your grandparents left."

"I don't know. Do you think it's possible to go to heaven, even if you're not baptized?"

"I—I'm not really the person to ask," I stammered. "I haven't been to church in years."

"But you went to church?"

"My dad was an elder."

"You left the church?"

"I stopped going, yeah."

"Do you worry about going to hell?"

"Do you?" I found it safer to deflect the question.

"Our bishop says the English don't go to heaven. I don't think Jesus was

Amish, though, and I don't think His disciples were. I think His disciples went to heaven."

"I think so. So...do you think you could live apart from your family? You seem so connected."

"I'd have Levi. And Grandma."

"I don't see my mom and sister. Sometimes, I wish things were better."

"Why don't you make them better?"

"It's complicated."

"You should try to make things better."

"Sometimes, people just get stuck. Why don't Levi and your dad talk?"

Before she could answer, footsteps sounded down the hallway. Before you could say "Spring Collection," Sara snatched up her pile of contraband and stashed it safely under the flooring.

***

I really did wish things were better with my family. The early nights at the Burkholder farm gave me lots of time to think about how much in my life I wanted to change.

But when it came to my mom and sister...what could I do? I couldn't be the daughter my mom wanted. She wanted the traditional good girl. I couldn't be that girl. She nearly had a heart attack when I drew on my Converse sneakers in ballpoint pen as a teen. My shoes didn't look like the other daughters' shoes. At least, they didn't look like the shoes worn by her friends' daughters.

I didn't care what they thought. Her friends' daughters smirked at me and whispered behind my back about the streak of purple in my hair and the band T-shirts I wore as they strutted around in their Tommy Hilfiger outfits.

Even though I grew out of the Converse-sketching, hair-dying phase, I don't know that my mom ever noticed.

And Beth...

I didn't know how to reach her. I didn't know how to be her sister.

What would it be like to live in a family like the Burkholders? To have my family mean so much to me that I changed careers to be near them, like Levi?

***

I dreamed about pie that night.

Odd, considering my fear of ovens and accidental pyromaniac tendencies. But the pie looked really good. I think it was a nectarine raspberry pie. I don't know where that came from. I don't think it's possible to have nectarines *and* raspberries together in a pie. Either way, it sounded really good. It sounded good as breakfast food. Pie was pretty close to toast and jam, wasn't it? Maybe more like toast, jam, and some fruit chunks, but it still sounded good.

Really good.

To my disappointment, Martha had not read my mind that morning. There were potatoes, sausages, and a steaming mound of cheese-topped scrambled eggs, but no pie.

I couldn't blame her, though. She'd made, like, a billion pies the day before. Maybe she had pie elbow, or whatever you call a pie-induced injury.

I helped clean up the breakfast dishes after the men left for work. "I was wondering," I said, as I scrubbed plates, "if you could teach me how to bake."

"What kind of baking?"

"I don't know. Bread—I've never made bread. The cobbler you made the other day was really good. Or," I paused artfully as I removed a stubborn bit of cheese, "there's pie. I don't know how to make pie."

Martha stopped drying dishes. "You don't know how to make pie?"

I shook my head.

"Your mother never taught you to make pie?"

"I wasn't much interested in baking when I lived with my mother."

To say the least. I couldn't be bothered to make toast at the time.

"The most important thing about the crust is not to make the shortening bits too fine."

And so it began.

When the last dishes were put away, Martha insisted that I measure out the flour myself, even with my injury. I dipped the cup measure into the flour bag, filled it, and then clumsily tried to scrape off the excess mound of flour on the top with my sore arm.

Martha shook her head. "You can't scoop like that. Dump it out."

Startled, I obeyed.

She removed a spoon from a drawer. "If you scoop, you may get air bubbles and your amounts won't be right. Use a teaspoon to add a little in at a time."

I tried to follow her instructions, but maneuvering the spoon and cup measure with my brace proved too difficult. Martha stepped in and offered to fill it, now that I knew the correct method.

After all the flour made it successfully to the mixing bowl, Martha taught me how to cut in shortening using two butter knives, drawing them across the bowl in opposite directions. "Many recipes tell you to continue until the mixture resembles coarse sand, but they're wrong. Only mix until it looks like little peas. Your piecrust will come out flakier that way."

After she rolled out the crust—another task I couldn't complete with a brace—she turned back to me. "What sort of pie do you want to bake?"

I bit my lip. "A fruit pie?"

"What fruit? We have apples, canned apricots, frozen berries…"

Apricots were kind of like nectarines. "Apricot? And raspberry?"

Martha lifted an eyebrow. "Never done that before."

We rinsed the apricots and let them dry a bit in a strainer. The raspberries remained frozen when we stirred them with the apricots, some flour, a little sugar, a half-teaspoon of cinnamon, and a pinch of nutmeg. After we poured the filling into the pie pan, Martha showed me how to fold over the top sheet of pie pastry and crimp the edges shut.

"Now you have to cut vents," she said, handing me the knife. "You could cut slits or make a design. You can also use your scrap crust as decoration."

I cut two hearts out of the leftover piecrust, and then I cut a heart in the crust itself as a vent. "How's that?"

"Good. Now put it in the oven."

Uh-oh. "Is the oven on?"

Martha gave me a blank look. "Yes. The oven must be hot when you put the pie in, or the pastry won't bake right."

Hot oven, hot oven. Oh, dear. "Um…"

"*Ja?*"

"Er…I don't think I can do it."

"You can't…"

"Lift. I can't lift the pie pan with one hand." I let out a forced chuckle. "Too heavy. Lot of fruit in there."

Never mind I removed the meringue the day before. But wasn't meringue lighter because of all that air?

"Oh." Martha grasped the pie with one hand and yanked the oven door open with the other. A wave of hot air greeted my face. She set it perfunctorily on the rack, closed the oven, and eyed me up and down. "You should eat more. Strengthen you up."

～⁂～

Leah wrinkled her nose. "What kind of pie is it?"

I tapped her kapp. "Apricot raspberry. Doesn't that sound good?"

"I ain't never had apricot raspberry pie."

"There's a first time for everything."

"It smells good," Elizabeth said.

"It smells like pie," Samuel corrected decisively.

"Who wants a slice?" I asked.

The pie had waited, uneaten, untasted, until the children returned from school. They greeted it with the enthusiasm reserved for strange things like sweetmeats and marzipan.

I cut into the pie with a knife, the crust still slightly warm under my fingers. After cutting the first wedge, I tried to lift it out with the flat edge of the knife.

What landed on the pie plate looked less like pie than it did a fruity train wreck.

Leah squinted at the plate. "I think you need a pie server."

"Oh. Right." I started fumbling through the drawers in front of me, but Leah pulled one out from a drawer across the kitchen.

"Here you go."

"Thanks." The next slices came out much prettier. I passed out forks and led the troops to the kitchen table.

My first bite melted in my mouth with an explosion of flavors. The tartness of the raspberries contrasted with the muskiness of the apricots.

Did everyone's first pie come out like this? I hadn't baked since I was in middle school home economics, and even then my muffins had collapsed like my mother's dreams for my future.

But the pie? The pie was special. Even as I devoured the rest of my slice and scraped the last bits of goo and crust from the plate, I wondered what other things I could learn to do while I was here.

～⁂～

Gideon took me aside after dinner that night.

Your daughter wants to leave your family to become a fashion designer, I thought.

"We'll be going to church at the Lapps' home, day after tomorrow," he said.

Clearly, he couldn't read minds. I had to think for a moment and shift gears. Was it Friday already? I'd completely lost track of days since my arrival.

"Sunday. Church. Okay," I said after I'd oriented myself in space and time.

"We don't allow outsiders into our church services."

"Not ever? I mean, observing the service would show me a lot about your culture. And I wouldn't talk. I could sit in the back—"

Gideon held up his hand. "No outsiders. I don't want to bring trouble to my door."

Trouble? What would that look like? Images of Amish men carrying pitchforks flashed through my mind.

"We follow the *Ordnung*," Gideon said.

I nodded. "I've heard the term."

"We must follow the *Ordnung* at all times. And we must never give anyone cause to be thinking that we're not."

"Okay..."

"Some people don't much like that you're here, is all. We see nothing wrong with it, but we don't need the bishop at our door for anything but a friendly dinner."

"I understand. That's fine," I said.

But inside I was disappointed.

⚬⚬⚬

Sunday dawned cold and drizzly. While the woodstove in the living room emitted a fair amount of heat, my feet still ached with cold. I put serious thought into turning on the oven in the kitchen, pulling up a chair, and reading a good book.

Maybe not my most brilliant idea, but thinking is tough when your feet are blue.

While I contemplated the state of my chill, the Burkholder family prepared for church. Their preparing for church resembled in no way my family's preparation for church.

In my family, there was a lot of rushing, arguments over bathroom space, and encouragement to finish breakfast quickly.

The Burkholder process resembled clockwork. Each child dressed and prepared himself or herself. The boys, including Amos and Elam, wore newer-looking pants and crisply pressed shirts. All the girls wore dresses I hadn't seen yet, in lighter colors and nicer fabrics. Where bedlam reigned in the Tate household every Sunday morning, the Burkholders moved with a peaceful sense of routine.

The routine continued until the family filed out the door, looking a bit like the von Trapp family.

From inside, I could hear their steps halt and the tension heighten.

"Daddy," Elizabeth asked, "where's the buggy?"

I stood up from the rocking chair and peered out the door, over the children's shoulders. The shed doors were open and the buggy was nowhere to be seen.

Chapter 11

"The buggy may be gone," Gideon said, with a nearly undetectable tightening of the jaw, "but we will still get to church. We will walk."

"How far away are the Lapps?" I asked.

"Two miles from here."

"I have my car now. I could drive you."

The entire family perked up like daisies in fresh water.

"I mean, I'd have to take two trips. You wouldn't all fit…"

Two minutes later Gideon, Amos, Elam, and Samuel were buckled in. I'd pulled an old University of Oregon sweatshirt from the trunk of my car over my Amish ensemble so I looked less like a driving Amish woman and more Mennonite, perhaps. It was just too much work to take off the organza kapp. The ride over was silent, and when I unloaded my passengers outside the Lapp residence, I turned around to pick up Martha and the girls.

"There is something I must show you in your room," Martha announced when I returned. Without pause, she marched me back to my bedroom and closed the door. "Take off your sweatshirt and kapp," she said.

I stopped myself from frowning, shrugged out of the warm garment, and dutifully began the kapp removal process.

From her pocket she retrieved a handful of hairpins. With quick movements, she pinned my short strands of hair up and fastened the kapp on top.

"Keep your eyes down. Stay in the back. Move your mouth during the songs. Don't let anyone notice you."

Before I could say a word of protest or thanks, Martha whirled out of the room and gathered the girls like chicks. "We're late," she said. "Thank Jayne for driving us."

Sara, Leah, and Elizabeth chorused their gratitude.

Martha instructed me to park a bit behind the buggies. I didn't know how it looked, an Amish woman behind the wheel, but then who was I to care how things looked?

For the first time in a long time, I realized I did care. I didn't care what people thought of me, but I did care what they thought of the Burkholders.

"Martha," I said just before she climbed out of the car. "I don't want people to talk. You've been very kind to me. I don't want you to have any trouble on my account."

"Keep your eyes down. You look Amish," she replied.

And with that she walked away.

I knew she was trying to give me a gift. A gift I didn't know if I could, or should, receive.

From what I remembered in my research, the men sat on one side of the room and the women on the other. So if Gideon sat on the men's side, and I sat in the back and didn't say a word...

If he sat toward the front, this could work. People slipped in and out of church unnoticed all the time, didn't they?

Come to think of it, "people" was me. I recalled slipping in less and slipping out more...at least when my dad wasn't looking.

So if I could sneak out of church without my dad knowing, chances were I could do it without Levi's dad noticing, either.

I followed the path to the door Martha had taken earlier. The sound of singing voices filled the air. When I cracked the door open, I could see that even the minister—pastor? preacher?—was facing away from the congregation. I slid into the back with the stealth of a cold war operative, minus the cyanide pill.

Benches served as the seating of choice. Old men, young women, small boys—every member of the community sat in this room, singing their hearts out. In German.

Even the children sat still and sang. I couldn't remember ever sitting that still in church, although I did remember singing.

The sermon began after the singing, not that I understood a word. It too was in the same dialect.

I remembered having a hard time as a teen staying awake and involved in the service. Here, everyone was bright eyed. I didn't see a single yawn, even though this minister didn't appear to be telling any family stories or funny moral anecdotes. He spoke firmly and directly, and everyone paid attention.

At least I thought he spoke seriously. He was stoic enough that he could be doing stand-up comedy and I wouldn't be able to tell.

I stayed through the service, hands folded, eyes cast down every time the minister looked in my direction. There was a recited prayer and another song, during which I stepped out and cut a trail for my car and the warmth of my sweatshirt.

My sweatshirt was firmly in place when Gideon returned. I searched his face for evidence of suspicion and found none.

Martha nodded at me. "Thank you for waiting, Jayne. We hope we haven't kept you from your work."

Tricky, this one. I denied inconvenience and watched as the men loaded up for the return home.

I sought Gideon out when we returned to the Burkholder farm. "What do you think happened to your buggy?"

"Probably stolen," he said with a shrug. "We will buy another."

"Shouldn't you contact the police?"

"It's Sunday."

"Okay. Tomorrow, then?"

"We can afford to buy another buggy. We don't got a need to seek revenge."

I shook my head. "I'm not talking about revenge, I'm talking about justice. Either way, eighty percent of stolen vehicles are found and returned. I don't know why a buggy would be different."

"Jayne—"

"By filing it with the police, you're at least doing what you can to protect your neighbors from the same thing happening to them."

I watched Gideon hear my words, watched his mind process while varying emotions crossed his face.

"*Ja,*" he said. "I think you are right."

"I have a cell phone. You're welcome to call the police with it."

He shook his head. "It's Sunday. It can wait until tomorrow."

<hr />

I had a bicycle stolen once, when I was a student. Well, maybe not stolen as much as swapped. I came out of History of Ancient Greek Art to find that my bike was gone and replaced with an older, less gently used one than my own.

Same lock. Different bike.

I even looped around the bike racks a few times to make sure I wasn't crazy.

I all but sprained my thumb, dialing the police. Or rather, 411 to get to the police. But either way, I wasn't letting moss grow under the worn tires of the bike in front of me.

I couldn't imagine not immediately reporting the theft of my primary mode of transportation. In an odd way, I kind of respected it.

The thief (or thieves) who removed the buggy from the yard may have complicated the Burkholders' morning, but Gideon refused to give him (or her) the power to disrupt their day.

Admirable. And oddly empowering.

Since my original bike was covered by my parents' insurance, I was able to replace it with ease.

I kept the swapped-out bike for two more years (with the police's permission before selling it to help fund a proper motorcycle jacket with Kevlar.

Maybe I hadn't needed to dial so fast.

The police, as I had suspected, treated the buggy theft pretty seriously. Although in monetary value the buggy was far less expensive than, say, a car, the theft carried the air of a religious hate crime. Officers came out and questioned Gideon and Martha, as well as the neighbors down the road.

Conversations were conducted outside, despite the light drizzle. I joined Sara, Leah, Elizabeth, and Samuel at the window, peeking from behind the curtain. When the cops finally drove away, Gideon and Martha returned to the house and behaved as though a valuable personal possession hadn't been snatched in the dark of night. They didn't seem at all bothered or stressed.

They may as well have had a PTA meeting.

Although the Amish probably didn't have PTA meetings.

Elam rode with his Mennonite buddy into town for work and didn't
require my taxi services. Life returned to a fairly normal schedule, until
Sara informed me that she was babysitting that afternoon and wanted me
to come too.

"You've got to be kidding."

Sara shook her head. "Why do you think I'm kidding?"

"Well, I, um…I mean…me? Babysit? I don't trust myself around Leah
and Elizabeth as it is."

Granted, I had no idea what to do with children. Whenever I saw Beth's
daughter, I froze up. I mean, I was messed up enough. It wasn't as though
I needed to share that with my little niece. Emilee was only five years old,
and I wasn't the sort of person a five-year-old ought to be with.

When I was fifteen, the woman in charge of the church nursery called
my mother and asked if I would volunteer. I showed up under protest with
no idea what to do and no desire to find out. The other ladies, as far as I
could tell, took one look at me, with my purple hair, Smashing Pumpkins
T-shirt, and perpetual scowl…

Let's just say I was never invited back.

And that was fine with me. Baby poop was never my thing, anyway.

Not that I would show up for childcare duty looking like a roadie these
days. I had grown up in the last ten years. But children remained a mystery
to me, and I'd always assumed it was for their own good.

Now Sara wanted me to babysit. And she wasn't taking no for an answer.
"They're good children," she said. "Because of the baby, I could use an extra
set of hands."

"Baby?" My panic grew. "I don't do babies."

"What's wrong with babies?"

"They're little. They're breakable. They don't use toilets."

Sara just rolled her eyes.

We showed up at Naomi Zook's home shortly after lunch. She pulled
Sara into a hug and introduced herself and the children to me.

Mary Ellen was the oldest at four years old, followed minutes later by her
twin, Becky. The little boy, Doyle, had celebrated his third birthday a few
weeks before. I shuddered at the thought of giving birth—again—a year
after having twins. Not that I could imagine giving birth at all.

Baby Ruby was, naturally, the baby of the house, a scant three months
old. Naomi placed Baby Ruby into Sara's arms the same way she might have

transferred a much-loved bag of flour. Transfer completed, Naomi waved goodbye and left for errands in town.

"Okay," I said when she was gone. "What do we do now?"

"You should play with the kids."

"How?"

She shrugged. "They're kids. They don't care much."

"That's not going to work. You're going to have to give me something else."

"What did you like to do when you were four?"

I stuck my hands on my hips. "Listen to rock and roll."

Okay, maybe not rock and roll. But I bet Raffi sounds a lot like rock and roll to the Amish.

"You don't remember doing anything else?"

"I try not to think too hard about my childhood."

"Why not?"

"Just because. Now that I'm remembering, though, I seem to recall a few games of follow the leader." I turned to Mary Ellen, Becky, and Doyle. "Follow the leader?" I said, my voice loud and clear. "Does that sound like fun?"

"They're young, Jayne, not deaf. But they might be if you keep yelling."

"Sorry." I lowered my voice and gestured with my good arm. "Follow me!"

We trailed around the farmhouse while acting like airplanes, elephants, football mascots, and newspaper editors, the latter two involving a lot of jumping and waving of arms. When that burst of energy, well, burst, I collapsed into a handy rocking chair.

As I rested, Mary Ellen whispered into Becky's ear, cast a furtive glance at me, and ran behind a corner. Becky followed. They stayed back there, giggling, peeking, and whispering.

"What are they doing?" I asked Doyle.

He looked away, shy.

"What are you doing, Mary Ellen?"

"We're sneaking!"

Amish children snuck? I had no idea. I turned to Doyle. "Do you like to sneak?"

He nodded without making eye contact.

The whispering continued. "Would you like to sneak with me?"

A pause…and a nod.

So we snuck. And after a successful campaign, Doyle, Becky, Mary Ellen, and I decided to turn our attention on Sara, who looked as though she had the easier time of it. She held the baby, and the baby was fine with the state of the union. But then, Sara had been around babies all her life. She probably knew exactly what to do.

We started behind the chair, then sprinted across the room to the stairwell, followed by a covert jaunt to the kitchen doorway and a shorter distance to where Sara stood, bouncing the baby and looking out the window.

"Oh good, there you are," she said, not at all startled by the children tugging at her skirts. "Can you hold Baby Ruby? I need to start dinner."

"Me?"

"Yes." She held Baby Ruby out.

I stepped back as if Baby Ruby were a smallpox blanket. Maybe "jumped" would be more accurate.

"I don't know what to do with babies. I've never been around babies."

"I thought you said your sister has a little girl."

"Yes, but—"

"And you saw her when she was tiny?"

"I did, but—"

"Baby Ruby is a baby too. And she's a real easy baby."

"You mean she doesn't poop? Or cry? Because that's my definition of an easy baby."

The children behind me giggled at my use of the word "poop." I guess such things are humorous to children across all walks of life.

Sara rolled her eyes. Teen eye rolls, I guess, are also the same. "Of course she has…movements…and sometimes she cries, but she's a real good baby and I need to start dinner."

"But—"

"She doesn't bite. She doesn't even have teeth yet."

Baby Ruby gave a smiley, toothless giggle, proving Sara's point.

"I don't think—"

Sara didn't give me a chance to think. She placed Baby Ruby in my arms in such a way that if I didn't take the baby, she would have fallen to the floor.

To my credit, I knew enough about babies to know that the whole floor thing would be bad.

Baby Ruby looked at me and blinked. Then burped.

"You need to hold her so her head is supported." Sara moved my arm until Baby Ruby rested just under my collarbone, with my hand propping up her lolling head.

"Is she okay?"

"She's fine."

"Are you sure?"

"Very. Can you take the children to the living room?"

"I have the baby!"

"They can entertain themselves."

And they did. They played happily, resuming their game of sneak while I held Baby Ruby.

Then the unthinkable happened. Baby Ruby urped and released a tiny cry. "Sara!"

Sara poked her head out of the kitchen. "What do you need?"

"She's not happy!"

"Bounce her up and down. Take her to look out the window."

"Can she see that far? I mean, is her vision that good?"

"If it makes her happy, does it matter?"

She had a point. I followed her instructions, and to my surprise it worked. Baby Ruby quieted instantly, her head nestling against me.

This wasn't so bad. In fact, it was rather nice.

Baby Ruby yawned. I agreed.

Chapter 12

Baby Ruby grew heavy, so I sat in the rocking chair. Mary Ellen and Becky herded Doyle into a game of house. Doyle found himself instructed to check on the cows. Often.

These were happy kids. Were all kids this happy? All Amish kids? I suddenly found myself beginning to rethink my previous opinions on the short end of the human race. Maybe they weren't so bad or difficult.

Corruptible, probably, but I'd been watching over this brood for thirty minutes and none of them had tried to wield knives or leap from windows. Perhaps I wasn't the terrible influence I thought I was.

Perhaps.

I might have sat in that rocking chair forever if Sara hadn't finished starting dinner.

"She hasn't bitten you yet, has she?"

"Not yet."

Sara leaned over my shoulder to look at the baby. "She's asleep."

"Really?" I craned my neck to see. Baby Ruby's soft eyelashes rested against her cheeks, just as Sara said.

No wonder she'd become so heavy. Had to say, Baby Ruby was awfully trusting. She didn't know me from Eve. How did she know I wasn't going to kidnap her once she lost consciousness?

I touched her head gingerly. "I can't believe she fell asleep."

Sara shrugged. "She'll wake up hungry at some point. Did she try to root?"

"Root?"

"Try to nurse?"

"You mean, on my—"

"I don't think she's nursed anywhere else."

90

the best time for asking. I can understand if you didn't want to wake us. If there's something real important that needs pulling, I can wake one of my sons to help you. Is there?"

Mike shook his head.

"Someone borrowed our buggy a day or two ago. Do you know where'n it might be?"

The boy looked away.

"Your foot does look like it's swelling. Do you want us to call someone for you? Take you to the clinic in town?"

"We took your buggy," Mike blurted.

"Oh?"

"We hooked it up to Nate's truck hitch."

Creative.

"Why did you take it?" Gideon sat on the ground.

Mike looked down, shame covering his features.

In that moment I was able to see him the way Gideon clearly did—not as a punk kid with an agenda of hate crime, but as a lost kid. A kid not beyond reach.

"It was just a joke," Mike said in a small voice.

"Hmm." Gideon thought on that. "Maybe it will be a funny one when we get it back. Do you know where it is?"

"Hight Street," Mike mumbled.

Gideon nodded. "That is a good joke. Would you like us to call some-one for you?"

The boy fidgeted. He had to be awfully cold down there, considering the whole saggy-pant thing. "My sister."

I retrieved my cell phone from the house and gave it to Mike to make the call. While we waited for her, Martha and Gideon helped Mike into the house and set him up by the stove. Martha clucked over his foot and wrapped with ice and a salve that smelled like the inside of the ton-ton from Wars movie *The Empire Strikes Back*.

His sister showed up about a half hour later, looking as though she might her brother with a pair of dull hedge trimmers. "You were with Sean again, weren't you."

He looked down. "They left."

"Of course they did. How bad is it?" She gestured toward his purple,

I could feel my cheeks turning pink. "But I, um, I don't…have any… you know."

"Babies don't know that. Don't worry. Naomi should be back from town soon."

A part of me felt disappointed inside. As disturbed as I was about the whole nursing thing, I was liking the sleeping baby, contented children experience.

Was it like this for Beth? Had my niece been anything like Baby Ruby? How much had I missed?

⁓⁓

I asked Gideon over dinner if he'd heard anything from the police.

"No," he said with a shake of his head. "There has been no call."

I didn't point out that the phone, such as it was, was in an exterior shed ten feet from the house and didn't have an answering machine.

But then, the police probably guessed that the Burkholder residence wasn't much of a telecommunications hub. I'd wished at the time that Gideon would have given them Levi's number, but that would have meant acknowledging Levi as a son, and Gideon didn't seem too keen on that.

Sara and I finished the dishes while Leah and Samuel finished their nightly school assignments. Elam and Amos still seldom spoke to me, although it seemed they avoided me less since the car ride to church.

Meaning that they didn't necessarily leave the room when I walked in.

I wrote in my journal on my computer that night, wanting to get the details of my time with the kids and the soccer team of conflicting emotions that kicked my thoughts in circles around my head.

Seriously. I was conflicted to the point that my internal metaphors were getting weird. I rolled my head around to the side, willing my tense neck muscles to relax. I remembered my Tylenol PM. And my melatonin. Seemed like a good idea—I could use a good night's sleep.

The household noises subsided as everyone went to bed. I continued typing until the warning bubble on my desktop advised me to save all my documents lest anything be lost when my computer died. That was fine with me; I could barely see straight.

I tucked my laptop into its case, resolving to drive to Levi's shop some-time the next day to recharge the computer batteries.

I yawned, burrowed under the layers of quilts, closed my eyes, and let the over-the-counter sleeping pills carry me away.

Noises outside reached my ears just before I fell asleep.

I burrowed deeper. Probably another one of Sara's many admirers. I'd been through this before, and tonight didn't strike me as being a good night to fly around in my nightdress.

The amount of clatter increased. For Pete's sake, this particular boy wasn't very good at the whole courting-in-secret thing. I heard a horse whinny, and then I heard another sound.

A word. Followed by several more, and not the kind I heard out here. The Amish weren't much for colorful language.

My eyes opened. Who would talk like that? I could hear the rumble of a motor. I knew some of the boys drove cars before they were baptized into the church, but it's not as though you'd drive to a girl's house, impress her with your command of expletives, and bring a horse along for kicks.

I edged out of bed and peeked out the window. Boys with backward-facing baseball caps and saggy pants were leading Shoe out of the barn and away from the house.

I racked my brain for any reason how this could be construed as something harmless. Came up empty. It's not as though horses need midnight walks when they can't sleep, and even if that were the case, I don't think saggy pants are high on the list of horse-wrangling wear.

Before I could talk myself into a different course of action, I shoved my feet into my shoes and pulled on my armored motorcycle jacket.

I don't know why it hadn't occurred to me last time to wear my jacket. Maybe I was getting better at the whole Amish-defense thing.

I burst out onto the porch and assessed the scene. Three boys in hooded sweatshirts skulked in the driveway. One of them held Shoe's reins.

"What do you think you're doing?" I yelled, deliberately making as much noise as possible.

Shouts of "Dude!" and "Get out, man!" broke out. They began to scatter, but the boy holding Shoe's reins made a mistake. In his panic, he tugged Shoe closer to him while extending his foot. Shoe's hoof landed solidly on the kid's thin Converse sneaker.

The boy cried out and yanked his foot back, the force of which sent him sprawling on his backside. He tried to get up but yelped when he put weight on that foot.

The other hoodlums didn't wait for him—they jumped into a beat-up Datsun and sped away, scattering gravel in their wake. The kid on the groun shouted obscenities at them, ending in a whimper.

"What is going on?" Gideon stepped out onto the porch. Behind him could see Martha, a quilt wrapped around her shoulders.

"Three boys were trying to take Shoe," I said. "This one got stepped o

The kid's eyes widened at the sight of Gideon, whose sleep-mussed bea gave him a fearsome expression. In desperation, the boy backed away i sort of crab-walk.

"If you are hurt, you should let us help," Gideon said. "It's fifteen m to town."

"Do you want me to call the police?" I asked.

"Not yet." Gideon stepped off the porch and approached the boy. "V is your name?"

The kid looked sideways and back. "Drew."

I didn't believe him, and I could tell Gideon didn't, either. "Oh. is your real name, Drew?"

This time "Drew" didn't break eye contact. "Mike."

"How is your foot, Mike?"

"It hurts."

"Can you take off your shoe?"

Mike looked from me to Gideon to Martha.

"If your foot is broken," I said, "it may swell to the point tha get your shoe off and they'll have to cut it off. Your shoe, not y

"Oh." He fumbled with the laces, which were halfway un When he removed his sock, the dark purple of the spreadin already be seen.

"Shoe has big feet," Gideon said.

"Shoe?" Mike shot a confused glance at the sneaker

"The horse," I answered. "The horse's name is Shoe

"He has big feet," Gideon continued. "He's a draft not for riding. Did you have something you neede

"Huh?"

"Were you taking our horse because you ne thing? A plow or a cart?"

Mike didn't answer.

"If you needed to borrow him, you only n

"Probably broken," Martha offered.

The sister reached for her purse. "Did he break, damage, or steal anything? Do you people take checks?"

Gideon held up a hand. "No need. He ain't hurt nothing but himself. Take him to a doctor—it'll be all right."

She tried to argue, but Gideon wouldn't budge. They helped Mike to the waiting car.

I think Martha gave them a loaf of zucchini bread on the way out.

When the headlights disappeared down the road, the three of us went back to our respective rooms.

Sara, Elam, and Amos stood in the hallway, concern covering their faces. Gideon spoke a few words in Dutch; everyone returned to bed.

I lay in bed, trying to sleep, not able to get the evening's events out of my head.

How could Gideon be so gentle, so gracious, so *forgiving* of Mike the hoodlum and yet refuse to have a relationship with his law-abiding, talented son? Levi's only crime was to leave the community and join a church with instruments. Mike had taken the family's main form of transportation and was caught removing one of their horses, and still he had received patience and kindness.

Why was Levi held to such a different standard? Wasn't he, as Gideon's son, worthy of a certain amount of grace?

───※───

I drove into town the next morning, citing the deadness of my laptop and cell batteries. Truth be told, it felt good to put on normal clothes and head toward civilization. I picked up Starbucks on the way in, filling a tray with an assortment of drinks and carbohydrates.

"Jayne!" Spencer's eyes lit up when I entered the office. "Nice of you to drop by."

"Hi, Spencer. I brought coffee for everybody. Did I bring enough?"

"More than. I think Levi's here somewhere—want me to get him?"

"Yes, please. I need to plug in my computer and phone—all my batteries are dead. This," I gave the tray a tap, "is my thank-you present."

"We feel thanked. Hold on."

He disappeared behind the shop door. Levi stepped through a moment later, followed by Grady.

"Hi, Jayne. How are things?"

"They're fine," I said, wondering what Spencer had told him. Knowing Spencer, it could be anything. "I really need to charge my laptop batteries. Do you mind if I plug in and hang around a while?"

Was it me or did the three of them brighten? "I brought coffee for everyone," I added.

"You're our new favorite person," Levi said. "Everyone's been dragging today. Do you want to come back to my office?"

"Sure," I said, not particularly wanting to be Spencer's verbal sparring partner while I worked. "If I'm not in your way."

Spencer didn't say a word as I headed down the hall with Levi. A quick glance revealed his face stuffed with scone.

Which was, in fact, the root of my intentions with the Starbucks trip.

"How are things with my family?" Levi asked, sorting through some papers and desk bric-a-brac to make space for me.

I sighed and relayed the events from the previous night.

"Have they said how they are planning to bring the buggy back?" he asked when I finished.

"No."

"I have a hitch on my truck. If it worked for the boys, I don't see any reason why it wouldn't work for me."

"Wouldn't you have to drive awfully slow?"

"I learned to drive a buggy before I learned to drive a car. I'm not a complete stranger to driving slow."

I narrowed my eyes. "How many speeding tickets did you get after you left?"

"Don't ask."

"What made you leave the community?"

"I wanted to go to school."

"That was all?"

He shrugged. "It was time."

"You know Sara wants to leave."

"Did she tell you?"

"She showed me her sketches."

"Do you mind taking back some contraband? I've got a stack for her."

"What are you going to do if she decides to leave?"

"Help."

I could feel my cheeks turning pink. "But I, um, I don't...have any... you know."

"Babies don't know that. Don't worry. Naomi should be back from town soon."

A part of me felt disappointed inside. As disturbed as I was about the whole nursing thing, I was liking the sleeping baby, contented children experience.

Was it like this for Beth? Had my niece been anything like Baby Ruby? How much had I missed?

———✦———

I asked Gideon over dinner if he'd heard anything from the police.

"No," he said with a shake of his head. "There has been no call."

I didn't point out that the phone, such as it was, was in an exterior shed ten feet from the house and didn't have an answering machine.

But then, the police probably guessed that the Burkholder residence wasn't much of a telecommunications hub. I'd wished at the time that Gideon would have given them Levi's number, but that would have meant acknowledging Levi as a son, and Gideon didn't seem too keen on that.

Sara and I finished the dishes while Leah and Samuel finished their nightly school assignments. Elam and Amos still seldom spoke to me, although it seemed they avoided me less since the car ride to church.

Meaning that they didn't necessarily leave the room when I walked in.

I wrote in my journal on my computer that night, wanting to get the details of my time with the kids and the soccer team of conflicting emotions that kicked my thoughts in circles around my head.

Seriously. I was conflicted to the point that my internal metaphors were getting weird. I rolled my head around to the side, willing my tense neck muscles to relax. I remembered my Tylenol PM. And my melatonin. Seemed like a good idea—I could use a good night's sleep.

The household noises subsided as everyone went to bed. I continued typing until the warning bubble on my desktop advised me to save all my documents lest anything be lost when my computer died. That was fine with me; I could barely see straight.

I tucked my laptop into its case, resolving to drive to Levi's shop sometime the next day to recharge the computer batteries.

I yawned, burrowed under the layers of quilts, closed my eyes, and let the over-the-counter sleeping pills carry me away.

Noises outside reached my ears just before I fell asleep.

I burrowed deeper. Probably another one of Sara's many admirers. I'd been through this before, and tonight didn't strike me as being a good night to fly around in my nightdress.

The amount of clatter increased. For Pete's sake, this particular boy wasn't very good at the whole courting-in-secret thing. I heard a horse whinny, and then I heard another sound.

A word. Followed by several more, and not the kind I heard out here. The Amish weren't much for colorful language.

My eyes opened. Who would talk like that? I could hear the rumble of a motor. I knew some of the boys drove cars before they were baptized into the church, but it's not as though you'd drive to a girl's house, impress her with your command of expletives, and bring a horse along for kicks.

I edged out of bed and peeked out the window. Boys with backward-facing baseball caps and saggy pants were leading Shoe out of the barn and away from the house.

I racked my brain for any reason how this could be construed as something harmless. Came up empty. It's not as though horses need midnight walks when they can't sleep, and even if that were the case, I don't think saggy pants are high on the list of horse-wrangling wear.

Before I could talk myself into a different course of action, I shoved my feet into my shoes and pulled on my armored motorcycle jacket.

I don't know why it hadn't occurred to me last time to wear my jacket. Maybe I was getting better at the whole Amish-defense thing.

I burst out onto the porch and assessed the scene. Three boys in hooded sweatshirts skulked in the driveway. One of them held Shoe's reins.

"What do you think you're doing?" I yelled, deliberately making as much noise as possible.

Shouts of "Dude!" and "Get out, man!" broke out. They began to scatter, but the boy holding Shoe's reins made a mistake. In his panic, he tugged Shoe closer to him while extending his foot. Shoe's hoof landed solidly on the kid's thin Converse sneaker.

The boy cried out and yanked his foot back, the force of which sent him sprawling on his backside. He tried to get up but yelped when he put weight on that foot.

The other hoodlums didn't wait for him—they jumped into a beat-up Datsun and sped away, scattering gravel in their wake. The kid on the ground shouted obscenities at them, ending in a whimper.

"What is going on?" Gideon stepped out onto the porch. Behind him I could see Martha, a quilt wrapped around her shoulders.

"Three boys were trying to take Shoe," I said. "This one got stepped on."

The kid's eyes widened at the sight of Gideon, whose sleep-mussed beard gave him a fearsome expression. In desperation, the boy backed away in a sort of crab-walk.

"If you are hurt, you should let us help," Gideon said. "It's fifteen miles to town."

"Do you want me to call the police?" I asked.

"Not yet." Gideon stepped off the porch and approached the boy. "What is your name?"

The kid looked sideways and back. "Drew."

I didn't believe him, and I could tell Gideon didn't, either. "Oh. What is your real name, Drew?"

This time "Drew" didn't break eye contact. "Mike."

"How is your foot, Mike?"

"It hurts."

"Can you take off your shoe?"

Mike looked from me to Gideon to Martha.

"If your foot is broken," I said, "it may swell to the point that you can't get your shoe off and they'll have to cut it off. Your shoe, not your foot."

"Oh." He fumbled with the laces, which were halfway untied as it was. When he removed his sock, the dark purple of the spreading bruise could already be seen.

"Shoe has big feet," Gideon said.

"Shoe?" Mike shot a confused glance at the sneaker in his hand.

"The horse," I answered. "The horse's name is Shoe."

"He has big feet," Gideon continued. "He's a draft horse, used for pulling, not for riding. Did you have something you needed pulled?"

"Huh?"

"Were you taking our horse because you needed to use him for something? A plow or a cart?"

Mike didn't answer.

"If you needed to borrow him, you only needed to ask. Though, daytime's the best time for asking. I can understand if you didn't want to wake us. If there's something real important that needs pulling, I can wake one of my sons to help you. Is there?"

Mike shook his head.

"Someone borrowed our buggy a day or two ago. Do you know where'n it might be?"

The boy looked away.

"Your foot does look like it's swelling. Do you want us to call someone for you? Take you to the clinic in town?"

"We took your buggy," Mike blurted.

"Oh?"

"We hooked it up to Nate's truck hitch."

Creative.

"Why did you take it?" Gideon sat on the ground.

Mike looked down, shame covering his features.

In that moment I was able to see him the way Gideon clearly did—not as a punk kid with an agenda of hate crime, but as a lost kid. A kid not beyond reach.

"It was just a joke," Mike said in a small voice.

"Hmm." Gideon thought on that. "Maybe it will be a funny one when we get it back. Do you know where it is?"

"Haight Street," Mike mumbled.

Gideon nodded. "That is a good joke. Would you like us to call someone for you?"

The boy fidgeted. He had to be awfully cold down there, considering the whole saggy-pant thing. "My sister."

I retrieved my cell phone from the house and gave it to Mike to make the call. While we waited for her, Martha and Gideon helped Mike into the house and set him up by the stove. Martha clucked over his foot and wrapped it up with ice and a salve that smelled like the inside of the ton-ton from the Star Wars movie *The Empire Strikes Back*.

Mike's sister showed up about a half hour later, looking as though she wanted to kill her brother with a pair of dull hedge trimmers. "You were out with Nate and Sean again, weren't you."

Mike looked down. "They left."

"Of course they did. How bad is it?" She gestured toward his purple, swollen foot.

"Probably broken," Martha offered.

The sister reached for her purse. "Did he break, damage, or steal anything? Do you people take checks?"

Gideon held up a hand. "No need. He ain't hurt nothing but himself. Take him to a doctor—it'll be all right."

She tried to argue, but Gideon wouldn't budge. They helped Mike to the waiting car.

I think Martha gave them a loaf of zucchini bread on the way out.

When the headlights disappeared down the road, the three of us went back to our respective rooms.

Sara, Elam, and Amos stood in the hallway, concern covering their faces. Gideon spoke a few words in Dutch; everyone returned to bed.

I lay in bed, trying to sleep, not able to get the evening's events out of my head.

How could Gideon be so gentle, so gracious, so *forgiving* of Mike the hoodlum and yet refuse to have a relationship with his law-abiding, talented son? Levi's only crime was to leave the community and join a church with instruments. Mike had taken the family's main form of transportation and was caught removing one of their horses, and still he had received patience and kindness.

Why was Levi held to such a different standard? Wasn't he, as Gideon's son, worthy of a certain amount of grace?

I drove into town the next morning, citing the deadness of my laptop and cell batteries. Truth be told, it felt good to put on normal clothes and head toward civilization. I picked up Starbucks on the way in, filling a tray with an assortment of drinks and carbohydrates.

"Jayne!" Spencer's eyes lit up when I entered the office. "Nice of you to drop by."

"Hi, Spencer. I brought coffee for everybody. Did I bring enough?"

"More than. I think Levi's here somewhere—want me to get him?"

"Yes, please. I need to plug in my computer and phone—all my batteries are dead. This," I gave the tray a tap, "is my thank-you present."

"We feel thanked. Hold on."

He disappeared behind the shop door. Levi stepped through a moment later, followed by Grady.

"Hi, Jayne. How are things?"

"They're fine," I said, wondering what Spencer had told him. Knowing Spencer, it could be anything. "I really need to charge my laptop batteries. Do you mind if I plug in and hang around a while?"

Was it me or did the three of them brighten? "I brought coffee for everyone," I added.

"You're our new favorite person," Levi said. "Everyone's been dragging today. Do you want to come back to my office?"

"Sure," I said, not particularly wanting to be Spencer's verbal sparring partner while I worked. "If I'm not in your way."

Spencer didn't say a word as I headed down the hall with Levi. A quick glance revealed his face stuffed with scone.

Which was, in fact, the root of my intentions with the Starbucks trip.

"How are things with my family?" Levi asked, sorting through some papers and desk bric-a-brac to make space for me.

I sighed and relayed the events from the previous night.

"Have they said how they are planning to bring the buggy back?" he asked when I finished.

"No."

"I have a hitch on my truck. If it worked for the boys, I don't see any reason why it wouldn't work for me."

"Wouldn't you have to drive awfully slow?"

"I learned to drive a buggy before I learned to drive a car. I'm not a complete stranger to driving slow."

I narrowed my eyes. "How many speeding tickets did you get after you left?"

"Don't ask."

"What made you leave the community?"

"I wanted to go to school."

"That was all?"

He shrugged. "It was time."

"You know Sara wants to leave."

"Did she tell you?"

"She showed me her sketches."

"Do you mind taking back some contraband? I've got a stack for her."

"What are you going to do if she decides to leave?"

"Help."

"You don't think she should stay?"

"I think it's up to her. If she makes the decision to leave, I'll support her."

"And if she decides not to go back?"

"That's up to her too."

"Will your dad cut her off as well?"

"I don't know. Probably. I don't know how many children he'd have to lose before he changed." Levi shrugged. "It's who he is, who he was raised to be."

"You were raised the same way."

"Mostly. Everyone's different. Is this enough space for you?" He pointed at the tidy desktop.

"I'm game."

"I'll let you work, then. Want to try to get the buggy with me afterward?"

"Sure."

He grinned. It was such an engaging grin, I didn't mind the prospect of driving at fifteen miles per hour, towing a buggy behind us.

checked my email in the quiet of Levi's office. There were the usual memos about sundry office happenings but nothing life altering. Then I poked around online, catching up on current events.

Bombings, earthquakes, corporate shenanigans…life seemed so much easier on the Burkholder farm.

Granted, the previous evening's events with Mike weren't exactly a picnic. But in relation to world destruction, the attempted horse theft didn't amount to much.

I pulled up my word processor, discovering that if I was careful I could still type with my left hand. I wrote about life at the Burkholders', learning to bake and sew, and my experience with Naomi's children.

Then there was my confusion over how to deal with Sara.

The part of me that grew up in the English world wanted to support her to be all that she could be, to believe in herself, dream big, stretch her horizons, reach for the stars—all of those cheesy sayings found on motivational posters.

But another part of me recoiled at the thought. I wanted to remind her she was Amish and, because of that, above the English desire to live life in the fast lane. Sara had a family who loved her, who would surround her with strength and love and food for the rest of her life.

Maybe that was it—the idea that being Amish set Sara and her family at a different standard. They were the last bastions of a nonconsumer existence so foreign to those of us who complained of being sucked into the rat race.

I don't think I was alone in that belief. The Amish clearly held themselves to a very high standard of behavioral expectations. Leaving their way of life was not included.

Gideon could forgive Mike because he expected Mike to behave badly, being English. It was his nature. But Levi…Levi was raised to join the church and follow in the footsteps of his father and grandfather.

A knock interrupted my thoughts. "Do you have a moment?" Levi's head appeared in the doorway.

My hands froze on the keyboard.

It really is awkward when the person you're writing about walks in. "What's up?"

"I need an opinion in the shop."

I closed the lid to my laptop. "Yeah?"

"There's a sideboard I'm working on and…well, you'll see. Put these on." He handed me a pair of safety glasses.

"I don't know why you'd want my opinion," I said as I followed him. "Design isn't really my thing."

"Do you own a Star Trek uniform?"

"No…"

"Then you're more qualified than one of the people I would have asked."

"Grady?"

"Spencer."

I squeezed my eyes shut as the visual flooded my imagination. "Wow."

"He goes to the conventions and everything."

"May he live long and prosper."

The shop was just as loud as I remembered. Bits of dismembered—or preassembled, I supposed—furniture littered the expanse of the space. A heavy layer of sawdust coated the floor.

"It's over here," Levi said, pointing toward the corner.

The sideboard stood six feet tall, and though it was clearly unfinished, the wood gleamed. "It's beautiful."

"It's a commission piece," Levi said, running his hand over the side. "The client was specific about some parts, but not the side shelves."

I examined the side shelves. The ones in the center were long, with short rows of shelves on either side. "Okay."

"I want to put a glass cabinet-cover over the side shelves."

"Can you do that?"

He arched an eyebrow. "Yes…"

"I mean, is that Amish? Do the Amish do glass?" I tried to think of instances of glass in the Burkholder furniture.

"Sometimes they do. Our customers aren't exactly Amish purists, though."

"No?"

"People read 'Amish' as code for 'quality wood furniture of simple construction.'"

"I think people read 'Amish' as a lot of things."

"You're probably right."

"So what did you need my advice for?"

"You agree that the glass would look nice?"

My hand stroked the smooth wood. "Yeah. I think it would look great."

"I've got a few kinds of glass over here..."

"Aside from the breakable kind?"

He rolled his eyes. "Different patterns. Some with a bit of tint to them."

I tilted my head. "I don't think you'd want color. The wood is so pretty, you wouldn't want to take away from that."

"It is good wood."

"What kind is it?"

"Walnut with a hand-oiled finish."

"It's beautiful."

"Thank you. Want to see the glass?"

He showed me panes of glass, and we talked about the merits and detractions of each one. In the end we picked water glass for the rim of the cabinet, with plain glass on the inside. Levi explained how he would use silver solder and place the glass insets into the finished piece. "Want to help?"

I jumped back a foot. "No, no, that's fine."

He laughed. "Why not?"

One of the other guys in the shop started a saw and I jumped again. "You know...saws...blades...death...not really my thing. Besides, I have a sprained wrist."

"It's your left wrist, and the swelling's going down. You still have your right wrist. I'll help."

"I don't think so..."

"You ride a motorcycle but won't try carpentry?"

My back stiffened. I knew what he was doing, and I wouldn't let him win. "I know how to ride a motorcycle. I don't know how to use power tools."

"I do. I'll help."

"I'm wearing safety gear when I ride."

"I wear safety gear when I work. You're wearing safety gear right now," he said, pointing at my goggles.

"Building isn't my thing."

"But you're a reporter. Reporters try new things. Weren't you baking something last week?"

"Baking is different."

"How?"

"It's hard to lose a finger while baking."

"I won't let you lose a finger."

"What if I suddenly spaz out toward the moving blade? How would you stop that?"

"Why would you?"

"Seizure."

"Do you have a history of seizures?"

I straightened. "Not yet. I might."

"You might develop a history of seizures?"

"You never know."

He shrugged. "It's okay if you don't want to. I just thought you might want to try something new, you know, being a reporter."

He was good. He was very good.

"You wouldn't let me lose a finger?"

"Nope."

I tucked a piece of hair behind my ear. "If anything happens, I'm blaming you."

"I would be surprised if it were otherwise." He smiled. "I have sisters. Are you ready?"

"Sure." I exhaled.

As patient as if I were ten, Levi helped me pick an appropriate piece of wood to cut into frame pieces. After I chose a piece, he helped me line it up under the table saw.

My face was in a permanent flinch as I made the cuts, but all of my digits remained in their original locations. They even remained after I cut the angles and finished the matching pieces for the opposite door.

I had to admit that the pieces didn't look half bad.

After a while, Levi checked his watch. "Want to go get the buggy soon?"

"Let me swap out the batteries I'm recharging, then yes."

I walked past Spencer's desk on the way back to the office. "How's it going, Number One?" I called over my shoulder.

Spencer scowled. "Who told?"

I gave what I hoped looked like a mysterious shrug and kept walking. Just as I'd expected, the first battery was completely charged. I switched batteries and closed the lid again.

"Did you bring a jacket?" Levi asked from the doorway.

"I'm an Oregonian," I said. "I'm impervious to rain."

"It might take some work getting the buggy hitched to my truck. You're welcome to borrow one of mine."

"You have more than one jacket at your workplace?"

"I don't like to be wet."

"And yet you live in the Pacific Northwest?"

"Do you want the jacket or not?"

I squared my shoulders. "I'll take a jacket."

"Smart." He tossed me a crispy-feeling parka.

"I wouldn't be smart without Gor-tex?"

"Just put it on."

"I'm not outside yet."

"You're exhausting."

"You invited me."

⁓

Two tarps covered the Burkholder buggy parked on Haight Street.

"Teen boys, you said?" Levi asked as he tugged the tarps to the ground. "Yup."

"At least they didn't damage it much." He ran his hand over the front, examining where the boys had towed it before. "There are a few scuffs, but nothing that can't be fixed or repainted."

"That's good."

"Let's get going, then."

Ten minutes later, Levi had his family's buggy attached securely to his pickup. I climbed in the cab, just short of drenched. The rain was really coming down, and I was truly glad I'd taken Levi up on his offer of water-repellent gear.

"Now the long road home," Levi said when he joined me in the cab. "I'm going to put my safety lights on. Thanks for coming with me."

"Thanks for dragging the buggy back to the farm."

"I help my family out when I can."

"Why?"

"Why what?"

"They're so awful to you sometimes. Why are you so good to them?"

"It's the right thing to do."

"That seems so simplistic."

He shrugged. "Things might not always be the way they are. I don't want to have regrets."

"Everyone has regrets."

"I don't."

"Must be nice to be perfect."

"I'm not. I've learned from the times when I've messed up. Maybe someday my family will come around. Families are complicated."

"Believe me, I know." I shifted in my seat. "I don't want to talk about this any more."

"That's fine." He drummed on the steering wheel. "How did you get into journalism?"

"I applied to the University of Oregon School of Journalism."

"No, I mean what got you interested?"

"I grew up in a very small, very touristy town."

"Lincoln City?"

"Right. I wanted to learn about other places, other people. I needed to be reassured that the world was bigger than my hometown."

"You lived on the coast. All you needed to do was look out on the ocean."

"But that was just one edge. I wanted to know about the other side. I read the *New York Times*, the *Washington Post*, the *San Francisco Chronicle*, the *Wall Street Journal*—everything I could get my hands on. I decided I wanted to work for a big newspaper."

"You stayed in Oregon?"

"I like the Pacific Northwest, but people in Washington don't know how to drive. That left Oregon, and Portland if I wanted a big city."

"Very logical."

"I got an internship at the *Oregonian*—"

"And the rest was history?"

"Pretty much."

"I get that. Let's see how this goes…" He released the parking brake and eased on the gas. The buggy creaked and then lurched forward with the truck.

I checked over my shoulder. "Looks good."

"All right, then. Buckle up. This will be a bumpy ride."

"Really?"

"No. We won't top twenty-five miles an hour."

I laughed. "We should probably call and let the police know we've recovered the buggy."

"Better to have my dad call. That way you have owner verification."

"I've ridden in that buggy."

"You're not the owner."

"What happens if we get pulled over?"

"We make a run for it."

"What?"

"Kidding. We explain and hope for the best."

"You're funny."

❋

Despite the downpour Martha, Sara, Samuel, Leah, and Elizabeth met us outside as we pulled up with the buggy in tow.

Levi slowed the truck. "Do you mind jumping out and herding the kids back?"

"No problem." I unbuckled my seat belt and swung my door open, despite the fact that the truck wasn't exactly stopped. "Step back, guys," I said, "you don't want to get run over."

"You found it!" Elizabeth exclaimed, hanging on my leg. "You found the buggy!"

I started to pick her up and stopped myself. Stupid arm. I hugged her close, bending awkwardly. "We did and brought it back home for you."

Levi parked the truck and got out. "It's been scratched a bit, but otherwise it's in perfect shape."

"Where was it?" Martha asked, her voice carefully measured.

"Exactly where Mike said it would be," I answered.

Martha took Levi's hand. "Thank you."

He beamed. I wished his father had been there to thank him also.

Levi and I drove back to the shop in relative silence. He turned to me after he pulled into his parking space. "Okay, Jayne. What's eating you?"

I sighed. "It just kills me."

"What does?"

"The way your family treats you. It's entirely unfair."

"Life isn't fair."

"I know, but..." I frowned. "I just wish things weren't the way they are."

"And I pray every day that they won't be."

"It's not right! Families shouldn't behave that way. They shouldn't decide who you should be and then turn around and punish you when it becomes clear that you cannot, will not be that person."

"Jayne?"

"What?"

"Are we talking about your family or mine?"

"I—" My mouth snapped shut. I paused. I couldn't think of when I'd said much on that subject to Levi. "What do you know about my family?"

"Not much. You hardly talk about them, and when you do, it's rarely pleasant."

I fixed him with a stare.

He ducked his head. "Grady may have said something."

"Grady?" My eyes widened in surprise. "What did he say?"

"You guys went to school and church together and knew a lot of the same people. He mentioned something along the lines of you being treated like the black sheep of the family."

I sat back in my seat, my head resting on the glass of the rear window of the cab. Grady knew. Surprising, considering the importance of image to my family. I tucked a bit of hair behind my ear. "I wasn't completely bad. That's what they'd have everyone think."

"Grady didn't say you were."

"I was a good student. I organized all of my scholarship and financial aid for college. I never went to my parents for a cent."

"I'm not accusing you, Jayne."

"Just because I listened to rock music and dyed my hair black my junior year, I was the bad daughter."

"You don't have to explain anything to me."

I ran a hand over my face. "I don't like talking about this."

"Have you ever tried to make things better with them? Your family, I mean."

"I hardly see them. Not since I left home for school."

"People change."

"Do they? Have your parents changed?"

"I've changed. I'm people."

"You're different. My mother has worn the same perfume for the past twenty years—Calvin Klein's Obsession. It doesn't matter what I've accomplished in my life—that I put myself though school, graduated, found gainful employment in a field that's not easy to break into—it doesn't matter. I'm not married. I don't have babies. I don't matter."

Then, to my embarrassment, I felt tears prick my eyes. I tried taking deep breaths, tried to calm myself, but it wasn't any use. It hurt too much.

Levi put an arm around my shoulders and I leaned into him, sobbing. I think he stroked my hair, but it was hard to tell. All I could think about were the times I'd been hurt by my family.

After a few moments the tears slowed and my breathing regulated. I swiped at the dampness on my face and tried to reclaim my dignity. "I'm sorry."

"Don't be."

"But I really am. I don't know why I got so…"

"It happens."

"But I—"

"Do you want some ice cream?"

I scooted back, aware that his arm was still resting around my shoulders. "Ice cream?"

"You've heard of it?"

"I'm not one of those hysterical women who have to be slapped and then placated with bonbons."

I'll admit that when I spoke, it came out a little high pitched and, well, hysterical sounding.

"I didn't say you were. I just thought that you had a very busy afternoon and might appreciate a scoop of chocolate brownie ice cream."

"I'm also not one of those women who has fits until she gets her chocolate fix."

"Didn't say you were."

"I'm not really a chocolate brownie ice cream kind of girl."

"No?"

"No. I think I'm more of a fudge mint."

We walked from the shop to the ice cream parlor under the gigantic umbrella Levi kept in his truck.

Some people might question the consumption of ice cream in fifty-degree weather, and that's their prerogative. I'm just not one of them.

We ate our ice cream at a corner table, me with fudge mint, Levi with cookies and cream.

"When do you return to work?" he asked.

"A week and a half." I took another lick around the edge of my cone. "A week and a half, and it's back to business as usual."

"Are you looking forward to it?"

"I don't know...parts of it. I miss riding my bike around town and being stopped by all the old men who used to ride Triumphs."

"What?"

"Triumph is one of the oldest motorcycle companies."

"I knew that."

"Well, there are a lot of old men with fond memories of Triumph bikes from their past. They like to tell stories."

"It doesn't hurt that you're cute."

My cheeks turned pink. "It happens to the owner of the motorcycle shop I buy my gear from, and he's in his sixties. Anyway, I miss that."

"But you can't ride right now anyway."

"Rub it in, why don't you?"

"What else do you miss?"

"Oh, I don't know. Good coffee. Noah's Bagel. Central heating..."

"It can get pretty chilly at my parents' house."

"No kidding. But, I have to say, there are a lot of things I'll miss when I leave the farm."

"Like what?"

"The sense of family. Getting to do new things."

"Such as working with wood?"

"Such as baking. Spending time with children. Doing things by hand and feeling that I've accomplished something concrete, you know?"

"I do. They're good kids, aren't they."

"Your siblings? The younger ones, anyway. Amos and Elam still think I'm weird. But Samuel and the girls are terrific. I used to think I never wanted kids of my own. Now…" I shrugged. "I think I could live with it."

"That's a vote of confidence you don't hear every day." Levi rolled his eyes before attacking another bite of ice cream.

"Listen. I never thought I'd want kids. But now, I don't know. I guess I'm open to it."

"Raising kids isn't easy."

"You think I don't know that? My parents reminded me on a daily basis. Probably why I wasn't wild about the idea in the first place."

"You have a sister, right?"

"Beth. She's older."

"What's she like?"

"Imagine the good kid."

"Okay."

"That's Beth."

"Ah. You're not close?"

"We can't relate. She listens to Sandi Patty, I listen to Sam Phillips. I went to school, and she got her MRS degree."

He laughed at my joke.

"Seriously," I said. "It's not like I've really tried with Beth. I need to be better about that. She's the only sister I've got." I caught a melted drip with my tongue and pondered that thought.

When I finished my cone and Levi finished his dish, we walked back to the shop.

"Thanks," I said, swinging my purse, feeling happy and full of ice cream. "That was fun."

"Thank you for joining me."

By the time we'd returned, Spencer and Grady were nowhere to be seen. Levi followed me back to his office where my laptop sat, as satiated of power as I was of sugar.

"I'll be praying for you and your family," he said as I wound up the laptop cord.

"I appreciate it," I said honestly.

He held my computer bag open as I slid the computer inside. "I know how much rejection can hurt," he said softly.

I felt myself grow teary again, but tilted my head downward so Levi wouldn't notice. "Yeah."

"Know that you're talented, funny, and a hard worker. You've earned my parents' trust, and that's not easy. Don't base your self-worth on what your family has told you over the years."

Levi's speech didn't help the impending waterworks, and this time I couldn't hide it. He frowned. "I'm sorry. Did I say something wrong?"

I shook my head. "No. You said everything right, and it was one of the nicest things someone's ever said to me. I'm sorry…"

And the tears fell, despite the fact I'd apologized in advance.

I slung my laptop bag over my shoulder. "I should go."

"Jayne—"

Levi reached for my arm. The feel of his hand stopped me in my tracks. "Everything will be all right," he said, and with the utmost care he caught one of my tears with his finger.

And then, as far as I can tell, I kissed him.

On the lips.

It was just a little kiss, more like a brush. At least it started that way. It started as the tiniest nothing, but Levi wrapped his arm around my shoulder and the kiss deepened. I responded; he tasted like cookies and cream and smelled like cedar. My hands dug into his hair

This is nice, I thought. I had stopped crying, focusing my attention on Levi and that moment until a single thought entered my consciousness.

Shane.

I stepped back, ending the kiss and disentangling myself from Levi's inviting hold.

I couldn't make excuses—I had started it. Couldn't apologize, because a kiss that good shouldn't be apologized for.

Levi looked at me, flushed and slightly stunned.

There was nothing to say. I left as quickly as my feet could move.

Hormones. I chalked it all up to hormones. If I thought about it, I remembered my monthly happiness should arrive next week, which would at least partially explain my erratic emotions and inexplicable behavior.

I dug through my bag until I found my phone. I plugged in my headset and then pressed buttons until I found Gemma's number.

"How's Amish country?" she asked when she picked up.

"Not there yet. Driving. If I get there and I still have reception, I'll tell you."

"You sound upset."

"I kissed someone."

"Oh." She paused. "Really?"

"Yes."

"Who? I'm guessing it wasn't Shane, or it wouldn't be newsworthy."

I winced. "Levi."

"The guy who drove your bike back?"

"That one."

"Kim said he was cute."

"Gemma!"

"What?"

"You're not supposed to encourage me!" I braked behind a slow truck. Why did trucks drive so slow when I was in crisis?

"If he was ugly, I wouldn't know what to say."

"It doesn't matter if he's ugly or cute, the problem is that he's not Shane."

"True. Are you guys still together?"

"Yes!"

"Do you want to be together?"

"Of course I do!"

"Then why did you kiss Levi?"

"I was emotional. He bought me ice cream…"

"Right. That makes complete sense. I always kiss men after they buy me ice cream."

"Gemma!"

"Our eyes lock over the mocha ripple, and I just can't help myself."

"Be serious."

"No," Gemma said, her voice turning serious, "you need to be serious with yourself. If you really like Levi, then maybe you should do something about it."

"But Shane—"

"Probably doesn't want to be with someone who's into someone else."

"I'm a horrible person."

"Yes, you are."

"Thanks."

"I'm a horrible person too. That's the story of being a sinner."

"Yeah, I know. I was at that church service too. I got the memo."

"You'll make the right decision. Either way, you need to talk to Shane."

I sighed. "I know."

~~~

After the crazy afternoon I didn't feel like a verbal sparring match with Shane. I drove back to the Burkholder farm, parking the car next to the buggy.

A light drizzle coated my head and shoulders as I crossed the driveway to the small porch. When I opened the front door, I found the family in the living room, gathered around Gideon.

Gideon looked pale. Martha looked worried.

"Is everything all right?" I asked.

"He's having trouble breathing," Sara answered.

All my senses jumped to alertness. "Has this happened before?"

Martha shook her head.

"Gideon?" I asked. "Does your chest feel tight?"

He shook his head. "It feels like Shoe is sitting on it."

"Same difference." I looked at Martha. "We need to get him to a hospital. Now."

Chapter 15

They say cell phones are best for emergencies, right? I reached for mine and flipped it open. No service. "Why! Of all times—where is the phone?"

Martha looked at me blankly. "The phone?"

"We need to call an ambulance, Martha. Gideon needs medical assistance."

Gideon shook his head. "I'm certain…I'm certain it will pass."

Martha ignored her husband. "Couldn't you just drive him in your car?"

"They have access to equipment I don't keep in my trunk. Where is the phone?"

"In the shed," Amos said, speaking up for the first time. "I'll take you there."

I followed him out the door, around the house, and behind the barn. I felt as though I should pray. Hadn't prayed for a while. Was I still allowed? Would God laugh at me?

For the sake of Gideon's life, I took the chance and asked for guidance and protection for the Burkholder family.

The shed sat adjacent to the barn, looking more like a place for an outhouse than a place to chat, which is probably why they didn't. I lifted the receiver, relieved to hear a dial tone in my ear.

Amos started walking back to the house. "Don't go!" I said, as I dialed 9-1-1. "I need the address, and they may ask me things I don't know."

He stayed, and it was a good thing. He gave me the street address, as well as Gideon's age. The operator advised giving Gideon a tablet of aspirin to chew. I looked at Amos. "Does your family keep any aspirin?"

He shook his head.

"I have some in my bags—"

Amos' expression turned bewildered. I spoke again into the receiver, asking if it was necessary that I stay on the line.

The operator asked a couple more questions about Gideon's general health before clearing me to end the call. After hanging up, I strode back to the house, trying to remember where in my bags I'd packed the aspirin.

"Why does he need aspirin?" Amos asked. "He doesn't have a head-ache."

"Aspirin also thins the blood," I said, not slowing. "I think your dad is having a heart attack, which means his blood is blocked and can't get to his heart properly. Aspirin makes it easier for blood to reach the heart."

I quickly found a plastic bag of miscellaneous vitamins and painkillers in my room and fished out an aspirin. I took it downstairs and gave it to Gideon, telling him the 9-1-1 operator said to chew it.

He must have started feeling worse, because he took the aspirin without an argument.

The EMTs arrived in a blaze of flashing lights; Elizabeth began to whimper. Sara pulled her up into her arms and spoke softly to her in Dutch. We watched as the EMTs loaded Gideon onto a stretcher and fitted an oxygen mask over his face. After the ambulance doors closed, the driver told Martha she could follow them to the hospital.

She turned to me. "Could you drive me?"

Amos stepped forward. "Us. Could you drive us?"

"Of course," I said, pulling my keys from my pocket.

Following the ambulance was easy at first, but after a while—and several red lights I couldn't run through—it disappeared into the darkness.

I realized I had no idea where the hospital was. "Martha?" I asked. "Do you know how to get to the ER?"

She nodded and proceeded to give me directions via landmarks.

I really hate when women do this. Men give street names, direction, mileage, and everything short of GPS coordinates. Women tell you to turn left at the second garden gnome. But Martha's husband was heading toward the hospital, fighting for his life, so I told my irritated self to hush up.

As I had this conversation with myself, Amos interrupted. "Take Queen and turn left on Elm."

I thanked him.

I pulled into the ER parking lot and performed what was not likely to be the best parking job of my life.

Inside, the administrative staff informed us that Gideon was having tests done and we would be informed when we could see him, and that we could take a seat and the coffee dispensers were around the corner to the right.

I stepped back. "That was a lot of hurry up and wait."

Martha frowned. "Hurry up and what?"

"Don't worry about it. Do either of you want coffee?"

Amos nodded, and I offered to go and discover exactly how awful the hospital coffee was.

Martha sagged against her son. "I need to sit down," she said.

"You both sit down," I said. "I'll find the coffee."

I followed the instructions and walked around the corner to the right. But the farther I walked the more I knew I needed to make a phone call.

I needed to call Levi. He deserved to know his father was in the hospital.

I passed the coffee station, not pulling out my phone until I'd walked down the hallway and found a second seating area.

"Levi?" I said when he picked up.

Oh, this was awkward…

"Jayne? Are you all right? I'm sorry things got…out of hand—"

"Your dad's in the hospital," I interrupted. "He had a heart attack."

"Is…is he okay?"

"They're running tests. We don't know anything."

"Where are you?"

"Past the coffee machines."

"At the hospital?"

"Yes. Your mom and Amos are here."

"I'll be over in ten minutes."

My eyes slid shut. I knew he would, but it didn't make my life any easier.

⸻

Just as he'd said, Levi rushed in like a windstorm ten minutes later. "Have they told you anything?" he asked, giving his mom a hug.

She melted into him. "Tests. We know nothing but tests."

He gave her a squeeze and strode to the front desk. "I need to know how my father is doing."

"Name of patient?" The receptionist looked peeved. But then, maybe her face was just stuck that way.

"Gideon Burkholder."

"He's having tests."

"I know he's having tests. I want to know if he's stable or if he isn't."

"I'll need you to wait, sir." She stood and disappeared behind a door.

Levi sighed. "I should call Rebecca."

I frowned. "Who's Rebecca?"

"My sister. She and her husband live in Washington." He reached for his cell phone. "She may not even answer. The phone is twenty feet from the house."

"Older? Younger?"

"Younger. She's between me and Amos." He winced. "Come on, Bex, pick up. You could hear when any of us were in trouble. I don't think your hearing's changed." He stood, leaning against the desk, head bent, clearly focused on the steady ring of the other line.

After several moments he straightened so fast you'd think the receptionist had returned and zapped him. "Karl? It's Levi—please don't hang up. My father's in the hospital, and I thought Rebecca would want to know. Thank you. I—" Levi sighed and closed the phone. "I should have had Amos call."

"Karl won't talk to you?"

"No. Rebecca will, but Karl…he's just trying to protect his family."

"You did the right thing, letting her know."

"She has my number if she wants to call." He shook his head as if trying to clear it.

The receptionist chose that moment to return. "Your father is in stable but critical condition."

I tilted my head closer. "What does that mean?"

The receptionist's voice softened. "It means he's not out of the woods just yet."

—⁓⧉⁓—

I finally went to get Amos his coffee. Retreated to the coffee is more like it. Now that I had—I shuddered to admit it—*kissed* Levi, a part of me worried that if I were in too close of a proximity to him, I might do it again.

And that would be bad.

First, because I was still in a relationship with Shane.

Second, because we were in the hospital waiting to see if his father would live through the night. Not wildly appropriate timing.

Around eleven, a person clad in hospital scrubs came and found us. I managed to tag along, pretending to be family. No one asked. I didn't tell.

A doctor met us in the hallway. "You're Gideon's family?"

Again, I said nothing as Martha, Levi, and Amos nodded.

"He's currently stable," the doctor said, "but he'll need surgery. I put a call into the cardio unit in Corvallis, but they're full. I recommend transport to OHSU. He needs a good cardiothoracic surgeon."

"Wait. What is this 'OHSU'?" Martha's face tightened in confusion.

The doctor took a breath. "It's the Oregon Health and Science University, ma'am."

"It's a school?"

"It's a teaching hospital."

"What kind of surgery?" Levi interrupted.

"Your father has severe coronary artery disease. That means there has been a significant buildup of plaque inside three of his arteries, blocking blood to his heart. I recommend a procedure called a coronary artery bypass graft, in which veins from his leg would be grafted to repair the damaged ones. It's a kind of bypass procedure."

Levi shoved his hands in his pockets. "His chances without it?"

"Difficult to speculate, but likely very poor. Medications can buy him time, but his chances of a second heart attack are greatly increased."

Martha's face showed her anguish. "Is he comfortable?"

The doctor nodded. "He is."

"Can we see him?"

"Yes. He's resting now, but it's fine if he wakes up."

We all filed into the room.

Gideon looked so small in the hospital bed. I'd heard people say that of their loved ones when they were unwell, but I had never witnessed it to be so true.

Levi patted his mother on the back. "I'll be outside," he said.

I followed a moment later.

"Why did you leave?"

Levi snorted. "Did you hear the doctor? He's still at risk for a second attack. Heaven knows that if he woke up and saw me in the room, it could happen right here."

"He might want to see you. Near-death experiences change people. Things could be different."

He gave a rueful smile. "They might. But I want him to be healthy before I find out."

"Does your mom have the money for the surgery? It can't be cheap."

"The Amish take care of their own. My parents have savings, and if that's not enough, the community chips in. They'll be fine."

"That's nice."

"It is."

Martha stepped out a few minutes later. "He'll be taken in an ambulance to the hospital in Portland. Tonight." She wrung her hands. "I want to go with him, but…"

"You can stay with me," I said, a little surprised even as I offered. "My apartment isn't that far from the OHSU campus."

"Amos needs to help maintain the farm," she said, clearly thinking out loud. "My mother can come and stay with the younger ones for a few days."

"Did the doctor say how long his recovery time would be?" Levi asked.

Martha shrugged. "Three days? Five? They don't know exactly."

"Amos needs to get back, and you need to pack some clothes. We'll drive to the house and go from there." Levi pulled his keys from his pocket. "Would Sara want to go with you to Portland?"

Martha considered it. "Yes, I'm sure she would."

I frowned. "Won't Ida need Sara's help with the children?"

"My mother can handle the younger ones just fine. Naomi is nearby if she needs anything."

I wondered at Levi's suggestion of taking Sara to Portland. Was he trying to encourage Sara to leave by giving her a taste of outside life?

Martha took a deep breath. "I will say goodbye to Gideon and then we'll go back to the house."

Her eyes looked watery, but her face was stoic. She knew as well as we did that if Gideon didn't pull through the surgery, this could be the last time she saw him. I felt myself tear up too. I couldn't comprehend what that must have been like for her. To be married to someone for as long as she'd been married to Gideon, and then to have everything change so quickly.

A light squeeze on my arm redirected my thoughts. "How many people can your apartment hold?"

I looked up at Levi, trying to figure out where his question led. "It's only two bedrooms, but it's fairly spacious. I was planning on giving Martha and Sara my room and taking the couch."

"I was just wondering," he said. "I'd like to be there too, but I can always find a room somewhere."

An argument raged inside my head. Being with Levi could be...dangerous. Having him stay in my apartment could be...more dangerous. A part of me enjoyed having him near, hearing his opinion on things, having someone else around to be strong and practical. I worried I'd enjoy it *too* much.

On the other hand, I did have room, and Martha and Sara would be there as well.

His father was in the hospital. And it would only be a few days, max. Surely he couldn't stay away from the shop for very long.

"No, it's fine," I heard myself say even before I had made up my mind.

"I can bring a sleeping bag and an air mattress."

I nodded. "You can sleep in the study."

Levi nodded back. "We'd best be going then."

⁓∿⁄⁓

I drove Martha and Amos back to the farm that night. I packed up what I would need while Martha packed for herself.

Sara had greeted us at the door, desperate for word. Martha explained the trip to Portland, and Sara began to pack.

I think that if her father weren't going in for triple bypass surgery, she would have been completely delighted.

An hour later we left for Portland. Sara sat in the front seat next to me, her nose pressed to the glass as the farmhouses disappeared. I began to relax when the streets became truly familiar and my apartment complex came into view.

We woke up Martha, who had fallen asleep in the backseat during the drive. Sara and I carried the bags up the stairs, I unlocked the door, and everyone walked in.

My apartment seemed colder than I remembered. Granted, I hadn't had the heat on for more than a week, but it was colder in a different way. It didn't feel like home.

Levi called a few moments later, telling us he'd be there shortly.

I had Martha and Sara sit on the couch while I tried to get my room ready for their use. Not that it was *bad*, per se, but certainly not the standard of cleanliness I'd experienced at the Burkholder farm.

You wouldn't want to eat off my floor. And maybe not the table, either.

I remade my bed with fresh sheets and checked the floor for stray underwear. I especially looked through the study before turning it over to a certain carpenter.

A knock sounded at the door, and I knew Levi had arrived.

He had a backpack over his shoulder, a sleeping bag under one arm, and a pillow under the other. "I really appreciate this, Jayne."

I gave a crooked smile. "You're welcome."

"Sorry I was running late. I didn't want to keep you up—you'll get little enough sleep as it is—but I figured you didn't have a whole lot in the way of groceries."

Hadn't gotten that far. "No...not really."

"I stopped by the grocery store to pick up some staples."

"You didn't have to do that."

"You didn't have to take care of my family."

"So where are they? Did you fit them in that backpack?"

"In the truck. I'll get them in a moment."

"I can do that—"

He tossed me the keys. "Thanks. I'll be out in a minute."

Didn't know quite why he said that. How much food did he buy?

I understood once I saw the bags piled atop each other in the cab. I unlocked the door to find milk, eggs, flour, sugar, shortening, butter, sausage, ground beef, baking soda, baking powder, deli meat, sandwich rolls, an assortment of condiments, and a lot of other things I'd have to dig through the bags to discover.

"I didn't know what you had," he said, coming up behind me.

"A little more than stale Pop-Tarts and beef jerky." Although not much more.

"Like I said, I didn't know what you had. And knowing my mom, she'll want to cook."

I'd give him that. "It's fine. I really appreciate it. Truly."

Between the two of us, we managed to haul all of it up the stairs in one trip. "Did you leave any food at the store?"

"The day-old sushi. I turned that down."

"Right." I set the bags on the kitchen counter and began loading appropriate items into the fridge.

"I'll finish this," he said, stacking boxes and cans. "You go to bed."

"Bed's over there," I said, pointing at the couch not ten feet from the kitchen. "I have trouble sleeping when someone's rummaging in my kitchen."

"Doesn't look like you've gotten yourself any blankets. I'm okay here. Go take care of yourself."

I was too tired to argue. I grabbed my college-era comforter from my closet as well as an extra pillow.

Sara and Martha were already fast asleep in my room, two in the morning being far past their bedtimes. I snuck in quietly and found what I hoped were matching pajamas.

As soon as I was in the bathroom, I discovered I had a cupcake-print top with Harley-Davidson logo bottoms.

Oh, well. I washed my face and brushed my teeth, and then I looked at myself in the mirror. Circles were already under my eyes, yet I was still completely keyed up. I found some sleeping pills—I would need them if I was going to be able to sleep with Levi around.

I made up my makeshift bed while he puttered in the kitchen, finding homes for baking items I'd never used and likely never would.

"Almost done," he said, wadding up empty plastic sacks.

"Not a problem."

"Does it feel good to be home?"

"Mmm." I climbed into my couch bed and snuggled against my pillow. The sleeping pill was kicking in.

"Thanks again for letting me stay."

"You bet."

And with that, I fell asleep.

blinked a few times, confused. Where was I?

Couch. Home. Gideon. Surgery…the last 24 hours filed into my memory like little marching soldiers.

I heard the clink of metal in the kitchen. Was Levi still putting groceries away? How long did it take?

My eyes opened a bit wider, wide enough to read the time on the wall clock. Half-past eight. I hadn't slept this late in more than a week.

I sat up and peered into the kitchen.

Martha, not Levi, stood in the kitchen. A collection of apple peels sat in a pile to her left; her forearms flexed as she rolled out what had to be dough.

Curious, because I didn't think I owned a rolling pin.

I swung my legs to the floor. "Good morning," I said.

Martha nodded. "Morning."

"What are you making?"

"Apple dumplings, hash browns, and sausage. For breakfast."

As I came closer, I saw that she was using two aluminum cans duct-taped together as a rolling pin. "I'm sorry. My kitchen isn't very well equipped."

"Most English kitchens aren't."

"Well, my friend Gemma has about every kitchen tool known to man…" She'd probably be willing to loan some of them out, at least for a few days.

"Have you heard anything from the hospital?"

"My phone hasn't rung. They said they'd call when he's out of surgery."

Martha nodded. I watched her. Her movements were jerky, her muscles taut. Dark circles had taken up residence beneath her eyes. In a moment, I understood. Making breakfast—a breakfast for nine that would be eaten by four—was her coping method.

And far be it for me to get in her way.

121

I heard a rustling from the direction of the study. I turned in time to see the door open and Levi emerge, face stubbled and hair mussed.

He gave a crooked smile. "Mornin'."

"Hey."

I was suddenly very aware that my pajamas didn't match.

Martha turned. "Levi."

"How'd you sleep, Mom?"

"Well enough."

"Is Sara still sleeping?"

"She is."

Levi turned back to me. "Mind if I use your shower?"

"Go right ahead," I said, even as I considered my towel situation.

"I brought my own towel."

"I wasn't worried," I lied. I could only hope I had two other clean towels for Martha and Sara. Even if I tried to run a quick load of laundry, my dryer took a good two hours to finish drying even a single towel.

Everyone froze when my phone rang. I dove for it, nearly tripping on my shag carpet. "Hello?" I was embarrassed to hear my voice shake as I answered.

The nurse on the other end of the line asked for Martha. I passed the phone over.

Martha held the cell phone awkwardly in her hand, but the awkwardness faded as she paid complete attention to the words coming from the tiny speaker.

"I will be right there," she said, before ending the call.

Or trying to end the call. Levi reached over and helped her close the phone.

"He is just out of surgery," she said, reaching for her apron strings and untying them. "He is well, the surgery went well. He is not awake, but we can see him." She looked from me to Levi. "We can see him!"

Clearly, breakfast was forgotten.

I looked at Levi, hoping he wouldn't miss the fact that I was unwashed, clad in mismatched pajamas, and not ready to be taken seriously by hospital staff.

"I'll shower really quick, Mom, and drive you down."

"And Sara?"

"Sara's not awake yet."

"She needs to be woken."

"Even then, she'll need to get dressed and put together. Jayne can drive her down."

"Yes," I chimed in. "I'll drive her down shortly."

"Okay." Martha brushed the flour from her hands and walked back down the hall.

"Cereal?" Levi said.

"Cereal," I agreed.

Levi showered while Martha woke Sara up, and then he took his mother to the hospital. I showered and dressed in clothes that matched.

"Is that what you're wearing?" Sara asked when she saw me.

"Yes," I said warily, suddenly understanding what it would be like to have a teenager in the house.

"But it's so…"

I raised my eyebrows.

"…dark."

"You're wearing a blue dress and a black apron."

"Because I *have* to. You can wear anything you want, and you're wearing a black sweater with jeans?"

"Gemma helped me pick out this sweater. It's one of the most stylish things I own."

Oops. Shouldn't have said that. Sara's eyes narrowed. "But…you're English."

"Yeah, well, just because someone's English doesn't mean they dress like they do in magazines."

"But you live in Portland."

"The Portland uniform is jeans, a sweatshirt, and Chacos."

"What are Chacos?"

"They're sandals…and beside the point. We need to meet up with your mom and Levi."

Sara looked down. "I'm sorry."

"I know you're excited about being in the city, but your dad's not out of the woods yet."

"People have bypasses all the time, right?"

"Yes, but it's still major surgery."

"Do you think he'll be okay?"

"If the doctors say the surgery went well, that's a very good sign."

"Okay." She cast one more look toward me. "You don't even have a printed scarf you could wear with that?"

I put my arm around her shoulders. "If your dad's fine and we have time at some point, I'll take you to Gemma's closet. The two of you will be very happy together."

⚒

I was afraid Sara would fall out of the car, her nosed pressed so hard to the glass as we drove up Terwilliger to get to the hospital.

"Do you want to stop by the gift shop on the way up?" I asked her. "We could pick up some flowers or a card or something."

Sara shook her head. "Flowers? He wouldn't know what to do with them."

Okay, then. "When we get inside," I said, deciding to broach the subject, "you need to tell the receptionist who you are."

Sara frowned. "I have to talk to them?"

"Yes, you do. Tell them you're Gideon's daughter and ask to see him."

"Can't you ask?"

"I'm not a relative."

"Oh."

"Technically, I should wait in the sitting area for you."

"I'm not going alone!"

"I didn't think so. That's why you have to talk."

Sara sulked for a little while, but when we reached the desk, she gave a concise speech to the receptionist that included the importance of my presence.

The receptionist nodded and directed us to Gideon's room. Our feet quickened when we saw Levi waiting outside.

"Is Martha inside?" I asked, pulling off my jacket.

He nodded. "Sorry," he said in a whisper. "I'm trying to keep a low profile."

I pressed my lips shut and followed Sara into the room.

Martha sat beside the bed, holding Gideon's hand. His eyes opened wider when he saw me.

"Ah," he said. "Jayne's here."

Martha patted his hand. "She's been very kind, letting us stay with her."

"Sit down, Jayne," he said, gesturing to the chair on the other side of the bed.

I sat.

"The doctors tell me that if I had gotten to the hospital just a little later, my heart would have died. But it was not God's will that I die yet. He sent you to call the ambulance. Thank you."

I nodded, a stab of guilt piercing my heart. He might have had even more time, had I not been eating ice cream and kissing his son. "I'm glad you're feeling better."

Gideon rolled his eyes. "I don't know that I'm feeling better. I'm full of needles. But at least I can breathe, right?"

"We're glad you can breathe," Martha echoed.

I checked her grip on his hand—her knuckles were white. It must have terrified her, seeing her husband so close to death.

I thought of Levi outside the door. "I'm glad you're still here with your family." I tried to think of something clever I might say about second chances and reconciliation, but everything sounded as though it belonged on an inspirational billboard.

A shadow passed over Gideon's face. Maybe I hadn't needed to say anything after all.

⁓⁓

While Sara and Martha kept Gideon company and Levi brooded outside, I excused myself to make a phone call.

The mention of Gemma's closet had made me think of Gemma's other talents. Namely, completing meal preparation without setting the kitchen on fire. At some point, members of the Burkholder clan would have to eat, and I didn't know how they would respond to Chinese takeout or the concept of beef-a-roni.

"Wow," Gemma said when we connected. "This is the clearest the line has been since you've been gone. I don't know what part of the field you're in, but remember it, will you?"

"Um, well, I'm not in Albany any more."

"Oh? Where are you?"

"OHSU."

"What! Why? Are you okay?"

"It's not me. Gideon had a heart attack, but listen. He had to come up here to have bypass surgery, and now I have three people staying in my apartment who can't live off crackers."

"Any vegetarians?"

"No. Definitely not."

"Any food allergies?"

"None that I'm aware of."

"How many people?"

"Four, including me."

"Four?" Gemma checked.

"Martha, Sara, me...and Levi."

"Levi's there?"

"Gem—"

"Levi, you kissed him, Levi?"

"There just aren't a whole lot of Levis in this world. Yes, same one."

"He's staying in your apartment?"

"In the study."

"Oh, that's kind of cute."

"Not helping!"

"Right. How about if I bring over some food from the restaurant?"

My shoulders relaxed. "Have I told you you're fantastic?"

"Not in the last ten minutes."

"Feel free to invite yourself over. Sara will want to analyze your outfit."

"I would, but I have study tonight."

"Oh." Study as in Bible study. "Well, have fun with that."

"I will. Have you talked to Shane recently?"

"I haven't."

"Just wondering. See you tonight?"

"Tonight," I agreed, and hung up.

Shane. Shane, Shane, Shane. Didn't know what to do with Shane. Didn't know what to do about Shane. I wanted to talk to him—well, catch up at least. But I didn't particularly want him to know I was back in town or to know I had houseguests.

If only I hadn't kissed Levi.

If only I could kiss him again.

———※———

"Everything okay?" Levi asked when I returned.

"Yeah. I just secured us food for tonight."

"You didn't need to do that. I can cook."

"You can cook? Like what, toast?"

"Pasta. Jambalaya. Chicken Cordon Bleu."

"I'm impressed. I thought most bachelors ate noodles with butter and salt."

"I do that too."

"No poor-person pasta tonight. My friend Gemma is either cooking or bringing food from her family's restaurant. Either way, we'll eat well."

"You have good friends."

"I do."

"Holding up okay? It was a late night."

"You're asking me? It's your dad hooked up to the machines in there. How are you?"

Levi sighed.

I gave him a sad smile. "It's okay. You don't have to say anything."

———

Gemma arrived promptly at six thirty that night, and I wondered if she'd kicked up her wardrobe a bit to make up for not staying. Despite the fact that she was carrying an armload of casserole dishes, Sara studied her ensemble from head to toe.

It doesn't hurt that Gemma's half-French, half-Italian, and wholly striking.

"Whatcha got there?"

"Rosemary chicken lasagna, rolls, salad, soup from the restaurant—"

"What kind?"

"Italian Wedding, I think. Maybe potato and leek."

"I confuse the two all the time."

"I just had Niko throw some into a container. I wasn't involved in the soup choosing."

"If it's good enough for your brother, it's good enough for the rest of us." I turned to my houseguests, assembled as they were in the dining alcove. "This is my dear friend Gemma. Gemma, this is Martha, her daughter Sara, and her son Levi."

"Good to meet you," she said, possibly paying more attention to Levi than Martha or Sara. "Let me get the food and get out of your way."

"Positive you can't stay?"

"Sorry. Bible study, and I'm bringing the snack."

Knowing Gem, the snack involved something wrapped in prosciutto or stuffed with candied marscapone. Being on the receiving end of Gemma's cuisine was a happy place to be.

"What kind of Bible study?" Levi asked, out of the blue.

Gemma paused, a funny little smile on her face. "We're going through Isaiah."

I shoved my hands into my pockets, not particularly interested in the ritual Christians go through to identify each other.

"I like Isaiah. Are you going through the whole book?"

"And studying the historical context, yes."

"That must be fascinating."

"Completely fascinating," I said. "Want us to transfer the food out of these containers?"

"No, that's fine. The study is also interesting because we're reading the Scripture out of four translations, including Amplified."

"You can get some remarkable insights from the Amplified."

"It just takes a while to read through."

They shared a laugh. I fought the urge to roll my eyes.

"I do need to go, though," Gemma said. "Jayne? Didn't you leave your scarf in my car?"

"Scarf?" I wasn't much of a scarf wearer, and I couldn't remember the last time I'd ridden in Gemma's car.

But then I read the look on Gemma's face.

"Right. Scarf. I'll follow you out." I turned to my guests. "Feel free to start without me. I'll be right back."

Gemma waved goodbye to everyone, and then I shut the door behind us.

"I don't wear scarves," I said when we were halfway down the stairs. "You couldn't think of anything else?"

"Nope. So, that's Levi?"

"Yes, Gem, that's Levi."

"I like him."

"Fine. He's all yours."

She glared at me. "No. I mean I like him for you. Jayne, why on earth are you still in a relationship with Shane?"

I sighed. "Why am I with Shane? He's smart. He makes me laugh. I enjoy spending time with him. We vote the same way, believe in the same things."

But on the inside, I knew the honest answer.

Shane was safe. He knew nothing about my past, and I liked it that way. He didn't pry into my life, at least not usually.

More than that, he was the first clean-cut, non-hick guy to notice me, to want to spend time with me. A part of me felt that I owed him for that.

I had a pretty good handle on Levi. He wouldn't let me shut him out of my life. Because of that, I couldn't afford a relationship with him. He would want too much.

I didn't tell Gemma that.

"Believing the same things doesn't make a great relationship. I mean, think of Meg Ryan and Greg Kinnear in *You've Got Mail*," I said instead.

"You do realize they were playing scripted characters."

"Fine," I said with a calculated shrug. "It's unprofessional to get involved with someone while I'm working on a story."

"You're not working on it for the newspaper."

"Still, I'm working on it. I'm on the job. I can't get involved."

"That's why half the family is staying in your apartment."

"Not half. Six, no, seven other members aren't here. Only thirty percent of the family are here."

"I stand corrected. You might just…think about it."

"Okay. I will. Here's your car," I said, as if, after three years of ownership, Gemma struggled with automobile identification. "Thanks so much for the food!"

"Are you getting rid of me?"

"Don't want you to be late for study."

Her mouth twisted into a wry smile. "That would break your heart, wouldn't it. You'll keep me posted on Gideon and everything?"

"Absolutely."

"You're not just saying that?"

"Absolutely not." I gave her a hug to make myself feel less guilty.

I watched Levi during dinner for signs that he was suddenly interested in marriage.

Not to me. To Gemma. Her cooking had that effect on men sometimes. They would envision themselves happy and well fed and that would be the end of that.

That Gemma was still single astounded us all, especially considering the quality of her meatloaf.

After dinner I found myself thinking that I was home, in possession of a TV, and wouldn't it be nice to watch Bill Moyers? I knew I had recorded shows on my DVR…but what was the protocol on television viewing when the Amish were about?

I could go with the strict interpretation and say I couldn't do anything they wouldn't, but then, I wouldn't be able to turn the lights on.

In the end I decided that using basic necessities was permissible (seeing as how I didn't own a Coleman lantern), but Bill Moyers was pushing it.

Martha beat the boredom by attacking my apartment with a vengeance. The dinner dishes were washed and put away into locations they had only ever dreamed of. After that, she swept the floor with a broom I didn't know I had before proceeding to hand wash the floor on her hands and knees. She used paper towels because I didn't own rags, a fact that completely amazed her.

I was completely amazed that I had a broom, so we were even.

"Thanks for letting her do that," Levi said in a voice quiet enough for Martha not to hear. "I think it's cathartic for her."

"I just keep feeling like I should tip her or something," I said, wrapping my arms around myself. "I'm not quite a slob, but I don't think this apartment was this clean when I moved in."

"It probably wasn't. The Amish have a standard for interior cleanliness that outsiders can only aspire to."

"I didn't say I aspired. I don't enjoy scrubbing on my hands and knees."

"The irony is that they'll walk barefoot through mud and wash less than we might have them wash, but the houses are always very clean."

"And the rest of us are the other way around."

"Like I said, thanks for doing this."

I shrugged, remembering the sight of Gideon nearly lifeless in his hospital bed. "You're welcome."

I walked the halls of a ward in a daze. There were doors on either side of me; they stretched as far as I could see. Some of the doors were open, some were closed. Some had people inside, others had puppies.

One had a green iguana.

I continued until I found the right door. I don't know *how* I knew it was the right one, because the name on the whiteboard to the side read "Artemus X," and I didn't know anyone named Artemus X.

I knew the person inside. People, rather. My father was on the bed, wires and tubes entering and exiting through his nose, his ears, his feet, his fingers. I'd never seen him so pale. If the machine to his left weren't beeping, I wouldn't think him alive.

My mother sat next to the bed, her face covered with a lacy black mantilla. I don't know why—she wasn't Catholic or Spanish. I could see her tears beneath the dark lace.

Beth sat next to her. In her arms she held my niece, Emilee, though instead of looking like Emilee she looked like Baby Ruby.

I stepped farther into the room when I saw Baby Ruby. "May I hold her?"

Beth clutched Baby Ruby tighter. "Since when do you hold babies?"

"Since I went and stayed with the Amish. I learned a lot of things."

"Like what?"

"I learned to bake pie, how to hold babies, how to—"

"Be loyal to your family?" Beth's eyes narrowed. "You took care of their father, but you wouldn't go near your own."

"But I'm here now!" I said, pointing to the figure on the bed. "I'm not too late!"

"Yes, you are," she said, and when I turned back to look at the bed, I saw the sheet had been pulled over my father's face.

"Why did you do that? He's still alive. Move the sheet, or it'll get stuffy in there."

"He's dead."

I pulled the sheet back. "No, he's not! He's alive! I just saw him alive! The monitor was beeping!"

She put a cautioning hand on my shoulder. "It's not beeping anymore. You're too late."

"I'm not too late!" I swatted away her hand. "Dad? Wake up! It's Jayne! Tell them I'm not too late. I know you can hear me! Please wake up. I'm not too late! Not too late!"

"Jayne! Open your eyes!"

I didn't know where the voice was coming from. Open my eyes? My eyes were already open. Someone was shaking my shoulders. Who was that? Beth had disappeared. My mother was gone.

But a person crouched next to me in the dark. The person was Levi. He released my shoulders. I realized I was awake and had been dreaming.

I frowned and pushed myself into a sitting position. "What are you doing? What time is it?"

"Late. Are you okay?"

I took stock. I was not okay. I released the knot of grief that had held itself captive inside my chest and shook my head. "No."

"Do you want to talk about it?"

"Did I wake you up?"

"You were crying out."

I winced. "S-sorry. Did I wake your mom or Sara?"

"No, don't worry about it. Were you dreaming?"

I nodded.

"That would explain the iguana."

"There was an iguana?"

"In the hospital room."

"Oh."

"I'm not crazy!"

Levi handed me the tissue box from under the end table. "Didn't say you were."

I wiped at my eyes. "I dreamed my dad was in the hospital. My mom and my sister were there. He was alive. I stopped to talk with my sister, and then he was..." A sob caught at my throat. "He was gone. I missed it. I wasn't there. And Beth was telling me about how I was there for your dad but not for mine and..." I shrugged. "She's right. *You* have been available to your dad, and he's all but denounced you."

"When did your dad pass away?"

"About four weeks ago." Had it been that long? Longer? Shorter? "I think."

"Do you mind if I sit on the couch? This is killing my knees."

"Okay."

He shifted himself up and onto the couch, sitting next to me.

"Do you...need to go spend time with your family?"

"I wasn't there. I don't know why they'd want me around."

"Who do you have left?"

"My mom. My sister."

"I'm sure they miss you."

I hugged my arms to myself. "I'm sure they don't."

"A daughter. A sister. They miss you."

"I don't know why."

Levi leaned back. "We're designed to want a relationship with our families. Even if things are strained, there is the desire for things to be better."

I thought about it. Did I wish things were better? Of course I did. Of course I craved beauty instead of ugliness. But I didn't want to concede the things I would have to in order to receive acceptance from my mom and Beth. I told Levi as much.

"What do you have to concede?"

"I don't know. My independence."

"Can I ask you something?"

I yawned. Hmm. Those sleeping pills were still in my system. "Okey-dokey."

"What's so great about independence?"

"Well, it worked for the American Revolutionaries."

"Personal independence can be overrated. Consider the Amish. Their families and communities are completely dependent on each other, and it works for them. They take care of their friends, family, and neighbors, knowing they'll be taken care of too when the time comes."

"I don't know," I said with a shake of my head. If I were more awake, I might have been able to come up with a better argument. My eyelids felt heavy.

"Are you getting sleepy?"

I forced my eyes back open. "I don't want to fall asleep again."

"Why not?"

"If I close my eyes again, the iguana might still be there."

Levi chuckled. "I think you're already falling asleep."

"Am not."

"You're worried about the iguana?"

"And my dad. Maybe he's haunting my dreams."

"I don't think so."

"He's angry with me."

"If he's in heaven, he's too happy to be angry."

I shook my head. "You don't know my dad."

"Are you sure you don't want to go back to sleep?"

"He'll be there. Angry with me."

Levi took my face between his hands. "If he's in heaven, looking at you the way I see you, it would be impossible for him to be angry with you."

A part of me registered that maybe I ought to enjoy that touch, or resent it, or something, but I was too fuzzy to pick one. "You think?"

"I know."

My eyelids felt like lead weights. Were they always so heavy? "You're nice."

"Thanks."

"It's too bad I can't fall in love with you."

I think he may have stroked my hair. "It is too bad. Why can't you?"

"You'd want to know."

"Know what?"

"Everything." I yawned. "I'm sleepy."

"I noticed."

"I don't want to sleep."

"The iguana again?"

"No." I sank back into the couch. "The puppies."

"I'm not going to ask."

"Fluffy puppies."

"I'm sure they were. Do you love Shane?"

"Probably not."

"Why can't we be together?" Was it the artificial sleep, or did he sound sad?"

I waved a hand. "I can't remember. What time is it?"

"Late. You should go to sleep."

"I don't want to close my eyes."

"Why don't you just rest your head on my shoulder?"

"Really?" I shifted so that his shoulder would be in range. He had a comfortable-looking shoulder.

"You don't even have to close your eyes."

"Okay."

The next thing I knew, I was curled up on my side on the couch. It was morning, and I was all alone.

~~·~~

I began to reheat Gemma's breakfast casserole per the instructions taped to the casserole lid. Even as I went through the motions of placing it in the appropriately warmed oven, I tried to piece together the events from the night before.

I remembered the dream vividly. The scent of hospital hallways still clung to my nose, though my logical self reminded me of my recent trips to the hospital. Then there was the oddness of the, ah, animals that also inhabited my dreams. I chalked them up to a snack of cheese and crackers before bed.

But after the dream…I remembered Levi waking me. I remember talking with him, calming down. After that, things were a bit fuzzy. And that was bad. I had a tendency to react to tiredness as if it were truth serum and not remember things I said, a fact Joely and Kim had attempted to exploit more than once.

Not Gemma, though. Gemma was too nice.

The fact that I was medicated probably hadn't helped, either.

I whipped around when I heard footsteps, hoping it was Sara or Martha and not the person who had witnessed me at my most vulnerable.

Again.

Levi stood on the threshold of the kitchen. "Hey."

"Hey back."

"How are you this morning?"

My heart sank. If only he had the same memory issues I did.

"Fine," I answered.

"You didn't seem to have any other disturbing dreams."

I winced. "Not that I remember. Listen, about last night?"

"Yeah?"

I almost didn't continue. His eyes, occasionally guarded, were open and full of a hope I hated to shatter.

"I, um, I don't really remember much after you woke me up."

Levi smiled. "I'm not surprised."

Fine, but I was. I expected him to be upset, not smiley. "You're not?"

"You were pretty out of it."

"Oh. What did I say?"

He shrugged. "Stuff about iguanas."

"Iguanas? You're making that up."

"Surprisingly, no." He stretched his arms. "Where do you keep your coffee? I'll start a pot."

"Um…I don't actually have a coffeemaker."

Levi froze. "You don't have a coffeemaker?"

"No."

"French press?"

"Which I believe is a kind of coffeemaker…"

"Instant granules?"

"I have green tea."

From the look on Levi's face, you would have thought I'd told him to raise a glass of hemlock to his lips. "So tell me," he said after he recovered, "is there any decent coffee to be found in this town?"

"Somewhere, yes. This is Portland, after all. Who do you think Seattle sells it to?"

"Want to help me find some after breakfast? I haven't had any in over twenty-four hours."

"Can't have that," I said, realizing without disappointment that I'd just agreed to go.

Chapter 18

Martha stopped dead when she walked into the kitchen and found breakfast prepared. "I'm sorry," she said. "I must have overslept."

"That's perfectly fine." I reached for a serving spoon. "Would you like some?"

She nodded. I didn't imagine people made breakfast for her very often.

Sara followed shortly after. "Any news on Dad?"

Levi shook his head. "I'm about to call the nurse and check."

"Or you could talk to him yourself," I murmured in the softest of soft voices.

"Not over the phone," he muttered back.

I made a face at him.

He made a face back.

"I can call," Martha said, oblivious to our moment. "I would like to hear his voice."

We ate in silence as Martha borrowed my phone for the call.

She listened carefully to the person on the other line, but her face lit up when Gideon came on.

I smiled as I watched. "He must be awake."

"And upset that he's still in a hospital bed," Levi added.

Sara rolled her eyes. "He's probably going crazy."

Five minutes later, Martha held the phone out to me. "How do I hang up?"

I snapped the phone shut.

"Oh. That makes sense. I'd like to go to the hospital soon."

"Is Dad okay?" Sara asked.

"He says he is, and the nurse agrees. But he wants to get out of bed, and I need to be there to stop him."

Levi and Sara exchanged glances.

Levi looked to me. "Another time?"

Another time for...oh, right. Coffee. "Of course." Probably for the best anyway.

——☆——

Levi took Sara and Martha to the hospital while I stayed behind to "work."

"Working" being code for figuring out what to do with my life.

I used to think that was what college was for.

Gemma was right. I either needed to make things better with Shane or at least move on. Staying with him because I liked him as arm candy wasn't fair to him.

And as far as my family went...if my dream was any indication, the dissonance had gone on long enough. They either loved me or they didn't. I either loved them or I didn't. I had to choose one.

It struck me as ironic that, really, my situation surrounding my family and my boyfriend were so similar.

Basically, I needed to make up my mind.

I sighed, picked up my phone, and dialed Shane for the first time in a while.

"Jayne? Where are you? The connection is the clearest it's been since you left."

"I'm actually in my apartment."

"Finally had enough?"

"Not really..." I gave him the short and sweet version of Gideon's heart attack. "So Martha and Sara are staying with me while he's at OHSU."

I sort of edited out the fact that Levi was sleeping in my study.

"I miss you," he said.

"I miss you," I echoed back, although I wasn't certain that I did. Maybe I did. I probably did. "Anyway, I called because I think I'm going to cut my time in Albany short and go to Lincoln City to see my family."

"Oh. That's nice."

"I was wondering..." I paused and then took a deep breath, "if you wanted to come with me."

"Why?"

"I thought...I thought you might want to meet my family."

"You want me to meet your family."

"Yes."

"You realize that would involve me talking to them."

"Yes."

"And you still want me to go?"

"Wait. Let me think about it…"

"Jayne!"

"Just kidding! Yes."

"And this isn't just because you're going and you need a buffer."

"No."

"No, you don't want me as a buffer?"

I couldn't lie. "Well, it's one of those side benefits. But not the only reason. At all." I released the breath I'd been holding. "This next weekend?"

"That's fine. I may need to bring some work with me."

"Bring whatever you need, as long as yourself is included."

"You're doing okay?"

"I'm…" I thought about it. Was I okay? I was conflicted. And confused. And not looking forward to the Lincoln City trip. Did that make me not okay?

I straightened my spine. "I'm fine."

I was alive and healthy. That made me okay enough.

⁂

I ran errands that afternoon, picking up a bag of Stumptown coffee for Levi as well as a coffeemaker, reasoning that at some point I might brew coffee at home.

It's also possible that I went to Powell's, because, well, I hadn't been to Powell's in more than a week and I was low on reading material.

The Martha who returned to the apartment seemed younger and, I don't know, lighter than the one who left. Not that she weighed less, but that there was less weighing her down.

"He's doing very well," she reported, her cheeks glowing. "The doctor said that if he continues to do so well, he can leave in two days. Two days!"

"That's good news!"

"I insist on making dinner," she said, tugging at her apron. "After a day of sitting around at a hospital, I need to do something useful."

I couldn't stop her, not without feeling horribly guilty. "Knock yourself out."

She frowned at me. "Knock myself…"

"Er…go ahead. The kitchen is yours with my blessing."

"Is that a thread on your shirt?" Sara glued herself to my side and picked at the hem of my cowl-necked T-shirt.

"It is," she said, before I could reply. "The hem's coming out. This wasn't sewn together very well. Would you like me to fix it?"

I figured if I let her fix it, she'd let go.

"Can you take it off?"

I had to physically restrain my eyes from darting to Levi for his reaction. Instead, I schooled my features and said, "Why don't we go to my room? You can mend this shirt, and then you can look for other garments in need of your care. Does that sound like fun?"

She all but skipped down the short hallway. I followed.

In the short expanse of time that followed, Sara found six T-shirts, two blouses, and three pairs of pants in desperate need of her service. Then she looked at me. "Where's your needle and thread?"

Seriously. "Sara, I don't have a needle and thread."

She rolled her eyes in such a way as to make me a believer that teenager-dom is a reality that crosses cultures. "You probably don't have extra buttons either, do you." It was a statement more than a question.

"I save the buttons that come with my clothes," I said defensively, and it was true. I did save them. I didn't know how to attach them if and when the need arose, but I had them just the same.

She pointed to the pile of clothes on my bed. "I can't fix these without thread."

I chose not to suggest dental floss, instead opting to bundle up and make a trip to Fred Meyer's.

Freddy's has everything.

"Need company?" Levi asked when I returned to the living room.

I shook my head. "Just a quick trip. I'll be right back. Did you see the coffee?"

"Coffee?" The look in his eyes turned a bit desperate.

"I bought coffee for you. It's on the counter."

"You don't have a coffeemaker."

"But not until after dinner," Martha called from the kitchen. "Sara, would you set the table?"

Sara dropped her eyes and moved back toward the kitchen as if driven by an invisible force.

When we sat down to dinner, I found myself struck again by the sense of family. I couldn't remember the last time the idea of family was so appealing.

My mind wandered before I could stop myself. I wondered what Martha would be like as a mother-in-law. Shane's mother was an interior designer (one of the reasons they'd never come to my place on a visit, since I had decorated the place in a postcollege eclectic style she probably wouldn't approve of) and married to her career. I couldn't see her preparing and serving dinner, unless it involved a caterer with excellent presentational skills.

I shook my head. Not that it mattered. I didn't see myself getting married anytime soon—or at all—and certainly not to a carpenter from Albany.

Seriously.

Even if he was good looking, handy, and an all-around enjoyable person to be with. Didn't matter.

※

The next few days flew by. Gideon continued to steadily improve, and the Burk-holders began to ready for departure. Levi and I never had a chance to go for coffee, which was fine with me. I was with Shane.

Sara and I never had a chance to paw through Gemma's closet, which was also just as well. As far as I knew, Sara hadn't yet made up her mind about her future with the Amish. Exposing her to Gemma's closet would just be unfair to her. I didn't know how the Amish could compete with a French and Italian wardrobe.

Levi never visited Gideon in the hospital. "I can't run the risk of upsetting him, not when he's like this," Levi told me when I pushed the issue for the last time. "I don't want to be responsible for killing him."

"At least there are health care professionals around, unlike at the farm," I reasoned halfheartedly.

Levi shrugged. "Another time."

His plan was to leave before I drove Martha and Sara to the hospital to pick up Levi. "I want to thank you," he said, his backpack slung over his shoulder.

"The box next to the coffee that says 'Mr. Coffee' on it."

I could hear his grin as the door closed behind me.

I found all sorts of things at Freddy's. Scissors made especially for fabric. Who knew such a thing existed? My mother, probably.

There were needles of all lengths and thicknesses, and a little more thread than I felt comfortable around. But I struck gold with what they called an "Emergency Mending Kit," which contained thread of assorted colors, needles, a miscellaneous button, a tiny measuring tape, tiny scissors, a tiny thimble, and two small safety pins.

I don't know what kind of emergency might necessitate this sort of kit, but I was pretty sure it had everything Sara might have asked for.

When I got back to the apartment, dinner simmered on the stove and the scent of brewed coffee filled the air. Martha bustled around the kitchen, putting the last touches on her meal. Levi sat on the couch, a book in one hand and a mug in the other, while Sara breezed in and out of the living room, putting away items that had managed to drift out (mostly by me) since morning.

The sense of family took my breath away. Was this what coming home to people was like?

I pulled the emergency kit from the plastic Fred Meyer sack and waved it in the air. "Hope this works," I told Sara, "otherwise we'll have to improvise. Yank thread from my duvet, that sort of thing."

Sara's eyes narrowed. "What is that?"

"A kit."

"What kind?"

"Emergency mending, and you're the field medic."

Her eyebrows pitched forward in an expression of complete confusion.

"She means you're an emergency doctor," Levi said, looking up from his book.

"Oh."

He looked at me, his eyes twinkling.

Sara began to peel away the plastic covering. "This has everything I need," she said. "I should have your clothes done right away."

I waved my hand. "It was nothing."

"You let the Amish take over your home for five days."

"They're good people."

"I noticed you have a lot of books."

"You're very perceptive."

"I thought I could make you a bookcase. As a thank-you gift."

I opened my mouth to protest but decided against it. "That would be nice."

"I was thinking a tall one, with short shelves to fit a lot of books, but two taller shelves in the middle."

"I could live with that."

"Light wood? Dark?"

"You're the carpenter."

"You're a special lady, Jayne."

He left, then, and I found myself wishing that maybe things could be different.

***

Gideon slept through most of the trip back to the Burkholder farm, but for that matter so did Martha. Sara sketched out a quilt pattern on her notebook.

I played Sixpence None the Richer softly over the car stereo; I knew the Amish weren't big music listeners—Sara had explained that recorded music was taboo—but I had to do something to avoid joining the communal nap.

The kids ran out into the driveway despite the downpour, and I understood how Levi felt about driving up to them. I managed to miss their toes but I did catch their hugs after I opened the door and stepped out.

I packed the rest of my things after Gideon was settled inside—my quilt squares, a pair of socks, and the dress Sara made me and insisted I keep.

Martha stepped inside the room just after I finished. She held a quilt in her arms.

"I would like to thank you for all of your help while Gideon was sick, Jayne. I—we—would like you to have this."

She held the quilt out to me.

It was exquisite. The shades of blues worked together to create a subtle three-dimensional effect that took my breath away. Black and purple pieces ran along the edges.

I ran my finger over the stitches. "Martha, it's beautiful."

"Take it."

I found myself hugging it close before pulling Martha into that hug. I didn't want to leave. "Thank you for letting me stay and be a part of your family."

Martha's body, stiff at first, relaxed. Her hand patted my back. "You're welcome."

I said my goodbyes to Gideon, Amos, and Elam, and hugged each of the younger children.

"Do you really have to go?" Elizabeth asked as she held onto my knees.

"I do," I said, stroking her braid one last time. "I need to be with my family before I go back to work."

"Will you write letters?"

I looked up to see Martha's encouraging nod. "If you want me to, I'll write."

Sara stood in the living room, her back straight as the ladder in the barn. "Take better care of your clothes," she said. "You really should learn to sew."

I gave her a knowing smile. "I'll miss you too."

I thought about stopping by Levi's shop on the way out of town, but I decided against it. Saying goodbye to the Burkholders had already made me more emotional than I wanted to admit.

Besides, a part of me needed a clean break from Levi. I needed to focus on Shane if that relationship wasn't going to dissolve into Oprah-discussion material.

Clean break. Need space. Getting back to my life. I reminded myself of all the reasons why it was okay to go home to a quiet, empty apartment.

Quiet as it was, the walls still seemed to hold the memory of noise, people, and laughter. The sound of pots clanging echoed in the kitchen. Sara's disbelief over my wardrobe still resonated in my bedroom.

And Levi...truth be told, he was everywhere. He was everywhere but I ignored it, unpacked my belongings from Amish-land and prepared for my trip to the Oregon Coast.

I couldn't sleep that night. My nights on the couch had been hit-and-miss, considering the mix of exhaustion and the fact that I wasn't used to sleeping on something with arms and a back, but this was different.

Every time I almost fell asleep, I heard something. A Harley roaring past. Skateboarder kids yelling. An emergency siren—no, two.

I hadn't heard a siren while I was sleeping since I'd left to stay with the Burkholders, and I couldn't believe how fast I'd accustomed myself to not hearing them. Now that I was hearing them, they annoyed me to no end. It was four in the morning! How much traffic could there be? Couldn't they flash their lights and make that *whoop whoop* noise when necessary, instead of waking up every resident within a one-mile radius?

Unfortunately for Shane, I woke up the next morning groggy and irritated. When he arrived, my things weren't packed, my hair was wet, and I had only just gotten dressed.

Who knew getting dressed could be so difficult? I'd spent more than a week without clothing options, and now pairing a shirt with jeans took mental calisthenics I'd never expected. Sara had made me twitchy about my clothes. I held up a shirt and wondered, *What would Sara say?*

It made the whole process rather time consuming.

"You're not ready?" Shane said, deciding, I supposed, that today was a good day to skate hard on thin ice.

I glared at him. "*No*, I'm not ready. And you're early. Why are you early?"

"No traffic. Why are you so defensive?"

"I told you! You're early and wonder why I'm not ready! Of course I'm not ready. If you'd been here on time, I might have been ready."

"Sorry, no traffic. Are your bags packed?"

"No. But they might have been if you'd gotten here when you were supposed to."

Shane checked his watch. "I'm ten minutes early. Would you have been packed and dried your hair in ten minutes?"

I crossed my arms. "Yes."

He just looked at me.

"Maybe," I amended. "At least I'm dressed."

"Congratulations." He sighed and took off his jacket. "Do you need help with anything?"

"No."

"Did you, um...not sleep well?"

"No."

"Ah. Take a deep breath. Go pack."

I did. Or I tried. In the end, I shoved most of my closet into my suitcase, then pulled it all back out. "I need to go shopping."

"What was that?" Shane called from the living room.

"I said I needed to go shopping."

"I didn't know you shopped."

"Everyone shops." I packed socks. You couldn't go wrong with socks. "Otherwise, we'd starve."

"I meant clothes shopping."

"I've got to get them somehow, and shoplifting seems out of the question."

"But you don't enjoy it."

"No." I tucked away a selection of underwear. "But it's like the dentist. Bad things happen if you don't go."

Especially according to Sara, a girl who made all her own clothes. I would have discredited her opinion, except that it sounded a lot like everything Gemma had ever said about my motley collection of garments.

"You got a coffeemaker." Shane, I guess, had moved from the living room to the kitchen. "Stumptown. That's good stuff. Need coffee? I'll make you a pot."

I winced. "No, I'm fine."

"Might help take the morning edge off."

"You want me cranky *and* caffeinated?"

"Never mind."

Thought so. I didn't need coffee in the air. It would remind me too much of a certain caffeine addict.

"Where exactly are we staying?"

I couldn't decide which jeans to take, so I brought them all. "The Sea Gypsy."

Shane grimaced. "Is it clean?"

"I'm going to forget you said that. Of course it is. It's pristine."

"Just asking."

"It's the coast, Shane, not the slums of Mumbai."

"Just checking."

"Stop checking," I said, dragging my bag down the hall. "Start loading. Please."

Shane eyed my bag in disbelief. "Tell me that's half empty."

"I like to think of it as half full."

"Jayne!"

"What? I'm an incurable optimist."

"It's two days! Unless I missed something…"

"No. Two days."

"You need all that for two days? And we're not scuba diving?"

"I hate scuba diving."

"What's wrong with scuba diving?"

I rolled my eyes. "The fact you're supposed to move away from the earth's main oxygen supply."

"You take air with you."

"Not the same. Why are we talking about this?"

"Because you have a suitcase you'd have to pay extra for to take on an airplane for two days on the Oregon Coast."

"It's not fifty pounds!"

"It's close!"

My voice hardened. "You haven't even touched it! Do you weigh things with your eyes now? How much do I weigh?"

"I—" He stopped. Took a deep breath. "I'm sorry. This morning started off wrong."

"You didn't answer my question."

"Which one?"

"How much do I weigh?"

"Hi, Jayne," he said, ignoring my question and taking my hand. "It's good to see you. I've missed you."

"I've...missed you too."

"Promise?"

I nodded. I really had.

"I'm sorry I was argumentative."

I shifted my feet. "I'm sorry I was irritable."

His other hand slipped around my back. "Can we make up?"

"Okay." I put my arms around his neck.

He leaned closer and kissed me.

I analyzed the kiss with a clinical detachment. Did I enjoy it? Was the chemistry the same? Had I imagined the chemistry before?

The kiss...well, it wasn't the best. Shane kissed with a great deal of precision. If he were being scored on technique, he'd be Olympian.

But I wasn't seeing rainbows, or feeling at the least as though I wanted the kiss to continue forever.

Another two or three seconds was perfectly fine. I could move on without much of a second thought.

Then the guilt hit. The reason I was rainbow-less was because I was being so pickin' analytical. Being analytical would kill any kiss. Even the one I shared with Levi.

Wait—I wasn't supposed to be thinking! I was supposed to be moving on, mending fences, revisiting my past in order to prepare for my future. I was doing everything Dr. Phil would want me to, dash it all, and thoughts about Levi wouldn't get in the way.

Shane pulled away. "You seem distracted."

"Oh?"

"You're really tired, aren't you."

"Yes."

"Let's get you in the car. You can sleep on the way."

I gave him a light hug. "You're sweet. Wait a minute!" I dashed back into my room, grabbing a small bag before returning to my behemoth suitcase.

"You forgot something?" I couldn't miss the irony in his voice.

I opened the bag and let him look inside. "My quilt squares are in here."

"Quilt squares?"

"Something I got into last week. It's very calming."

"You sew?"

I put my hands on my hips. "I cut."

"And then what?"

"Haven't gotten that far. I just like cutting them out."

Shane shook his head. He continued to shake his head even as he dragged my suitcase down the stairs to the car.

⟡

Shane's offer of travel time slumber was sweet, if impractical. If I couldn't sleep in my bed, logic followed that sleeping in a car while he griped about other drivers wasn't particularly likely.

I closed my eyes anyway.

He shook me "awake" once we entered the town of Rose Lodge. "Mind if we get something to eat when we get there? I'm starved."

"We're close to Otis Café, if they're not too busy."

Shane studied the sparse, rural buildings and lots littered with the occasional mobile home on cement blocks. "Busy?"

"There are only about eight tables and the café's been written up in a lot of national press—*USA Today* included. It's quite popular."

"What kind of food?"

"Farmer's breakfast-type fare. Man food. A lot of potatoes. The bread's really good." *The Burkholders would love it.*

Shane shrugged. "I'm game if you are. I thought you avoided carbs."

"I've been living with the Amish."

"Right. How close are we?"

"A mile or two."

We drove for a while.

"Is that it?" he asked.

"Does it have a large sign that says 'Café'?" I didn't open my eyes.

"Yes."

"Is it on the right?"

"Yes."

"Then pull in. We're here."

I sat up straight and opened my door, looking out my window at the familiar sight that was Otis Café.

My family came here every year for Beth's birthday, and often drove down for lunch after church.

It wasn't too busy inside—we managed to slide into a table before an onslaught of diners entered on our heels.

The waitress kept looking at me while she took our order. It probably had something to do with the fact that she graduated a year before I did, and we had geometry together.

She brought the food without saying anything about it, and that was fine with me.

As I ate my potatoes, I remembered all the reasons I'd stayed away.

I didn't like small towns. I didn't like being remembered. Trouble was, people in small towns remembered you because there was little else to do.

Not only did they remember you, but they had an opinion on you, or whatever you were doing. Or not doing. Living in a small town was like being followed by a Greek chorus who lamented your latest mishap. Maybe that was why God and I weren't close. He paid too much attention.

I didn't need a chorus. I didn't want a chorus. I wanted everyone to mind their own business. But I, of all people, knew that was simply too much to ask for.

~~~

"Looks like there's a nice view," Shane said, when we pulled up to the Sea Gypsy.

"And a close walk to the beach, if you don't mind the cold. Or the wind. Or the rain." Secretly, I didn't mind. But it hurt my anti-home image to say so.

Shane offered to carry my suitcase; I declined, choosing instead to lug it up the stairs myself. After sitting in the car for so long, the idea of physical exertion appealed to me.

"Reservation for Tate," I told the receptionist once we'd managed to schlep our belongings inside.

"First name?" the receptionist asked, looking to Shane.

"Last name," I corrected. "First name Jayne."

The receptionist bobbed her head and clicked her mouse. "Jayne Tate. Two double rooms." She left the computer to retrieve the keys from the back room.

"Two rooms?" Shane asked.

"Mm-hmm," I said, distracted by the one key on my keychain that refused to slide into the side pocket of my shoulder bag.

"I thought..."

"What was that?"

"I thought this was a getaway weekend."

"It is, kind of. We're seeing my family, but we're also away."

"I thought we'd be sharing a room."

"We'd be...oh." I stiffened. "But we've never..."

"I thought you might—"

"On a weekend to see my mother?"

"At the coast!"

"That's where she lives!"

"So who's paying?"

"What?"

"What if I wanted a different room?"

"I'm paying for it. I figured it was the least I could do for bringing you with me. If you want a different room, that's up to you. You just can't have mine."

"Shall I show you to your rooms?" The receptionist returned with our keys and either hadn't heard our conversation or should have been sent to Hollywood.

I grasped my suitcase. "Lead the way." I looked back to Shane. "What are you going to do? I can rent a car if I need to."

He frowned but shook his head. The receptionist started walking and he followed.

But he wouldn't look at me.

Even after we found our rooms, Shane had no desire to speak with me. Maybe car rentals were in my future, not that I cared. I wasn't in the mood for one of Shane's tantrums.

Granted I'd thrown my own earlier...but if it's unflattering for a woman, it's worse for a man. Especially when it was about the subject of sex.

I hadn't slept with Shane. Ever. Even more, I had no intention of doing so unless we at least went through a legal civil ceremony first. Thing was, I'd spent the first eighteen years of my life living with my parents. And for better or for worse, my mother's voice resonated through my cranium whenever things became a bit...involved.

Why buy the cow when he can get the milk for free? If there's any sort of passion dampener, it's your mother comparing you to a cow. Until I was married, that voice wasn't going anywhere. Truthfully, I had concerns about it even then.

And here I was, back in Lincoln City, trying to make amends with the keeper of that voice.

I fished my phone out of my tote bag and dialed the home number.

No answer.

I tried her cell, bearing in mind that I had a fifty-fifty chance of her not hearing or noticing the ringing of her phone.

Nothing.

I hung up and chewed on my lip in frustration. Would Beth be around? I tried her number, which rang until a voice message announced that I could leave a message for Steve as long as I left my name and number.

Beth wasn't married to a Steve. She was married to a Gary.

Wow. I didn't even have my own sister's current number.

I didn't feel like sitting at the motel all day, and I had no deep desire to putter around and see the sights. I grew up here. The sights had been seen.

The reason I came was to see my mom. If I was serious, then I would do exactly that.

I got off the bed and left the room, walking down the corridor to Shane's door.

I knocked. He opened his door, still looking grumpy, his cell phone crunched between his ear and shoulder.

"I'll call you back," he said before hanging up.

"Hi."

"Hi." His voice sounded wary.

"I can't reach my mom or my sister over the phone. I don't want to sit around here all day. I'm just going to go to the house and see who's home."

"How are you getting there?"

"That's up to you. You can calm down and we can go together. Or you can go home and I'll rent a car."

"Harsh, Jayne."

"I don't think so," I said with a frown.

"Come inside. I don't want to argue in a breezeway."

I shrugged. "Up to you." I stepped inside and he closed the door.

"I've asked you this before." Shane pulled up a chair, sat, and leaned forward. "Are you serious about us?"

"I told you that I was. I asked you to come, to meet my family."

"I mean, are you wanting to take us to the next level?"

"'The next level.' Makes us sound like Donkey Kong."

"You know what I mean."

"You're asking if I want to sleep with you."

"Well, yes."

"Haven't we already talked this to death?"

"I thought you were saying no because you weren't ready to commit to us."

"No, I was saying no because..." I sighed. "I was raised to believe in certain things, Shane. Even though I'm no longer that person, some of those concepts stuck."

"Concepts like..."

"Unmarried sex." The words came out in a whoosh. If he pressed any harder, I'd spill about my mother's voice and the whole thing could get very ugly.

His shoulders tightened. "Oh. You could have just said that."

"It makes me feel like Emily Brontë."

"And you won't change your mind?"

"Positive." My mother's voice could be very insistent.

"Do you want to get married?"

A vein of panic welled up inside me. "Ever?"

"In the nearer future."

"To you?"

"You think I'd ask you about someone else?"

I fought to keep Levi's face from my mind. "I don't know. I would like to get married, I think—someday. I haven't spent a whole lot of time thinking about it."

"We've been dating for six months!"

"I didn't know you were wife shopping!"

"I'm not—" he exhaled hard. "I'm not wife shopping."

"That's good, because I didn't mean for this trip to be an opportunity for you to offer my mother an assortment of goats for my hand in marriage."

A smile tugged at his lips. "Oh, I think you're worth at least a couple camels."

I may have kicked him.

—————

"Stop checking your hair," Shane said, a minute after we pulled up in my mom's driveway.

"Her car is here."

"Good. That means she's home."

"And because she's here, she'll see me."

Shane's head quirked to the side. "Am I missing something?"

"She'll see me. She'll see if my hair is in place—or out of place. If I have excessive lint on my clothes or if I'm missing a button." I tugged on my blouse to inspect the front.

"You've got to relax, Jayne."

"This is my mother we're talking about!"

"Right. Your mother. She's not going to throw anthrax in your face if you've got a scuff on your shoe."

"There's a scuff? Why didn't you say so earlier?"

"Your shoes are fine. That was just an example."

"*Why* would you say something like that?"

"You're really worried about this."

"Now that you mention it, yes, I am." I rolled my eyes.

"I've never seen you this dramatic."

"You've never met my mother." I gave my hair a final shove behind my ear and opened the car door, moving more on impulse than anything else.

I had decided this was the best course. I would move forward. Even if it was hard.

Even if it hurt.

I strode up to the front door, Shane trailing behind me. He reached for the doorbell but I slapped his hand back. "She doesn't like the doorbell being used."

"Then why is it still there?"

"Because it would look funny to not have a doorbell." I knocked on the door.

And waited. Nothing.

I knocked again.

Shane cleared his throat.

I folded my arms against my chest. "What?"

"Maybe you should ring the doorbell."

"She's home. She's somewhere."

"And you're going to knock until she hears you? Why wouldn't she have answered the phone?"

"Sometimes she doesn't hear it."

"But she hears knocking?"

"Not hearing her cell phone is because she leaves it in her purse and forgets about it. It's not like she carries it from room to room."

"But she has a landline, doesn't she?"

"If she's in the garage, she can't hear it."

Shane blinked. "So if she can't hear it, how will she hear you knocking on the door?"

"If she were in the garage, she wouldn't hear the doorbell, either. Do you need to go sit in the car?" I knocked a third time. Seriously. She had to be in there somewhere.

"Jayne—"

"Do you hear that? There's music playing. She's home."

And to prove it, I heard footsteps. The bolt creaked back and my mother unlocked the door.

"Jayne! This is a surprise," she said. "Have you been here long?"

She looked different since the last time I'd seen her. Grief still clung to the edges of her eyes, but her hair was shorter now, and blond instead of gray. Had it been that way at the memorial and I hadn't noticed?

"We've just been a few minutes," I answered, hedging.

"I'm sorry I didn't hear you. I had the KitchenAid on. Come on in, both of you." She opened the door wide and extended her hand to Shane. "We haven't met—I'm Nora Tate."

Shane shook her hand, a bemused expression on his face. "Nice to meet you."

She patted his hand before leading us to the living room. "Sorry you were standing outside for so long—it's awfully drizzly out. You should have rung the doorbell."

⊰⊱

"How long are you in town for?" Mom asked when she returned with tea and coffee.

I took the teacup she offered. "I have work on Monday, but I was hoping to stay until then."

"Do you have your bags with you? I can set you up upstairs."

"I, um, checked in down at the Sea Gypsy."

She froze, her gaze darting from me to Shane.

"In separate rooms." No use torturing her.

Mom tried a nonchalant shrug. "I didn't ask."

But she was thinking.

"It's up to you, but I have plenty of space for the both of you. If you'd like to stay here—it's entirely up to you."

I looked to Shane. He nodded. "That'd be really nice."

She beamed. "Excellent. Have you seen Beth yet?"

"No," I said, my face turning red. "I don't think I have her current number."

"She switched phone services. Why don't I give her a call? Do you have dinner plans?"

We said no, and I watched as my mother all but skipped to the phone to call Beth.

"What were you so worried about?" Shane set his coffee cup down. "Everything seems cool. Your mom even makes good coffee."

I smiled, thinking it was a comment Levi would have made. I forced myself back to the present. Standing, I walked around the living room and looked at the pictures sprinkled around the room.

Beth and me as little girls, dressed for Easter Sunday. Beth looking like a princess, me looking like a princess who would rather be the scullery maid. There was Beth's graduation photo, followed shortly by the wedding pictures, she and Gary smiling and looking so very young.

There were other photos I appeared in—my first day of kindergarten, that sort of thing. But after my graduation, there were no more photos.

I knew why. I had made it a point to not be available for photo ops.

There were other pictures I hadn't seen. Beth holding a newborn in her arms, a smiling Gary sitting on the edge of the hospital bed.

I knew I'd visited briefly weeks before the baby was born and sent a card shortly after. But there were moments I'd missed, moments I'd never get back. I always thought I was fine with that. Now…I wasn't so sure.

My mom came back to the room. "I just got off the phone with Beth. She and Gary are free tonight, so they'll be over soon. They'll bring little Emilee with them. I can't believe how fast she's growing up!"

"How old is she now?"

"Turning five next winter."

I think I might have sent her a birthday present. Once. I certainly wasn't in line for any "Auntie of the Year" awards.

"They'll be a little while, coming in from Neotsu," my mom continued. "If you like, you could check out of the motel and get settled in here."

A part of me hesitated. If things blew up over dinner, I wouldn't have anywhere to go.

However, it also meant that I would have to stay and sort out my problems.

Which was technically the reason for the trip.

"That sounds nice," I said.

"I'll go start dinner." She frowned. "You're not vegetarian, are you? Either of you?"

Shane emphatically shook his head.

"Excellent. When you get back, will you want your old room, Jayne?"

I shrugged. "Fine with me."

"And Shane, there's a bed in the sewing room."

"Sewing room?" I didn't know Mom sewed.

"Beth's old room." She sighed. "It'll be so nice to have everyone here. I just wish…"

Her voice trailed off, but I knew what she meant. She wished my father were there.

I didn't know if I could agree with her or not.

※

The receptionist gave us an odd look when we checked out. I imagine it looked a bit shady that we'd only checked in a little while ago, but we were in separate rooms, for Pete's sake. "My mom invited us to stay with her," I explained, trying to make the woman's expression go away.

"That's nice," she said, but the expression only slightly softened.

Back at my mom's house, she led us upstairs to the rooms, even though I'd grown up there. Maybe she thought I'd been gone so long I'd forgotten.

My room looked very little like I remembered. Granted, it had been eight years. My striped bedspread had left with me for university life. In its place was a floral-print quilt that coordinated with the soft green color of the walls. It was very soothing, very pretty. Made me think of my room at the Burkholders.

Speaking of the walls, they looked different than I remembered. Probably because ACDC no longer scowled down on anyone who walked in.

I went to check on Shane once I had put my bags down.

Beth's room really had been converted to a sewing room. Tubs of fabric lined a wall. Plastic sets of pull-out drawers held thread, scissors, and measuring tapes. A table against the wall held a massive sewing machine. Next to the machine sat a stack of…

"Quilt squares!" I rushed over to pick them up. They looked so nice, so organized, their edges trimmed just so.

Shane came up behind me. "Explain to me what you'll do with them? Seeing as how you don't quilt…"

I narrowed my eyes at him. "Cut more squares so they'll be with friends."

"You just have stacks of quilt squares?"

"Aren't they nice?"

"Do you collect three-by-five cards too?"

"Shane—"

"Do you stack them as well? Or I guess you don't need to. They come out of the shrink-wrap that way."

"You're impossible."

"You like me that way."

I leaned over to give him a quick kiss. "Define like."

Shane deepened the kiss but pulled away when the doorbell rang. "That's probably your sister. *She* rang the doorbell."

I rolled my eyes and stepped away. "Seriously, the doorbell used to be very taboo in this house."

But it had changed. Obviously. I just wanted to know what other things—aside from our bedrooms—had changed as well.

Chapter 21

Shane and I headed downstairs, following the sound of people—chatter, the rustle of coats, Velcro, and zippers.

As we came into the entryway, I could see Beth, Gary, and Emilee. My little niece looked a lot larger than I'd imagined. I hadn't seen her at the memorial. Beth had elected to get a sitter rather than put a four-year-old through that.

Beth looked up. I smiled. Her chilly expression caused me to stop where I was. Shane nearly ran over me.

"Hi, Beth," I said, hoping that maybe her expression was an anomaly.

The corners of her mouth moved a fraction of an inch up. "Hi, Jayne."

"This is my boyfriend, Shane," I said, attempting to distract everyone. "Shane, this is Beth, my sister, and her husband, Gary." I flashed my most winning smile. "And Emilee is my niece."

Shane shook everyone's hand, charming as usual.

"Shane and Jayne?" Beth asked. "Do you date because you rhyme?"

I heard Gary chide his wife under his breath, but Shane jumped in before I could form a non-incendiary reply.

"More like, we date, therefore we are. I've always tried to be existential about my romantic relationships," he said, and because he's witty and charming, everyone but Beth laughed, even if they didn't understand.

Existentialistic humor not being for everyone.

"Dinner's going to be a little while," Mom said, taking coats to the hallway closet near the utility room. "Settle in and get comfortable."

"Do you need any help in the kitchen?" I asked. Sitting around in this crowd wasn't my idea of relaxing.

Mom stopped still. Beth stopped still. It's possible the earth froze in its orbit for a moment, at least until my mother caught her breath.

"I'd love help." My mom glanced at my brace. "Are you sure your wrist feels well enough?"

Beth snorted. I refused to look at her. "It's nearly healed."

"I thought I'd put a pie together. Would you like to help with that?"

I could feel Beth's gaze shifting from me to Mom.

"I love pie."

"She can eat it, but she can't bake it," Beth mumbled, and I heard Gary mumble something back.

Shane squeezed my hand. I left for the kitchen.

"Do you have an apron I could borrow?" I asked, thinking for the first time that I might want an apron of my own. Not that I'd necessarily travel with it, but I kept going places and wanting one. At some point, I'd probably want one at home too.

My mom produced a flowered apron that triggered childhood memories of cookie frosting and postdinner dishes. I slipped it over my head and tied it behind my back

Something strange happened in that instant. Before the apron, a part of me felt out of place, like the object on Sesame Street that Big Bird would decide didn't belong. But after the apron—I felt more settled. More centered, as though I were back at the Burkholder farmhouse, with a garden in the back and a loose pig and children underfoot and everything in a state of rightness.

I measured out the flour the way Martha had taught me. I placed the measuring cup inside a slightly larger bowl, spooned the ingredient into the cup, then leveled off the top, all with my good arm.

I could feel my mom watching as I worked, but I didn't care. I was in my happy place. When Mom offered to help with the rolling, though, I didn't turn her down. Within minutes, the lower dough layer was in place in the bottom of the pie pan.

"What kind of pie are we making," I asked, fingering the edge of the crust.

"How does cherry sound?"

"I didn't know cherries were available," I said, thinking about how much more they would cost at the coast.

Mom raised a finger to her lips. "Don't tell Beth." She opened a cupboard and retrieved three cans of prepared cherry filling.

I stifled a laugh. I'd never known my mom to bake anything *not* from scratch. Even brownies never came from a box.

"I drain them, so there's less of the cherry syrup in the pie."

"Very clever." Feeling like a coconspirator, I helped open the cans and dumped their contents into the sieve in the sink. We gave the sieve a tiny shake, then emptied the ripe, sugar-coated cherries into the pie pan. I watched as my mom made a lattice top out of the remaining dough, cutting strips and laying them out just so.

When she finished, I went around and crimped the edges so that they waved in a perfect circle.

I let Mom put it in the oven.

She brushed the excess flour from her hands. "Do you bake often these days?"

"Not until recently."

"Oh?"

I ducked my head and smoothed my apron. "I, um, went to stay with an Amish family for a while."

"Really? What was that like?"

What was it like? How could I begin? "Hard to describe," I started, realizing I wasn't making any mental headway. "It's a society that makes so little sense to me. But there's something really beautiful about it."

"Will you go back to visit again?"

"I hope so."

And before I knew it, I was telling her about Martha and Sara, Gideon and the boys, about Leah and little Elizabeth. I told her about Ida, Naomi Zook, and her twins Mary Ellen and Becky, little Doyle and Baby Ruby.

Woven throughout their stories was the ever-present Levi, whose face had followed me ever since I left the farm.

I told her more than I had told anyone, even Gemma. I didn't know why, either. I had never been one of those girls who had been able to confide in her mother. When I was a teen, I thought she'd criticize me for what I said.

"Tell me more about this Levi," Mom said when I was through. She stood at the stove, stirring a sauce. "He sounds like an interesting fellow."

I listened for a quick moment for Shane and the others in the living room. Shane was saying something, Gary was laughing.

"Levi…is a puzzle. He left the Amish to use his mind, and then he left his corporate job to be back near them. He could befriend anyone."

"Like Shane?"

Shane would befriend, yes, but name-call later. "Yes. And no. They're different."

"How long have you and Shane been seeing each other?"

"Six months."

"Is he serious?"

"Yes."

"Are you?"

The chatter in the living room died down. I shrugged, rather than incriminate myself audibly.

"The sauce is done, and I think the roast is too. The pie will bake through dinner. Shall we call everyone in?"

⌁

"How's the pie?" Shane asked when I returned to the living room.

"Cheery cherry."

"Cherry?" Beth's eyebrows lifted in surprise. "Where'd Mom get cherries this time of year?"

"She has her ways, I guess," I answered with a straight face. "Dinner's ready, if you'd all like to come in to eat."

"I don't think I heard," Beth started, pointing at my arm, "how you wound up with a brace."

I opted for the condensed version. "I fell down."

"Out of nowhere?"

The Beth I grew up with never pressed this hard. Somewhere along the line, she had become quite a pain. A pain with a backbone.

"There was a short trashcan involved."

"Was that at the Amish house?" Shane asked.

"No. It was…in town."

Gary chuckled. "There's a lawsuit waiting to happen."

Hmm, I didn't like where this was going. I pointed to the dining room. "Dinner—hot—in there. Good stuff."

"Is the pie sanitary?" Beth asked innocently.

I saw Gary give her a dirty look.

"It should be," I said with a straight face. "At least, once the E. coli cooks out."

Shane snorted.

"Who's Ecoli?" little Emilee asked, the first time I'd heard her speak.

She had a sweet little voice. Reminded me of Naomi's twins. Come to think of it, they were about the same age.

"Don't worry about it, honey," Gary told his daughter. "E. coli is a kind of germ, but there won't be any in your pie. Your aunt was just joking."

"Where is everyone?" Mom called from the dining room. "Dinner won't be hot forever!"

"Coming!" I called, walking in her direction and willing everyone else to follow suit.

I could hear Beth and Gary arguing softly behind me, but their voices never seemed far away, which I took as a good sign. Shane came up beside me and squeezed my hand.

I squeezed it back.

"Shall we pray?" Mom asked, once we'd all settled at the table. "Gary, would you like to pray for us?"

"We should check with Jayne first," Beth said.

My stomach sank.

"Is it all right if we pray?" she asked me, her voice heavy with sarcasm. "It won't disagree with your religion, will it?"

"Beth—" Mom warned.

"We don't know if it would offend her, Mother. We've seen so little of her. She could be Baha'i by now. Or Buddhist. Are you Buddhist, Jayne?"

"What is your problem, Beth?" I asked, crossing my arms. "I'm here. Need to get something off your chest? I don't want you to wear yourself out. Potshots can be exhausting."

"I can't believe you!"

"What can't you believe?"

Gary pulled Emilee's chair back out. "Honey, why don't you go play upstairs for a little while? The grown-ups need to talk."

Beth reached to still Emilee's chair. "She needs to eat, Gary."

"She doesn't need to hear you—"

"Hear me what? It's past her normal dinnertime."

Gary lifted Emilee from the chair. "There's a granola bar in your bag. That should tide her over."

With that, Gary and Emilee retreated to safety upstairs.

I knew exactly how they felt.

"I can't believe you'd not visit for three years, barely show up at Dad's memorial, and then waltz back here like nothing was wrong. Did you notice how Mom's lost twenty pounds in the last month? Who helped take care of Mom when Dad was in the hospital? Who brought her meals? Who organized the caterer for the memorial, made the phone calls, wrote the thank-you cards for the bouquets?"

"I'm sorry, Beth." I struggled to keep my voice steady. "You want to know why I came? I came because I didn't like the way things were. Because I wanted to try, *try*, to make things right."

"Why didn't you try five years ago? Did it occur to you that you might be five years too late?"

"Beth, that's enough!" Mom chided sharply. "If you can't be pleasant, you can leave."

"Let me answer, Mom." I looked back to Beth. "I did consider that it was probably *eight* years too late, but I wanted to try anyway."

"What if," she said, "I wanted a sister that whole time?"

I sighed. "What if I did too?"

"I was here! We all were!"

"You didn't want a sister who was a reporter in Portland. You wanted a sister who could look through children's clothing catalogs with you. I couldn't do that."

"No. Instead, you ran away to the big city, doing big-city things so important that you didn't need us anymore."

The room at the Sea Gypsy called my name, but I remained in my seat. "I'm sorry, Beth. I don't know what to tell you. I'm trying. I'm doing what I can. The rest is up to you."

Beth closed her mouth, though she looked as though she had a lot of words still hanging around on the tip of her tongue. When she finally spoke, her voice was controlled.

"Would someone please pass the peas?"

⁂

"The pie was good," Shane said, settling himself on the floor next to the couch where I was stretched out.

"The cherries were canned."

"They were good."

"The crust wasn't as buttery as Martha's."

"Martha…"

"Burkholder."

"Right, the Amish lady. Just use more butter next time."

"You don't use butter in pie crust."

"Then how…never mind."

"My sister hates me."

"She doesn't hate you."

"Where's my mom?"

"Talking to Beth outside."

I groaned and buried my face in a throw pillow with an appliqué butterfly. "It's like we're six years old again."

"I can't understand you when you talk into pillows."

"Sorry." I lifted my face. "I said it's like we're six years old again, and we need Mommy and Daddy to help us get along. Never mind she's married with a kid and I'm a working professional. We're not adult enough to work this out."

"She's not adult enough. You were amazing in there. I just about took her out when she started choking on the pie."

"If the crust had come out like Martha's, she wouldn't have."

"The only way she wouldn't have is if Martha had made the pie. The pie had nothing to do with it. It was the fact that you made it."

"You're a whiz at making me feel better."

"Just saying."

I heard the front door close and a single set of footsteps walking in our direction.

I was glad it was only one, that Mom hadn't made Beth come in and make an attempt at an apology.

"You all right there?" Mom took a seat in the chair next to me.

"I'm fine." I turned my face away from the pillow when I spoke. If Mom caught me accidentally drooling on that butterfly, that could have been the end of things.

"Jayne, well…give Beth time. She'll get over it."

I didn't believe her, but I chose not to argue.

"Heaven knows you're both too stubborn for your own good. You take after your father that way."

I masked my wince with a cough.

"I'm sorry the night went the way it did," Mom continued. "I was so glad you came. I just wanted it to be special."

I pushed myself up. "Beth's right. I've been gone, and I haven't been much of a daughter or sister for the past several years. I never expected to show up and have everyone welcome me with open arms."

"Well, you're welcome here anytime. Both you and Shane," she said, nodding in his direction. "Anytime."

I got up then, and gave her a hug. She hugged me back. I shoved my hair from my face. "It's good to be home."

Chapter 22

Mom made smiley pancakes for breakfast, though they weren't served that way. The fruit had been rearranged into a more sophisticated arrangement in the middle—but the red juice from the strawberries and raspberries left their indelible mark on the surface.

She had started making me a smiley pancake and thought better of it. It made me a little sad; I think I would have enjoyed a breakfast that grinned back.

But it probably would have weirded Shane out if he too had received such a breakfast, and it would have been unfair if they didn't match.

Thus the rearranged fruit.

Mom sat down a few moments later.

"Do you both have plans for the day?" she asked, cutting into her own elegantly topped pancake.

Shane and I looked at each other. "Not particularly," I answered. "Although I thought about taking Shane to Kyllo's for lunch."

"Oh," Mom said with a nod. "Kyllo's is nice."

I played with the edge of my black sweater for a moment before I asked the question I really wanted the answer to. "So…I saw some quilt squares in Beth's old room."

Shane snorted and covered it with a cough. Anyone under the age of five might have been fooled.

"Anyway," I continued, flashing a warning glare at my boyfriend, "I was wondering…do you quilt?"

"I do." Mom took a sip of her coffee. "I started a few years ago when I bought that sewing machine. Why?"

"I went to a quilting bee when I was staying at the Burkholders'."

"Really? An Amish quilting bee? What was that like?"

"Crazy. A lot of women and a lot of quilts." I though for a moment about Rachel, Levi's perfect ex-girlfriend. I wondered what she was doing.

Probably cleaning something.

"That must have been fascinating."

"It was. Sara—the teenager—taught me how to cut quilt squares. She wanted me to do something useful."

"Good idea."

Shane choked again. I turned to him. "I hope you're not coming down with something. You seem to be having trouble swallowing. Airway closing up?"

Shane wisely returned to his breakfast.

"She taught me to cut quilt squares, and I kinda got hooked on it. Except I don't know what to do with them now."

"You just keep cutting squares?"

"Yes."

"How many do you have?"

In truth, I didn't know. After breakfast we went upstairs and counted through the bag I'd brought. Mom counted one-half, I counted the other. After several moments, I put my stack down. "I have fifty-two."

Mom fingered through the last of hers. "This is tricky…I should have gotten my reading glasses."

"You have reading glasses?"

"They're a part of life at my age."

"Oh. I don't think of you as being of the age that would need reading glasses."

She gave a soft smile. "That's very sweet of you."

Another few moments passed before Mom set her stack down. "I have forty-seven here. You've been busy."

"Ninety-nine? I cut ninety-nine squares?"

"You could have Shane count to check."

No, thank you. "I had no idea. I wasn't paying attention most of the time." I looked up at her. "What should I do with them?"

"First," she said, "I think you should cut one more so you have an even hundred."

"Oh. Is one hundred a better number to have in quilting?"

"No. I just thought you might like to be able to say you cut a hundred squares."

"True." I smiled. "I can do that. I have fabric in my room."

"You're welcome to mine. It's all going to be cut up, anyway."

"Oh. Thank you."

"After that, I think you should make a quilt."

"Really?" My mind reeled. Me? Make a quilt? "But there...there isn't enough, is there?"

"You don't have to make a full-sized quilt. You could make a lap quilt or a throw."

"Oh." I mulled it over in my head. "Hmm. I never thought of that."

"You won't know how large it'll be until you piece it together."

"Oh." I fingered the squares. "I have no idea how to do that."

Mom smiled. "I think I could pitch in a bit."

"My stomach's growling," Shane called from down the hall.

"I know, I heard." I pinned another square onto the fabric amoeba on the floor.

"I'm really hungry."

"That's nice."

"We should give the boy a break and get him some food, don't you think?" Mom said, pinning a square before straightening. I heard her spine crack.

"I guess." I put the straight pin I'd been holding back onto the metallic pin base.

"I might pass out," Shane's voice sounded fainter than before.

"You're such a drama queen!"

I try not to reward such behavior, but when he's that whiny, there's not much to do but feed him.

We invited Mom to join us and ended up driving her car, since the last time Shane sat in the backseat of my car there was a lot of sighing and comments about cramped toes.

A deluge of memories filled my brain as we pulled into the parking lot. "I don't know if I told you," I said to Shane, "but I used to waitress here."

"Oh, yeah?"

"Yeah. It's kind of a Lincoln City thing. About everyone under thirty has either worked here, at Salishan, or been in construction."

"As in plastic surgery?"

I swatted his arm. "Houses. Condos. You know what I mean."

"What's Salishan?"

"A spa and golf resort south of here."

The hostess who seated us did not look familiar, thank goodness. We settled into our cozy booth and eyed the menu.

Shane studied his. "I'm impressed."

"I thought you would be."

I had almost relaxed when our waitress arrived.

"Jayne?"

I looked up. My heart sank. "Gretchen! Wow."

We hadn't seen each other since graduation. We were best friends in middle school, slightly less so in high school. After graduation and my leaving for college, we lost track.

Or rather, I lost track. I think she had tried to email me a few times, but I was busy with school and not particularly desirous of maintaining a connection to home.

"How have you been?" she asked, her eyes brimming with curiosity. She probably thought I'd run away with the circus.

"Jayne's been working as a reporter for the *Oregonian*," my mom answered.

I turned to look at her, surprised at the pride in her voice.

"Really?"

"She's written some terrific features in the last few months."

My mom read my work?

"That's so exciting!"

"This is my boyfriend, Shane," I said, collecting myself.

"Nice to meet you," Gretchen extended her hand. "Jayne and I went to high school together."

"What have you been up to?" I asked, feeling as though I had to return the question.

Gretchen shrugged. "This and that. I've been making jewelry lately, but this pays the bills. I'm so glad to run into you! I heard your dad passed away recently—I'm really sorry about that."

"Thanks." I didn't know what else to say.

"So cool to see you. Can I get you guys started with drinks?"

After lunch Shane and I dropped Mom off at the house, bundled up, and drove down to the beach for a walk.

"Why haven't you visited?" Shane asked, taking in the coastline. "The food's good, the people are friendly. You had friends here."

"I had to get away."

"Your mom is great. I wish my mom was as laid-back as yours."

"You never met my father."

"True, but how bad could he be?"

"I frankly have no memory of him telling me he loved me. As a child, as a teen, as an adult. Not that I gave him much opportunity later on, but maybe he could have left it as a voice mail message."

"Never?"

"Maybe when I was a toddler, but my memory doesn't stretch back that far."

"I'm sorry."

I sighed. "I am too."

<hr />

Beth was not invited to dinner that night. "I hope everyone likes lasagna," Mom said when we returned.

"Mom makes a mean lasagna," I told Shane.

"I don't think there's a man alive who doesn't like lasagna." Shane clapped his hands together. "Sounds good."

"The lactose-intolerant ones are probably a bit leery."

"They probably are."

An hour later, Shane and I helped set the table. Mom brought the food out, and we sat down to a much quieter, drama-free dinner.

Until halfway through. Mom said, "Church is tomorrow. Were you two interested in coming along?"

I froze.

I had a million memories of sitting in that sanctuary and not being able to sit still enough. Not wearing the right clothes. Not paying close enough attention to the sermon to be able to answer the questions my father asked afterward.

"Miss Lynnie will be there. I'm sure she'd like to see you."

"Miss Lynnie's still alive?"

Shane asked, "Who's Miss Lynnie?"

"My kindergarten Sunday school teacher." I put my hand to my chest. "I can't believe she's still alive!"

"Ninety-six last December."

"Wow." I sat for a moment and basked in happy Miss Lynnie memories. I turned to Shane. "Imagine the sweetest, tiniest old lady in the world. I think half the reason we liked her was because she was about our height. She always told us that when she went to heaven, she wanted her job to be bathing the little babies."

"Babies in heaven get dirty?"

"Even if they weren't, I think God would let her wash them," I said. "I don't know that even He could deny her that."

I thought for a moment. Most of the time I didn't spend a lot of time thinking about God or believing in heaven, but I believed, with all my heart, that when Miss Lynnie passed away she would be in heaven bathing those babies. I didn't want to believe that someone like Miss Lynnie would simply cease to exist.

A part of me wanted to believe better, so that I could join Miss Lynnie and hand her the soap, if they use soap in heaven.

"I'd like to go. I haven't seen Miss Lynnie in ages." I turned to Shane. "Would you like to come too?"

"I'm probably due for a trip."

Mom gave the gentlest of smiles. "Attending church isn't like a dental cleaning."

"It's not? Could've fooled me," he said with a chuckle. "Pass the salad?"

⁓⁓⁓

I spent Sunday morning in a panic. What did people wear to church these days? I mean, I knew now what Amish people wore to Amish church, but I didn't think that counted.

"You know, it makes it tricky to get out of my room when quilt squares are everywhere," I heard Shane grouse down the hall.

"The quilt is at a very delicate stage right now," I said. I didn't know if that was true or not, but his whining was annoying me and I decided he could take it.

In the end I decided on gray trousers and a soft, black wool wrap sweater.

I paired it with a red, five-strand beaded necklace that Gemma gave me for Christmas the year before.

I even paid attention to my makeup that morning.

Shane whistled when he saw me. "You look nice."

"Thanks."

"You've been dressing snappier since you went to stay with the Amish."

"It's what happens when a teen in an apron critiques your wardrobe. And I don't think you're supposed to whistle at a woman before church."

"Probably not." He leaned over for a kiss. "Are you ready?"

"Did you smudge my lipstick?"

"You're wearing lipstick?" He rubbed at his lips. "Am I wearing lipstick?"

"There's a bit of shimmer, but it suits you."

"Gross!" He pulled an about-face and all but ran for the bathroom mirror.

"Hurry up!" I called, walking downstairs.

Mom stood in the living room, Bible in hand. "You look lovely," she said, looking up as Shane descended. "Both of you."

"Thanks." I gave her a hug.

The drive to the church was quiet. In truth, my heart pounded. "Will Beth be there?" I asked.

"She might be." Mom turned on the car's blinker. "We didn't discuss if they'd be there today or not."

I sighed, but I reasoned in my head that being in church would give Beth cause to at least keep her voice down while she ripped my head off.

She couldn't kill me during a sermon or worship. There would be witnesses.

The inside of the sanctuary was as beautiful as I remembered, the wood paneling glowing in the pale morning light.

I didn't see Beth or Gary. We followed Mom to where my family sat traditionally, four rows back on the right-hand side.

The worship music was in full swing, and I realized I had been gone so long I didn't know many of the songs.

I also realized Shane couldn't sing. His pitch was approximate rather than accurate, and if I didn't know better I'd wonder if his voice was still changing.

I'd never known that about him before.

We followed along with the projected PowerPoint slides as best we could. People weren't turning and staring the way I'd feared, only singing.

In Shane's case, singing badly.

Halfway through "Here I Am to Worship" I heard a rustling to our right as people slid into our row.

I turned to see Beth and Gary clutching their Bibles and rain gear. I waved a hand and smiled, hoping for the best.

Beth waved back. The expression in her eyes could only be described as hope.

Chapter 23

Or maybe her expression wasn't hope, but indigestion. You know, when you eat breakfast right before church, it can do funky things to you. I didn't want to get my hopes up. As much as I wanted things to be okay between me and Beth, I was a realist.

I'd never known my sister to make a decision or change her mind with anything resembling speed. She dated Gary for two years. The engagement lasted another year, partly because she couldn't pick a wedding date for the first six months. The likelihood of her deciding in thirty-six hours that I wasn't the cause of the breakdown of the American family and global warming was fairly low.

I said hello to her and Gary after the service. She didn't bite my head off. No barbs, no snarky comments.

So as not to test my luck, I spotted Miss Lynnie in the back and made a run for it before Beth could change her mind.

Miss Lynnie greeted me with the biggest smile I'd ever seen.

"Look at you, all grown up," she said, reaching up to pat my cheek. "Are you busy doing big things in the world?"

I gave her a careful hug. She smelled the way she always had—of lavender and Jean Nate bath powder. "I think so," I said.

"I thought you would. You were always a special girl. Are you loving your Lord and Savior with your work?"

My mouth opened and closed for a moment as I tried to figure out how to answer that. Was it possible to love God through reporting?

"I hope so," I said, feeling that answer was positive and yet vague enough not to get me into too much trouble.

She gave me a knowing look. "I hope so too. Now, tell me, who is that handsome young man? He looks like he knows you."

I turned to find Shane lurking a few feet away. "Miss Lynnie would like to meet you." I gestured for him to come closer.

Shane stepped forward and offered his hand to the tiny woman. She took it and gave it a pat. "What's your name, young man?"

"Shane Colvin."

"Do you love Jesus?"

"I…" Shane paused, clearly taken aback by Miss Lynnie's directness. I didn't remember her being so direct. Must have been old age. "I have a great deal of respect for Him," he said finally.

"That's very nice," she said, still patting his hand. "But so do the demons in hell."

Shane forced a polite smile. "It's very nice to meet you." He turned to me. "I'll be waiting in the car."

Miss Lynnie did not seem sad to see him go. "Mark my words, Jayne dear. Marry someone who loves the Lord."

<hr>

I said goodbye to Miss Lynnie and headed out for the car. Shane was standing beside it, hugging his coat to protect himself from the fine, chilly drizzle.

"I realized I don't have a key."

"I'm sorry."

"Your Sunday school teacher just told me I'm condemned to eternity in the underworld."

"She's a ninety-six-year-old Sunday school teacher. What did you expect?"

"You just stood there!"

"What was I going to say? I didn't want to upset her—she's fragile. She could go at any moment."

"Can we leave, please?"

"I don't have a key either."

"We should have taken my car."

Mom emerged from the church moments later, followed by Beth, Gary, and Emilee.

"Beth's joining us for lunch," Mom said.

"Oh. Okay. Good."

"We can't stay long," Beth said. "Emilee needs her nap."

"No, I don't." Emilee twirled under her father's hand. "I don't need a nap."

"Yes, you do, little girl," Gary said, picking up his daughter. "We'll see you at the house?"

Mom unlocked the car; Shane all but leaped inside.

"Don't worry." Mom nodded to me after the doors were closed. "I talked to Beth. She said she'll be on her best behavior."

"I wasn't worried," I lied.

At lunch we rolled out leftovers from the previous two nights, the microwave buzzing away and bringing renewed life to the lasagna and pork roast.

I helped Emilee with her lunch while Beth talked to Mom and Shane chatted with Gary.

"Would you like potatoes?" I asked

Emilee nodded.

"Broccoli?"

Emilee shook her head.

"Would your mom like you to eat broccoli?" I said, turning to Beth.

Beth looked at Emilee. "Two pieces. Two baby trees."

I picked out two from the Rubbermaid container. "Two baby trees, coming right up."

Emilee wrinkled her nose. "I don't like baby trees."

"They're good for you. Broccoli helps your eyes to see well and helps prevent colon cancer."

She looked back at me, blankly.

"Broccoli will help you to stay healthy and maintain a svelte, princess-like figure."

"Broccoli will make me look like a princess?"

I chose my words carefully. "You already look like a princess," I said, "but eating broccoli will help you to keep looking like a princess, even when you're a grown-up." *When you're a grown-up, and your hormones are out to get you.*

She stood up on her tiptoes and examined the broccoli spears on her plate. "I want three."

Beth stepped in. "I want three, *please.*"

"Please!"

I placed another broccoli floret on her plate.

Lunch passed companionably. Emilee ate all of her broccoli. When she started getting a bit cranky, Beth asked Mom if she could take a nap in the sewing room.

"Maybe Jayne's old room would be better," Mom said. "Jayne and I have a quilt on the floor of the sewing room."

"A quilt?" Beth's eyebrow lifted. She turned to me. "You quilt?"

"I cut quilt squares. Haven't actually made a quilt yet."

"You will," Mom said before taking a sip of ice water.

"When are you coming back to visit?" Beth asked.

I paused. When was I planning on visiting again? I hadn't contemplated the possibility of a return; I didn't think anyone would want me to. "Um…" I stalled. "I'll have a lot of work to catch up on come Monday morning."

Mom's and Beth's faces fell.

"But," I continued, "I don't see any reason why I couldn't come out weekend after next."

They both brightened.

Mom took a satisfied bite of lasagna. "The guest room is always available for you."

"Unless Emilee's napping in it," Beth said drily, "but it wouldn't be longer than a two-hour delay."

Everyone laughed.

"Why is that funny?" Emilee asked, sending everyone in chuckles all over again.

After lunch Mom and I cleared the plates while Beth put Emilee down for a nap upstairs. Gary and Shane settled in the den in front of a baseball game.

When the kitchen was cleared, Mom and I went back to work on the quilt while Beth offered her two cents about the layout and design of the squares.

I packed up my things after Emilee woke, cranky and fuzzy, from her nap. Shane carried my suitcase down to the car with minimal grousing while I hugged everyone goodbye. My heart melted when Emilee wrapped her arms around my neck, kissed my cheek, and said, "Goodbye, Auntie Jayne!"

Mom promised to take good care of my quilt squares in my absence. Beth gave me a hug and didn't utter a single insult, even professing to be looking forward to seeing me next.

Shane and Gary exchanged man hugs, with a good deal of thumping on the back for extra measure.

I retreated to the car as my eyes grew damp; I didn't want to leave.

I sighed as Shane drove around the corner and the house completely left my sight. "That was wonderful."

Shane nodded. "Yeah. Gary's a cool guy. Things seemed like they went better with your sister today. And your mom...she makes a really good lasagna."

"What about little Emilee? She's so cute."

"Yeah. She's a great kid."

"You know, I never really thought I'd want to do the kid thing. I mean, kids, you know, they ooze, they smell, they're terrible communicators. Why would someone create them on purpose? But then I meet Naomi's kids and Baby Ruby, and now little Emilee. Even if they don't have a complete vocabulary, they're excellent at showing how they feel. They're better at body language than, I don't know, a mime."

"A mime?"

"Or something like that. They're very expressive." I turned to him. "I never thought I'd want kids. But now I think I do."

I almost missed how Shane's hands tightened on the steering wheel.

"We've never talked about kids before," he said.

"No, I don't think so."

"I like kids, don't get me wrong. I've just never wanted any of my own."

"Even a little girl like Emilee?"

"No."

His words started to sink in. "You really don't want children, do you?"

"I don't."

I turned to stare out the window.

We didn't speak again until we were nearly back to my apartment.

"Jayne, what do you think about us?"

I looked at him. "I...I like us. I like you."

"Where do you see us in the future?"

I tried to imagine us dating for another year—I could visualize that. After dating though...

"What I'm trying to say is, do you *want* to marry me?"

My eyes widened. "Are you proposing?"

"I'm asking. Sometime in the future, do you want to be married to me?"

"You don't want children? Not ever?"

"No."

Miss Lynnie's words floated back to me. *Marry someone who loves the Lord.* I couldn't begin to call myself a good Christian, although I had asked Jesus into my heart two decades ago. As much as I liked Shane...

"I don't think I could marry you," I said, in sudden realization.

He sighed. "I didn't think so."

"It's not just the kids," I blurted out in a rush. "It's..."

He held up a hand. "I know. The church thing. I thought you were over that."

Believe me, I thought I was too. "Being with the Amish—it made me realize things about myself. About my life."

"I noticed. Quilting?"

I gave a half smile. "I know. Who saw that coming?"

"Not me."

"So...are we breaking up?"

"I think...yes."

"Huh." I ran a hand through my hair. "I feel like one of us should be yelling or something."

"You yelled a couple days ago."

"We didn't break up a couple days ago."

"I think we both saw this coming."

All I could think of was Levi. "Maybe."

⁓⁓⁓

Shane and I broke up so graciously, Nora Ephron would have been proud. He drove me to my apartment and helped me carry up my luggage. I found a couple of his books that had been lurking on my own shelves, as well as a jacket he'd left behind a few months prior.

He promised to bring over my copy of Ken Burns' *Jazz*, my volt meter (for my motorcycle battery), and the fleece blanket I'd loaned to his couch since his apartment ran so cold.

I gave him a hug. He leaned in for one last kiss and I couldn't turn away.

He rested his forehead against mine when the kiss ended. "I loved you, you know."

I laid a finger on his chin. "I know."

I just hadn't loved him back.

After Shane left, I lay down on my couch and stared at the ceiling.

Huh. I hadn't been single for so long, I'd forgotten what it was like.

For starters, Shane wouldn't be calling to make plans with me anymore. True, he had a few things he needed to bring by, but we weren't headed to dinner and a movie anytime soon.

Interesting.

I unpacked my bags, really and truly this time, taking care to check my garments for damage and wear. After starting a load of laundry, my stomach rumbled. I walked to the kitchen to investigate the food situation.

I shouldn't have been surprised. My freezer was full of labeled leftovers from Martha. My pantry was more full than I'd ever seen it.

On a whim, I picked up the phone and called Gemma, Joely, and Kim. "I have tons of food," I said. "Come over and eat with me."

Somehow, everyone was available. Joely was the first to arrive. "Look at you with your all-weather wrist brace! You look great. And I've never seen your apartment this clean."

"Yeah, I decided the open sewage finally needed to be taken care of."

"You survived the Amish okay?"

"They were wonderful. Challenging, but wonderful."

"You called just in time. I just got off my shift and I'm starving."

"Did you break speed laws getting here?"

Joely had the grace to turn a bit pink. "I was really hungry."

Kim and Gemma showed up shortly after. "Where's this food I was hearing about?" Kim asked, seeing that I hadn't really taken anything out.

"I was waiting for you. It's in the freezer."

With Gemma's help, I had dinner on the table in fifteen minutes.

"I just can't believe how clean everything is," Kim said between bites.

I rolled my eyes. "It's not like this place was a safety hazard or anything."

"But it wasn't this...this *spotless*," Gemma said. "The backsplash of the sink is clean, and the ridge around your sink has been cleaned with a tooth-brush."

I grimaced. "How can you tell?"

"That's the only way I know of to get the ridge to look that way, unless the Amish know something I don't. I'm assuming Martha—was that her name?"

"Yup."

"I'm assuming Martha was cleaning up. Unless you decided to hire some-one."

"You don't think I'm capable of being this clean by myself?"

Gemma, Kim, and Joely broke out into simultaneous laughter.

I rolled my eyes. "Flattering. Thank you."

"It's just not your style," Gemma said. "You're more comfortable. Lived in. You've never been obsessive about tidiness."

"And that makes me a slob?"

"No," said Kim, "cluttered."

"We're only pointing it out," Joely said. "It's not like my place is all that clean. There are parts of my bathroom that will probably get up and walk away someday."

Gemma grimaced. "Gross. That's why I never use the bathroom at your place."

I clapped my hands over my ears. "Too much information!"

"Changing the subject," Kim said, holding out her hand. "Have you seen Shane since you got back?"

I shifted in my seat. Now was as good a time as ever to tell them.

"I did. We actually went to visit my mom this weekend."

"That's nice. A little weekend getaway?" Kim asked.

"Something like that. But we, ah, we broke up."

Kim put her fork down. "You broke up at your mom's?"

"On the way back."

"So who dumped who?" Joely asked.

"Whom," Kim corrected.

"It was mutual." I swished the water around in my glass. "Anybody want anything else to drink?"

"I never liked Shane," Kim offered.

"Well, not dating him anymore."

"Any plans, now that you're free?" Gemma had a glint in her eye.

I knew exactly what she was referring to, even if she wasn't going to come out and say it.

"Oh, catch up on work." I kept my voice light and vague. "I've been gone so long, things will be crazy."

Gemma's eyes danced with questions, but she didn't say a word.

Which was fine, because I wasn't about to tell.

Chapter 24

I actually made myself breakfast the next morning before work. Before I went to stay with the Burkholders, I seldom ate a morning meal.

Martha had spoiled me with biscuits and hash browns and bright yellow eggs. In her absence I fed on leftovers and cereal.

Since my little dinner party the night before, I'd made a decision. I was going to try to keep the apartment in its post-Amish state.

Along with that, I was going to learn to cook, bake, and quilt. If the Amish could do it, I could do it.

I had to stop myself from clapping my hands over my ears as I sat at my work computer. Since when was the newsroom so loud? People talking, people working. Brian typed loud. Laura, two cubicles away, was still complaining about her sunburn and the resulting peeling skin on her face.

I jumped when my phone rang. It was Sol, wanting to see me in his office.

In five.

The whole thing felt very familiar.

"Jayne," Sol said when I walked in. "You look good. Rested."

I sat down. "Thanks."

"How are things?"

"Broke up with my boyfriend."

He winced. "But you're fine?"

"It was mutual."

His face relaxed. "Good."

For a second there I think he was contemplating firing me. I mean, it's not like I was going to take two mental health breaks in one month. That's what unemployment was for.

"While I was gone," I said, "I stayed with an Amish family in Albany."

"Really." Sol leaned back in his chair. There are days I'm surprised he doesn't fall over altogether.

"I thought there might be a story there."

He shook his head. "I put you on mandatory leave and you went story chasing?"

Um, yeah.

"I should be surprised," he said with a sigh. "But I'm not. Go on. Did you get a story?"

I reached into my briefcase, retrieved the printout of the story I'd written, and plopped it on its desk.

The pages splayed with a satisfying *slap*.

Sol lifted them from his desk. "Did you pick up your flair for the dramatic from the Amish?"

"Just read it," I answered.

"I don't have my reading glasses."

I saw them at the corner of his desk and handed them over.

"Thanks." He settled them on the bridge of his nose and started reading.

He didn't talk while he read. When he finished, he flipped through the pages again before tapping them onto the desk to align the sheets.

"Aside from a split infinitive near the end, this is good." He tapped the pages against the desk once more. "Really good."

"Thank you."

"You've got your groove back, Tate."

I grinned. "I'd hoped you'd say that."

"We'll run it Saturday after next. Human interest. You changed the names, right?"

"I did."

"Good. Don't want any issues with Legal."

"There won't be."

"Until then, there's an urban garden southeast of town that's been vandalized several times despite security upgrades."

"Security at an urban garden? Aren't those things pretty open?"

"They are until people dig up plants and spray paint racial slurs on the fencing."

"I'm on it."

"Your piece looked good. Glad to see you're back."

"I'm glad too," I said before retreating to my cubicle.

───※───

I collapsed on my couch after work. The busyness of the day had sapped every last bit of energy from my body. I fought the urge to pull the afghan over my head.

Because that would just be silly.

Instead, I channel-flipped for a while until I realized I'd left my jacket, purse, and keys in the entryway, and if Martha had seen it, she would have cleaned it up by now.

I hoisted myself up from the couch, hung my jacket up in the hallway closet, and looked around for a place to put my purse.

There was the chair, and I could place it there to look artful, but then it might lead to other things being dumped on the chair.

I needed a hook or a shelf of some sort. Or a shelf with hooks under it. Maybe Levi could make me a shelf with hooks underneath. Nice, large hooks, suitable for women's motorcycle accessories.

After all, he'd promised to make me a bookcase. Maybe he could make me a shorter bookcase and a shelf.

With hooks. Couldn't forget the hooks. They were the most important part.

But until that day when such a shelf magically appeared (whether through Levi or Home Depot), I set my purse on the floor of the hallway closet, tucking my keys inside my jacket and removing my phone before I closed the closet door.

I flipped my phone open. One missed call. One new message. I lifted the phone to my ear to listen.

I almost dropped the phone when I heard Levi's voice.

"Jayne," he said, sounding (let's face it) devastatingly sexy in the process, "two things. I wanted to talk to you about the bookcase. It's almost done. Wondered if there was any way you'd be able to give it a once-over before I finish up. Or I could send pictures, I guess, so I'd need your email address. Secondly, Sara would like to write to you but realized she doesn't have your mailing address. I think I remember what street you're on, but

not the apartment number. Give me a call if you have a moment and I'll
pass that on to her. And your email address, if you want pictures. Or let
me know when you can stop by, if that works out. I know it's a long drive.
Just let me know."

I snapped my phone closed.

Levi had called.

I flipped it back open.

Closed.

Open.

Closed.

Open. Who was I to deny Sara my mailing address?

"Jayne? Thanks for calling me back!"

"You're, um, you're welcome. Anytime. I mean, I got your message. And
I'd love it if Sara wrote to me. That'd be great. Really great."

Wow. When was I smacked with the idiot stick? Before I could say anything else that was completely inane, I recited my address while he wrote
it down.

"Are you going to be able to see the bookcase anytime soon?"

"The bookcase? Sure. I can come down. That's no problem."

"Really?"

"Yeah. I, um, have some time this weekend."

"This Saturday?"

"Okay."

"What time?"

"Noon?"

"Great." He sounded unreasonably happy. I mean, I was just going down
there to inspect his carpentry. Nothing to get excited about.

———— ···※··· ————

The week sped by. I called Gemma Saturday morning.

"I'm so glad you're back in town," she said after she picked up. "Things
were much too quiet without you."

"Glad you thought so. What are you doing?"

"Right now? Working on a few freelance pieces."

"Little tired? Little cross-eyed? Need a break?"

"What's up?"

"I'm driving back to Albany."

"Oh. Are you doing some more Amish research?"

"Um…"

"You're not going to go see Levi, are you?"

"Maybe."

I held the phone away from my ear as Gemma squealed. "And you, all broken up with Shane, you're so available! Wait—Levi isn't a rebound, is he?"

"He's not an anything. I'm just going down there to look at a bookcase."

"A what?"

"He's been building me a bookcase as a thank-you for housing his family while his dad was in the hospital."

"Really."

"Yes, really. And he wanted to know if I could come by and take a look before he finishes it."

"He couldn't send pictures?"

"Pictures wouldn't do it justice."

"Your words or his?"

"Mine."

"So you're going to Albany. What's my part in this?"

"I don't know what to wear."

"Oh. And what's my part in this?"

"Gemma!"

"Just kidding. I'll be over in a few minutes. Do I need to bring anything?"

"You've seen my wardrobe. You tell me."

"I'll bring a few things."

"Thought you might."

<hr />

Before I knew it I found myself driving to Levi's shop wearing my own jeans, a floral-print silk shell of Gemma's (I didn't know it was a shell—I would have called it a blouse, but she corrected me), and a coordinating black cardigan that was woolly enough to keep me warm.

I'd asked Gemma if she thought I looked as though I were trying too hard and didn't look like myself.

She assured me I looked casually beautiful, and she pointed out that Levi had only really known me a couple weeks and wasn't likely to have pinned down my personal style during that time.

She had a point.

Spencer whistled when I walked into the shop office. "Look at you, all nice and cleaned up."

"Yes. I traded in the apron," I said, before I got an eyeful of his ensemble. "You wore a Star Trek uniform? To work?"

"Hey," he said, smoothing the tunic or the shirt or whatever they call the part that covers your torso in space. "It's casual Saturday."

"I thought casual day was Friday."

"Saturday's casual too."

"And casual is code for being ready to uphold the Prime Directive?"

"I used to think you were nice."

"I am nice. Is your boss in?"

"He is, hard at work on a bookcase." He clucked his tongue. "It's nice."

I tucked a piece of hair behind my ear. "I'm sure it is."

"*Really* nice."

"Am I going to get a chance to see it?"

"I'll page him." Spencer lifted the phone, dialed a set of numbers, and set the receiver back down. "You been staying busy? Liked that piece about the urban garden."

"You read it?"

"I did."

"Did you get your copy of the paper from your onboard replicator?"

Scowling, he stood up, walked to the shop door, and threw it open. "Hurry up, man. She's killing me in here."

The sound of power tools drowned him out.

"I don't think he heard you."

"We have a connection, he and I. He heard."

"You're telepathic? What does that make you...Beta-something? Beta-tape, Beta-version..."

"Betazoid," he corrected through clenched teeth. "The Betazoids were telepathic."

"Right. Betazoid. Tip of my tongue."

Spencer opened his mouth for a comeback but found himself interrupted when Levi stepped through the door.

I'll admit my breath caught.

For just a teeny moment.

"Jayne," Levi said with the most beautiful smile. "I see you've met Number One."

Spence pantomimed stabbing himself with a knife. "Et tu, Brute?"

Levi gestured to me. "Wanna come see it? It's out here. I'll have the guys shut down the tools. They need to take lunch anyway."

He made some sort of signal and the noise ceased. We stepped into the shop, Levi leading the way.

"I went with cherry," he said as he walked. "I saw that you didn't get a lot of light in that room, so I figured a nice, bright wood with a sheer red stain would help to liven it up."

I looked ahead. "Is that it?"

He beamed. "It is."

I closed the distance in three more steps. "Wow," I said, running a hand over one shelf. "It's beautiful."

"Thank you."

The sides, rather than being plain, had carved rectangles the same height as the shelf. I remembered now what he'd described before he started, how it had shorter shelves at the top and bottom and taller shelves in the middle. The top had a carved crown molding, and a divot ran along the center of the shelves' edge as well as all the way around the front edge.

And the wood...the wood glowed. "It's perfect."

"Not quite perfect. I still need to do the finish."

"You haven't? It's so smooth and pretty now!"

Levi chuckled. "It'll be even smoother and prettier when it's done. I'm planning on a hand-rubbed oil finish. It will prevent dust and water rings."

"In case I set a drink down on a bookshelf in the office?"

"Or you have a vase of flowers and condensation leaks out."

"Ah, true." Not that I had a vase of flowers back there, either, but it was a pretty thought. Shane had never been much for flowers, and I never bought them for myself.

I crossed my arms, not knowing what to do with my hands anymore. "Well, it's absolutely perfect. And beautiful. I can't wait till it's done."

"Glad you like it."

All right. I'd done it. I'd looked at the bookcase. What next? I maintained eye contact with the bookcase and shoved another stray piece of hair behind my ear.

Levi checked his watch. "Wow. It's past lunchtime."

If he meant fifteen minutes past noon, then yes.

"Hungry?"

My head snapped to look at him. "Hungry? Me?"

"Want to grab something to eat? I know a good spot for lunch."

"I'm hungry."

"Yeah?"

"Starved."

He smiled. "Then let's get out of here."

Chapter 25

When Levi and I pulled up to Pastini in Corvallis I began to wonder. Was this a date? Like, a real date? I mean, I knew we were sharing a meal together, but lunch isn't necessarily the "date meal."

I changed my mind as we sat down. Levi held out my chair and pushed it in for me. Any lunch with chair assistance is a date.

All of a sudden, I wasn't hungry at all. In fact, I felt distinctly sick to my stomach.

"Are you all right?"

I looked up to face Levi, who had taken the chair opposite me. "Fine. Dandy. Why?"

"You started frowning and turned pale just now."

"Oh." I felt color rise to my cheeks, which was probably good. "I was just thinking about...work."

"What's it like being back?"

"Good. Weird." Almost as weird as my inability to form sentences. I put a little more thought into my next statement. "It's good to be back, but I definitely grew accustomed to a different pace." I sucked in a breath. "Busier and quieter at the same time."

"That is what it's like with the Amish, isn't it? More activity and less noise."

"Less random noise. More people noise. I like people better."

The waitress arrived at our table with a bright, if tired smile, asking for our drink orders. I asked for Sprite, Levi for coffee.

Big surprise.

He unrolled his silverware and placed his napkin in his lap after the waitress left. "You were talking about seeing your family. Did you?"

"I did."

"How did it go?"

"They hated me less than I thought." I unrolled my own silverware.

"Yeah?"

"My mom didn't hate me at all. My sister? I think she'll thaw. Things were…" I searched for the right word. "Satisfactory."

"Glad to hear that."

I shifted in my seat. "And I, um…" My mouth felt dry. I took a sip of my water. "Shane and I broke up."

"Oh." He ducked his head, rendering me unable to read his expression for a moment. "Are you…?"

I shrugged. "I'm fine with it. It was a mutual decision." Didn't talking about your ex break all sorts of dating rules? "Anyway, it's over. I'm glad. I'm making a lot of life changes right now."

"Like what?"

"I want a relationship with my family. I want…I want to like who I am."

"You don't right now?"

"I've let myself get lost. I want to start going to church again."

Levi gave a kind smile, his eyes crinkling at the edges. "You're always welcome to join me for church down here. I'm sure Spence's mom would be happy to have you for a weekend."

"That's sweet," I said, knowing I'd never take him up on it. Finding a church and attending was something I needed to do without a man. And who knew what the mother of Spencer would be like? "Have you heard anything from your family?"

"Ida drove Sara to the shop a couple days ago."

"Really?" Ida was such a rebel.

"She—Sara—said everyone's well. The boys have picked up the slack around the farm, making up for Dad. The younger girls are doing fine. Sara says they miss you."

"And Sara herself? How is she?"

"I think she'd like to leave, but Dad's health is stopping her. At least for the time being—"

I couldn't take it anymore. "Levi, are we on a date?"

"Technically, yes."

"Technically?"

"I asked you to lunch, you said yes." He spread his hands. "Ergo, date."

"But what if you'd asked Spence to lunch?"

"I wouldn't. He tends to talk with his mouth full."

"Or Grady. Or whomever. You get my point."

"*My* point is that I didn't ask anyone else. I asked you."

My shoulders sank. "Why?"

"You're good company."

"So is Grady."

"Jayne, you're funny, smart, and compassionate. I don't think I said it today, but you look," he paused, his eyes taking in my carefully chosen ensemble, "really, really good."

I felt my face flush. "Thanks."

"I asked you to lunch because I wanted to spend time with you. I want to keep getting to know you."

"I live in Portland."

"I know."

"Seventy miles away."

"Right now, we're eighteen inches away."

I sighed and sipped my water. "I'm not very good at dating."

"Me neither. I don't know what to do when a buggy is out of the picture."

I snorted. "And not climbing into girls' rooms through their windows?"

"Without windows and buggies, I'm out to sea."

"Sorry. I'm fresh out of buggies."

"What was that?" Just then, the waitress appeared at our table. "What did you say you were out of?"

I lifted my eyebrow, daring Levi to tell her "buggies."

He didn't take the bait. "We may need another couple minutes to order."

When she left, Levi reached across the table and took my hand. I almost yanked it back out of shock but thought better of it.

Having my hand held felt nice. Having Levi hold it—nearly divine.

"I think we should date."

"How old are you?"

"Does that make a difference?"

I feigned indifference, pulling my hand away to toy with my napkin. "Maybe."

"You tell me first."

"I'm twenty-six."

He lifted an eyebrow. "Awfully young for a reporter in your position."

I bristled. "It's not my fault I'm good. You haven't answered my question yet."

"Thirty-two."

"Wow." I sat back. "You're old."

He kicked my foot under the table. "Thanks."

"Okay. Maybe not *that* old."

"Do I pass? Will you go out with me?"

"I'm not in town anymore. I mean, I'm here now, Levi, but I can't be here every weekend. I don't know how—"

"Do you have to know?"

"Yes."

He leaned forward. "I don't. I'm perfectly capable taking things a day at a time."

"I'm a reporter. We're trained to think ahead of schedule."

"What would happen if you let someone else do the worrying for a change?" He nodded toward my menu. "What sounds good?"

"What are you having?" I hated choosing something before the guy, preferring instead to match my order to his. If he ordered a sandwich, I'd order a sandwich. If he ordered a steak, I'd check out the menu's pricier items.

He folded his menu. "Rigatoni with meat sauce Bolognese."

"Yeah?"

"Yeah. Do you like artichoke dip?"

"I do."

"Then we'll get artichoke dip. I got hooked on artichokes in college."

"Artichokes not figured into Amish cuisine?"

"Not often."

When the server came back, Levi recited his lunch order before gesturing to me.

I closed my menu. "I'll have the Rigatoni with chicken cacciatore."

"That's my favorite," the server said, as she scribbled on her order pad.

She probably said that to all her customers.

"So?" Levi said, bringing my attention back to the topic at hand.

As if I could think of much else.

"Do you want to be adventurous with me? Want to give it a shot?"

"Us dating?"

"No, us going deep-sea diving. Haven't you been paying attention?"

I gave him a playful smack on the arm. "You're high-maintenance. Fine. Let's give it a go."

⸺⁂⸺

After lunch we walked around downtown Corvallis for a while. He didn't try to hold my hand, but he stayed close to my side as we walked and talked about his family, my family, our jobs, and whatever else came up. My feet were sore by the time we returned to the truck, but I didn't care. I couldn't remember the last time my heart felt so light.

"I need to get back to work after this," Levi said as the familiar form of the shop came into view. "When do I get to see you next?"

"I told my mom I'd visit her next weekend," I answered, already feeling the tension of a long-distance relationship.

"In Lincoln City?"

"Yes."

"I'd love to meet your family."

I frowned. "You're joking."

"It's only fair. You've lived with mine."

"But—"

"It's up to you. You can let me know later."

"I'll think about it."

"Thanks."

"Have a good rest of your weekend."

"Jayne," he laughed and shook his head. "Relax!"

"I am relaxed!"

"That's why your shoulders are up to your ears. Just relax. We're having fun."

We were. And that was the problem.

⸺⁂⸺

To my eternal shame, I ducked away from the shop and back to my car before something along the lines of a goodbye kiss could be discussed.

Instead, I think I reached out and squeezed his elbow, fast, or something ridiculous like that. Can't be certain what, the whole thing was a blur.

Pretty sad, really.

On the drive home, I felt a strong urge to call my mother. Strange, because I don't believe I've ever had the desire to call her just to talk.

But there I was, dialing her number on Highway 20 anyway.

As the phone rang, I worried she wouldn't answer. As far as I knew, she had all sorts of activities lined up on Saturdays. As the phone continued to ring, I debated telling her I'd gone to Albany at all. Back in Lincoln City, I'd told her I couldn't come this weekend because of work. Well, work certainly hadn't stopped me from driving seventy miles to see my new...boyfriend? Significant Male? Gentleman caller?

Before I could think better of the whole mother-calling action, I heard her voice. "Hello?"

"Hi," I said, sounding much more breathless than I'd meant to. I sounded like a bad Marilyn Monroe impersonator.

"Jayne?"

"Yeah, Mom, it's me."

"Oh. Good. How are you?"

"I, uh, I broke up with Shane."

"I'm sorry to hear that. Did it just happen?"

"No. Actually, it was on the way back from visiting you."

"I hope—I hope it wasn't anything that happened here?"

"Not really. It was just time."

"*Not really* sounds a lot like *partially yes*," she said drily.

"It became clear that we were going in different directions."

"You should run for political office."

"Thanks, Mom."

She sighed. "I'm not surprised. About you and Shane, that is."

"You're not?"

"You seemed like good friends, but there wasn't...chemistry. Not love chemistry, at any rate."

"Well, I'm glad you're not disappointed."

"He seemed like a nice man, but no."

"I'm also...seeing..." I exhaled hard. "Someone else."

"Oh? Was it that boy you met researching your Amish story?"

Wow. She was good. "Yeah. It's Levi."

"How do you feel about him?"

"I…" was it possible to know how I felt? I'd hardly known him a few weeks. Had it only been a few weeks? Crazy. "I like him a lot."

Which was code for, "I can't stop thinking about him."

Being new to the whole mom-talk thing, I kept that to myself. I didn't need her picking out baby names.

Come to think of it, I didn't know if she was the picking-out-baby-names type.

"I'm very excited for you," she said.

I licked my lips. "I know I said I'd visit next weekend."

"If you can't, we understand."

"What I'm asking is…can I bring him?"

"Of course!"

"Would that be too weird? What am I saying? Of course it would be too weird. That's two guys in two weeks."

"It's up to you."

Of course it was. "He wants to meet my family."

"You lived with his, didn't you?"

Naturally, she'd have to throw that back too. "I did."

"Bringing him or not bringing him is your decision. If he's fine sleeping in a room covered in quilt squares, then he's welcome to join you."

I brightened at the mention of quilt squares. "They're still on the floor?"

"They are. Waiting for you."

Such faithful quilt squares.

"I'll talk to Levi." Who knew? By next week we might have thrown in the towel. "Either way, you'll definitely have at least one guest next weekend." A stray thought stuck in my head. "Mom?"

"Yes?"

"Will Beth mock me if I bring over a different man?"

"She wants to see you happy. She really does."

That so didn't answer my question.

Or maybe it did.

⚬⚬⚬

I called Gemma when I got home. "You go to church, don't you?"

"Every week. Why?"

"Can I come with you?"

"Of course. You really want to?"

"You know I grew up in the church, right?"

"Jayne, you…you don't talk about yourself very often."

I ran a hand through my hair. "I know. I'm sorry. I don't want to be that person anymore. And that means going back to church. So can I meet you there?"

"You can meet me or I can pick you up."

"I need to be as independent about this as possible. I need to drive myself."

"You're independent, so you're letting me help you choose a church?"

"It's a springboard. And no woman is an island."

"Amen, sister."

"Save it for church, Gem."

"Touchy."

"Nervous. It's been a crazy day."

"Like how?"

I told her about my date with Levi.

"Really! Good thing you looked so nice. Are you guys an item now?"

"Working in that direction."

"Are you terrified?"

I sighed. "Petrified."

"It's good for you. Gosh, I can't remember the last time I felt that way about someone."

"You've had a bit of a dry spell, haven't you."

"Like the Sudan."

"You know," I said, "Levi has several employees. One of them is really into Star Trek. You guys might hit it off."

"You're cruel. Besides, dealing with my family isn't for the faint of heart."

"That's the flip side of growing up with so much great food."

"Very true. So tomorrow?"

"Tomorrow."

Heaven help us all.

Chapter 26

I took a nap Sunday afternoon. I'd forgotten how much I loved my post-church naps. When I was growing up, my entire family napped after church. No one emerged before four forty-five.

Church with Gemma went well enough. The pastor was highly educated and highly able to make me uncomfortable with the probing nature of his scripturally based remarks.

But I wasn't attending church to stay in my comfort zone, so I stayed in my seat.

It's funny to me how many churches in the last ten years have made the swap from pews to interlocking chairs. While the chairs make it harder to slide into your seat, they are more comfortable and better delineate personal bubbles.

Not that personal bubbles matter much with Gemma's family. Her Italian father wrapped me in a hug while her French mother air-kissed me on each cheek.

Really, it's amazing Gemma's as normal as she is.

Being surrounded by Gemma's family and multiple siblings made me feel for the briefest moment as though I were back with the Burkholders.

Which made me think of Levi. Thinking of Levi, until recently, had only made me feel guilty.

Now it made me happy. Unabashedly happy.

Even as I lay down for my nap, I couldn't stop smiling.

※

My first letter from Sara arrived Monday.

Jayne,

We miss you very much. I had a very nice time at your apartment, although I regret that we could not go to see your friend's closet. Maybe another time?

Leah and Elizabeth say hello. Things are well here. Father is mending, although he complains about eating fish and not being able to work the farm as much. Mainly the fish. Mother has begun cooking with less butter and fat for the sake of Father's heart. I think he would rather have another heart attack than give up fat, but I don't say anything. The boys are complaining about so much fish, but only when Mother is out of the room. They haven't complained about going fishing more often.

Levi said you'll be writing an article about us. You aren't going to write about me thinking about leaving, are you?

I hope that you will visit us sometime. Are you still cutting quilt squares? Have you tried to piece them yet? I'm sure if you called my grandmother, she'd be able to tell you what to do.

It would be nice if you wrote back.

Sara

I smiled and refolded the letter. After a long day of writing and editing written material, hearing from Sara made me miss the Burkholders' farm-house.

Things were simpler there. Of course, things were more complicated now that I was seeing Levi. I didn't know how Martha would feel about me dating him, but I could guess that in her heart of hearts, she would want him to return to the community. Dating an outsider would hinder that.

I felt I knew Levi well enough to know he had no intention of ever returning, so I couldn't feel guilty for holding him back. Furthermore, I met him before I met his family.

What would drive me over the edge would be Sara. How do you know when to give the girl-power speech or encourage her to live the life of her ancestors?

I knew I wouldn't want to live that life. Here I was trying my own version, and already scuff marks had resurfaced on the tile and my shower was turning pink where water pooled. But there was something about knowing that somewhere everything was perfect, orderly, clean. Peace and simplicity reigned in that place, even if it wasn't here.

Not that I wasn't trying. I mopped my floor the other day for the first time in eighteen months, and that wouldn't have happened if I didn't find the Swiffer commercials so convincing.

I found paper and an envelope in the study.

> *Dear Sara,*
>
> *I miss you all terribly. Sorry about all the fish, but from what I hear it really is good for the heart. Don't worry. I didn't put anything about your thoughts of leaving into the article. Also, I changed everyone's names for your privacy.*
>
> *I'm back at work and wishing I was still baking in your family's kitchen. However, I did help bake a pie at my mom's house and surprised everyone. I also started a quilt with my mother; we'll work on it again this weekend.*
>
> *You told me about your dreams of designing clothes. That took a lot of trust. I don't know if Levi's mentioned it to you, but we've decided to try a relationship. I guess we're dating. I hope you're okay with that. Levi is a very, very special person. I don't know how serious we are—or not. We've agreed to see what happens. I just wanted you to know.*
>
> *Give the children hugs for me. I miss all of you.*
>
> *Jayne*
>
> *P.S. Don't worry—I've been very careful with my clothes since you left. No missing buttons.*

I addressed and stamped the letter, but decided against sealing it. Instead, I walked down the street to the convenience store and picked up a glossy magazine with a "Best Dressed" section before going back home.

Once I was behind closed doors, I perused the pages and found the parts I thought Sara would like most. I pried the staples from the magazine before cutting out the pages.

I folded the contraband to fit inside the letter, slapped on another stamp, and headed outside to the mail drop.

~~~

People don't usually whistle at me when I show up for work, but the next morning I received two before arriving at my cubicle.

Once I saw my desk, I understood why.

"Those are some serious flowers," said Laura, who apparently decided to make my reaction her next story.

Thing was, she wasn't exaggerating. On my desk sat a bouquet of a dozen light pink, long stemmed roses.

Upon closer examination, I realized it wasn't a dozen, but a baker's dozen. There was a card tucked among the blossoms. I opened it to find a printed message:

> *Because I couldn't climb through your window, the least I could do was send you flowers. Have a good day at work.*
>
> *Levi*

I smiled and put the card back into the envelope before sliding it into the top drawer of my desk and away from the prying eyes of my colleagues.

I worked with a roomful of investigative reporters. I knew the only thing stopping Laura from going through my desk was the threat of what I might find in hers if I returned the favor—rumor had it she kept quite the chocolate stash and the odd prescription medication in her left-hand drawer.

Calling Levi at that moment would have provided more fodder for the entertainment section of the office, so I opted to wait until lunchtime rolled around.

It wasn't raining at noon, so I stepped outside, taking my phone and my jacket with me.

"Did you see your surprise?"

I couldn't help but smile. "Yeah, me and every one of my coworkers."

"Hope it didn't bother you."

"Not too much. Hey, I hope you don't mind. I told your sister about us."

"She wrote you already?"

"She did."

"I don't mind. She'd have to find out eventually, and she likes you."

"Yeah?"

"Yeah."

"I talked to my mom the other day."

"Always a good way to continue the relationship."

"She said you're welcome to come with me this weekend."

"Only if you want me to."

A bitter breeze nipped at the edges of my jacket. I tucked my free hand deeper into my pocket. "Sure."

"You sound excited."

"It's the right thing to do."

"Your decision, Jayne."

"I mean, I'm feeling kinda pressured here."

"Whoa, whoa—where is this coming from?"

"You send me a dozen roses—"

"Thirteen. I wanted to be unique."

"Whatever. Thirteen. You send me this big statement in front of all my coworkers and you think that will smooth the way for you to insinuate yourself into my weekend and my life. What if I'm not ready?"

"Then you're not ready. And that's okay."

"You won't resent me?" I stepped aside as the door behind me opened and two women from archives emerged from the building, cigarettes in hand.

"Nope."

"Do you want the flowers back?"

"Jayne, the roses had nothing to do with me meeting your family. I don't see you often because we don't live in the same city. The roses were me trying to, I don't know, make up for that in my clumsy guy way. I told you. I'm not good at dating. I thought girls liked roses."

"I do like the roses!" I shouted into the phone. The archive ladies backed away even farther.

"The weekend thing is really bothering you, isn't it."

My shoulders slumped in defeat. "It feels too fast."

"And that's fine."

"I want you to meet my family."

"I'd like to. But only when you're comfortable."

"Then come with me this weekend."

"But you don't want me to."

"Yes, I do."

"Why?"

I ran a hand through my hair. "Because I won't get to see you this weekend otherwise. Because I know it's the right thing to do. And I want to go to church on Sunday, and Miss Lynnie is getting old, and I know she'd like to meet you."

"Who's Miss Lynnie?"

"My Sunday school teacher."

"And you want me to go to the coast with you this weekend because she's old and you want me to meet her before she dies."

"Yes!"

"Okay."

"Okay?"

"Okay."

He was exhausting.

"Why don't I drive to your place on Friday and bring your bookcase?"

And then he'd go and do nice things like that. "That sounds good."

"Are you positive?"

"Yes."

"I didn't want you to feel about the bookcase the way you felt about the roses. This isn't a manipulative bookcase. It's a thank-you bookcase."

"I consider myself adequately thanked. And I like the roses."

"Miss me?"

I smiled. "Yeah."

"I miss you too."

Friday couldn't arrive soon enough.

⁘

I dreaded the arrival of Friday with all my heart.

In the meantime, I finished up part two of the urban garden story with the help of my police insider. Joely was more than willing (for the price of a coconut cupcake) to get me past the red tape and into the initial police reports and list of witnesses present when the crime was reported.

I interviewed community members, took pictures, and wrote up a nice yet haunting story of senseless vandalism to conclude the piece I had written earlier.

Wednesday, I readied my study for the arrival of the new bookcase. I tidied up the papers that managed to cover every flat surface and vacuumed into the corners of the room.

When I finished, the study was spotless. The rest of the apartment was not.

I don't know where all the clutter came from. Seriously. I was a professional, not a slob. Maybe little messy elves came out when I slept. I don't know how else my jackets found themselves stacked up on the chair by the door, and how I'd taken to playing a round of hide-and-seek every morning with my keys, finding them under banana peels or inside my laundry closet.

When did I last buy bananas, anyway?

Thursday I came up with the brilliant idea of cooking dinner for Levi before we left for the coast.

Martha cooked dinner every day after spending the day working—why couldn't I? I tracked down Gemma that afternoon at her desk.

"Got a minute?"

"Always." Gemma turned her chair around and folded her hands in her lap. "What's up?"

"I want to make dinner."

"Noble."

"Tomorrow. After work. For Levi."

"Oh." She thought for a moment. *"Oh."*

"Stop saying that."

"You're cooking for a *man*."

"Which means he'll eat anything in large quantities, right?"

"Usually. Not always. If he's related to me, yes, but I've never seen Levi eat."

"Do you have to observe someone eating before you can cook for them? Are there hidden cameras involved?"

She rolled her eyes. "You're funny. Does he like Italian?"

"Yes. He took me to Pastini in Corvallis."

"Last weekend?"

"Yes."

"So that's why you've avoided me all week."

I folded my arms. "I haven't avoided you."

"Returned any of my calls or emails lately? Or clothes, what about clothes?"

"You know, of all of us, people say you're the nice one."

"I am the nice one. So, you went on a date with Levi."

"I didn't say it was a date."

She tapped her pencil against her desk. "A man took you to an Italian restaurant in a town separate from the one he lives in. It's a date. And it was nice, otherwise you wouldn't be cooking for him." She tapped her hands on her desk. "Are you sure you don't want me to bring over some of the food from the restaurant? It'd be like having a catered dinner."

"That's sweet, but no. I want to cook."

"Okay." She thought for a moment. "He's a meat eater, right?"

"Yup."

She began scribbling notes on a piece of paper. "Good. That's good."

"What are you doing?"

"Writing out your recipe. That's why you came, right?"

"It's a simple recipe?"

"It is. Add a salad and a box of Rice-a-Roni, and you're done."

"You eat Rice-a-Roni?"

"Don't tell my mom. I'd be disowned."

"Your dad wouldn't care?"

"He doesn't believe in Rice-a-Roni the way adults don't believe in Santa Claus."

"Interesting. Family is complicated, isn't it."

"Kind of like men," Gemma said, sending me a significant glance. "But both are very, very worth it."

Chapter 27

I shopped for groceries Thursday night, following Gemma's list like a scavenger hunt guide.

Pork. If only she had been more specific! She did say boneless, but there was the thin cut pork that was light, and the thick cut pork that was dark. Most of the time, the thick cut was cheaper—did that make it lower quality?

I stood there in the meat section for five minutes, a package of light pork in one hand, dark in the other.

Not one of my prouder moments.

I called Gemma and explained the problem. She said, "Go with the pork sirloin—the darker one."

"You've decided on that?" I asked.

"I've listened to my parents debate about the finer points of recipes since I was in my mother's womb. Don't argue with me."

"Yes, ma'am." I hung up.

Cream. Pretty straightforward. I didn't see any difference between the store-brand cream and the name-brand cream, so I stuck with the store brand and figured the cows weren't stamped with a product name, so why should I care?

Unless they selected the cows differently...

I pushed my cart forward before I could talk myself out of the store-brand cream.

I checked the rest of the list—one lemon, one bunch parsley, one package hazelnuts, four red potatoes...for Pete's sake, I was going to be there all night.

Parsley—I found it in the produce section. Trouble was, there was Italian parsley and flat-leaf parsley.

I pulled out my phone again. "Gemma?"

"Tell me you're not still at the grocery store."

"I'm not at the grocery store."

"Are you lying?"

"Yes. It's the parsley."

"What's wrong with the parsley?" She sounded frustrated.

"Italian or flat-leaf?"

"They're both green, you know." Her voice grew practical again. "Use the Italian."

"Thanks!"

"Anything else you've got a question about?"

"I don't know yet. I don't grocery-shop that often."

"It builds character."

"And you really can't come down and help me?"

"I'm thirty-five-minutes away. By the time I'd get there, you'd be done."

"No, I wouldn't. I'd wait." Really. I meant it.

"You can do this."

"I am a skilled person."

"Very true."

"I can order off a Chinese menu with agility and accuracy."

"I don't know if I've ever ordered Chinese takeout."

It boggled the mind. "If you ever need help, you can call me. I'm great with Indian and Thai too."

"I will defer to your vindaloo knowledge. Until then—keep shopping."

I sighed and hung up.

<hr />

That night I dreamed I cooked dinner for Levi. I put the pork chops in the oven. When I opened the oven to check on them, they'd turned into chickens. Whole, roasting chickens. I had to call Gemma to see if the recipe would turn out okay with chicken. She told me that it wouldn't work with chicken, but it might work with veal or lamb. So I closed the oven door for twenty minutes.

Twenty minutes pass, I check, and there's a rack of lamb in my oven.

Instead of marveling at my oven, I reasoned that all was well because Gemma said lamb would work. Then I went to start the salad and found that the whole thing had wilted overnight.

Then Levi showed up, and I had to explain to him that I didn't have salad. He stood up really straight, saying he couldn't eat dinner if there wasn't any salad.

That's when I woke up. Sweating.

I marched down the hall to the kitchen, flung open the refrigerator, pulled open the produce drawer, and retrieved the bag of salad.

Fresh and crisp and green. Just like I'd remembered.

Rolling my eyes, I went back to bed.

I looked at the clock. Five thirty. Levi had told me he planned on arriving at a quarter till.

Problem was, the pork chops were nowhere near done, and I had a horrible suspicion that I had overzested the lemons. I'd remembered reading one of Gemma's articles once about the white stuff being bitter. Unfortunately, I didn't remember this until I'd dumped the lemon zest into the sauce mixture.

I jumped when my cell phone buzzed on the laminate countertop. "Hello?"

"Hi, Jayne, it's me," Levi said. "I'm running late. I had trouble closing up, but I should be there soon. Do you want to pick up some dinner on the way out? I was thinking something quick, like sandwiches."

My eyes darted to my still-pink-in-the-middle pork chops "No, we can't pick something up!"

"Why not?"

I bit my lip. "I just...don't want to."

"Do you want to eat something at your place and I'll pick something up for myself?"

"Can't you wait until you get here? How far out are you?"

"Thirty minutes."

Surely the pork chops would be done in thirty minutes. They'd been cooking for nearly an hour.

"Okay. I'll see you in thirty minutes."

"So what are we doing about food?"

"I'll think of something," I said and then hung up.

Thirty minutes. I looked at the pork chops, picked my phone back up, and called Gemma. "They're not cooking!"

"Who they?"

"The pork chops! He's going to be here in thirty minutes, and the pork is still really pink."

"How long have they been on the stove?"

"An hour!"

"Um, Jayne, I don't mean to insult your intelligence, but is the correct burner *on*?"

"Of course it is!"

"And there's heat coming from it?"

"Yes!"

"Keep your pants on. Are the chops browning at all?"

"A little."

"What temperature do you have the burner on?"

I examined the little black dial. "How should I know?"

She sighed. "Okay. I think I told you to start with medium-high heat, brown both sides, and then cook covered on medium low."

"Oh." That would do it.

"Use your words, Jayne."

"Where on the dial would you call medium-low?"

"Between medium...and low." She cleared her throat. "Jayne—"

"Closer to the medium or the low?"

"Middle."

"Oh."

"Where is it?"

I yanked the black dial into the appropriate position. "In the middle."

"Right. Where was it before I asked."

"Um..." I winced. "Maybe...more low than medium?"

"Did you ever have them on medium-high?"

"Not so much?"

"Well, if they've been there for an hour they're at least making progress. Turn the heat up to just under medium."

"You speak words of confusion."

"You get odd when you're cooking. Turn the dial to not-quite medium. Cover them and ignore them for ten minutes or so."

"Or so?"

"Check in ten minutes. Call me back."

I would like to draw a veil over my memories of the food preparation and phone calls that ensued.

Twenty-six minutes later, my phone buzzed again.

"I'm really close," Levi said, "but there's an accident on I-84."

"Can you get off?" I asked as I set the table. "I can give you back-road directions."

"I'd get off if I could, but nothing's moving at the moment. I'll call you back when that changes, okay?"

"That's fine."

"Are you all packed?"

"Just about."

Kind of, sort of, not really. I had the clothes I wanted to bring in a pile. They were clean. This was progress.

"Okay. Let's try to leave pretty soon after I get there. How late does your mom stay up?"

"She'll be up if she knows we're running behind. I'll call her when we know what our actual estimated time of arrival will be."

"I miss you."

A smile broke out across my face. "Yeah?"

"And I hate being stuck in traffic when I'm so close to seeing you."

"I'll be praying it breaks up soon," I said and then hung up.

Then sat down.

Pray? I didn't pray. Not anymore, and not unless it was a life-threatening situation. But it had occurred to me, just the same.

I closed my eyes. God and I were doing better these days. I'd gone to church with my mom and Gemma. I'd sung the songs. Spontaneous prayer shouldn't be far behind.

Would God listen to a prayer like that? Was He actively concerned with Portland's traffic troubles? More important, would He pay attention if I asked?

I knew the answer to that question even as it passed through my mind. Years of Sunday school had that effect on me.

He would pay attention. He just wouldn't necessarily answer the way I wanted to.

Did that mean I shouldn't ask?

Before I could talk myself out of it, I bowed my head and uttered the silliest prayer of my life, "Lord, please help the traffic to regulate."

That was all.

I let out the breath I'd been holding. My tense shoulder muscles relaxed.

My cell phone buzzed again.

"It's me," Levi said when I picked up. "I just wanted to tell you traffic's moving and I'm coming up to an exit."

I gave him directions to my apartment, all the while wondering if the traffic had cleared before or after I prayed.

⁂

When Levi arrived at the door, my eyes gravitated to the bag in his hand. "You got dinner."

"Just fries." He wrapped his arms around me in a hug, but I was too upset to enjoy the sensation.

"Are you still hungry?"

"Wha—" he stepped inside and saw the set table, the serving plates, and bowls covered in foil. "You made dinner."

"It was supposed to be a surprise. Are you still hungry?"

"Of course." He beat the bag with his hands into a wad. "Of course I'm hungry. It smells amazing in here."

Actually, it smelled like I spilled something on the burner, but it was sweet of him to say so. "There's pork chops and rice and salad. I even had time to run around the corner and get a loaf of bread."

"I'm sorry I'm late."

"That's okay. I called my mom. Everything's fine."

"I've got your bookcase in the bed of my truck."

"Shall we bring it in?"

"Sure." He planted a short kiss on my lips.

"How heavy is it?" I asked on our way down the stairs. "Can just the two of us handle it?"

"I was clever and designed the back to attach with pegs; we'll be fine. You look wiry."

Fifteen minutes and a lot of grunting later, we had all of the pieces up the stairs. Didn't tweak my wrist once. Levi dragged the parts into the study, where I had cleared a space for the new piece of furniture. "The pegs, see, go in like this."

I watched as he aligned the back with the body and connected the two. "It seems like it would be hard to design it to match perfectly."

"It was. I'm that good. Shall we get it into position?"

At that moment, my stomach growled. Loudly.

"Let's eat," he said, turning my shoulders toward the table.

I lifted the foil from the serving plates, checking to see if the food was still warm. "Let me get this for you." I began to scoop food onto his plate. "What do you want to drink? There's filtered water, Coke, and milk. I've been drinking milk ever since your mom was here."

"Hopefully not the same carton."

"I bought new milk. Even finished the last one before it got chunky. Do you want pepper? I think I have a pepper shaker around here somewhere."

"Sit down. Get yourself some dinner."

"I'm trying to do this right." I shoved my hair behind my ear. "I wanted it to be...you know..."

He smiled. "It's very special. I appreciate it a lot. May I?"

I nodded, and watched as he filled my own plate with food.

"When do you think you'll be able to be brace free?"

"I don't know. Another week, maybe. Maybe less."

"You've managed well."

"I improvise. How does it taste?"

"Wonderful. Really, really good."

"Really?" I took a bite, expecting the worst. "Hmm. You're right."

After a few moments Levi pushed his plate away. "I can't eat another bite. That was amazing."

My eyes narrowed. "You didn't eat very much."

"It was filling."

I looked at my plate. I'd already put away the same amount and wasn't yet near full. I put my fork down. "You filled up on fries."

"Jayne, I didn't know you were making dinner for us."

"I asked you not to get dinner!"

"I didn't get dinner."

"No, you got a giant deep-fried appetizer."

"I'm sorry. My hands were shaking on the road. And I didn't think you cooked."

"I'm broadening my horizons! I'm perfectly capable of cooking a single meal. Your mom makes meals in her sleep."

"That's because she's been doing it since she was eighteen."

"And I'm twenty-six, so I'm behind and it's time I started catching up."

"You're not seriously angry about this, are you?"

"No. Yes. No. I don't know."

"Finish your dinner."

"I'm not hungry anymore."

"Right. Just look at those juicy, perfectly cooked chops."

"You're not going to make me hungry."

Trouble was, they were really, really good. But I didn't particularly feel like giving him the satisfaction of being right.

I reached for my fork.

"It's Gemma's recipe. Of course they're perfect."

My resolve lasted for another thirty seconds. "These are really good."

He sat back in his chair. "You look pretty."

I smiled. "Thanks."

I knew I looked rumpled, and I had yet to take off my apron, but the way he looked at me made me believe him.

"Want to get the new bookcase settled?"

"Sure." I followed him down the hallway.

We pushed together until the bookcase was flush against the wall. I stepped back. "That looks really good." I hugged him around his torso. "Thank you."

"You're welcome," he said, turning me so I faced him. "Always."

Under his gaze, I couldn't move. With a single smooth gesture, he cupped the back of my head with his hand and drew me close, his lips touching mine with infinite care.

So this was what it was like to kiss Levi on purpose. I ran my fingers through his hair and kissed him back.

Lincoln City could wait.

Chapter 28

Levi held my hand until we hit the Van Duzer corridor. By that time, the sky was black and the road slick with new rain. Levi kept two hands on the wheel; I rested my head against the seat back. I couldn't see the ocean in the dark, but I knew it was there, close by.

I didn't worry about my mom meeting Levi. I knew she'd love him.

The houselights were on when we pulled up in my mom's driveway. They cast dappled light patterns on a car to our left.

My sister's car.

"Beth wants to meet you."

"Oh?"

I nodded toward the Subaru Forester with the telltale booster seat in the second row. "She's here."

"Isn't it late for your niece?"

"With any luck, Beth came by herself."

"I'm not afraid of them."

"That's good. That's very good. Hang on to that. Beth can be a pain when she wants to be, but her meds seem to be kicking in lately."

"I'll stand up for you."

"I know." I clasped his hand. "Shall we go in?"

"Want to grab bags first?"

"If my sister's going to be here late at night to scope you out, she may as well help carry luggage."

"I don't have that much—"

"Yeah, but because of your sister, I do."

"How is your bag Sara's fault?"

"Have you met her? I'm barely qualified to wear my clothes, much less choose them and pack them with the care they deserve. So I bring everything these days. Sara's doing, all the way. When I went to stay with your parents, everything I needed fit into my motorcycle panniers."

"And then Sara."

"And then Sara."

"I think your clothes always look good."

"I've been letting Gemma pick out stuff for me lately."

He rolled his eyes. "Trying to compliment you here. Are we going to sit in the car and talk about your wardrobe or go inside?"

"I have a choice?"

"Jayne—"

"Because I can talk buttons."

"Let's go." He leaned over and pressed a quick kiss on my lips before opening his door and stepping out.

I sighed and opened my own door.

He held my hand on the way up the walk. When we arrived at the door, I knocked.

Loudly. Because I could.

Two footfalls and the door opened. I had to wonder if *someone* was peering out the kitchen window.

"Jayne!" My mother's face glowed. "Come in, both of you." She closed the door, shutting out the wisps of the damp night breeze.

Levi extended his hand. "I'm Levi. I'm very glad to meet you, Mrs. Tate."

"It's very nice to meet you, Levi." She clasped his hand. "May I take your coat?"

"Oh, thank you," Levi shrugged out of his jacket. When his back was turned, Mom winked and gave me a thumbs-up.

She liked him. I knew she would.

From the corner of my eye, I could see Beth and Gary in the living room.

Poor Emilee. With any luck, she was asleep upstairs, curled up with Beth's old stuffed dog, Sniffy.

The rundown of the following events:

Gary shakes Levi's hand. I admire Levi's firm grip.

Beth eyes Levi, presumably checking him for, I don't know, suspicious rashes. When he turns to greet her, her face transforms into the smiling visage of the girl-next-door.

Emilee stumbles in, hair mussed, eyes half shut. She must have conked out on the couch.

Levi kneels and introduces himself. The women in the room not already in love with him are now.

Or at least, they ought to be.

"We should be going," Beth said. "We just stopped by because Mom said the car's brakes were making noise."

Yes. And what better time to check them out than eleven p.m. on a Friday night? She probably mentioned the car to Gary at least a week ago.

"I just need to replace the brake pads," said Gary. "I'm going to come back over and work on them tomorrow."

"Want a hand?" Levi asked. "I've spent some time under cars."

"I never turn down free help."

"I'll throw in lunch," Mom said. "I don't expect you to work on the car for free."

Beth pulled Emilee's coat from the closet and began the fastening process. Gary reached for his jacket.

"We'll walk out with you," I said innocently. "We need to get our luggage."

"We can help with that," Gary volunteered. "Come on, Beth."

Score.

The men left for the bags. I stayed inside with the warmth.

"Are you ready to go home and sleep, Miss Emilee?" I knelt and tugged on Emilee's left braid.

She shook her head. "I'm not sleepy."

"She'll fall asleep in the car." Beth pulled the hood to cover Emilee's head.

"No, I won't."

"Okay, you won't." Beth patted her back.

"If the guys are working on the car tomorrow," I started, wondering how such words could trip from my mouth, "would you all like to go shopping with me?"

"Of course," Mom answered right away. "I'd love to."

"Shopping?" Beth said the word as if I'd just suggested a skinny-dipping trip off a jetty.

"I could use some new items…and help picking them out."

Beth tilted her head and studied me.

I refused to flinch under her gaze.

"I can be there as long as Emilee holds out. She can be a pretty good shopper. Can't you, Emilee?"

Emilee nodded absently.

Maybe she was right. She wouldn't fall asleep in the car, but on the way to the car.

I never felt like this with Shane. I scrubbed my face in my mom's guest bathroom, door closed, washing off the day's makeup and travel grime. The feeling of vulnerability was new to me. I didn't know how I felt about it. Would I be able to sleep knowing he was down the hall?

A knock sounded on the door. I cracked it open, mouth full of toothpaste foam.

"You okay in there?" Levi asked.

I wanted to smack the look of amusement right off his face, but it might have caused the toothpaste to splatter. I nodded instead.

"Can I brush my teeth at some point?"

I spat into the sink. "Sure. Of course. I'm about done."

"Really."

"You know, there are other bathrooms in this house."

"I didn't want to dirty up another sink. I thought you'd be done…" he checked his watch. "Twenty or so minutes ago."

"I'm done."

"Am I making you uncomfortable?"

I tucked my hair behind my ear, noting its slight oiliness. "Why would you think that?"

"Because you've never struck me as the kind of girl to hold herself hostage in a bathroom."

"You think you're so funny."

"You're not answering my question."

"You grew up around girls who never spent any time hogging a bathroom. Your parents don't even have a mirror in there."

"You weren't like this when I stayed at your apartment."

I put my toothbrush down. "It's just kind of weird."

"My being here? How is that different?"

I shrugged.

"If you want me to leave, I will. I won't be mad."

"No—not at all. I'm sorry, Levi." I folded my arms across my chest. "We're just so…new. When you were at my apartment before, we weren't, you know, together. I mean, we had our first dating kiss just a few hours ago."

"Still doesn't make sense, but okay. What can I do to help you feel more comfortable?"

"Tell me something embarrassing about yourself."

"I used to have the same haircut as my brothers."

"That's not embarrassing. That's who you were."

"I found a toy in town and kept it hidden from my parents. I realized a couple years ago it was just a little McDonald's toy with a cartoon character."

"You don't have any embarrassing stories, do you?"

"Wanna go for a drive?"

"Right now?"

"Sure."

"It's almost midnight."

"You're all keyed up. I doubt you'll sleep anytime soon."

"My teeth are all brushed."

"The car won't change that, unless you find gummy bears under the seat."

"Mom's already in bed."

"Leave her a note. You're not seventeen."

"Not seventeen, Amish, and climbing out of windows with boys? I almost pulverized one of Sara's callers."

"He probably had it coming."

I forced my shoulders to relax. "Let me throw on my coat."

"You're okay working on the car tomorrow?" I asked, as we curved down Highway 101.

"I like to be helpful. I want to get to know your family. It seemed like a good place to start."

"This whole night-drive in your pajamas is very comfortable. You should try it sometime."

He squeezed my hand.

The sky had grown even darker, but this time I could just make out the line of ocean foam against the sand as we drove down the coast. The rain had lessened and the sky had cleared. A couple of stars peeked out from behind black clouds.

I'd forgotten how dramatic the Oregon Coast could be. After moving to Portland, I'd spent much of my time reviling my roots. Now I found comfort in them.

We didn't talk during the drive. Before I knew it, I felt a gust of cold air and strong arms reaching around me. My eyes opened, which meant they must have been closed.

"Was I asleep?" I asked, except that I'd been sleeping, and I wasn't quite awake, so it came out "Wha ay as-eep."

With horror I realized I had a line of drool on the left side of my chin.

If Levi noticed, he didn't say anything. "You relaxed."

I nodded, and surreptitiously swiped at my chin.

Levi helped me the rest of the way out of the car, borrowed my key, opened the front door, and gave me an arm up the stairs.

"Are you ready to go to bed? Anything else to do in the bathroom?"

To his credit, there was only the tiniest shred of irony in his voice. I shook my head.

He nudged my bedroom door open with his foot. I leaned into the doorframe while he turned my bedcovers down. When he finished, I shrugged out of my coat, sank into the bed, and nestled my head into the down feather pillow.

I think he may have brushed a kiss against my lips, but I could have been dreaming.

The next thing I knew, it was morning.

Morning, and someone was using tools. Loud tools. Either loud tools, or Mom was having it out with a cast-iron pan.

Against the wall.

What was so important that it had to make this much noise on a Saturday morning at...I checked my watch.

A quarter till eleven? I checked again.

Still quarter till. How did that happen? I never slept that late.

I pulled the covers back and sat up. Too fast—I laid back down. Sat up again, this time slower. Okay so far. Two feet on the ground...check. I stood with unsteady legs.

I checked the lower half of my face for drool. Negative.

The noise continued. It was lower than the sound of a cast-iron pan. It sounded like a hammer. A hammer being used by someone with a steady swing.

My mom didn't handle a hammer like that, unless her upper-body strength had suddenly increased overnight. Protein-enriched night cream, that sort of thing. Not likely. That left...

"Levi!" I called from the top of the stairs.

The racket stopped. "You're awake?"

"This relationship isn't going to work!"

"Oh?"

"What are you doing?"

"Fixing your mom's shelf."

"Why?"

"It was falling down. Do you want to come the rest of the way down the stairs?"

"If I come down, I might be angry with you for waking me up."

"It's almost eleven."

"You woke me up."

"I helped you go to sleep."

"Hammer!"

"Jayne—" my mother's voice floated up the stairs. "Would you like to come down for some breakfast?"

"Hammer!" I ignored the petulant, four-year-old tone to my voice.

"I made caramel-pecan rolls."

Oh. I thought about it. Weighed my options.

Weighed my options until I was in the kitchen, smelling the rolls.

"Hi." Levi's face creased into a wide smile. "How'd you sleep?"

"Fine, until you woke me up."

"Eat a roll, Jayne." My mom handed me a plate with an oozy, gooey roll, a fork sticking out of the top.

"You knew I'd come down."

She patted my shoulder. "It's not rocket science."

Plain Jayne

I pulled the fork out and cut a bite. The caramel melted in my mouth the way I'd remembered. "Mm-mm-hm-mm-hmhm."

"I thought it was good too. Did you sleep all right until your boyfriend helped your mother with a shelf that nearly fell and crushed the rolls?"

I clutched my plate, horrified that my yummy, yummy caramel-pecan roll had nearly met with a certain, flattened end. I swallowed my bite and looked to Levi. "Boyfriend?"

"I'm sorry." Mom's forehead creased and her face flushed. "Are you not…"

"We are," Levi interrupted. He snagged a pecan off the side of my plate.

I didn't look at him. "My boyfriend has courage." Boyfriend, boyfriend, boyfriend. The word rolled around my head. I tried it again, to see how it felt on my tongue. "Boyfriend."

"Want to sit with me?"

I nodded, hair falling in my face and dangerously close to the caramel residue on my lips. He reached over and tucked it behind my ear before kissing a bit of the caramel off.

I looked around. Mom had disappeared from the kitchen.

Sneaky.

"I didn't mean for you to wake up on the wrong side of the bed, but your mom said these were your favorites."

"They are."

"I didn't think it was that loud."

"Sound carries in this house."

"I'll remember that."

"If you're my boyfriend, does that make me…"

"My girlfriend? I think that's the way it works. I don't know. I never went to a traditional high school."

I wove my fingers through his. "I really…" I sighed. "I want this to work."

"Me too."

Looking into his eyes I felt hope. "If this is going to work…" I locked eyes with him. "You have to keep away from my pecans."

Chapter 29

My sister was a shopping machine. I think even Gemma would have been impressed by her skills. My original intention for the trip to the outlet malls was to pick up some nice pieces that would allow me to create decent-looking outfits without much effort in the morning.

Beth created a "wardrobe scheme," finding me a pile of clothes that all seemed to coordinate and yet not look like a bad mix-and-match puzzle. She managed to do all that *and* keep me under budget.

"I do it for myself all the time," Beth said while we stopped for lunch in the deli section of Sip Wine & Bistro. "It's not like I can spend a lot of time figuring out what to wear these days." She glanced at Emilee. "The goal is that I can pick up four things from the floor, and at least two should go together."

I reached over and tugged on Emilee's blond braid. "You're a very good shopper's assistant."

She pulled her thumb from her mouth. "I get two cookies when we get home."

"And you will have earned both of them."

Mom pointed at her bowl. "This potato salad is really good."

"Speaking of very good," Beth said, leaning toward me, "when are you going to talk to us about Levi?"

"What about?"

She pinched the bridge of her nose. "Jayne, the last time you came, you brought Shane. Now it's Levi. At some point we need to lean in, whisper, and giggle. Where did you guys meet?"

I didn't point out that Beth and I had never been whisper-and-giggle sisters. But in the interest of improving our relationship, I lowered my voice and answered. "His woodshop. He was a source for the Amish story I wrote."

"Were you instantly attracted to him?"

"No."

"Oh."

"Sorry. Trumpets weren't playing, and I didn't see an armed Cupid in my peripheral vision."

"Well, what changed? Something must have happened."

"I stayed with his family for a week and a half. I interviewed him a couple times. We just kept seeing each other. After a while…"

Let's face it. After a while, I was gone. Embarrassingly gone.

"After Shane and I broke up, we had an opportunity to explore things," I finished.

"Nothing happened while you were with Shane?"

Define nothing… I bit my lip.

Beth snapped her fingers and pointed at me. "You're doing it. You're hiding something."

I batted at her pointed finger. "Put that away."

"You get that look on your face when you don't want to tell. What did you do?"

Pined for Levi until Shane and I ended.

"We met. I really liked him, but we didn't start having a relationship until after Shane. Shane ended, and Levi and I got together."

"Just like that?"

"He took me out for a really nice lunch."

"You like him."

"He's my boyfriend. I'm supposed to."

"You really, really like him. You didn't look at Shane the way you look at Levi."

"Beth, you only saw me with Shane over one weekend. We were together for ages. You don't know how we did or did not look at each other."

Mom patted Beth's arm. "Are you ready to get back to the shops? I'd like to hit Kitchen Collection."

Mom was distracting Beth. I knew it. Beth knew it, but no one except Emilee said anything, and Emilee only announced her need to use the ladies' room.

⁂

We returned home, arms full. I couldn't remember the last time I'd shopped and returned with so many logo-emblazoned bags. I felt like a character in a chick flick during the scene when she gets a makeover and goes on a shopping spree. Hadn't felt like that before. I was more likely to return with yoga clothes I'd wear to the gym for a week before using them mainly in front of the TV, utilitarian work pieces, pants I bought because they were long enough for my legs and didn't pucker oddly in the back.

Not inspiring stuff. But for the first time I was kind of excited about my purchases.

Gary and Levi were still working on the car when we returned. Emilee ran to her dad, but Gary lifted his hands out of the way. "Careful there, sweetie. Daddy's messy."

Beth closed the car door. "How'd you both manage to get so greasy? I thought you were just changing out the brake pads."

"This is just brake dust," Gary answered.

I tilted my head, waiting for the full answer. There were undeniable grease spots on Levi's face.

"We decided to change the oil while we were at it," Levi said, his eyes charged with unreleased laughter. "I dropped the oil plug in the drain pan." He held his own hands out. "And I got brake dust."

I smiled. "See you inside?"

"Only if you agree to walk on the beach with me. It's dry right now."

"We'll see." I gave my best attempt at coyness. From Levi's expression, I guessed that it worked.

⁂

Thirty minutes later, Levi was grease free and we were walking along the beach at Road's End. The wind whipped at our clothes; Levi held my hand inside his jacket pocket.

"I like your family," he said, avoiding a crab shell in the sand. "They're very..."

"Defiant of classification?"

"Fun. Talkative. Protective of you."

"They are not."

"Gary threatened me with bodily injury if I didn't treat you right."

"Oh. Wow" Impressive, considering I'd seen him maybe four or five times since he and Beth married.

"He was pretty specific about his methodology."

"Sorry about that." I wondered if Shane had received that speech. But then, Shane had never participated in a one-on-one activity with Gary. Poor Levi. No good deed went unpunished, I guess.

"I don't mind." He squeezed my hand. "I'm glad you have people who care about you."

"They're different than I thought they were. I wish I hadn't missed out on so much time."

"You're here now."

I took a breath. "Your parents aren't going to be happy if we...stay together." I didn't think I should bring up marriage this soon, but I knew I had a point. "They want you to go home and marry Rachel." I hated myself as soon as I said the words, but the thoughts had been worrying me for too long.

Levi didn't seem perturbed. "I've been worshipping a personal, gracious God for too long. I can't go back. I like the drums in my church service too much."

"You don't miss Rachel?"

"How did you know about Rachel?"

"Ida."

He sighed. "No, I don't miss Rachel. She wanted the life her parents had. I didn't. In fact...now's as good a time as any to bring this up."

"What?"

"I'm thinking about selling the shop."

I pulled my hand away in shock. "Honestly? Why?"

"I bought it and built up the business to be near my family. Near my siblings if any of them wanted to be like me. Sara's the only one who's expressed any interest...I don't know. I worked so hard to leave and learn and do something different. Now I'm building furniture."

He ran his hand through his hair, an ineffective gesture since the wind restyled his hair moments later. "I've been looking around at some other jobs. I've even thought about maybe starting my own firm."

"Would you stay in Albany?"

"I...don't think so."

I felt my heart twinge. "Don't do this on account of me, Levi. What would Spencer and Grady do?"

"I'd offer to sell them the business first." He shrugged. "I haven't figured everything out yet. I just wanted you to know what I was thinking."

"What about Samuel? And Leah and Elizabeth?"

"If they need me, there is a phone on the farm. And they've got Grandma."

"You're okay not having contact with them?"

"I don't have contact with them as it is, Jayne. From what I hear from Sara, my dad's home all the time now. I couldn't visit if I wanted to."

There had to be something else. "Why would you voluntarily choose to return to corporate life?"

"I was never a workaholic corporate guy. I took vacations. Sure, I wasn't traveling up the ladder at the speed of sound, but I liked my job and felt good about what I did during the day."

"And you don't at the shop?"

"I feel like I've done my brain a disservice."

"You feel like that because of the shop, and not because you're overdosing on coffee?"

"Hey now!" He reached out to tickle me, but I was too fast. I sprinted ahead, my feet digging into the sand.

⁓⁓⊱⋇⊰⁓⁓

"What are you thinking?" Levi asked as we were driving back to my mom's.

"Just woolgathering," I answered.

Truthfully, I couldn't get my mind past the conversation we'd had on the beach. I felt myself moving toward the ideals of the Amish: simplicity, family, faith. I craved the way I'd felt at the Burkholder farm—for the first time, I didn't feel my life was spinning out of control. Since then I'd restructured my own life, repairing my family relationships and reconciling with a God I'd ignored for too long. I was learning to quilt, bake, and make my apartment mold resistant.

Basically, I was moving from big-city life to the simple life.

And now Levi wanted to move in the opposite direction.

I knew he wasn't about to abandon his faith; he was stronger than that. The idea that we were otherwise moving in different directions scared me.

My mind took it one step further.

What if he did move to Portland? What stood in the way of us having a real, serious, adult relationship? The kind that led to "save the date" cards?

Nothing.

I was terrified.

⚜

I remained terrified through dinner, and our family-sans-Emilee viewing of *Witness*, with Levi pointing out all of the inaccuracies.

"An Amish woman would never be so forward toward an English man," Levi said. "Ever. Even if she were in one of the least restrictive communities, she wouldn't speak like that with a man she'd just met."

"Sara would swoon for clothes so tailored," I added.

Levi chuckled.

"What was it like, growing up Amish?" Beth asked, not caring that the movie continued.

"I have a wonderful family. We were very close. I was raised to be a farmer, but I didn't want to be one."

He explained how he left, turning his back on everything he was raised to be, and how he returned to be near his family.

"Now you're leaving them all over again." Suddenly all eyes were on me. "Well, he is."

"Jayne—" Levi started.

"And it doesn't matter that they need you or that they're your family. You're outta there, because they weren't smart enough, or old enough, to follow you."

My mom stood. "Why don't I check on dessert?"

"I'll help you," Beth said. Gary joined her.

Outburst over, I took that moment to study my hands. In detail.

"Thanks, Jayne. Appreciated that."

"Sorry," I said, although I knew a part of me wasn't.

"Does it bother you that much that I want to leave Albany?"

I didn't know what to say.

"Your family has welcomed you with open arms." Levi's brow wrinkled. "You show up on the doorstep, and they let you in. I go home, and my brothers won't look at me. They won't look at me!"

"Your sisters look at you."

"My father pretends that I am dead. I don't exist to him."

"Your mother misses you."

"But I'm not welcome in her home."

"Sara talks about leaving."

"If she leaves, she'll be just like me. She'll never see her older sister again; Rebecca's husband will see to that. And why do you care if she leaves? You're mad at me for leaving a second time."

"I…" Anything I said made me look like a hypocrite.

"I need to take a walk."

"It's raining outside."

"I don't care."

He stood, crossed the room, and retrieved his jacket. In an instant, he was out the door.

I stood and walked to the kitchen.

"You can stop skulking now." I ran a hand through my hair.

"We didn't want to interrupt," Mom said.

"If you'd interrupted, I might have stopped talking, and that might have been for the best."

"Communication is the key to relationships," said Gary, his sage words punctuated by a swig from his root beer.

"We should take Emilee home," Beth said. To my amazement, she reached out and gave me a hug. I forced myself to relax. "Everything will be okay."

I was glad she thought so. I wasn't so sure.

Levi returned half an hour later. I was on the couch reading Mom's *Reader's Digest* when he came back, jacket soaked, hair dripping.

I studied his face. "I'm sorry."

He hung his jacket on the closet knob. I heard tiny pats of water hit the tile.

"Beth and Gary went home?"

I nodded. "And Mom's in bed."

"Do you really want to be with me, Jayne? Or do you just like the idea of me? I'm not a quilt. I'm not your path to a more simplistic existence or whatever else you think you need."

"I'm just trying to figure things out."

"So am I. But you didn't answer my question."

Beth's words at the mall floated back through my head. I was crazy for

Levi. I knew it. That scared me to death. What I didn't know, exactly, was *why* I was so crazy for him. Maybe he was right. Maybe he was the human version of my quilt squares.

That would be the easy answer. Life would be simple if I were crazy about him for all the wrong reasons.

Being with him for all the right reasons? That was serious.

He still waited for my answer.

"I couldn't stop thinking about you when I was with Shane. You, who you were. I don't know if how much of how I see you has to do with your job. I honestly don't know, Levi. All I know is that I couldn't get you out of my head."

He took a step closer. "You need to see me for who I am. I'm not my job."

"I…I want to see you for who you are. We just need time." I took a step closer to him.

His hand glanced over my hair and then caressed my face. I closed my eyes. "I hope so," he said.

I did too.

Chapter 30

I don't know anything about makeup sex, on account of my mother's voice in my head making me think about cows.

Makeup kissing on the other hand...hadn't really experienced that one either.

Until now.

We stood in my mother's living room, cradled in each other's arms. If I'd believed in ghosts, I might have worried about my father's disapproving glare. But Dad wasn't here. His body was in the urn on the mantle, and his spirit was in heaven.

My thoughts concerning Levi were wildly conflicting. I hated the idea of him selling the shop. I met him at the shop. I think I fell for him at the shop. I loved everything it stood for.

Without the shop, though, Levi was still Levi. He still smelled the same. His eyes still crinkled when he laughed. I knew he still cared about his family. I knew he still cared about me.

I knew this, because one of his hands was buried in my hair, the other nestled in the small of my back, holding me steady. His lips caressed mine, over and over.

We came up for air a couple moments later. His eyes burned into mine as he stroked my hair. "I love you," he said.

I froze. I knew I was crazy about him. I knew I didn't want to be without him. But love?

Love was a big deal.

Rather than answer, I kissed him.

Kissed him and hoped he didn't think too deeply about it.

Before church on Sunday, Mom and I worked on piecing my quilt. It didn't take us long to get the whole thing pinned into strips. Levi checked in from time to time.

"Are things all right with you two?" Mom asked after Levi offered to bring us refreshments.

I didn't know how to answer. "How did you know that you wanted to be with Dad?" The question was difficult to ask, but I had to know.

"He was everything I was looking for—a believer, a leader. Handsome. I loved him very much. When everything fits together like that, you know."

I wanted to ask a thousand questions. There were pictures of my dad smiling; I just hadn't been born yet to witness those smiles myself. Had he always been like that? What had happened—or who? Was there something about me that was so wrong?

"He loved you, you know," Mom said, using the mind reading abilities she'd picked up the second she gave birth.

For a moment, I was confused. Did she know about Levi? But then my mind reoriented itself, and I knew she was talking about my father. My stern, unyielding father.

"He...he had trouble showing it. I know that parts of your childhood..." she took a deep breath, "couldn't have been easy. I'm so sorry about that. He was proud of you, though. Proud of your going to the university, proud that you had your job at the paper. Whenever you wrote an article, it spent a week on the fridge. After that, he put it into a notebook. It's around here, somewhere."

"I didn't know."

We both knew that I might have known, had I bothered to return home for more than a few minutes around the occasional holiday. My mom was gracious enough not to point that out.

I looked over my shoulder, checking the hallway for listeners. "Levi... told me he loves me."

"Of course he does."

"Not helping."

"Do you love him?"

That's the question that frightened me. I didn't have a chance to even try to answer; as soon as I heard Levi's footfalls on the stairs, I turned my attention back to the prickly quilt.

After arriving at church, I received compliments on my flippy navy skirt, printed blouse, and tangerine cardigan, and reveled in the fact that I was the recipient of such comments. On my clothing, no less.

Sara would be so proud.

Miss Lynnie found me after the service. "Who is *this* young man?" she asked, not looking at all upset that I had a new husband candidate with me.

"This is Levi," I answered, performing introductions.

Levi shook her hand carefully and complimented her brooch. Miss Lynnie smiled, delighted. "I like this one," she said.

"Me too," I answered. "He's also a believer," I added, before she could ask.

"Of course he is," she said with a wave of the hand. "How else would he know all five verses of *Come, Thou Fount of Every Blessing*?"

She shuffled away after patting both of us on the cheek, her version, I think, of a blessing.

"She approves," I told my mom after Miss Lynnie was out of earshot.

"Of course she does," Mom answered, smiling at Levi. "Shall we all find something for lunch? Emilee's hungry."

We ended up voting for lunch locations, and Hawk Creek Café won unanimously. We started with a large Thai chicken pizza and ended with the crusts drizzled with honey. Near the fireplace in the back, I almost fell asleep.

Levi and I packed up after lunch, despite my yen for a nap. We gave final hugs to Mom, and began the drive back to Portland.

For the duration of the drive, we listened to Levi's Trace Bundy CD. Levi wasn't feeling talkative, clearly, and I certainly wasn't either. I closed my eyes and allowed myself to drift off.

I awoke to the feel of turning into a driveway. I opened my eyes. It was the driveway to the parking lot at my building. We were home. My home, anyway.

"Sorry," I said, trying to sit up. "I didn't mean to sleep the whole way."

"That's all right." The tone of his voice told me it probably wasn't. "Need help with your bags?"

"I…sure." I'd assumed he'd come in and we'd spend a little time together. Apparently I was wrong.

Levi carried my duffel bag. I carried my purse, windbreaker, and tennis shoes. I opened the door; he walked through it, took my bag down the hall, and deposited it in my bedroom doorway.

"Thanks," I said, dumping my things in the chair by the door and kicking off my shoes.

"You're welcome. I should get back."

"Oh—okay."

"Bye."

"Bye." I watched in confusion as he started to walk out the door. "So that's it?"

He stalled in the doorway but wouldn't look at me. "I don't know."

I crossed my arms. "You have to talk to me."

"What's there to talk about?" He closed the door, so at least my neighbors weren't getting their live *As the World Turns* installment from me. "I told you I loved you. You didn't say anything."

"I seem to remember kissing you. If I didn't like you at all, I probably wouldn't have engaged in any sort of physical contact with you."

"I don't know that."

"Levi!" I laid a hand on his shoulder. "You know I care about you. A lot. I just…didn't know what to say."

"Because you don't love me."

"You don't know that!"

"Don't I?"

I retracted my hand. "I told you, I care about you."

"But you don't love me."

"I want to be with you!"

"You don't love me."

For Pete's sake, he was slow. "We've been together such a short while. Love takes time."

"You're saying I don't love you?"

"No. I believe you. I just need more time."

"How much time?"

"I don't know."

"What about if I sold my carpentry business? Would you still love me? If I decided to think practically instead of allowing my life decisions to be made on the basis of wishful thinking and sentimentality, would you still be there?"

I hesitated, just the tiniest second.

"Thanks. That's all I need to know."

"Levi—"

He reached again for the doorknob. "Jayne, I love you. No matter what you do."

I pulled myself up. "Obviously not, if you're leaving like this."

"I love you." He shrugged. "I can't help but love you. I've loved you since you scheduled an interview with me on a day when you didn't have anything going but pretended you did and then rode away on your motorcycle. That was the first day I met you. You're not being honest with me, and you're not honest with yourself. You like the idea of me. If the idea shifts..." his voice broke. "It makes me sad. I wish you felt the same way about me that I do about you."

"You don't know I don't."

"Do you love me, Jayne?"

"Yes!"

The look in his eyes wrenched at my heart. "I wish you were telling the truth."

"It's not that easy—"

"Sometimes it is. Goodbye, Jayne."

He left, closing the door behind him.

I jumped to my feet and threw the door back open. "Levi! Wait!"

He kept walking down the stairs. I followed him, the damp soaking into my socks. "Levi!" I could hear my voice shake, but I didn't care what anyone thought. "Please!"

His steps didn't slow. He didn't turn around, didn't do anything to acknowledge that he'd even heard my voice. Levi, the man I couldn't stop thinking about, climbed into his truck and drove away.

Just like that.

⁓⁓∿⁓⁓

I spent the night in the living room next to my phone, in case he came back or called.

I left the door unlocked, so that if I fell asleep he'd still be able to come in, wrap his arms around me, and tell me everything was all right. I cried myself to sleep sometime around three.

Because I'm a creature of habit, I woke ninety minutes before I needed to leave for work. As usual.

I stumbled down the hall, but I locked the door before I did so. I didn't need a weirdo entering my apartment while I was in the shower. I peered at my reflection in the bathroom mirror.

I looked like a typhoid patient.

Thoughts of calling in sick shot through my mind. The idea of not dealing with people appealed, but staying at home and continuing to cry my eyes out appealed less. I went through the motions of washing my hair, drying my hair, dressing in my most comfortable, work-appropriate clothes, and finding my keys. I couldn't eat breakfast—the thought of food turned my stomach.

I managed to arrive at work without getting into an accident. Brian leaned over the joining cubicle wall after I sat down. "What happened to you?"

I didn't feel the need to look up. "Bad weekend."

"I've got a couple aspirin if you're hungover."

"I'm not hungover."

"Sick?"

"No."

"Woman's issues?"

I slammed my pencil down. "Since when is that any of your business?"

"Sorry. My eyes have been opened to the difficulties of being female ever since I got married."

Somehow, I doubted his increased sensitivity, and I guessed his wife would agree with me.

"I'm not sick, hungover, or experiencing untoward hormonal fluctuations."

"Are you sure? Because ovulation can cause mood swings too—"

"Brian!"

"Sorry."

But he wasn't sorry enough. When I got up to use the restroom, I came back to find Kim and Gemma at my desk, textbook concerned looks on their faces.

"Brian, you just couldn't help yourself." I looked to Kim. "Do I get my chair back?"

"What happened?"

"Bad weekend. I was out drinking."

"No, she wasn't!" Brian said from behind the cubicle wall.

"Your pupils aren't dilated. We don't believe you." Kim tossed her head.

Gemma lifted an eyebrow. "I'm impressed."

"Come on. Am I the only one who listens to Joely's cop talk?"

"She lost me at Miranda rights."

Seriously. "If I were hungover, you two would be giving me a headache. But I'm not. I'm just sad. Not hungover or hormonal or sick. Just sad."

Gemma reached for my arm. "What happened?"

"We broke up, okay? Levi and I broke up. And I'm sad. But I'm moving through it."

They went through the motions of trying to comfort me. It felt like rubbing a wool blanket over soft skin. "Don't worry about it, okay? I mean, I'm a breakup pro. Me and Shane, me and Levi. I'm old hat."

Gemma frowned. "I've never understood that phrase."

"It means I am weathered or experienced. I think. If I'm using it wrong, you certainly wouldn't know. Don't you both have jobs? Food to taste, politicians to expose?" My phone rang. "I've got a job to do. You guys can drown me in ice cream and *Love Story* later."

"Bleh," Kim said, sticking out her tongue. "I hate that movie."

Second ring. "Fine. *The Way We Were.* Bye!" I lifted the receiver and swiped at the dampness near my eye. "Tate."

"Tate? Sol. Come in for a visit, why don't you."

I stood and leaned to the right so I could see through his office window. "Can't we just chat about this over the phone?"

"Not while you've got a three-ring circus at your desk. Move."

So I moved.

"If you'd managed to check your email," Sol began as soon as I closed the door, "you would have seen that we've had a huge reader response from that Amish piece you wrote."

"Really?" My outlook on life almost brightened. Almost, because it reminded me of the family of the man who never wanted to see me again.

"What's going on? You look like—well, it would be ungentlemanly for me to say what you look like."

"Flatterer."

"Waiting."

"Boyfriend. Broke up."

He narrowed his eyes. "I thought you broke up with that architect boy last week. What's new?"

"Different boy. The family I stayed with?"

"You dated an Amish boy?"

"No, and he's hardly a boy. He's thirty-two. And he left the Amish, but they're still his family. And…he left."

"That's no good. I called you in here to ask you to do another installment on the Amish series."

"It's a series?"

"It is now. Are you up for it?"

"Yes." The word came out in a whoosh. "When?"

"Soon as you can. Might want to clean yourself up a bit. You'll frighten the Burkholders."

Knowing Martha, she'd probably feed me and wrap me in a warm blanket. The thought of being back at the farmhouse made me ache for the warmth of the kitchen and Elizabeth's gapped grin.

We went over the word count and angle he wanted. I jotted a few notes and stood to leave.

"And Tate—"

I stopped, my hand on the doorknob. "Sir?"

"Take better care of yourself. Can't afford to lose you."

"Thanks."

"New reporters annoy me."

"I'm sure they do."

⁓

I packed up later that morning, my emotions impossibly mixed. I longed to see Martha; I dreaded seeing Martha. In fact, I felt that way about the entire family. The last thing I wanted was to see Levi's resemblance to his brothers, his sense of humor in Sara…

I was pathetic.

If only I had been able to tell Levi I loved him.

If only I knew I was telling the truth.

If only my intense attraction and affection for him had been enough. I knew I'd screwed up that night at my mom's when I'd practically attacked him in front of the family. Not one of my prouder moments.

He didn't want any less than all of me. Less than that was unacceptable. So unacceptable that he walked out as if I'd never meant anything to him.

Rethinking that night and that week and every other encounter made me cringe, but my mind wouldn't stop the instant replays.

Was this part of God's plan? Now that I was going back to the faith of my childhood, was this His way of making sure He had my full attention?

"That's not playing fair, God," I said out loud to make sure He was listening.

I ripped apart the Velcro holding my wrist brace together and then wiggled it off.

My wrist felt naked and unprotected without it. I flexed my fingers and rotated my hand. So far, so good. Maybe it was...

I winced and replaced the brace. Okay, not yet. But soon. I missed my motorcycle, and this would have been a nice trip to take on it.

I stretched my back and neck and tried to recenter myself. I had to be stronger than this. I couldn't be the girl who fell apart when a guy left. I had to hold strong to what I believed.

So what did I believe?

Chapter 31

On the way back to the farm I took a detour and drove out to Silver Creek Falls. There were a few other cars in the parking area, but I couldn't see any people. With my hands shoved into my pockets, I hiked the short way down to the North Falls. The question I'd considered at the apartment had haunted me during the drive and stayed with me as I walked down the concrete path.

What did I believe?

I believed in God.

What was He like?

Was He someone I could trust? It was one thing to be told by a pastor that, yes, God was trustworthy, and entirely another to believe it for myself.

I could hear the falls as I approached. A fine mist filled the air.

The water was magnificent. I felt myself relax just watching.

I knew God was a father, and yet the only father I'd ever personally experienced wasn't one I'd readily recommend. Did my feelings about God have anything to do with that?

Standing in front of the falls, I realized if I continued thinking along this vein I'd be here all day.

With a mixed-up heart I went back to my car and pulled onto I-5.

———※———

The moment I saw the farmhouse, I had a strange desire to get out of my car and race toward it, arms outstretched.

The breakup was making me crazy. I made a mental note to avoid romantically inclined relationships in the future. I wasn't a fan of the fallout.

Having decided not to run to the farmhouse, I grinned at the sight of Leah and Elizabeth running toward me.

Then I started worrying about running them over. I remembered Levi complaining of the same thing—and the memory stung.

I stopped, yanked at the parking brake, retrieved my keys, and stepped from the car.

Leah and Elizabeth hugged my legs, asking so many questions I couldn't understand a single one.

"What are you two doing out of school?" I tried my best to pick them up, one arm per child, but I couldn't manage to get them two inches off the ground. "You've grown!"

"Teacher's sick today. I lost another tooth," said Elizabeth, pointing at a new hole in her mouth.

"Yes, you have. Is your mom inside?"

Leah nodded. "She's in the kitchen. We're going to have dried peach pie tonight!"

"Sounds yummy! Walk me in?"

The moment I stepped inside, I was embraced by warm, dry air filled with the scents of yeasty bread and roasting meat.

"Jayne!" Martha's smile when she saw me was welcome enough. "This is a surprise."

"I wish I could have written first, but my boss wanted me to write a follow-up piece for the paper."

"Would you like to help with the pie dough?"

"Of course." I took off my jacket, washed my hands, and picked up the rolling pin Martha had left on the counter. "I was planning on staying in town a few days."

Martha frowned. "Why in town?"

"I didn't want to be underfoot."

"You must stay here. I insist, and Gideon will too."

"How is he?"

Martha rolled her eyes. "He's in the fields with Elam and Amos."

"Not working too hard, I hope?"

She shrugged. "They're keeping an eye on him. He's stubborn."

Reminded me of someone else I knew.

A thought struck me—this time around, if my computer battery died, I'd have to go to a coffee shop. Levi wouldn't be opening his office electricity to me anytime soon.

"That looks thin enough," Martha said, glancing at the pie crust dough. "You can probably stop there."

"Oh." *Thin enough* was being kind. There were places where the dough was near translucent in its papery thinness.

That's what I got for thinking about Levi and trying to bake at the same time.

Sara chose that moment to swing around the corner. "Oh. It's you."

If I hadn't read her letter, I would have thought she was completely indifferent.

"Yes, it's me. What gave it away."

Sara shrugged. "I heard you from upstairs. You're really loud."

"Nice to see you too."

I turned my back, but I could feel Sara analyzing my outfit. Because she didn't depart immediately, I knew she approved.

Success!

⁓⁓⁓

"We are very pleased to have Jayne back," said Gideon at the dinner table that evening. "And very pleased that on the night she returns we are not eating fish."

"I hear fish is good for your heart," I said, mainly because I could get away with it.

"Good for your heart, but maybe too much is not good for your soul."

Interesting theology. "How have you been feeling?"

"I feel like I am young again."

Somehow I doubted that.

"Well, I'm just here to observe for a few days. I don't want to get in anyone's way."

I think I heard Elam snort.

Punk.

"Grandma is coming the day after tomorrow," Sara said. "We're going to quilt together."

"Really!" An idea popped into my head. "I've been working on my quilt. I'll have my mom send it down."

The shipping would cost an arm, leg, and a kidney, but I didn't want to miss out on quilting with Sara and Ida.

Everyone needs something to look forward to.

⁓⁓⁓

As far as the breakup was concerned, I think I'd moved from denial to anger. I lay under a stack of Amish quilts that night, stewing.

Levi knew I'd just come off a relationship with Shane. He knew I was going through a lot of major life changes. Who was he to give me a "love me or leave me" ultimatum?

I wondered briefly if he had a brain tumor. I spent a few minutes worrying about him before I reverted back to anger.

———※———

I broke a plate at breakfast that morning. I may have been thinking about Levi at the time.

———※———

"You're wearing your normal clothes," Sara commented as we washed the breakfast dishes.

"I can switch, but there weren't any other options in the guest room, and I forgot to ask."

She looked around, checking for little listeners. "Your clothes look better than before."

"Thank you. I went shopping."

"With Gemma?"

"My sister."

Sara gave an appreciative nod. "She did a good job."

"And I pulled out my debit card with exceptional skill."

"What's a debit card?"

I explained, realizing the Amish weren't exactly regular bankers.

"How are you and Levi...you know."

"You mean are we still together?"

"Yes."

"We aren't." I sighed.

"Oh." She scrubbed another plate. "That was fast."

Too fast. "It happens."

"Was it you or him?"

"Meaning...?"

"Which one of you did something to ruin it?"

"Sometimes, relationships don't work out. Not for things people did or didn't do, but just because those people don't work together."

"You find out that people don't work together by what they do or don't do," Sara pointed out.

"Stop being so smart."

"Am I right?"

"Sara, give me a break. I'm trying to be a good ex-girlfriend and not speak badly of he whom I dated. Can I get credit for that?"

"You still like him."

"We need to finish the dishes and start the laundry."

"You still like him."

"Be nice to me. I sent you contraband."

"Do you think he'll change his mind?"

I didn't want to cry, not in front of Sara. "No, I don't. What about you? Any boys sneaking through your window these days?"

Her eyes grew wide. "It's a secret!"

"Well, so was Levi. Spill."

"There's no one."

Was that because she planned on leaving? I didn't want to know. We dropped the subject of the opposite sex altogether and paid very close attention to the rest of the breakfast dishes.

***

My mom agreed to overnight my quilt strips. I didn't tell her about Levi. I couldn't get myself to explain that I had ended two relationships in one month.

When the package arrived the following morning, I saw that my mom had also included enough fabric to back the quilt, as well as some edging and batting.

Ida arrived shortly after, and we set to work. I asked Martha for assistance with the treadle sewing machine, but she deferred to Sara.

Sara instructed me to practice with scrap fabric until I got the hang of the treadle sewing machine. Then she showed me how to thread the needle and fill the bobbin, place the fabric, and then run a line of stitches.

I watched her do it first. She turned the wheel on the right-hand side, using it to start the rhythmic movement of the needle slowly before beginning the pedaling movement with her feet. "Don't push the treadle too fast," Sara advised. "You want to keep control of the stitches. When you pedal, put your right foot ahead of the left, like this—" she lifted her skirt out of the way so I could see her feet with an unobstructed view. "It keeps your ankles from getting tired. Your turn!"

"I think I should watch a bit longer," I said, not that she was listening. She'd already sprung from her seat and waited expectantly for me to replace her.

I sat. "Which direction do I turn this?" I asked, touching the wheel on the right.

"That's the balance wheel. You always turn it toward you."

"Toward me. Okay."

"Do you want to practice the treadle?"

"Sure." I pedaled a few times. Sara knelt, adjusted my feet, and had me do it again. "That's good. Now try it with fabric."

I tried a line of stitches. To my surprise, they didn't veer off and begin a trip to Jersey. "That's not bad."

Ida nodded. "You have good quilting hands."

I studied my hands. I hadn't thought of them that way before.

Sara began to rattle about the finer points of basting, reversing, and tension, and I just barely kept up. When she was talking about sewing and fabric, she came alive. I got the feeling she could talk for a week about hems.

If she stayed, those skills would translate into sewing for her family, likely with a quilting business on the side. Would that be enough for her?

I thought about Levi. Keeping his family's accounts wouldn't have been enough for him, and running the woodshop clearly wasn't either. Was I kidding myself to believe he would be happy there forever?

Sara, Martha, and Ida continued to quilt long after I begged off with sore calves. The sky was clear outside, and I resolved to take a walk around the farm to stretch the rest of my muscles. I stopped still when a familiar green pickup pulled into the drive. I saw the truck slow suddenly, as if the driver braked hard in surprise.

I couldn't move as Levi climbed from the cab. He looked to Ida's car, parked next to mine in the driveway. "You're back."

I nodded.

"My grandma's here?"

I nodded again.

"I'm looking for my dad."

"Oh."

He didn't ask why I was there.

Not that it mattered much to him.

I watched as he walked toward the barn. When he was sufficiently away, I took an alternate route to the same location. Every one of my reporter's instincts urged me to move faster, to think harder, to remember all of the details.

When it began to rain, I didn't care. There was a back entrance to the barn that would allow me to listen to any words spoken. Granted, the gas-powered generators were loud, but people had to shout over them anyway. The shouting I could hear. And knowing Levi and Gideon, the likelihood of shouting was present.

I don't know what farm equipment was in use, but some of it quieted.

"Do you have a minute, Dad?"

I didn't need to be in the room to see Gideon's scowl. I positioned myself just outside the back door.

"Don't call me 'Dad.' You are not my son."

"Did you know I left my job in the city to work in town, to be near my family?"

"You don't have a family."

"I'm sorry I had to leave. I'm sorry I couldn't be the son you wanted me to be." I could hear the rising tension in Levi's voice.

"Don't upset him, please," said Amos' voice. "His health—"

"My health is *gut*," Gideon snapped.

"I was never baptized, Dad. You don't have to shun me."

"I had a son. I had a son and he turned his back on his family and his God."

"God is still with me."

"Are you baptized?"

"Yes."

"Into an Anabaptist church?"

"No."

"Then I fear for your soul."

There was a pause. "You won't change your mind, will you."

"No."

"I love you, Dad."

Gideon grunted. There was quiet, and then I heard Gideon's voice telling Amos and Elam to get back to work.

I moved from my hiding place to see Levi walk back to his truck, his gaze steady ahead. I knew in an instant that he'd expected for the conversation to go the way it had, and yet he'd done it anyway.

The truck engine started up. I could see the women watching from inside the house.

I fought the urge to run up to Levi to comfort him, to talk to him. He didn't want to talk to me.

He didn't look at me as he got back into his truck and started the ignition. I watched as the tires moved against the gravel drive and he drove away. Out of my life, and as far as I could tell, out of his family's lives.

I turned to go back to the house. My eyes caught Ida's as I neared the door. Her old eyes regarded me with an expression I hadn't seen before.

She met me at the door. "I need my sewing box. Would you mind helping me carry it from my car? My back ain't what it used to be."

I agreed, following her back out.

"He's in love with you, isn't he." She made the statement mere moments after the front door closed.

"We were together for a little while. He broke it off." I knew any attempt to hedge on the truth with Ida would be pointless.

"Do you still love him?"

"He left."

"He still loves you."

I shook my head. Ida opened her car door and pointed at the box. I leaned in and pulled it out, noticing that only a person with significant movement loss would have difficulty carrying it.

"He looks at you with love in his eyes. There is hurt, too, but Levi has never been good at hiding his thoughts from his face. Even as a boy. I knew he would leave. If only he could have been Mennonite, his family might have forgiven him. But once he grew his wings, he couldn't help flying far." She patted my cheek. "I don't know what happened between you. He loves you, though, Jayne. Don't worry."

She turned and walked back to the house with impressive speed. I followed her with the sewing box. All I could think of was the raw memory of Levi leaving my apartment and not coming back.

Chapter 32

Samuel, Leah, and Elizabeth returned home from school that afternoon, cheeks rosy and eyes bright. Ida, Martha, and Sara were all still in the throes of a large mending session, so Martha asked me if I'd mind helping the children.

"Your mom told me I'm helping you with your homework," I announced, trying to sound energized and pro-education.

They nodded.

"Where do you normally study?"

"The kitchen table," Leah answered.

"Okay." I clapped my hands together. "Do you eat a snack while you do homework?"

Three shaking heads.

"Okay. What kind of homework do you have?"

They each pulled their books out of their knapsacks. I picked one up.

The textbook would have looked at home in Punky Brewster's book bag. I flipped to the copyright page and checked the publication date—1979.

The map in the social studies book showed the USSR covering half the world in bright red. Germany remained divided.

I forced a smile. "Let's get started."

I made a point of flipping through whatever books weren't in use as the children studied. "Do you ever study science?" I asked, trying to sound nonchalant.

Samuel shook his head. "We learn reading, 'riting, and 'rithmetic."

Which would explain my having to introduce Sara to the world of spores and molds several weeks before.

I wanted to talk to Levi. I wanted him to explain to me why the eight years of education these children were afforded were so poor.

He must have worked hard to get to where he was if his schooling was the same. I rubbed my forehead. I knew from some of my reading that it wasn't always like this, that some Amish children attended public school or studied under trained teachers.

I answered their questions about math figures as best I could. When they came to a point when they understood the material, such as it was, and the questions ceased for the foreseeable future, I wandered back to the sewing group and my own quilt strips.

"Did Sara tell you she's getting baptized next week?" Martha asked.

I nearly impaled my finger on one of the straight pins. "Really?" My head whipped around to where Sara sat. "That's...exciting."

Ida's eyes watched my every move. I could feel her gaze.

"Sara, tell Jayne about the baptism service," Martha said, encouraging Sara with a nod.

Sara cleared her throat. "It's part of the church service. Before the baptism, the bishop will ask applicants to leave the service, and then he asks if we're sure we want to be baptized. It's kind of silly, since we've all taken a class about it."

"We'll be asked a few questions before we return to the hymns and the sermon. Afterward, the bishop will have us go to the front. He'll remind us we're making a promise to God. Then he and the deacon—Mary Lapp's John—will take the bucket and cup. John pours water over the bishop's hands and then onto our heads three times in the name of the Father, the Son, and the Holy Ghost." She shrugged. "And then we're told to rise and such, and Mary, being the deacon's wife and all, will give me and the other girls the Holy Kiss."

"Of brotherhood," Martha added.

"Of brotherhood," Sara finished. "But shouldn't it be sisterhood?"

"It's family," Ida said, "whichever way you look at it."

I tried not to look confused. When we'd spoken over the breakfast dishes, Sara hadn't said a word.

"Don't baptisms usually precede weddings?" I asked, fishing.

"Often," Martha said, not looking up from her sewing. "But not always."

I smiled at Sara. "I'm glad for you." If that was the path she had truly chosen for herself, I really did wish her all the best.

~~·≈∜∕⋘∼~~

The rest of the day was a blur. After helping the children with their homework, I finished sewing the front of my quilt together.

I should have felt better about it than I did. As a first quilt, it wasn't the shoddiest specimen.

But something wasn't right. It wasn't Amish enough.

My thoughts traveled back to Levi. I thought briefly of giving Shane a call, but I thought better of it. Shane and I were over, and I was okay with that. Levi and I on the other hand—we were over, but I *wasn't* okay with that.

Not that it mattered anymore. I tried to think of something else. I couldn't think of anything else. I tried harder.

At some point while trying harder, I fell asleep.

And dreamed about Levi.

~~·≈∜∕⋘∼~~

I woke when the rooster crowed, horrified to hear several sets of feet moving throughout the house. I threw on my clothes and hurried out to join the others.

Leah met me in the hallway. "Today is Sara's birthday!"

"Really?" I gave her a hug as we walked toward the kitchen. "How old is she?"

"Eighteen!" Sara announced from behind us.

"I remember being eighteen," I said, smiling ruefully.

Of course, my eighteen and her eighteen were two different things entirely. If I remembered right, I celebrated by registering to vote, showing up at the elections office with my purple-streaked hair and Smashing Pumpkins T-shirt.

Sara, on the other hand, wouldn't be voting anytime soon, and her lovely brown hair was twisted up under her kapp.

"Will you celebrate today?" I asked.

Leah nodded and swung my hand from side to side. "We'll celebrate at dinner. *Mutter* will make a cake and roast a ham."

"Sounds delicious! Do you get presents?"

"Yes," Sara straightened her apron. "Probably some new shoes."

I stopped my sarcastic "Oh goody" comment from leaving my lips just in time.

"My sister Rebecca and her family might take a taxi from Washington and stay with Grandma," Sara added. "You haven't met Rebecca."

"Not yet, but it sounds like I will."

We ate a breakfast of dried apple muffins, eggs scrambled with peppers and bacon, fried potatoes, and sausage patties. After helping with the dishes, I made my excuses and drove into town, determined to find an appropriate birthday gift for Sara.

I may have driven past the shop. I wasn't *stalking* Levi, just checking to see if there was a sale or lease sign in front of the building. Just in case.

There wasn't. I proceeded to Fred Meyer's. What do you buy for an Amish teenager that you can give her in front of her family? If it were only between the two of us, and if she weren't being baptized, then I would go a little crazier, maybe find her a pair of sequined flip-flops for the summer. Or a bright scarf with fringe.

Probably should have checked with Martha first.

I wandered out of Fred Meyer's, got back into my car, and drove around until the red glowing sign of inspiration appeared: JoAnn Fabrics.

Inside, I chose several bolts of fabric I thought Sara might like and bought a yard each. I drove back to Freddie's for a gift bag, tissue paper, and a card.

I didn't know if the Amish did birthday cards, but I bought one anyway.

After wrapping the fabric in paper and stuffing it elegantly into the sack, I signed the card and drove back to the Burkholders'.

"Something's baking," I called as I stepped inside. I found Martha in the kitchen. "It smells wonderful, whatever it is."

"Sara doesn't have a single favorite cake, so I make a five-layer cake with every layer a different flavor."

"Oh!" That could either be very good or very bad. "What flavors?

"Pumpkin, coconut, chocolate, raspberry, and lemon poppy seed."

"Oh." The jury might remain out for a while on that one. "Need a hand?"

"I'd appreciate it. Sara's birthday is the second most difficult of all my children's."

"Who's the first?"

"Elam. He doesn't like cake, so I make varieties of ice cream for him."

"From scratch?"

"Yes," Martha answered, but at that moment her gaze became shifty. "Well," she said with a lowered voice, "last year I was very busy with Rebecca's baby's quilt, so I…" her voice dropped still lower, "I *bought* ice cream."

"Martha!"

"And I made sure I got three flavors I hadn't made before so they wouldn't be able to compare."

I couldn't help but laugh. "Very sneaky. I would have done the exact same thing."

Actually, that wasn't true. I wouldn't have gotten conned into making three batches of ice cream in the first place. My mom used to make ice cream, and even with an electric ice-cream maker, it was labor-intensive. She would stand at the stove for ages, stirring the custard. Make three batches of heat-sensitive custard and then churn it? No, thank you.

"Do you make the same cake combination every year?"

"No. Last year it was carrot, yellow, ginger-pecan, chocolate chip, and Jell-O orange."

I couldn't even imagine, but a part of me wished I could. I wondered what it would be like to spend my days in a kitchen, cooking and baking for my family. To know what my children liked best for their birthdays.

The birthday party unfolded through dinner. Sara arrived at the table in her favorite dress—her favorite, I knew, because it was the brightest-colored one she owned. The rich brick red of her dress, covered by her black apron, accentuated the color in her cheeks and the green of her eyes.

Rebecca and her family arrived via taxi moments later. Out of all the siblings, she bore the strongest resemblance to Levi with her dark eyes and fair skin. She carried Baby Verna on her hip, while her husband, Karl, held young Henry.

Karl's genial smile faded the moment he saw me, dressed as I was in blue jeans and clearly not Amish. But Gideon jumped in and explained how I had called the ambulance for him when he'd had his heart attack and sang my praises about the way I'd cared for Martha and Sara while he was in the hospital, or, as he referred to it, "the clink."

He clearly didn't know that Levi had also been with us, but that was information for another day.

Ida appeared at the door, bearing a giant smile, and the gathering was complete. Complete except for Levi.

We crowded around the table and gazed at the beauty of the dinner provided. Martha had prepared—on top of the five-layer cake o' wonder—a ham crusted with brown sugar, creamy mashed potatoes, fresh green beans, buttery rolls, and homemade peach butter.

Everyone ate and laughed and told stories about Sara. When we'd all had our fill of dinner, we retired to the living room for a round of Parcheesi while we digested. Sara won, although I suspected everyone let her.

I came in second.

After the game, Martha called Rebecca and me to the dining room. Ida joined us. Within moments we had the dinner dishes cleared and cake plates out. Everyone else filed into the room, and Martha brought in the lit cake, all five layers of it.

I half expected the weight of it to send her toppling over, but after a lifetime of manual labor, Martha had untold brawn beneath her sleeves.

Applause broke out as she approached the table. Elam and Rebecca teased Sara about the flavors, throwing out potential candidates, such as licorice, pork roast, twigs, and bark.

The latter two were suggested by Elizabeth.

As we sang Sara "Happy Birthday," my eye caught something through the kitchen window. I dismissed it as one of the animals on the farm. Sara opened her gifts one by one—fancy molded soaps from Rebecca, a new pair of shoes from Gideon and Martha, a set of thimbles from Elam, a new dress from Ida. Sara's face lit up when she lifted the fabrics from the gift bag I'd chosen.

"Do you like them?" I asked, although there wasn't much I could do if she didn't.

"Very much," she answered, hugging them to her slim body.

Something moving outside the window caught my attention again. For the briefest moment, I thought I saw Levi in the darkness.

�≈⚬⚬≈�

I went to bed that night, warm from the time of family happiness and yet aching in my heart. I didn't want to leave the farm. Not ever.

⚭≈⚬⚬≈⚮

With the weather just beginning to warm up, Martha spent the majority of her day in the vegetable garden.

I watched from the window and spent a moment envying her ability to provide for her family through the work of her hands. I felt the familiar wrench in my chest at the calm in her life, the lack of distractions, how much purer things were in the shelter of the farmhouse.

Why couldn't I be like that? Why couldn't I keep my apartment clean? I didn't even have children, and clutter still accumulated. My quilt looked like a child's attempt, and I wasn't about to garden anytime soon.

This is not where I have called you.

I stepped back from the window as if I'd been zapped and looked around.

Are you sure? I asked back to the voice, so familiar and unfamiliar at the same time. *If I'm going to follow You, can't I follow You better here? Fewer distractions, no television, no internet—just You and me and the land?*

My questions were met with silence, but it didn't matter. I had already heard the voice.

I sighed and decided to take another walk.

———

The wind whipped my hair into my face; I kept brushing it away, even though I knew it would be back in the shortest of moments.

I wanted to stay at the farmhouse. It was that simple. But the more I thought about it, the more I realized the reason why I wanted to stay was because I liked myself better when I was with the Burkholders. I liked helping with the children. I liked being useful.

Could I still be useful in the outside world? Probably. Most likely. Yes. But it was so much more picturesque at the farm, with the bonnets and the buggies.

And yet, I knew the "picturesque" part wasn't entirely real. Levi's family was every bit as dysfunctional as my own. More, if you considered that at least my father acknowledged me as his child until the day he died. I had watched Gideon readily forgive a buggy thief but turn Levi away.

I knew the children were not receiving a quality education, so much more detrimental considering they only had eight years of it. Did it matter? I thought so. We were called to minister to the world, and it was hard to understand the world if you were unaware of the goings-on for the past thirty years.

Even though my return to the church was recent, I still knew in my heart that my God was a personal God, a gracious God, a God who cared less for our deeds than the quality of our hearts.

I didn't know what He was calling me to, or where, but I wanted the quality of my heart to matter. I wanted my actions to stem from love rather than tradition, guilt, or habit. Just because my life wasn't simple didn't make it insignificant. Owning a cell phone didn't make me a lesser person.

I sighed. It was time to go home.

Chapter 33

Are you packing?"

I turned to see Sara in my doorway. "Hi there. Yes, I'm packing. It's time for me to leave."

"But—you only just got here."

"I need to get back to the paper." And to the rest of my life, such as it was. "It's time."

"Your quilt! You haven't finished your quilt!"

"I will."

"Do you have a sewing machine at your apartment?"

"No..."

"Then how?"

"My mom. I'll take it with me when I visit."

"Oh," Sara said, her rosy mouth stretching into a frown.

"You can still write me," I said, continuing to fold. "Although, I probably shouldn't include..." I let my voice drop, in case we had listeners. Little ones. "You're getting baptized soon, after all."

Sara shuffled her feet. "Yeah."

I wondered if she was really ready, but it wasn't my place to question.

"I'm looking forward to it. Getting baptized."

She said it with the enthusiasm most people show toward dental work.

"I'm glad," I said. "I don't suppose anyone's taking pictures."

Sara rolled her eyes. "We don't believe in posing for pictures."

"You wouldn't be posing. You're already there, getting baptized. Speaking of photos—would anyone mind if I took a couple shots before I left?"

"I don't know. Ask my mom."

"Good idea."

I tucked a few more items away and left to find Martha. I found her in the kitchen, scrubbing her hands free of soil. "I think I'll be leaving this evening," I said, not knowing how else to start.

Martha dried her hands on the checkered dishtowel by the sink. "We'll be sorry to lose you, but I'm sure you have work to get back to."

"I do. I was wondering...would you mind if I took a few pictures? Nothing intrusive, but it would be nice for the piece I'll be writing."

She shifted uncomfortably. "No faces, no posing, please." She gave a slight smile. "I trust you."

I returned her smile. "Thank you."

~≈≫≪≈~

With Martha's blessing, I pulled my digital Canon SLR from its protective case, checked my battery and memory card, and set out on the farm.

I didn't profess to be a photographer of any skill, but it's one of those things that proves to be a useful skill when working for a paper in the day and age of media-downsizing.

And photographing the Amish. Seriously. As long as the photo was in focus, it looked amazing. Amish laundry was like that. To them it was just wet clothes drying—to us, mystical art.

The weather, while warmer, was still damp enough to mean there were dresses, pants, shirts, and aprons of various sizes drying inside on the rack. Not as picturesque as items flapping in the breeze on a sunny day, but they would do.

I took some shots of the buggy, some shots of the tidy white farmhouse from the road. Back inside, I watched as Martha puttered in the kitchen preparing lunch.

I kept my word. Every time I snapped the shutter, her features faced away from the lens.

Using a telephoto lens, I zoomed in on her hands as she worked, hoping I caught the lines and signs of labor on her skin. I snapped away as she immersed her hands in a bowl of bread dough.

"This ain't much interesting," Martha commented. I could hear the chuckle in her voice.

"Everyone's hands are interesting."

"You can see my hands?"

"With this lens, yes."

She brushed the flour residue away. "May I try?"

"Of course." I gave her the camera, telling her where to place her eye, where the digital sample showed up, and how to move the lens in and out.

"May I take a picture?"

I grinned. "Be my guest. The button is on the top."

She pushed it and then jumped when the shutter snapped. "I think I took a picture of the floor."

"Try again."

She pointed the camera out the window, snapped, and then peered at the tiny image at the back of the camera. "That's pretty." She tilted it toward me. "See? Oh. It disappeared. Is it gone?"

I shook my head. "It only shows for a moment after you've taken the picture." I pressed the right combination of buttons to bring the image back. "That is nice. You have a good eye."

Martha looked at the camera, looked outside, looked back at the camera, and then looked at me. "Are you done taking pictures?"

"Almost. Would you like to take some?"

"Such a fancy camera—I'd be afraid of a-breakin' it."

"Company camera. Have at it."

I made a point of returning to my packing, giving Martha the freedom to experiment how she wished. From the living room window, I could see her examining the mailbox, the barn, and the cows in the pasture. I watched as Sara walked out to meet her and said something—I couldn't hear what.

Not that I was spying or anything. Just watching out for the camera.

Martha nodded, Sara departed, Martha shot for a little while longer before returning to the house.

I busied myself folding the pile of dishcloths on the counter.

※

I didn't see Sara for the rest of the afternoon, and for that matter, I didn't see much of Martha either. I was making sure I had enough shots of the farm and checking under the bed for stray socks.

The kids came home from school, rowdy and energized. Martha sent them outside for chores; when they finished, they began a game of pickup volleyball in the field, using the summer clothesline as the net.

Martha reappeared for the dinner preparations. But everything became clear after the meal—as I stood in the entryway with my bags packed, I realized what I'd forgotten. "My quilt," I said, looking around. What had happened to it? It hadn't been in my room. "Sara, you haven't seen my quilt around, have you?"

Her expression turned guilty. "I...um...let me look."

We waited. When she returned, she was carrying my quilt in her hands, but not the way I'd remembered it. "Sara..."

"I finished it."

She had. The strips were all sewn together, and it even had a back. And batting in the middle. "You didn't have to—"

"Yes. You wouldn't have been able to finish it before summer."

Okay. Likely true. I gave her a hug. "Thank you, sweetie."

"I worked all afternoon on it."

I examined the quilt in closer detail. "It looks fantastic." I thought of her one-time hope to leave and become a fashion designer. Sara had such talent. I wished her all the best—and hoped that she'd be able to use her talent within the culture she'd chosen.

An expression passed over her face, but I didn't have long to decipher its meaning. Martha brought me a light cloth bag to carry my quilt in, and Elam offered to carry my luggage.

I thanked him and walked toward the door while Leah and Elizabeth clutched my good hand and begged me to write them too.

"Do you want your things in the car or the trunk?" Elam asked.

"Car is fine," I said, trying to twirl two little girls with one hand and nearly falling over in the process. Dusk had fallen. I had trouble seeing the keyhole for the car door. The Amish weren't much for outdoor lighting.

I said my goodbyes to everyone. Or was it everyone? "Where's Sara?"

Martha patted my arm. "Don't know where she got off to. I think she's a mite sad you're goin'. She misses having Rebecca in the house. You've become like an older sister to her."

All the more reason to say goodbye. I thought about looking for her, but the farm was just too big, and I wanted to make it back to Portland early enough to unpack and sit for a while before bed.

I sighed, waved goodbye, and climbed into my car.

Time to go.

My heart still broke a little when I returned home. I would be alone, again. Maybe I should think about a roommate. I supposed I could rearrange things. I could move my office into my room, even if sleep specialists advised against working in the room you slept in. But after being with the Burkholders, living alone held little appeal.

I parked my car in at the base of the stairs, got out, and started removing bags.

That's when I heard it. Or did I?

I held very still and waited.

There it was. A thump. A thump from the back of my car. The trunk.

Why would there be a thump?

My mind raced over all the reasons for a thump in a not-running car.

There could be a serial killer in the trunk, waiting to kill me when I was stupid enough to lift the lid.

There could be a spare bowling ball in my trunk, and it was still rolling around after I parked. I dismissed that idea quickly, considering I didn't own a bowling ball.

A small animal could have jumped inside, but I couldn't remember when it was last open.

Another thump.

I sent up a short prayer for my safety and opened the trunk with my key.

"Hi, Jayne."

"Sara!" I exploded. "What are you doing there?"

She sat up. "I'm out!"

"No you're not, you're still in my trunk. What were you thinking? Is this why you disappeared earlier?"

She stretched her arms. "I'm *out*, you see?" She held out her hand—I thought she wanted help out, but I realized what she had in her fist. It was her kapp.

"You're…leaving?"

"Yes. Can I get out of your trunk?"

"Please." I stood back and watched her climb out. Naturally, once both of her feet touched asphalt, the heavens opened and a torrent of rain fell from the sky. To make things better, a nice, strong Columbia Gorge wind blew the water sideways.

I closed the trunk as quickly as I could, grabbed my things from the backseat, and raced up the stairs with Sara right behind me.

Once inside, I slammed the door behind us and plopped my things on the floor. "You're soaked through." Sara hadn't thought to bring a coat or cape of any kind; her cotton dress clung to her shoulders and dripped on the entryway tile. "You can't wear wet clothes. You didn't bring anything?"

"Why would I bring any of my Amish clothes? I want to stay here."

"Oh, I don't know. So you'd have something to wear?"

"We're about the same size."

If I wasn't careful, she might alter my things to fit her. "We'll find you something dry, and then we're going to talk."

"I'm not going back."

"I want you to tell me that when you're dry, not before."

In my bedroom, Sara took charge of the clothing situation, parsing through my little closet and choosing items for herself.

Incidentally, they were mostly items I'd picked up in Lincoln City.

When she was dried and dressed, and I had changed into thick, woolly socks, I steered her out to my dining room and sat her down at the table.

"First," I said, although so many thoughts clamored for the title of "first" that I hardly knew what to say, "it was very dangerous for you to ride in my trunk like that. What if I had gotten rear-ended? You wouldn't have had any protection."

"But we didn't."

"What if we had?"

She squinted at me. "But we didn't."

All right. Excellent progress. "Did you tell anyone you were planning on doing this?"

"No."

"Not even Ida or Levi?"

"No."

"You realize your mother thinks you're getting baptized on Sunday?"

Sara looked at her lap. "I know. I couldn't do it. I didn't want to live a lie no more."

"Sara—" I searched for words. "I left home at eighteen. I went to college, and I rarely went back. Things with my dad were never good, but I also never tried to meet with my mom or my sister. I never tried to make things better. It wasn't a priority, and I was hiding. I missed out on a lot. Lately, I've been able to go back and have a relationship with my family. They've forgiven me—things have been good. I'm still me, still a journalist, still living in the city, but I can visit them whenever I want. It won't be like that for you, not with your father. He may never be able to forgive you. I want to help you in whatever ways I can, but you need to know what you're giving up."

Her gaze was direct and calm. "I know what I'm giving up. I've thought much about this. I want to design clothes, wear lipstick, and meet a boy I haven't known since I was born."

"I'm sure your family visits relatives in other communities—"

"They're all the same. They're all Plain. They all want wives to cook and give them children. I cook, and I would like children, but maybe not eight. And maybe not cook every meal, every day. I look at my mother and wonder how her arms have not fallen off. I don't want that life." She reached into her pocket and said, "I've kept this with me so that when you left, I could go too."

I peered at the contents of her pocket—a fold of cash and a Social Security card with "Sara M. Burkholder" printed above the nine-digit ID number.

"I'm not a minor anymore," Sara continued. "I don't need my parents to sign for me. I have my card and the money I saved up."

"How much?"

"Three thousand six hundred fifty-three dollars."

My eyebrows flew upward. "Where did you get that kind of money?"

"I sold two of my more complicated quilts. Some babysitting. I saved up."

I couldn't save like that at eighteen, and I'd thought myself fairly motivated at the time.

I was about to ask if she had any specific plans, aside from the lipstick-wearing, when my phone buzzed in my purse. I almost ignored it, but a tiny thought encouraged me to take a look at the caller.

It was Levi.

Chapter 34

Jayne, please tell me Sara is there with you." I could clearly hear the panic in Levi's voice. His alarm broke my heart.

"Levi...hold on." I pressed the mute button and looked to Sara. I almost asked if it would be all right for me to tell him, but thought better of it. I couldn't lie to Levi.

"She's here," I said, after reconnecting the call.

He exhaled into the receiver; it sounded like a windstorm. "That's good, because I'm halfway there."

A part of me bristled. The way he'd left before—I didn't know if I was ready for him to come back, much less uninvited.

He must have read my mind, or at least my silence. "I'm sorry. I know I should ask first, or be sensitive, but she's my sister, Jayne. You can drop her off at the corner if you want to."

"Drop her off at the corner? In this rain? In the middle of Portland at night? Are you insane?"

"I'm sorry, really sorry. I was just trying to think of a way that you wouldn't have to be involved."

"She hitched a ride in the trunk of my car and is wearing a pair of my jeans. I'm already involved."

"I didn't—I didn't want it to be like this between us."

"I have no idea what to say to that."

"Can we talk about it?"

"*I* wanted to talk about it. You left."

"I was upset."

"And you're not now?"

"I never meant to hurt you."

"Too late," I said, and then I realized I'd revealed too much. I hung up before I could say anything more. "So," I turned back to Sara. "Maybe before your brother comes you should tell me how you got into my trunk in the first place. That was pretty slick. Have you been practicing?"

"I took your keys when you told me you were packing."

"Oh?"

Her eyes shifted downward. "And I opened the trunk. There was a little ridge on the inside, just enough for me to pull it closed."

"But I saw you right before I left. I had my keys in my pocket."

"I left after I gave you the quilt. I didn't close your trunk all the way earlier."

"What would you have done if I'd decided to put my things in the trunk? Your brother would have seen you!"

She shrugged. "When you came, I saw you had stuff on the seat of your car. I figured you would do the same when you left."

"For Pete's sake." I rubbed my head. "Have you ever thought about working for the CIA?"

"What's the CIA?"

"People who can sneak around almost as skillfully as you."

"People who sneak are called CIA?"

"Never mind. Did I tell you how dangerous it is to ride in a trunk like that?"

"Yes. What happened between you and Levi?"

"I don't want to talk about it. Want something to drink? Bear in mind I haven't grocery-shopped."

We passed the time over tea, a stale package of Oreos, and *I Love Lucy* until there was a knock at the door.

A knock I recognized. I opened the door and there he was—six feet, three inches of gorgeous heartbreak.

I wanted to hate him. He made it difficult. But my feet felt cold just remembering the night I ran after him. My back straightened. "Come on in."

"Thanks." The door closed behind him; he kicked off his shoes. I wish he'd kept them on. Being in stocking feet together felt much too intimate. "Sara...are you okay?"

I rolled my eyes. "Of course she's okay. She's had tea and cookies and is watching *I Love Lucy*."

"Sara?" Levi persisted. "You didn't tell me about this. I wish you had."

"You don't have to baby me anymore," Sara said in a soft voice. "I'm eighteen now. Girls my age are getting married and starting their adult lives. I'm starting mine the way I want to. The way I've always wanted to."

I sat back down and gestured for Levi to follow. We formed a triangle: Sara and me on the sofa, Levi in the overstuffed chair by the door. I turned down the TV volume. The antics of Lucy and her cohorts cast flickering silver light on our awkward little gathering.

"I just want you to know what you're getting into." Levi tented his hands as he spoke. "Dad won't acknowledge me as his son. Mom has to obey him, but she'll be conflicted. Amos and Elam never forgave me; Rebecca might talk to me if her husband allowed it. Grandma will support you. You know I will…I just want you to be prepared."

When Sara explained to him about her Social Security card and cash stash, Levi's eyes widened. "That's very good."

"Have you thought about what you want to do, specifically?" I asked.

"I want to get my GED and attend the Art Institute of Portland. I want to study apparel design." She reached into her other pocket, pulling out a much-folded school brochure. "I will apply for financial aid. I will get a job and earn money. If I need to, I will make quilts and take in mending to support myself."

"Why did you leave with Jayne?" Levi asked in a quiet voice. "What you did was dangerous. You could have come to me."

"You are too close. I could have changed my mind and walked home."

Levi gave a wry smile. "You can stay with me at my house. Get your GED at Linn Benton Community College. Come to Portland when you're ready."

"Too close." Sara shrugged. "Here, I can't go back."

<hr />

An hour later Sara's adrenaline began to fade and the fact that she'd been awake since five kicked in. Levi checked his watch and looked at me. "Let's go check on that bookcase I made for you."

I wasn't stupid. I knew that was code for "I want to talk to you without Sara hearing, and it probably wouldn't be appropriate to go to your bedroom, so let's hit the study."

I didn't mention how I'd had an urge to chuck the bookcase from the landing. The fact that I couldn't lift any of it—dismantled or not—without personal injury was the main factor stopping me. That, and the fact that I had too many books.

We both rose and walked down the hall. I turned to check on Sara just in time to watch her eyes close in sleep.

Sleep, or she was sneaky enough to pretend. I didn't care either way. The powwow was Levi's idea, not mine.

He closed the door behind us. Like that wasn't suspicious. "I'm so sorry about all of this," he said.

"Yeah, I'm sure you are." I ran a hand through my hair. After all, Sara being in my apartment meant that I was being dragged into the center of a complicated family issue—one I was sure I didn't fully understand the implications of. That, and it meant Levi's continued presence in my life.

I didn't know how I felt about that.

"Thing is," Levi continued, "unless you ask her to, I don't think she'll leave here."

"I was getting that."

"Are you okay with an eighteen-year-old roommate?"

"She's not a normal eighteen-year-old, Levi. You know that. She's been groomed since birth to be ready to run a household and raise a family. Most girls—women—her age can barely do their own laundry. Sara can do it without a connection to city power."

"She's my baby sister."

"No, Elizabeth is your baby sister. Sara's grown now, and you're her hero. She watched you leave and make a life for yourself. She wants to do the same."

"I made a life, and then I compromised that life."

I hated the bitter tone I heard in his voice. "You came back so you could be available to your family, available to Sara."

"And she hopped a ride in the trunk of your car."

"She wouldn't have done that if she didn't have a goal. You gave her those brochures, didn't you?"

"I did."

"She's owning this, can't you see? She's not leaving because you pressured her into it. She strategized, planned—it's hers. You should be proud."

"You're okay with her moving in with you?"

"Sure. She's more qualified to live without adult supervision than I am."

"Trunk, Jayne. Trunk."

"Yeah, well, she probably won't let as much mold grow in the fridge as I do."

"True." He looked around the study. "Where would you put her?"

"Probably in here."

"I'll bring up a bed tomorrow from the shop."

"She left the Amish and you'll bring her an Amish-style bed?"

"If she's going to be a student, she needs to learn not to look a gift horse in the mouth."

A bed. One more object from Levi, one more arrival to be nervous about. I didn't want involvement with him. I couldn't take being hurt again.

"I'm sorry about earlier," he said.

I wanted to punch him for being considerate. "Oh?"

"I wish things didn't happen the way they did."

That was vague.

"Okay. Um…well, if she's going to stay here tonight, I need to make up a bed for her on the couch."

Levi opened his mouth as if to say something, but he must have thought better of it. "I'll be back tomorrow."

"If I'm not here, Sara will let you in."

"What hours are you working tomorrow?"

"Don't know."

"Guess?"

"Wouldn't want to say, in case I get a call."

"What kind of call?"

"The 'Jayne, there's a breaking story' kind of call." I didn't mention that since I'd been in features, a whole series of people would have to be extraordinarily unavailable for me to get that call. It could happen, I suppose. Gas leaks aren't an urban myth.

"I can always wait around for you here, if you're late getting home."

"What?"

"It's a long day for Sara to be home alone. I'll come up whenever and keep her company."

There was no getting around him. "Sure, whatever. Anything else?"

He took so long to answer that I lifted my hand. "While you think, I'm going to make a bed up for her."

In a matter of moments I had my spare bedding gathered, and this time Sara was truly asleep.

"She's a heavy sleeper," Levi commented.

"No kidding." I struggled to lift her head high enough to put a pillow underneath.

"Let me help." He reached under his sister and lifted her gently from the couch. While Sara was aloft, literally, I tucked a sheet under the back of the cushions and arranged the pillows. After he laid her back down, we both tucked a comforter over her sleeping form.

We stepped back, neither of us daring to look at the other. I'll admit that a part of me wanted to be next—I wanted to be tucked in too.

Cold feet. Cold feet.

"Have a safe drive," I said.

Levi took the hint and walked to the door. "Thanks. I'll see you tomorrow."

I thought about imploring him to leave me alone, to keep me out of things, to treat me as Sara's roommate, nothing more. Instead I said nothing as I watched Levi put on his shoes, thread his arms into his coat, and leave, pretending he hadn't broken my heart.

And pretending I hadn't broken his.

***

Sara woke up at her usual time, five a.m. I came to that realization shortly after deciding that my apartment hadn't been broken into, and the person making a loud breakfast for herself in my kitchen had in fact been invited.

I tried the traditional techniques; burying my head in my pillow, pulling the covers over my head. What no one ever tells you is that doing either of those things makes the air too warm to breathe.

Finally I swung my feet around to the floor, threw on my college sweats, and walked down the hall to the kitchen.

"Good morning!" Sara greeted me with a bright smile and a hug. "I woke up this morning when the sun streamed through the window over there. You get such very good light in here! I thought about staying in bed—I slept so well! But I decided to get up and make us some breakfast."

My brain really only caught the last bits of her speech. "Us?"

"I made pancakes and eggs, and I found some bacon in your freezer, so I scrambled it with the eggs and put cheese on top, hope you like that, I couldn't remember. Do you have potatoes? It's so nice to have potatoes around. Potatoes and onions. You never know when you'll need a good onion, and they go with every meal. Potatoes too—"

I held up a hand. "We'll shop for groceries later. Can breakfast wait until I've showered?"

Sara nodded.

"Okay. I'll be back." I turned and all but stumbled into the bathroom. I considered it a success to get into the shower without finding that I'd brought a sock in with me. Afterward I felt better, the sleep cleared from my eyes and some of the mental cobwebs cleared out of the way. I dusted on a bit of light makeup and went back to my room to dress, knowing all the while that Sara might find fault with my ensemble.

To my surprise, she didn't say a word about my clothes as she served our respective breakfasts onto two plates. Instead, she asked when we were leaving for work.

"We?" I asked, my fork hovering halfway between my mouth and the plate.

Sara nodded. "I thought I'd go with you this morning and then come home at lunch."

My first thought was, "I'd lose my parking spot." This was Portland, by the way. I had never parked illegally until I moved here. But my second thought was that it wasn't fair to leave her alone in my apartment all day. There wasn't a farm to run; she would be bored to tears. I could get her a visitor pass, especially considering that her family was the focus of the piece I'd be writing.

"If I bring you this morning, you'll need to bring a book or something to keep you busy." There was a computer bay, but throwing Sara into the internet would be like chucking her into the deep end of the swimming pool without arm floaties.

She nodded. "I'll just sit. I'll take my sketchbook. I can watch people and get ideas."

"Yeah, maybe I'll take you to the ad department for that. They're usually a little snappier than reporting and editorial."

"Can you take me shopping soon? I would like to buy some of my own clothes."

"What's wrong with my jeans?" I said, rolling my eyes before I smiled. "Sure. I'll see when Gemma's available. Or Kim—she can be good at finding sales."

"I like sales."

I knew Levi would have to figure into all of this at some point.

Which meant I would have to call him.

I mulled that over as Sara showered and readied herself for her first day as an English girl.

Chapter 35

Sara and I ran into Kim inside the foyer of the *Oregonian* offices.
Of all mornings.

"Jayne! You're back. Who's this?"

Thinking I could be saved by brevity, I smiled and kept it short. "This is Sara. She's my new roommate."

"Sara?" Kim looked at me, looked at Sara, and then looked back at me. "The Amish girl?"

I could see Sara wilt. "Look, she left and she moved in with me. She's hanging out with me this morning until lunch."

"It's 'take your Amish roommate to work' day? Wish I'd gotten the memo." She touched Sara's shoulder. "Sorry, great line, couldn't resist. Want to grab lunch with us? We'll make Gemma take us out."

I was going to protest, but Sara's face had taken on an almost unearthly glow of joy. "Lunch sounds good," I said. "But right now I need to get her a visitor's pass—"

"Wait." Kim held out her hand. "This isn't Levi's sister, is it?"

"Um, yeah, it is. So, we'll see you at lunch—"

"Any changes on that front?"

"Have a good morning!" I all but yanked Sara's arm as I tried to make a break for it.

"She asks a lot of questions, doesn't she," Sara said as we'd turned a corner and I'd determined a safety level that allowed us to walk at a normal pace.

"Occupational hazard."

Once Sara was processed and armed with a badge, I set her up on a couch not far from my cubicle. I left her with written instructions on how to find me, my phone extension, and an assortment of dollar bills if she wanted something from the vending machine.

At my desk I plugged my camera's memory card into the USB reader and took a look at the images I'd gathered. The buggy, the barn, the stone path up to the door of the farmhouse. My pictures were fairly straightforward. Then others began to load, and I realized they were Martha's.

Martha. Where was she in all of this? A mixture of guilt and grief clutched at my heart. Her daughter had left, and she used me to accomplish that. Martha had taken me into her home, treated me like family, and this is what had happened. I couldn't help but feel it was my fault.

Had Levi communicated back to Martha that Sara was safe, dry, and had a roof over her head? The thought worried me so much I picked up the phone to ask.

"Jayne? Is Sara okay?" Levi asked as soon as he answered.

"She is. She's at work with me. I was just wondering—did you tell your mom? Does she know Sara's with me?"

"I told her Sara is safe, but I didn't say where. I wouldn't put it past Elam and Amos—or my father—to try to bring her home."

"Drive all the way up in the buggy?"

"No, they'd take a taxi."

"Oh. But they're pacifists. The worst they would do is spend the night on the landing."

"You don't think that would be a little traumatic for Sara?"

"She's stronger than you realize. Your mother needs to know where her daughter is."

"Jayne, you don't understand—"

"I have a pretty good hunch that mothers, no matter where they live or what they believe, generally want to know where their children are, even if it's just a general idea. Your mother's been very kind to me. It's the least I can do."

He sighed. "It's your call. It's your apartment. Don't underestimate the mail brigade, though."

"The male brigade? Are we talking about your brothers again?"

"Mail, as in the post. Rebecca wrote me letter after letter telling me how Mom cried herself to sleep every night and how much my siblings missed me. I asked my grandma once. It wasn't *that* bad. Does anyone at the house have your mailing address?"

"Sara did. It's probably written down somewhere in her room."

"Mom will find it."

"I'm not afraid of Amish mail."

"Sara's doing okay with everything?"

"Honestly?" I looked all around, making sure she hadn't snuck up on me. "I don't think it's all sunk in yet. She's running on a lot of adrenaline. How was it for you when you first left?"

He exhaled. "It got harder as I realized what I'd done, but I didn't go back."

I sat up, feeling particularly mature. "How are things on the job front? You are looking, aren't you?"

"I have a couple interviews in Portland next week. Another in Seattle."

"Good luck."

"Thanks." I could hear a smile in his voice. I missed his smile, the way it made me feel like melted chocolate on the inside. Before I could think too much about missing him, I mentioned work to be attended to and hung up.

At least I was telling the truth—I had a lot of work to do. But before I got to it, I had to talk to Martha. I dialed and listened to the line ring. And ring. And ring. And ring. And that was okay. I didn't expect differently.

After what seemed like half an hour, a voice answered. "Who is this?"

The voice was young and male. Amos or Elam? "This is Jayne. I need to speak with your mother."

"Do you know where Sara is?"

"I need to talk to your mother."

"Do you?"

"Who is this, Amos or Elam?"

A pause. "Elam."

"Elam, please go get your mother." He sighed, and there was silence. I had the distinct impression that the receiver was dangling over the ground as he went to fetch his mom.

Moments later I heard commotion and voices. Then, "Jayne? Is that you?" Martha's voice held a note of panic that broke my heart.

"It's okay. Sara's in Portland with me."

"Oh, I'm so glad. Oh, goodness. Why did you take her? Her baptism is in three days!"

"I didn't take her, Martha. She left. She climbed into my car when no one was looking. I didn't discover her until I was home."

"She is in your apartment?"

"Yes."

"She's safe?"

"Yes, she is."

"She doesn't want to come back?"

I didn't know what to say. "Not...right now."

"Sara is stubborn. She's a lot like her brother."

And we both knew how *that* turned out. Levi wasn't about to go back, marry a nice Amish girl, and grow a moustache-less beard.

"Will you...watch over her?"

I nodded, not that she could see. "I will."

"Could you write to me about her?"

"Of course."

"Don't send it here—send it to my mother."

"Do you think Gideon will ever—"

"No."

"I'll take care of her," I said.

I could hear the tears in Martha's voice. "Thank you."

─────※─────

I worked straight until lunch without thinking twice about it or taking a coffee break. If Brian's wife hadn't sent him to work with curry-smelling leftovers, I might not have noticed the time.

I gathered my things in a rush and hurried down the hall to find Sara, half expecting her to be holding court with Kim and Gemma.

Instead, I found her chatting with a heavyset, African-American man who looked an awful lot like my boss.

"Jayne!" Sol said when he saw me. "I was just talking to your new roommate here. Young Amish woman leaves home to pursue an education and career—story there?"

"Right now, she's my roommate, not a source."

Sol scowled. "You know, Jayne, I've heard rumors about reporters who listen to their editors."

"I think it's a good idea," Sara piped up.

I turned to her in surprise. "Are you sure?"

She shrugged. "Maybe having an article about me would help my chances at design school."

Sol lifted a dark eyebrow. "Kid's got a point."

"We'll talk about it."

Sara crossed her arms. "I'm an adult. It's my decision. Besides, you've already written stories about my family. Why would this be different?"

"Uh, let's see, I changed all the names? Hey, if we're going to get lunch, we need to leave now."

"What about your friend Kim? And Gemma?"

So much for keeping a low profile. "I'll call them, we'll eat, I'll drop you back at the house."

Sol reached for Sara's hand. "I'm sure we'll talk later."

I rolled my eyes as we walked away. "Seriously. He may be an editor now, but the man's a diehard reporter at heart."

⁓⁓

At Gemma's family's restaurant, DiGrassi & Elle, Gemma's father kept bringing us plate after plate of lunch specials until he came and found there was no room left on the table. Without room, he simply scraped the contents of the serving plate he was carrying onto our respective dishes. After that, Gemma waved a white flag—possibly her napkin—and the barrage of food ceased.

Until dessert.

To my surprise, Sara blended in with my friends seamlessly. Everyone asked her questions; she answered them openly. Gemma promised a shopping trip while Joely offered to teach her to drive. Kim volunteered to look into the area's GED programs and college financial aid options.

Sara moved differently away from her family, spoke differently. It was as if she was no longer looking over her shoulder, making sure no one guessed her secret.

I wished Levi could see her. Maybe he'd stop worrying.

⁓⁓

The rest of the afternoon flew by. When I wasn't thinking about Levi, I managed to get an impressive amount of work done. But when I was thinking about Levi? Forget it. I may as well have stuck a Post-it Note on my head that read "Out to Lunch."

Eventually, however, the day ended and it was time to go back to the apartment and greet whomever I found there.

Because of my profound internal strength and fortitude, I did not step into the restroom for a hair check before getting in my car to drive home. I really wasn't that girl, though I impersonated her from time to time.

I saw Levi's truck even before I parked outside my apartment complex. Bracing myself, I walked up the stairs and tried the door handle.

Locked. I started with the bolt and then unlocked the door handle. But as I turned the key in the door handle, I heard the bolt scrape closed.

Okay. I unlocked the bolt again and tried to push the door open. The knob was locked.

I banged on the door. "Hello? Sara? I'd kind of like to come in, please." Nothing.

Fine. I unlocked the handle and turned it in my hand halfway; holding the knob, I unlocked the bolt. I felt the person on the other side try to lock the knob again, but it didn't catch since the knob was still turned. Before the bolt could be turned again, I turned the knob, shoved the door open, and just about knocked Spencer over.

"Spencer?" I put my purse down. "Pleasant to see you."

"Jayne?" Levi appeared down the hall. "Are you okay?"

"Spencer locked me out." I turned to the offender, who didn't look the least bit sorry. "What are you, twelve?"

"He locked you out?" Levi rolled his eyes. "Sorry. I brought him so he could help haul the bed up the stairs. He has his own car and should be going home anytime now. Right, Spence?"

"Come take a look at the office." Levi motioned for me to follow him down the hall. As I approached the doorway to the study, I could see what he'd done so far—the bed was flush against the far wall, but it wasn't what I'd expected. Instead of bringing a standard twin bed, Levi had brought a lofted bed and managed to fit a desk and a narrow dresser underneath.

My eyebrows lifted. "I'm impressed."

Levi put his hands on his hips. "Not bad, huh? With small spaces, the best thing to do is go up. I'm sure she'll need some additional closet space, but this way, moving her in takes over less of your life."

I nodded, still admiring his handiwork.

"I'm looking for an apartment in Portland," he said.

"Oh?" I turned to face him, surprised. "What about the shop?"

"Grady is buying it. He and Spence will keep it going, along with one of the shop guys who's got some brains. I'll be selling my house too. I know the market's not good, but I'm willing to sell it for less if it means getting out of it." He gave a sad smile. "Time to move on."

Move on. Did *I* want to move on? My life had undergone some huge changes, but there was one piece I couldn't let go of.

As I thought about it, I felt myself move toward him. "I hope things work out for you."

He stepped closer. "Thanks. I appreciate that."

I leaned closer to him. "You deserve to be happy."

"I don't know about that." His eyes studied mine, flickered to my lips, and returned.

I held my breath. His lips edged closer to mine until I could feel his breath against my face. He smelled like cinnamon. Our lips brushed together. I felt his hand glance over the ends of my hair.

"You guys hungry? I'm starved."

We jumped apart. Spencer stood with his hands braced against the door-jamb, eyes innocent. "Mexican? Italian? Pizza? What sounds good?"

⸙

In the end we chose sushi, partly because Spencer was against it. I thought about inviting Kim, Joely, and Gemma to dilute the amount of Spencer-ness in the dinner party, but decided against it. I wanted my friends to still be my friends afterward, and Spencer was in full loose cannon mode.

That, and Joely would probably kill him. With her police-issued shoe-laces.

Levi and I didn't look at each other throughout dinner. At least, I didn't look at Levi. I suppose if he had been looking at me, I wouldn't have known.

Chapter 36

Levi and Spencer left after dinner. Sara sketched on the couch while I read a book in the chair. A movement caught my eye—Sara's shoulders shook, almost imperceptibly.

"Sara?" I put my book down. "What's wrong?"

Her shoulders stilled, but I could see her lips waver as she tried to regain control. I moved to sit beside her on the couch. "Talk to me."

She hugged a pillow cushion to herself. "I'm afraid I won't go to heaven now when I die. I thought I could forget about it, but I can't."

I frowned. "What are you talking about?"

"I left. I won't be baptized." She shrugged. "I don't have the hope of heaven anymore."

"What...what did your deacon teach about salvation?"

She shrugged. "It's boastful to think I can *know* I'll go to heaven, I know that..."

"Sara," I took her hand. "It's not boastful." I took a deep breath. "I haven't been a model Christian for a really, really long time." Had I ever been? "Okay, never was," I admitted. "I should probably ask someone like Gemma to have this conversation with you. I've been kinda rude to God for a while. Thing is, I decided to make Jesus my Savior when I was a kid, and Jesus has been after me ever since. I know that, and I know that I want an active relationship with Him now. Scripture tells me I'll go to heaven, and I believe that."

Sara wiped at her eyes. "You think I can still go to heaven?"

"I do." I sighed. "Even if you're not Plain anymore, Jesus still loves you. He still wants to have a relationship with you. Do you want a relationship with Him?"

Sara nodded.

We prayed together. The words felt awkward on my tongue. I'm sure it wasn't the most eloquent, grammatically correct prayer of all time, or even this month, but it was a prayer, and it meant something.

⌒⌇⌒

Sara and I attended church together that Sunday with Gemma.

Throughout the week, Sara had taken in her new surroundings with wide eyes, from Elephant's Deli to the Portland Art Museum, but nothing amazed her as much as the experience of a worship service. When the music started, she clapped her hands over her ears.

"Are you all right?" I asked.

She grinned and nodded.

It occurred to me that she hadn't likely heard much music, much less amplified by the sort of speakers this church had hanging from the ceiling.

Looking at her broad smile, I stopped trying to monitor Sara's every reaction and sang out, even if I didn't know all the words.

⌒⌇⌒

Sara sat with rapt attention throughout the sermon, which, appropriately enough, was about grace. She nodded when she agreed with the pastor, and tilted her head when she seemed to have trouble absorbing the words.

And me? I felt ashamed of having lost so much time being angry with God and angry with my family. Had I transferred that anger to Levi? Was I the sort of person who wasn't happy unless she was mad at someone? The thought troubled me.

⌒⌇⌒

"I have a job!"

"Really?" I steadied my phone headset to keep it from leaping out of my ear as I drove. "Sara, Levi has a job!"

Sara beamed from the passenger seat. "Is he moving back to Portland?"

I wondered that myself, but I asked the question that puzzled me most first. "They called you on a Sunday?"

"The corporate world doesn't take days off."

"Will they expect you to work seven days a week too?"

"No, but the person hiring wasn't an economist. He's just the head of the department."

"Crazy. Where's the position?"

"Portland."

"Oh, wow," I said, as my heart began to race. "So…you'll be moving?"

"As soon as I can. Job starts next week."

"Are you glad?"

He sighed. "Very."

"Then I'm happy for you. Truly." I shot a look at Sara. "What are you doing tonight?"

"Not much, why?"

"You could come up so we can celebrate. Knock back a few cups of coffee—I bought a machine. Besides, Sara would like to see you."

"I'd love to see her. I'll leave in a few minutes."

I hung up and pulled off the cell phone earpiece. "He's coming up. He found a job here. We're going to party like it's 1999."

"He's moving to Portland?"

"He is." More cardiovascular palpitations at the thought. "The position starts next week. In the meantime, he'll be here this afternoon."

Watching Sara's smile, I felt myself grow glad on the inside.

＊

By the time we returned home from church, the sun was out. We opened all the blinds and pulled back all the curtains, filling the apartment with warm, sunshiny light. After making a lunch of deli sandwiches full of tomatoes and avocados, Sara settled on the couch with a book.

Sunny day, and my wrist felt fine—I decided I was ready for a motorcycle ride.

That was the downside of the roommate thing. I had to work a little harder to have a moment to myself, as opposed to living in total seclusion all the time.

I supposed it was probably healthy for me.

I suited up and headed out. My bike took a moment to start; it hadn't been used in so long. But once I got it started, riding it felt incredible. The wind rushed through the vents in my jacket. The sun warmed the exposed spot on the back of my gloved hand.

Levi was coming. He was coming because I'd asked him to. I thought back to how we'd met, at the woodshop. The way he'd taken me to the emergency room when I hurt my wrist. How we towed the buggy back to the farm together. Our date at Pastini. The weekend at the coast when everything fell apart.

I lived a lot of my life expecting people to let me down, expect the worst of me, and shut me out. Had I expected that of Levi?

The root of our breakup was that I couldn't tell him I loved him. Sure, we hadn't known each other long. I'd needed time. Well, time had passed. Did I feel differently?

Or did the time not matter? Had I loved him all along but been afraid to admit it to myself?

I never wanted to live a life of fear, but I realized that I had done that anyway despite my best efforts. I had hesitated pursuing a relationship with my mom and sister because I was afraid they would hate me. Because of my fear, I'd missed out on so much. I didn't want to miss out on Levi, not if he loved me back.

I'd hurt him. I knew I had. Should I apologize? Beg his forgiveness? Not say anything and just add it to my feminine mystique? I felt confused. When I returned home, I found my phone and dialed my mom's number.

She picked up, sounding groggy. "Did I wake you?"

"It's Sunday," she answered, by way of explanation. "Is everything all right?"

I explained my situation.

"Well, dear, you fix it the way women have been fixing their man problems for hundreds of years."

"How's that?" I asked, ready to be horrified if somehow my mom had reversed her position in the milk/cow arena. If she had, I was back to square one.

"Easy, dear. You make him a pie."

Chapter 37

Pie. Pie. Pie. What did I have to make a pie with? "Sara, I need you!"

Sara got up from the couch and joined me in the kitchen. "What are you doing? What's wrong?"

"I need to make Levi a pie."

"Okay…what kind of pie?"

"Any kind of pie. We don't have time to go shopping."

"Oh." She joined me in fervent cupboard-checking. Then she moved on to the freezer, digging past boxes of frozen ravioli and grilled chicken strips. "What about these?"

"I'd forgotten about those." In her hand she held a bag of frozen peaches. "I was going through a smoothie phase for a while."

"Smoothie?"

"Blended fruit. Then I broke the blender. Sticking a fork in to loosen the fruit was a bad idea. I moved on to less dangerous cuisine." I winced as I heard myself babble. Was I always like this under stress?

"You've got peaches, apricots, and…" she held the last bag close for examination. "Organic Oregon marionberries."

"Think there's enough for a pie?"

Sara shrugged. "Sure. Do you have shortening for the crust?"

"Levi bought it when you and your mom stayed here."

An expression of longing passed over Sara's features. I knew she missed her mom. I knew she wouldn't talk about it.

At her suggestion, we placed the fruit in a colander and ran it under warm water, just long enough for the fruit to lose most of its ice. I mixed and rolled out the piecrust, enjoying working gently with my hands without the brace, while Sara mixed the fruit with flour, sugar, cinnamon, nutmeg, and a little lemon juice.

Like an experienced team, we put the thing together—I put the bottom of the pie into the pie pan, Sara dumped the fruit inside, I put the top on, trimmed off the excess, and crimped the edges all nice and pretty. As a last thought, I carved LEVI into the top. We were congratulating him on the job, after all. Nothing says job congratulations like a pie.

Sara insisted we not put the pie in the oven until it was fully preheated. So I stood, staring at the oven until the heating light blinked off. We placed strips of tinfoil around the edge before putting it in the oven.

"How long?" I asked, my fingers hovering over the timer function on the microwave.

"Forty minutes, remove the foil, and then another ten should do it."

I set the timer for forty minutes.

And waited.

⁓⁓⁕⁓⁓

By the time Levi knocked on the door, the apartment smelled almost as good as Martha's kitchen.

I opened the door. "Hi," I said, aware my voice sounded flight attendant perky. "Glad you could come up."

He smiled. "Me too."

I couldn't read the expression on his face. He seemed happy, but…guarded? Was that it? Hard to say.

Sara gave him a hug. He ruffled her hair; she made a face. He looked around. "Smells good in here."

I gave a careful smile. "We made pie."

"What kind?"

"Peach, apricot, and marionberry." Sara tugged on his sleeve. "Take off your coat."

He began to shrug out of his jacket. "I don't think I've had that before."

"It's Jayne's specialty." Sara took the jacket and hung it up in the closet.

I began to panic. What was I thinking, that he would walk into the apartment and I'd suddenly know what to say? In front of Sara? It was one thing to try to make amends with the man who could very well be the love of your life, but another thing entirely to do it with his sister in the room.

Awkward.

I jumped when the microwave timer went off. The pie was really done this time—we'd removed the foil ten minutes ago. I walked to the kitchen and started to pick up every hot pad I could find.

"Sure you don't want me to do that for you?" Levi asked. I turned in time to see the glimmer in his eye. I knew he was remembering the time I'd set the hot pad on fire at the farmhouse.

I handed him my stash. "Be my guest."

He kept two and discarded the others. He beamed when he saw his name. "I don't think anyone's made me a pie with my name on it before."

I pulled out plates and forks. Sara frowned. "Doesn't it need to cool for a while?"

"I like my pie a bit runny," Levi said. "Makes the fruit stand out."

He waited while I carved it into wedges; I handed him the first slice.

"What, no ice cream?" he teased.

"It's not a perfect world."

He didn't need to know that we'd essentially cleaned out my freezer with this pie.

We took our dessert to the living room and sat down while it cooled on the plates.

Sara ate hers with surprising speed before lifting a hand to her forehead. "Oh."

I frowned. "What's wrong?"

Her eyebrows furrowed. "I…I just got a headache all of a sudden."

"I'm sorry."

"It's like a throbbing behind my forehead. It's really bad."

Levi looked to me. "Jayne, do you have any painkillers?"

Sara held up a hand. "No, I don't want to take anything. I think I should just lie down."

With that, she got up, went into her bedroom, and closed the door.

Levi leaned back. "And then there were two. She's always been a terrible liar."

"What? How can you tell?"

"Her ears move when she lies. Always have." He looked out the front window. "It's a gorgeous day outside. Want to go for a walk?"

My hand itched to hold his. I dug it farther into my jacket pocket.

"The position is a good one," Levi said, as we walked under newly leafing trees. "I'll be doing what I love. Pay's all right. Certainly enough to where I can help pay for some of Sara's living expenses while she's starting out."

"I wouldn't tell her that just yet. I think she's liking independence."

"You think she's doing okay?"

"I do." I recounted to him the spiritual conversation Sara and I had had the other night.

Levi nodded. "I felt the way she did when I left. I'm glad she had you to talk to."

"Me?" I scoffed. "I'm the last person she should be talking to about spiritual matters."

"Why do you say that?"

"I've only recently gotten my life back on track. I spent too much time giving God the cold shoulder, pretending that if I didn't believe He existed, He might leave me alone."

"Did He?"

I snorted. "No."

"Glad to hear it."

Maybe this was my moment. I tucked my hair behind my ear. "Levi, I—"

He held up his hand. "Jayne, before you say anything, there's something I need to tell you."

"Okay."

"That night I left? I'm sorry. I handled things badly. I shouldn't have left like that."

"You had every reason to."

"No, I didn't."

"I hurt you. You told me you loved me and I...I was afraid. And here I was thinking I was going to stop living out of fear. Look," I said, trying to piece together a coherent thought. "I know I made a mess of things. Badly. Could you...forgive me?"

"Of course." His answer was immediate. He pointed to the right. "Let's go this way," he said, indicating a quiet alleyway.

Fine with me. I hated feeling as though I were having this conversation with an audience.

"What I'm trying to ask," I said, starting again, "is if you'd be willing to start over. With me."

"Start over?"

"Yes."

"All the way? Meet each other all over again?"

"Start over from where I screwed things up."

He stopped and turned to face me. "I want to, but I need to know you're not going to freak out on me again like that."

I shook my head. "I can't promise I'm not going to get scared again."

"Will you at least talk about it with me when you do?"

"Just don't leave."

"I won't." He cupped my face.

Not caring that we were standing in a Portland alleyway, Levi pulled me close and kissed me. Kissed me like a man who had lost his love and found her again.

He pulled me closer when the kiss ended, as if he were afraid I'd slip away.

"I missed you," I whispered.

"I missed *you*."

"You've driven me crazy for the longest time," I said with a sigh.

He stroked my hair. "Back at you. Ever since you rode away on your motorcycle."

"Yeah?"

"Yeah." He squeezed my hand. "Let's go back and tell Sara she doesn't need to have a headache anymore."

"Okay."

We walked back into the sunshine, hand in hand.

Six Months Later

Sara, Levi, and I watched from the window as the mail van parked to the side of the complex's mailbox unit.

"Can you see anything?" Sara asked.

Levi stretched to stand on his toes. I tried not to giggle. "No, he's behind the unit. I can't—wait."

"What?" I craned my neck.

"Sorry, wrong box. Yours is the one in the middle, right?"

"One of, yes."

"He stuffed something into one of the end ones."

I rolled my eyes. "Okay, guys, let's back away from the window and check the mail like normal people."

Levi kept his eyes on the mail van. "I'm not normal."

Moments passed in silence. Finally, Sara straightened. "He's gone. Let's go."

We hurried down the stairs, probably annoying the downstairs neighbors in the process. I carried the mailbox key; Sara plucked it from my fingers. When we got down to the boxes, she unlocked the door while Levi made an adept grab for the contents.

"Envelope from Portland Community College?" Levi fanned his face with the envelope in question.

Sara squealed and snatched the envelope from him before carefully tearing along the top fold to open it.

I crossed my arms. "The Apocalypse is ever nearer, Sara. Just open the thing."

"I don't want to tear anything that's inside."

I looked to Levi. "Just think. If today weren't Saturday, we would have missed this."

Sara awarded my sarcasm with an elbow to the ribs. In the time she'd spent living with me, she'd certainly learned to fend for herself.

She grinned. "I passed. I got it. I got my GED!"

Levi wrapped her in a bear hug. "I knew you could!"

"Let me see!" I managed to pry the letter from her fingers. "You scored well too."

She nodded. "It'll help with my entrance to the Art Institute."

I squeezed her shoulder. "You should set up that entrance interview."

"I'm going to go call Gemma!"

Levi and I watched as she ran back inside.

"She did it."

I nodded. "I knew she could."

"And it's design school from here."

"Yup."

"Does she ever talk about the family with you?"

"Nope."

He exhaled. "I offered to take her to visit Grandma a couple weeks ago. She declined."

"Give her time. She's still Plain in her heart, as much as she doesn't want to be. I thought she'd cut her hair months ago." I hugged my arms to myself. "I lost out on time with my dad. I hate to think of what she'll miss."

"Not every story has a happy ending. I tried to make peace with him—it didn't work. You were there. I don't know that he'd treat her any different."

"God can change hearts."

"Yes, He can. My dad's is particularly stubborn, though."

I made a face.

"Until that time," Levi continued, rubbing his thumb over my diamond-and-garnet engagement ring, "we're her family."

I squeezed his hand. "People can change."

"Yes, they can."

"Sara passed."

"She did."

I looked up at him. "Let's make her a pie."

*The stories of Jane, Levi, the Burkholder family,
and especially Sara continue in*
Simply Sara.
Here's a sample...

Chapter 1

With the letter still clutched in my hands—the letter that told me I had passed my GED examination—I walked to my room at Jayne's apartment. My hands pushed the door closed; I sank against it.

Me, Sara, an Amish woman, passed her GED. Not only passed, but scored highly. I allowed myself to feel a little pride.

A little would not hurt.

Instead of calling Gemma, Jayne's friend and now mine, with the good news, I crossed the room, sat in my desk chair, and thought about what this GED meant.

I knew without thinking too hard.

I had to stop hiding.

After moving to the big city of Portland, Oregon, six month ago, I worked with the singular purpose of earning my GED. My brother, Levi, got a job at a business and moved to the city shortly after I ran away from home.

I don't know why people say "ran away," because for most people I don't think there's a lot of running involved. I think a lot of people take the bus. I hid in the trunk of Jayne's car.

She's still not very happy about that. Says it wasn't safe.

It probably wasn't. Maybe that's why I've been extra safe ever since.

I'm not the person I thought I would be after I left. I look in the mirror in Jayne's bathroom (so funny that it's called a bathroom, because Jayne's apartment doesn't even have a tub), and I think the person in the mirror is the same person who hid her fashion magazines underneath the floorboards.

I know in my head I'm not the same person. I don't even much know what I looked like before; I didn't grow up with many mirrors. But the image in my head and the image in the mirror seem the same.

The same, even though I have earned my GED and live in the city with my brother's girlfriend.

I must stop hiding. I must change.

I want to find clothes I like, not just modern versions of the things I wore all my life. I want to learn to drive. I want to find a job so Levi can stop leaving money in my purse when he thinks I'm not looking. I want to apply for college.

College. The idea makes me sit up straighter. I, Sara Burkholder, an un-baptized Amish girl, could go to college.

⁂

"Of course you passed," Gemma said when I called a few moments later. "Listen, do you have plans for dinner? It's Saturday night—come on down to the restaurant this evening. We're trying a new special."

Gemma's parents' restaurant tried new specials a lot. I think it was Gemma's excuse to get everyone together and made sure we all ate properly. By telling us there was a new special, we felt a bit less like culinary charity cases.

I told her I'd ask Jayne and promised I'd call her back shortly.

"Gemma wants to feed us again," I said, entering the living room.

Jayne and Levi stood in the kitchen surrounded by mixing bowls, measuring cups, miscellaneous utensils, and a generous dusting of flour.

"What are you doing?" I asked.

They exchanged glances.

"We're making you a pie," Jayne said, pushing her short dark hair behind one ear and leaving a trail of flour in the process.

"Oh." I brightened, and then I lifted the phone in my hand. "Gemma wants to feed us?"

"Again?" Levi dusted his hands off. "Another special?"

"Is that a yes?"

"Only if you can eat Italian food *and* pie."

I shrugged. "I'll find a way."

⁂

Two of Jayne's other friends met us at the restaurant—Kim, who also worked at the *Oregonian* with Jayne and Gemma, and Joely, a policewoman. Joely tugged on my braid. "How's life, Ethel?"

Ethel was her pet name for me. She thinks I'm an old soul.

I gave her a hug, mainly because Joely isn't a huggy person. "I passed my GED."

"I heard. Planning for college now?"

"College." I exhaled, mentally steadying myself. "Yes. But I would also like to find a job."

"Really?" Kim asked as she slid into the restaurant booth. "I may be able to help you with that."

Before I could answer, Gemma's father arrived at the table with a steaming platter of appetizers. The conversation broke off and everyone dove in.

"You guys are really quiet eaters," Gemma said, a slice of crostini in her hand.

"We're chewing," Levi answered. "With our mouths closed. Doesn't lend itself to easy conversation."

"Italians don't let a little chewing slow them down," Gemma retorted. "You need to speed it up a bit. Talk, chew, swallow, and repeat."

"And repeat." Jayne took a sip of her water. "Repeat, repeat, repeat."

"I never said my family wasn't dinner and a show." Gemma lifted her water glass. "A toast for Sara, to her courage and success."

Everyone else raised their glasses and clinked them around.

It was sweet of Gemma to say so, but I didn't feel that courageous. Or successful. Finishing my GED was like crossing a creek when I had a river ahead. Just thinking about it made me dizzy.

But I had determined I wouldn't hide anymore.

"What are your plans?" Kim asked.

"I need to start on my school applications," I began. "I want to see more of Portland than Powell's and Elephants Deli."

"Not a bad combo, though."

"And learn to drive. I would also like to find a job."

"Any particular kind of job?"

"Something that would fit around a school schedule."

Kim pointed at me with her fork. "My mom's cousin Rich owns a bookstore. It's pretty close to the Art Institute's campus, and he's always looking for good help. I'd be happy to introduce you."

I couldn't help grinning. "A bookstore? Really?"

"She's been reading like crazy ever since I found her in the trunk of my car," Jayne said.

Levi elbowed her.

"Well, it's true!" Jayne protested. "I found her in the trunk of my car and she started reading everything I own."

"That's a lot of books," Kim said, smiling. "Anyway, I'd be happy to introduce you. We can go over tomorrow, if you're available. We'll just leave out the part about you and the trunk when we talk to Rich."

About the Author

Hillary Manton Lodge graduated from the University of Oregon's School of Journalism. When not working on her next novel, Hillary enjoys photography, art films, and discovering new restaurants. She and her husband, Danny, reside in the Pacific Northwest.

Check out Hillary's website at
hillarymantonlodge.com

Acknowledgments

Writing acknowledgments for a book is hard. At least I think so.

It takes a village to write a novel, and two villages to get it published.

I couldn't have written this book without my husband, Danny (who also took my fantastic author photo), whose calm suggestions helped me climb my way out of writer's block. He knew I was a writer and married me anyway—that's how great he is.

Exceptional thanks to the people in my life as I began my writing journey—my parents, Scott and Ruyle Manton, who filled my childhood with books and stories. Thanks to my brother, Geoff, who keeps me laughing, and my sister, Susannah, who reads my chapters every week.

Many huge thanks to my dear friend Kara Christensen, for reading aloud chapters with me and asking critical questions.

Many thanks to Bobbie Christensen (mother of Kara), who took me to Oregon Christian Writers' conferences, advocated for me, and introduced me to wonderful people like Kara Christensen and Bonnie Leon.

Many thanks to Bonnie Leon, who read my manuscript when I was sixteen and told me I was "publishable," helped me with my book proposals, and answered my questions about publishing houses.

Many thanks to my parents-in-law, Ray and Denise Lodge, whose assistance with wood and coronary bypass knowledge proved invaluable.

Thank you to my draft readers: my mom, my sister, Aimee, Diane, Rachel, Kara, and Bobbie.

Many thanks to my agent, Sandra Bishop, for all of her help and encouragement, and to the Harvest House team as they've seen this project through. Kim and Carolyn—I couldn't ask for better editors!

Additional thanks to the mentors and encouragers I encountered throughout my journey to publication—Lorna Eskie, Esther Barton, Helen Kelts, and the rest of my extended family. I love and appreciate you all!

Mystery, romance, and a beautiful Amish setting are all found in...

Englischer Kristie Matthews' move to an Amish family farm in Lancaster County, Pennsylvania, couldn't have started on a worse note. The young schoolteacher is bitten by the farm dog, and on her trip to the local ER she has a strange encounter with a man who has just had a heart attack...

> Suddenly he raised his head and looked at me with an intensity that made me blink. "Will you do me a favor, Kristie Matthews?"
>
> I leaned close to hear his weak voice. "Of course."
>
> "Keep this for me." He fumbled in his shirt pocket..."But tell no one—*no one*—that you have it." He slipped a key into my cold hand and folded my fingers over it.

When her life is endangered, Kristie suspects a connection to the mysterious key. While solving the mystery (and trying to stay alive), Kristie must decide whether her lawyer boyfriend, Todd Reasoner, is right for her...or if Jon Clarke Griffin, the local man she's met, is all he seems to be.

Book One in the Amish Farm Trilogy

WHAT SHADOWS DARKEN THE QUIET VALLEYS OF AMISH COUNTRY?

SHADOWS of LANCASTER COUNTY

MINDY STARNS CLARK

AUTHOR OF *WHISPERS OF THE BAYOU*

*A*nna Bailey thought she left the tragedies of the past behind when she took on a new identity and moved from Pennsylvania to California. But now that her brother has vanished and his wife is crying out for help, Anna knows she has no choice but to come out of hiding, go home, and find him. Back in Lancaster County, Anna follows the high-tech trail her brother left behind, a trail that leads from the simple world of Amish farming to the cutting edge of DNA research and gene therapy.

Following up on her extremely popular gothic thriller, *Whispers of the Bayou*, Mindy Starns Clark offers another suspenseful standalone mystery, one full of Amish simplicity, dark shadows, and the light of God's amazing grace.

ISBN: 978-0-7369-2447-4 $13.99   Read a sample chapter: www.HarvestHousePublishers.com

CHRISTIAN INSIGHT
✠ MEDITATION

FOLLOWING IN THE FOOTSTEPS OF
JOHN OF THE CROSS

Mary Jo Meadow, Ed.

By Mary Jo Meadow, Kevin Culligan,
and Daniel Chowning

Foreword by Joseph Goldstein
Preface by Thomas Ryan, CSP

WISDOM PUBLICATIONS • BOSTON

Wisdom Publications
199 Elm Street
Somerville MA 02144 USA
www.wisdompubs.org

Library of Congress Cataloging-in-Publication Data
Meadow, Mary Jo, 1936–
  Christian insight meditation : following in the footsteps of John of the Cross / by Mary Jo Meadow, Kevin Culligan, and Daniel Chowning ; Mary Jo Meadow, editor.
      p. cm.
  Includes bibliographical references.
  ISBN 0-86171-526-8 (pbk. : alk. paper)
  1. John of the Cross, Saint, 1542–1591. 2. Spiritual life—Catholic Church. 3. Spiritual life—Buddhism. I. Culligan, Kevin G. II. Chowning, Daniel. III. Title.
  BX4700.J7M43 2007
  248.3'4—dc22
                                    2007014694
11 10 09 08 07
5 4 3 2 1

Cover design by Pema Studios. Interior design by Gopa&Ted2, Inc. Set in Perpetua 12.5/15.

The material in this book is a revised and expanded edition of *Purifying the Heart: Buddhist Insight Meditation for Christians* by Kevin Culligan, Mary Jo Meadow, and Daniel Chowning

Wisdom Publications' books are printed on acid-free paper and meet the guidelines for permanence and durability of the Production Guidelines for Book Longevity of the Council on Library Resources.

Printed in the United States of America

This book was produced with environmental mindfulness. We have elected to print this title on 50% PCW recycled paper. As a result, we have saved the following resources: 31 trees, 21 million BTUs of energy, 2,689 lbs. of greenhouse gases, 11,161 gallons of water, and 1,433 lbs. of solid waste. For more information, please visit our website, www.wisdompubs.org

To the participants in our Silence and Awareness retreats,
who have inspired and encouraged us.

Blessed are the pure in heart, for they shall see God.
—Matthew 5:8

When you are purged of all impurity,
and the stain of all passion is gone,
you can enter the blessed abode of the saints.
—*The Dhammapada,* 236

Table of Contents

Preface

OBSERVERS OF THE RELIGIOUS SCENE have noted in the past fifty years or so the turning of many Western Christians, in search of meaningful practices to deepen their spiritual lives, to Eastern religions. Seeing this, the Dalai Lama has graciously said on various occasions, "We don't want you to become Buddhists. But we would be happy to see you take what you find of value in Buddhism back into your lives to help you become better Christians."

Easier said than done! Entering into another religious universe sends you back into your own with new and complex questions. Experienced guides are necessary to help pilgrims of interreligious dialogue negotiate the delicate passage of exploration without losing their footing.

Few are those who have worked as perseveringly in the role of guides as the authors of this book. It is a challenging task to become familiar with not one but two universes of religious discourse, and to find the themes in each that resonate with one another. And it is even more challenging to then develop a program or, in this case, a retreat model, that renders that resonance operational.

This the authors have done, based on three assumptions: First, that insight meditation, derived from Theravada Buddhism, is essentially a spiritual practice available to all and does not require belief in any of Buddhism's religious tenets. Second, that Christians can deepen their faith in and love of Jesus through this particular method of meditative practice. And third, that insight meditation can even offer a way into the self-emptying, purifying action of Christ's embrace of the cross, and serve as a doorway to a deeper experience of God's love.

Those who understand that there continue to be different religions in the world because there are some real differences between the religions, will appreciate that works such as these are "works in progress," witnessed to by the very fact that this is a revised and expanded version of an earlier work. But such works, though they will never be finally "finished" this side of the End-time, are important and necessary in a world that has come to see itself as a global village; a world in which the Spirit of God is at work among all people in every place, culture, and religion; a world in which peace among people of religion can only come through a positive appreciation for the gifts each brings.

While this book devotes considerable space to measuring the resonance between the teachings of the Buddha and John of the Cross relative to some aspects and objectives of meditation practice, it remains a work ultimately oriented not toward theory but practice. Where theory is concerned, there are bound to be differences of interpretation; but it is harder to argue with the experienced reality of beneficial effects accruing from one's personal practice over time.

It is in one's personal practice that "the rubber hits the road" as they say. Over the years of their own practice and of guiding others on the Silence and Awareness retreats, the authors have come to the conclusion that the insight meditation practice of Theravada Buddhism contributes positively to Christian contemplative life. But I suspect they would be quick to say, with the Buddha, "Don't believe it because you heard me say it. Put it to the test in your own experience, and judge for yourself."

Today's religious pilgrims can be grateful to Mary Jo Meadow, Kevin Culligan, and Daniel Chowning for their pioneering work and conscientious exploration of a segment of the new frontier in our religiously plural world.

Thomas Ryan, CSP

Foreword

IN 1996 AND 2002, I had the good fortune of attending two Buddhist-Christian conferences at Gethsemani Abbey in Kentucky. This is the monastery where Thomas Merton, one of the great pioneers in Christian-Buddhist dialogue, lived and wrote, both in community and in the solitude of his small hermit cottage. Over the four or five days of each conference, as different participants spoke of various aspects of their traditions, one feature of the dialogue stood out: When people were talking over points of theology and metaphysics, there were often striking differences between these two great spiritual traditions. But when the conversation turned to the core values that each of them taught and embodied—values like love and compassion, renunciation and wisdom—the similarities were very obvious.

Christian Insight Meditation builds on those early dialogues and takes them a step further. The authors of this seminal work are unusual in their in-depth experience of both Buddhist and Christian practice, and based on their own practices of transformation, they have seen how even the differences of language and philosophy are often rooted in the same process of purification. Using the language and methods of Buddhist Insight meditation and the teachings of St. John of the Cross they lead the reader to his or her own rich arena of direct spiritual experience. Although both of these traditions have profound theoretical understandings of the spiritual journey, they both value experience over theory, practice over speculation.

Something quite remarkable happens when we drop from the level of conceptual thinking to the level of direct, non-judgmental, awareness. We begin to see the limitations of our own particular conditioned patterns of thought; and we open to the possibilities for understanding ourselves and the world from a place emptied of self-centeredness. The following pages draw on two great paths of wisdom to show us how to accomplish this challenging task of spiritual awakening.

H.H. the Dalai Lama expressed very well the great value of staying open to different teachings. He wrote, "I have found that extending our understanding of each other's spiritual practices and traditions can be an enriching experience, because to do so increases our opportunities for mutual respect. Often we encounter things in another tradition that helps us better understand our own." *Christian Insight Meditation* serves this commendable end with great integrity.

Joseph Goldstein

Editor's Preface

ASCENDING MOUNT CARMEL was the metaphor of St. John of the Cross for seeking God. To show the most direct route, his drawing of the mountain had *"nada, nada, nada"* (nothing, nothing, nothing) written on it all the way up. This path of emptying out, of relinquishing everything, and of seeing the "nothingness" of objects to which we might cling is also the way of Theravadan Buddhist *vipassana* (insight) meditation. Christian insight meditation uses this time-honored, precise meditation method to implement John's ascetical and mystical teachings.

Since my co-authors and I published *Purifying the Heart: Buddhist Insight Meditation for Christians* in 1994, many more Christians have discovered Buddhist meditation and appreciated its helpfulness in supporting their spiritual work.[1] We are happy to offer a revised edition of our book under its new title: *Christian Insight Meditation: Following in the Footsteps of John of the Cross*.

We addressed the first edition of this book to Christians who long for the happiness of seeing God as Jesus promised to the pure in heart. By offering an ancient Buddhist meditation practice within a Christian prayer tradition, we hoped to teach our readers a process of inner purification that we believe can lead to deeper Christian faith in this world and the direct vision of God in the next.

Since that time, we have also found Buddhists interested in the teachings of St. John of the Cross. We offer this new edition for any readers who might feel that exploring the spiritual traditions of John of the Cross and Theravadan Buddhism could enhance their spiritual life.

Eastern Riches for Christians

Despite the long history of mysticism within Christianity and its many and varied approaches to meditation and contemplative prayer, more and more Christians have turned to Eastern religions to find guidance for their interior life that they did not find in Christianity. Some have completely abandoned the religion of their childhood, believing they have found the "pearl of great price"[2] in Eastern meditation.

Since our first edition, many Christians who are interested in or practice Eastern meditation have come to our retreats. Some had discovered for themselves Christianity's rich mystical tradition. They set out on their own to build a bridge between their Eastern meditation practice and Christian contemplative prayer. Such persons, who often call themselves Buddhist Christians or Christian Buddhists, draw equally upon both traditions to assist their interior development and growth in faith.

Other Christians who began with Buddhist meditation have experienced its physiological and psychological benefits; however, they are uncertain how to relate meditation to their faith. They are open to integrating their meditation practice into their Christian life if someone can show them how. Some worry about syncretism in their religious practice or fear becoming New Age dilettantes, believing it safer to keep religion and meditation separate.

We cannot know how many Christians, not yet familiar with our work, have at least some experience with Eastern meditation, but we suspect there are many. This book offers all these Christians reliable guidance for integrating at least one form of Buddhist meditation into one tradition of Christian contemplative prayer.

The Silence and Awareness Retreat

This book grew out of our eight-day Silence and Awareness retreat, which we have directed since 1989.[3] Some readers of our first edition have attended this retreat, and others have worked privately with the published tapes of our 1991 retreat. The retreat teaches the Theravadan

Buddhist practice of *vipassana,* or insight meditation, within the framework of Christian contemplative prayer found in Carmelite spirituality, especially in the life and writings of St. John of the Cross.[4] His Carmelite contemporary, St. Teresa of Avila, also appears in our work.[5]

As we developed this retreat from year to year, we gradually recognized the need for this book. We wanted to make the basic instructions for insight meditation available in writing for Christians who wanted to work with this practice on their own. We also wanted to set down, as clearly and simply as possible, our understanding of how this venerable Buddhist practice can be integrated with Christian prayer.

Our intent in this book is primarily pastoral and practical. We recognize, but do not discuss, many important questions that occupy professional scholars in the Buddhist-Christian dialogue and in the study of Christian spirituality. We are also aware of, but again do not elaborate, the social and political implications of collaboration between persons of differing religious faiths.

We want simply to teach the practice of Christian insight meditation, providing only as much history and theory as seems necessary to show the compatibility of this simple Buddhist practice with Christian prayer. We believe that Christians who are faithful to this practice soon discover for themselves its power to bring inner peace and healing, its implications for Christian life, and the inseparable connection between wisdom and compassion known for centuries to both Christian and Buddhist meditators.

Our Interfaith Perspective

This book invokes the spirit of the Second Vatican Council, which exhorted Catholic Christians to "acknowledge, preserve, and promote" the spiritual and moral goods and cultural values of Hinduism and Buddhism.[6] Vatican II also challenged missionary members of religious institutes to reflect attentively "on how Christian religious life may be able to assimilate the ascetic and contemplative traditions whose seeds were sometimes already planted by God in ancient cultures prior to the preaching of the Gospel."[7]

We have tried to be as faithful as possible to the integrity of both Buddhist insight meditation and Carmelite spirituality. At the same time, we attempt to point out the similarities between these two traditions that enable Christians to assimilate Buddhist insight meditation into Christian prayer and to practice an authentic Christian insight meditation.

We deeply believe that the Christian insight meditation taught in this book, a twenty-five-hundred-year-old Buddhist meditation practice integrated into Carmel's eight-century tradition of contemplative prayer, can satisfy the hunger of American Christians for spiritual nourishment—one of the most pressing pastoral challenges to Christian churches. To feed this desire, we offer a meditation practice that not only purifies our hearts, but also draws us directly into the paschal mystery, the self-emptying death of Jesus Christ that gives new life to our world.

Emptiness is a common theme in the spiritual teachings of both the Buddha and John of the Cross. Emptying our lives of attachment to everything contrary to God's will and opposed to the free movement of the Holy Spirit within us is the essential process that prepares us for transformation of our lives.[8] By fostering this emptiness, by leading us securely along a lifelong path of poverty of spirit and purity of heart, Christian insight meditation disposes us for this unfathomable blessing that alone satisfies all our longings.

Plan of the Book

Part I briefly lays the foundations of our approach. It first presents Jesus' call to purity of heart. Next it gives a historical outline of the Buddhist tradition of insight meditation and the Carmelite tradition of prayer.

Part II gives the instructions for insight meditation as they are taught during our retreats. This enables the reader to learn and experience the meditation practice directly. It also offers some new material giving guidance on setting up a practice, and discusses how to find help.

The unit's final chapter presents, more fully than the first edition did, the overall path of practice as both traditions see it.

Part III compares the teachings of John of the Cross and the Buddha on interior purification. This comparison provides the primary theoretical basis for our effort to integrate insight meditation into Christian prayer.

Finally, Part IV discusses some questions people attending our retreats often ask about using insight meditation as prayer. The last three chapters in this unit are new, written for this edition, to address the more recent questions we have been asked.

Two appendices offer additional information. Appendix I recaps our own work in drawing from Christian and Buddhist scriptures and other teachings the contemplative practice we call Christian insight meditation.[9] Appendix II lists resources for help in continuing the practice of insight meditation.

Because insight meditation focuses on self-emptying purification, we refer only briefly to the Buddhist loving-kindness *(metta)* meditation practice. However, *Gentling the Heart: Buddhist Loving-Kindness Practice for Christians* teaches this practice in detail within Christian perspectives.[10] Together, these two books show both the interior and social implications of Theravadan Buddhism for Christian spirituality.

Terminology

Deep meditation in Buddhism, called *jhana* or absorption, is experienced much the same as contemplation in Christianity—as receptive, passive, and not under our "control." However, Buddhists and Christians see the causes of development in meditation practice somewhat differently. Buddhists attribute it to deepening concentration, or stability of mind.

Carmelites, especially John of the Cross, generally regard contemplation as the inflow of God into the human person, a gift of God's love that we cannot achieve by our human actions alone. They teach that we can use various ascetical techniques and spiritual practices to dispose ourselves for contemplation, but the increase of divine life in us is always grace, God's gift. To avoid confusion, we reserve the term "contemplation" in this book to John's understanding.

We use the words "contemplative prayer"—or synonyms like "contemplative practice" or "contemplative method"—for the non-discursive meditation practices we use to dispose ourselves for contemplation. We discuss the concepts of meditation, contemplative prayer, and contemplation in greater detail in Part IV. Until then, when we speak of contemplation, we mean it as John of the Cross did—as God's unmerited gift; when we speak of contemplative prayer, we mean meditative practices that dispose us for that grace.

Language Usage

Three persons wrote the first edition of this book. I am responsible for the revised edition. I have done my best to give you a smooth and consistent text, both in style and content, and to iron out stylistic differences among the authors. Some content from the original edition has been rearranged, and some additional content added. The initials at the end of each chapter indicate whose work is found in that chapter. Where only minor changes were made in the second edition, I did not add the initials of others' work appearing in it. Where greater ones occurred, I did, with the first set of initials indicating whose is the major portion of the work.

For a text that reads more easily, I take several liberties with language usage. To preserve a smoothly reading text, I do not indicate minor deletions, which do not change meaning, in citing other authors. I also avoid most use of titles. This means that I commonly refer to Christian saints without putting the appellation "St." in front of their names. I often refer to St. John of the Cross and St. Teresa of Avila simply as John and Teresa.

In citing Christian scripture, I give only the name of the evangelist instead of prefacing it with "the gospel according to." For epistles, I name only the recipient rather than stating "the epistle of X to Y." Finally, because the words *"Nibbana"* and *"Dhamma"* are what Christians would consider God-concepts, I capitalize them, although some

Buddhists do not. I italicize non-English words that recur frequently in their first appearance only.

I take the liberty of offering a contemporary translation of Teresa and John, working from a Spanish text and the two English translations most common in the West.[11] This makes the text easier for most readers, and keeps the work flowing without the interruption of many unfamiliar terms or archaic ways of phrasing expressions. I do the same for Buddhist scriptures and works of Buddhist scholars that are in translation. These changes make the quotations more readable.

Notes of Gratitude

When we first presented Christian insight meditation, we recognized that we are latecomers in demonstrating the relevance of Eastern meditation for Christian prayer. We express our gratitude for Bede Griffiths, Thomas Merton, Abhishiktananda, John Main, Sister Ishpriya, Hugo Enomiya-Lassalle, William Johnston, Pascaline Coff, Yves Raguin, Raimundo Panikkar, Anthony de Mello, and many other pioneers in the field of ecumenical spirituality upon whose work we stand. You will easily discern their inspiration in our work. However, because we want to capture in this book the atmosphere of our Silence and Awareness retreat in both the meditation instructions and spiritual conferences, we provide notes for only direct quotations in the text. All our other sources are included in the general bibliography.

We thank Wisdom Publications for their interest in offering the revised edition of this work, and Josh Bartok of Wisdom for his helpfulness in bringing the second edition to press. We remain grateful to Clarence Thomson, former director of Credence Cassettes, and Michael Leach, formerly with Crossroad Publishing Company, for their original interest in our work and their encouragement to share our retreat with a larger audience through audiotapes and the first edition of this book.

We are also grateful to Joseph Goldstein, Buddhist author and cofounder and guiding teacher at Insight Meditation Society (IMS) in Barre, Massachusetts, and Kieran Kavanaugh, O.C.D., a founding member of the Institute of Carmelite Studies and American translator of John of the Cross, for their critical reading of our first edition and their helpful comments. They have both contributed immensely to this book, although the authors alone are responsible for its final form. I, the editor, am especially grateful to the teachers at IMS, especially Joseph, for expounding the Dhamma to me. Their wisdom pervades this book.

Finally, we thank all who have joined us for our Silence and Awareness retreats. Their longing for genuine spirituality, their openness to our teaching and guidance, and their constructive criticisms of our work have made it possible for us now to share this experience with a wider audience. To these men and women, we dedicate this book.

Mary Jo Meadow

✠ PART I

FOUNDATIONS

✤ 1 ✤

Purity of Heart:
The Teaching and Example of Jesus

"**B**LESSED ARE THE PURE IN HEART," Jesus taught in his sermon on the mount, "for they shall see God."[1] For Jesus, the heart is more than the bodily organ that sustains physical life; it is the interior center of our being from which all life flows. The New Testament depicts the heart primarily as the source of our feelings, desires, and passions; of our thoughts and understanding; of our will and its choices; and of our moral and religious behavior.[2] Accordingly, Jesus taught, as did the Buddha, that we must purify our entire interior life if we want the happiness of reaching our highest spiritual aspirations.

Jesus Demanded Purity of Heart

That Jesus demanded such inner purity is clear from his challenge to the Pharisees about ritual purification. "Listen to me, all of you," he said, "and understand. Nothing entering from outside causes a person to be unclean; rather it is what comes out of the person that makes for uncleanness."[3]

Impurity Jesus later explained to his close disciples that ritual food leaves the heart unaffected. It simply passes through the body into the sewer. All foods, therefore, are clean. However, persons become unclean by what comes out of them. "For it is from within, from the heart, that evil intentions emerge: fornication, theft, murder, adultery, avarice, malice, deceit, indecency, envy, slander, pride, folly. All these evils come from within. They make a person unclean."[4] The Buddha taught similarly: "Indeed, by oneself is evil done. By oneself is one defiled. Purity and impurity depend on oneself."[5]

To see God, our hearts must be pure, free of all evil. God is holy, and only the holy can rejoice in the divine presence. We cannot live before God with a heart filled with evil, with murder, deceit, envy, pride. We must first purify our hearts—our desires, thoughts, memories, emotions, and choices—of everything that might cause wrong behavior. As we gradually cleanse our interior life, we begin to know the happiness, the blessing, and the joy of seeing God. The Buddhist *Dhammapada* says, "Mindful of speech. Restraint of mind. Never allow your body to do harm. Follow these three ways with purity and you will achieve the Path."[6]

Seeing God In this world, seeing God does not mean physical vision, but experiencing God in the events of our daily lives. It means knowing God in dark faith and constant love. Yet experiencing God in faith and love in this world leads, as the apostle-evangelist John assured us, to seeing God directly in the life beyond this world. He wrote in his first epistle:

> Beloved, we are already God's children although what we are to be in the future has not yet been revealed. However, we know that when he appears we shall be like him, for we shall see him as he really is. And those who thus hope in him purify themselves as he is pure.[7]

Our true happiness in this world consists in embracing the purity of life we see in the teachings and example of Jesus, trusting that we shall be totally transformed in him when we finally see him face to face.

Finding Happiness

This happiness, Jesus reminded us, belongs not only to the pure of heart, but also to the poor in spirit, the gentle, the merciful, peacemakers, and to those who mourn, who long for holiness, and who suffer persecution for his sake.[8] His teaching on happiness implies a connection between all these ways of being in the world.

Beatitudes The pure of heart are also poor in spirit. Just as no one who is pure of heart can be a murderer, an adulterer, or a liar, so the truly pure of heart also work for peace, show mercy, and strive for holiness. These are the qualities that bring us true happiness.

The happiness Jesus proclaimed is thus paradoxical. The things we naturally expect to make us happy—money, prestige, power, security, pleasure—make us very unhappy when they become our only desire and close our hearts to God. The Buddha also taught, "By giving up lesser happiness, one may have a greater one. Let the wise give up the lesser."[9]

Purity, meekness, and simplicity, on the other hand, bring happiness because they cleanse our hearts and open them for God, who alone makes us completely happy. The kingdom of God, therefore, belongs only to the poor in spirit, the meek, the mourners, and the peacemakers—to those who make room in their lives for God. There is no other way to establish the reign of God in our hearts.

Hardness of heart Jesus, of course, did not expect us to purify our hearts by our own efforts alone. He knew too well what is in us.[10] He knew especially our hardness of heart, our *sclerocardia,* to put it in medical terms. Of all human diseases, hardness of the heart is the worst, worse even than cancer or AIDS, because it closes us to the Word of God and isolates us from God's love.

We can be so absorbed in our own plans, desires, pleasures, thoughts, memories, and emotions that we exclude God from our hearts. As the divine physician who comes to heal us, Jesus' primary focus was to cure the hardness of heart that prevents the growth within us of faith, hope, and love, and that excludes the transforming power of God's love from our lives.[11]

Dying to Self

To heal our hardness of heart, Jesus called us to die with him.

Those who want to follow me must renounce themselves, take up their cross, and follow me. Those who want to save their life must lose it; those who lose their life for my sake, and for the sake of the gospel, save it. What gain is it to win the whole world and ruin one's life? And, indeed, what can one offer in exchange for one's life?[12]

The example of Jesus As Christian discipleship demands dying to self, so too does purity of heart. We cannot achieve the purity Jesus taught in his sermon on the mount unless we die interiorly. We die interiorly every time we refuse to let harmful intentions or movements of rage, envy, lust, injustice, avarice, pride, and slander take root in our consciousness, not allowing them a place in our hearts.

As these movements pass through us, the heart's natural purity and simplicity emerges, grows stronger, and prepares us to experience God in new and unexpected ways. After a lifetime of dying daily to disordered internal movements, we one day die finally into the complete, never-ending, unchanging presence of God.

Jesus exemplified his teaching with his own death on the cross. Although public preaching, teaching, healing, and community-building were essential to his ministry, Jesus established God's reign in the world primarily through his death and resurrection. Similarly, his reign becomes established in our hearts as we daily share his death and resurrection. There is no other way. "Unless a grain of wheat falls into the ground and dies, it remains just a single grain of wheat; but if it dies, it bears much fruit."[13]

Teachings of the apostle Paul Recognizing the good that comes to the human family through Jesus' death and resurrection, Paul increasingly emphasized union with Jesus in his paschal mystery—his dying and rising—as central to Christian living. In his letter to the Christians at Philippi, Paul challenged them in these words:

In your minds you must be the same as Jesus Christ: his state was divine, yet he did not cling to his equality with God but emptied himself to assume the condition of a slave, and became as all human beings are; and being as all humans are, he was humbler yet, even to accepting death, death on a cross. But God raised him high and gave him the name that is above all other names so that all beings in the heavens, on earth, and in the underworld, should bend the knee at the name of Jesus and that every tongue should acclaim Jesus Christ as Lord, to the glory of God the Father.[14]

Speaking for himself, Paul went on to assure the Philippians of his own commitment to the paschal mystery: "All I want is to know Christ and the power of his resurrection and to share his sufferings by reproducing the pattern of his death. That is how I can hope to take my place in the resurrection of the dead."[15]

The mind of Christ We assume the mind of Christ when we embrace the process by which Jesus emptied himself for the human family in his suffering and death on the cross. His self-emptying was not a denial or renunciation of his unique personhood, but nonattachment to the divine honor and glory he could rightly claim. Jesus thus entered freely and completely into the depths of human suffering. The Father did not abandon Jesus in his self-emptying, but raised him from the dead and restored him to eternal glory. Now all creation praises and honors him as Lord. Similarly, purity of heart involves a self-emptying that does not destroy our personhood; rather, it opens us to the fullness of life as we share the spirit of the risen Lord who is given to us.[16]

The Holy Spirit purifies us interiorly for God. As we cannot pray without the help of the Holy Spirit,[17] neither can we purify our hearts without the Spirit's assistance. Paul reminded the Corinthians:

You know perfectly well that people who do wrong will not inherit the kingdom of God: people of immoral lives, idolaters, and adulterers. These are the sort of people some of you were once, but now you have been washed clean and sanctified, and justified through the name of the Lord Jesus Christ and through the Spirit of our God.[18]

The Holy Spirit The Holy Spirit within us continually supports our efforts to put to death the self-indulgent passions and desires that cause our disordered behavior; moreover, the Spirit produces in our conduct the enduring fruits of interior freedom—love, joy, peace, patience, kindness, goodness, trustfulness, gentleness, and self-control.[19]

Thus, we imitate Jesus in his self-emptying, not as an ascetical practice for its own sake, but because it purifies our heart and opens for us the door to freedom, love, peace, and life everlasting. This is the mystery of Christian faith. This is our daily rhythm of life. Indeed, purity of heart, poverty of spirit, mortification, non-attachment, and self-emptying not only lead to eternal life; they are eternal life already possessed, a risen life under the Holy Spirit's constant guidance lived here and now in this world, a life that promises joyous completion in the eternal vision of God.

Purity of heart, then, is like the little mustard seed in Jesus' story that grows from a very small seed to a large bush providing shelter for the birds of the air.[20] It is a hidden and humble activity, yet it brings us every blessing—happiness, gospel living, healing and transformation in Christ Jesus, the gifts of the Holy Spirit, eternal life. These permit us to experience God now in faith and to see God later in heaven.

Purifying the Heart

But how, precisely, do we purify our hearts? First, by our love for Jesus. Our hearts become pure as we listen to his words, practice his teaching, follow his example, and, most importantly, die daily to self-love in union with his death on the Cross.

Ancient traditions We can also learn from others. Long before the time of Jesus, the Hebrew Bible psalmist prayed, "A clean heart create for me, O God, and a steadfast spirit renew within me."[21] Like this ancient poet, we can purify our hearts by humbly asking God each day for this blessing in our lives.

In addition to prayer, we can learn the ancient practices of the pure in heart. Following his own enlightenment around the year 500 B.C.E., the holy man of India, Gotama, the Buddha, taught his followers the importance of purifying the heart by abandoning evil and doing good. He stated, "Strive quickly. Get insight. Purged of impurity and passion you shall enter the blessed abode of the saints."[22] Meditation, he taught them further, is the practice that cleanses the heart. "From meditation arises wisdom. Knowing this, conduct yourself that wisdom may arise."[23]

Meditation purifies the heart of disordered desires, hateful thoughts, harmful memories, fear, and other negative emotions. It replaces these conditions with sharp mental awareness, clear understanding, strength of will, and attentiveness to each passing moment. It develops wisdom and compassion, and finally opens one to ultimate truth, unconditioned being, or Nibbana. Over the centuries, the Buddha's followers have preserved their meditation practices with such care and precision that they are now available to those who wish to use them in response to Jesus' call to purify the heart.

Meditation and purification Christians, too, have developed effective methods for purifying the heart. The sixteenth-century Spanish Carmelite friar John of the Cross meticulously described in *The Ascent of Mount Carmel* and *The Dark Night* the progressive interior purification necessary for union of the entire person with God. He gave counsel on how to systematically purify desires, thoughts, memories, and emotions so that our hearts may be disposed to receive God's love in contemplation. Contemplation purifies, heals, and, ultimately, transforms all of the human personality, both sense and spirit, and unites it with God.

John taught that only God's love for us fully purifies our hearts and unites us perfectly with God's will. Divine love makes us God by participation, enables us to experience God in this life through faith, and after death to see God and live forever in God's presence.[24] Nevertheless, through the faithful practice of meditation and continual recollection, we can attain a purity of heart, a poverty of spirit, and an emptiness of self that irresistibly invites God into our lives and frees us to receive God's purifying and transforming love in contemplation.

Purifying our hearts and reforming our lives each day according to the gospel make us fit to know God. "It is not those who say to me, 'Lord, Lord,' who will enter the kingdom of heaven, but those who do the will of my Father in heaven."[25] We try during daily mental prayer to empty sense and spirit completely and surrender ourselves totally into God's hands as Jesus did on Calvary. This prepares us fully for liturgy, where we celebrate Jesus' paschal mystery and apply its fruits to our lives.

Christian insight meditation The chapters that follow in this book bring these two venerable traditions—Buddhist meditation and the Christian spirituality of John of the Cross—together into an ascetical practice we call Christian insight meditation. This contemporary approach to purifying our hearts lets us know, as Jesus promised, the happiness of seeing God—first in this world by dark faith, then by direct vision in eternity. This practice aims, in the spirit of the beloved disciple's first epistle, to help Christians purify their beings as Jesus is pure. Then their hope of seeing him and being finally transformed in him can be fulfilled.[26]

In Christian insight meditation, regular attention to the breath develops a growing consciousness of the presence of the Spirit whom Jesus breathes upon us. It readies us to follow where the Spirit leads, even into unfamiliar territory. "The wind blows wherever it pleases; you hear its sound, but you cannot tell where it comes from or where it is going. That is how it is with all who are born of the Spirit."[27]

The meditation discipline of staying in the present moment, refusing to give mental energy to thoughts of the past or the future, trains us for moment-to-moment attention to the here and now. This enables us to live fully in God's presence as we involve ourselves in the endless tasks that make up our day. "Do not worry about tomorrow," Jesus reminds us, "for tomorrow will have its own worries. Let each day's problems be sufficient for the day."[28]

Close attention to present experiences also puts us deeply in touch with our beings. This brings understanding that helps us manage problem thoughts, emotion, and impulses. It results in better conduct, calmer minds, and greater purity of heart.

Although not all of us pray in the same way, the goal of all Christian prayer remains the same: continual communion with God and transformation of our lives in Christ. Christian insight meditation brings this. Before explaining this practice further, we look first at brief historical overviews of the Buddhist tradition of insight meditation and the Carmelite tradition of prayer.

KC/MJM

✦ 2 ✦

The Buddhist Tradition of Insight Meditation

GOTAMA, the historical Buddha, was born into a princely family about 500 B.C.E. in an area of India that is now part of Nepal. His father arranged a very sheltered life for him because he strongly wanted his son to be an important worldly leader. However, stories from the child's young life indicate that he was bound for future spiritual greatness. When he finally came into contact with the human suffering of illness, aging, and death, the young prince resolved upon a spiritual life. He left his palace and sought spiritual teachings. Several teachers taught him all they knew, but he remained unsatisfied.

The *bodhisattva* (Buddha-to-be) then spent years trying in various ways to break through to his goal of full, clear seeing of spiritual truth. Finally he hit upon the method of awareness practice. Various temptations of lust, greed, fear, and self-importance then launched a massive assault on him. After he overcame the final temptation of self-doubt, his enlightenment unfolded over an entire night during his thirty-fifth year, and he came to full understanding.

From this time on, he was known as the Buddha, "The Fully Awake One" or "The Fully Enlightened One." This fulfilled his vow made many lifetimes earlier to become a Buddha for the good of all beings. He then lived a long life of teaching and healing, and performed many miracles. His dying concern was with the well-being and spiritual illumination of his followers. He exhorted them to remember that all worldly things end, and to work out their salvation diligently.

The Basic Teachings of the Buddha

The Buddha said that he taught one thing, and one thing only: suffering and the end of suffering. This emphasis on suffering is not pessimistic; the great point of the Buddha's teaching is that suffering can be overcome, that there is a path that frees us from suffering.

Four noble truths In his first sermon after his enlightenment, the Buddha taught the four noble truths that form his core message. The first noble truth is about suffering, only some of which is evident pain or hardship. He said that our earthly lives themselves are ultimately unsatisfactory because they can give us no lasting, permanent, and true satisfaction. Nonetheless, we all are born strongly inclined to put great effort into passing and fleeting outcomes even though we know that aging, illness, and death come to all of us eventually.

The second noble truth is the cause of suffering: craving. Whenever we have a pleasant experience or see the possibility of one, we are conditioned to react with greed. Those who have wrestled with addictions probably best understand the suffering that craving brings. However, all of us who have something we feel we cannot live without—a person, a job, or a possession—know the truth that craving means suffering.

Whenever we are faced with unpleasant experience, we want to strike out at it or push it away, become fearful or angry, or grieve over it. We feel driven to say the hateful word, shrink away from a frightening duty, or indulge in self-pity. This also is craving, wanting things to be other than they are, being unwilling to accept the present moment without reacting against it.

Whenever our experiences do not grip us strongly, we become careless, bored, restless, or inattentive; we "space out" on the present moment. We are "excitement junkies," and resist giving careful attention to routine details of life. This puts us in voluntary ignorance or delusion. Willingness to pay attention only to intense experiences is also craving.

The third noble truth is that suffering ends when we stop craving. When we no longer react to experiences with greed, aversion, and delusion, we no longer suffer. One meditator delightedly described her freedom from torment in a relationship. When faced with a co-worker who had always annoyed her, she became aware of how unpleasant it was, but realized that she could choose not to react with animosity.

The fourth noble truth tells us how to end suffering by following the eightfold noble path. Traditionally, the path is broken into three main parts: morality or purity of conduct, meditation or purity of mental contents, and wisdom or purity of heart. Each of these frees us from some suffering—transgression, mental obsessing, and lack of wisdom, respectively—and brings about a corresponding satisfaction.

Walking the path The first task is to establish basic morality and rectify behavior. Until this is done, we cannot know the happiness of freedom from guilt, remorse, and shame. Discordant conduct harms others or ourselves, and causes suffering.

Purifying mental contents is the second task. Meditation practice works directly on this by making us fully present and attentive. The practice clears the mind of such remnants of psychological ill health as envy, resentment, greed, anger, vanity, and so on. When such attitudes no longer dominate mental contents, a second level of happiness comes. This calm, peace, and stillness of mind is the happiness of concentration, which leaves no room for the mental baggage that agitates us or might even move us to unskillful action.

Finally, latent tendencies toward unwholesomeness cling to us, the results of past bad choices we have made. The hidden inclinations they have left in our hearts can ripen into wrong thought or behavior with sufficient provocation. Because of impurity in the heart, we easily move to coveting, and might even misbehave. Work on this condition is the deepest and most radical purification.

Our task is simply to be present and to let the work be done in us. The resulting purity of heart, when all that is unwholesome has been uprooted, finally brings the end of suffering. We enjoy the happiness of wisdom that culminates in experiencing the Ultimate Reality, which Buddhists call Nibbana. Others use different names, such as God, *Brahman,* the Absolute, *Allah,* Great Spirit, the Transcendent, or the Higher Power.

Three characteristics The Buddha taught that only Nibbana is unconditioned—that is, unborn, undying, unchanging, and truly satisfying. Everything else is conditioned reality, dependent upon causes. The entire world, including ourselves, consists of three types of conditioned reality: matter, consciousness, and mind-states. Our bodies are matter, and consciousness is the knowing faculty. Mind-states, which color experience, include moods, emotions, mental sets, states of awareness, and various "housekeeping" functions of mind.

Meditation practice shows us that all conditioned reality has three universal characteristics. We have already discussed one, suffering or unsatisfactoriness. Another characteristic of conditioned reality is impermanence—that things are continually changing; nothing lasts. Things keep being born and passing away. We easily see in meditation how rapidly our thoughts and emotions change. Our bodies also are always passing off dying cells and creating new ones.[1]

The third characteristic of all conditioned or created reality is essencelessness or no-self. This is one of the Buddha's hardest teachings to understand. However, if we reflect, we realize that what we call ourselves is a combination of ever-changing processes of body and mind. It is not a solid and permanent "thing." Our science of physics tells us that even the most solid looking matter is mostly empty space with flecks of "stuff" floating in it. All that we know of this world is processes within larger processes, combinations of constantly changing processes. There are no static or enduring "things," just changing processes. This is what "no self" means; nothing in conditioned reality lasts in any essential form. All is never-ending flux and flow.[2]

Trappedness and freedom The Buddha taught that everything happens dependent on causes; every experience that arises is born from something else. He described laws of cause and effect in areas that Western science recognizes: laws that explain how matter, living forms, and mind work. His teaching on dependent arising discusses another law, the law of cause and effect in the moral sphere. It shows how we are trapped, and how we can become free of our conditioning that causes suffering.[3]

The basic problem is that we are not willing to accept things as they are without unhelpfully reacting to them, without craving. We are trapped in our reactions to experiences—and the suffering that this brings—because of our past choices. We have conditioned ourselves into a prison from which awareness practice, insight meditation, can release us.

This practice is beautifully summed up in one of the Buddha's shortest teachings. He simply said, "In seeing, let there be only what is seen; in hearing, let there be only what is heard; in sensing, let there be only what is sensed; in cognizing, let there be only what is cognized."⁴ The point is to be fully aware of our experience, without adding interpretation or commentary, without getting lost in it, clinging to it, or pushing it away. This means simply being with what is happening right now, being fully present to the moment. It means surrendered acceptance of "what is," whether agreeable to us or not, without reactive emotions. It does not mean passivity in the face of evil or when action is called for, but only that we act out of the needs of the situation and not from our own reactivity.

Awareness practice shows us our trappedness in clear detail. It is also our way out, and actually works the needed purification in us. In freeing us from being trapped in unhelpful choices, the practice eventually brings the fruit of "touching" Nibbana, the only true satisfaction. "There is no wisdom for one without meditation. There is no meditation for one without wisdom. If you have both meditation and wisdom, then you are indeed close to Nibbana."⁵

Development of Buddhism

The Pali canon of Buddhist scriptures began in a meeting of monks after the Buddha's death. Of early Buddhism, based solely on the Pali canon, only the Theravadan school remains. Its stronghold is in Southeast Asia—in Myanmar (Burma), Thailand, and Sri Lanka. The awareness practice we teach is from a Burmese Theravadan school. Part II of this book gives you practice instructions.

Other Buddhist schools What is now called Mahayana Buddhism began within centuries of the Buddha's death. The larger Mahayana tradition developed as the Buddha's teachings went north and east to China and, by way of Korea, to Japan. The Mahayana takes many forms: from Zen, which contains some practices similar to Theravadan meditation; through groups emphasizing chanting or other rituals; to forms of "churched" Buddhism, influenced by Christian missionary activity. Mahayana Buddhism also traveled into Tibet where it merged with Tibetan folk religion to produce Tibetan Buddhism. This highly stylized and ritualistic Buddhism has a very deep meditative tradition.

In its various forms, Buddhism is now a major world faith, found in all parts of the globe. However, the meditation practice itself is not considered a religion, but just a spiritual practice; sometimes considered an "ethical psychology," it can also simply be called Dhamma practice.

Meditation writings of Buddhism We now look at some written bases of the 2500-year-old awareness practice, mindfulness practice, or insight meditation, in more detail. In the Pali language, this practice is called *vipassana* (vih-*pahs'*-sah-nah), or "clear, wide seeing through."

The Pali canon contains the Buddha's sermons *(suttas)* that describe awareness practice. Most important for our purposes is the *Mahasatipatthana Sutta,*[6] which details how to practice mindful awareness. Another large collection of early scriptures, the *Abhidhamma,*[7] contains Buddhist philosophical and psychological understandings.

Apart from scriptures, the major work on Buddhist meditation is the fifth-century monk Buddhaghosa's *Visuddhi Magga,* or *The Path of Purification.*[8] It details one thousand years of experiences of many thousands of meditators. It tells exactly what to expect at each stage of meditation practice from the signs that it is starting to those signaling its end. These fifteen-hundred-year-old Asian writings accurately describe our own experiences when we meditate in the twenty-first-century Western world.

History of insight (vipassana) practice For a long time insight meditation remained a monastic discipline because it was thought suitable only for monks and nuns who had dedicated their entire lives to spiritual practice. Lay people were seen as not having enough time to develop sufficient concentration to do awareness practice.

Early in the twentieth century, some monks began to teach the practice to lay Buddhists in Southeast Asia with a method that developed mindfulness and concentration together. A chief figure in this was Burmese Mahasi Sayadaw, whose school is the most widespread in the West. He is also considered one of the great meditation masters of all time. Mahasi Sayadaw wrote extensively on insight practice, but many of his works are not yet available in English.[9]

By the middle of the twentieth century, Westerners were studying insight meditation in Asia. Some returned home and began teaching the practice. A major American development was the 1976 founding of Insight Meditation Society (IMS) in Barre, Massachusetts.[10] The books of Joseph Goldstein,[11] one of the IMS founders and a major teacher of the practice, are a good place to start reading about insight meditation. Vipassana (insight) practice is also available at various other Buddhist centers. With the 1987 founding of Resources for Ecumenical Spirituality, sponsor of our retreats, the practice became regularly available in the context of Christian Carmelite spirituality.[12]

Understanding Insight Meditation

Insight meditation practice is rigorously empirical. It is quite simple conceptually, but achieving proficiency in practice takes patient, persistent effort.

Development of the method Centuries of meditators described their experiences to knowledgeable teachers. They, in turn, monitored meditators' progress, assessing it against what was already known about the practice. The result is a very precise and elaborate developmental psychology that has remained valid, accurate, and helpful to the present day. Because wanting or expecting certain experiences might distort practice, teachers typically explain stages of meditation in detail only after students are already familiar with them in their own practice.

The precise method is certainly one important feature of this

practice. Equally important is the discouraging of metaphysical speculation. We need not agree with any belief items, or be willing to call
on any supernatural beings, to do the practice. This makes the meditation method available to all people without any conflict with their
existing religious loyalties. The practice is simply a way to pay fine-
grained, continuous awareness to all of our experiences of mind and
body. Although it is this simple, it leads us to the highest stages of spiritual unfolding as the major spiritual traditions and figures, including
John of the Cross, see them.

Fruits of practice Buddhist insight meditation is primarily a purgative or purifying form of practice. It dredges up our unfinished moral,
emotional, mental—and even bodily—experiences to purge and heal
them, and to unify the personality. This meditation practice reveals the
depths of our own being to us, and forces self-honesty on us. This
process can profoundly improve physical, emotional, and mental
health.

Meditation practice helps us in various ways. Some of its fringe
benefits are physical: lower blood pressure, lower resting pulse rate,
relaxation, release of tension—even medical healings. It has healed
many psychosomatic ailments, bodily ills that have a large emotional
component. There are also directly emotional benefits: calming and
clarifying emotions, and getting us in touch with emotions before they
start to move us around. It has proven very helpful with managing
impulses to action, which helps with habit management and improves
behavior. Mental benefits include better concentration, the ability to
focus and stay focused, and freedom from fretting, stewing, worrying,
and other mental activity that causes distress.[13]

Spiritual benefits are the chief purpose of the practice, although
those who practice for these other benefits do get them. Some of the
named benefits are only indirectly spiritual ones, but whatever
improves self-management and betters personal functioning is helpful for spiritual practice. Whatever shows us ourselves clearly, and
empties us of clinging, satisfies criteria of John of the Cross for knowing God.

Buddhists' spiritual goal is the unmanifest Ultimate Reality, Nibbana, the only unconditioned, unborn, undying, unmoving, unchanging reality. Insight practice directly prepares us for this. To "touch" Nibbana, or to "know" God, requires a very deep purification of conduct, mental contents, and the heart. "Be virtuous and wise. Swiftly clear the way that leads to Nibbana."[14] The purgatory of insight meditation practice leads to that purity of heart of which the beatitude says: "Blessed are the clean of heart, for they shall see God."[15]

MJM

✛ 3 ✛

The Carmelite Tradition of Prayer

THE CARMELITE TRADITION of prayer began around 209 C.E. on Mount Carmel in the Holy Land. A group of laymen, most likely disillusioned crusaders from Europe, gathered as hermits near a spring named in honor of the Old Testament prophet Elijah to live in solitude and prayer after the example of that great prophet.

Early Carmelites

Little is known about these Western hermits except that they petitioned Albert, the Patriarch of Jerusalem, to give them a rule of life. This rule, known as the Rule of St. Albert, embodies the earliest elements of Carmelite spirituality.

The Rule The hermits were to live a common life committed to following Jesus Christ, serving him with "a pure heart and a good conscience." Sacred scripture nourished their prayer life. They assembled daily for the communal celebration of the Eucharist, and weekly for meetings to discuss their way of life.

The Rule especially enjoined constant prayer in solitude, calling them "to meditate day and night on the law of the Lord." In imitation of Jesus Christ, who retired alone on the mountain to pray, the hermits dedicated themselves to solitary, unceasing prayer. In medieval times, "meditation" on the scriptures meant much more than reasoning, which became the usual understanding of the word. Meditation was a matter of the heart. It involved the constant repetition of a word or phrase from scripture, allowing those words to sink deeply into the heart to purify it of all that was not God.

Mary and Elijah For inspiration in their life of prayer, the hermits of Mount Carmel looked especially to Mary, the mother of Jesus, and to the prophet Elijah. Just as Mary surrendered herself to the Spirit of God overshadowing her, and thus gave birth to Jesus the redeemer of humanity, the early Carmelites strove to yield themselves completely to the Spirit of God to become vessels of Christ's healing presence in a world marred by sin.

The prophet Elijah represented for them a man totally dedicated to God who walked zealously and lived continuously in God's presence. To imitate this fiery prophet, the hermits sought God alone in all things. They endeavored to live with purity of faith and to walk always in God's presence with unswerving fidelity and love.

The Carmelites in Europe

The Saracen invasion of Palestine in the middle of the thirteenth century ended the hermits' life of solitary prayer on Mount Carmel. The Carmelites returned to Europe to establish their eremitical life there.

Early life in Europe Europe posed difficulties. No longer could the Carmelites survive in solitary places as they had in the Holy Land. The change in culture and the ministerial needs of the thirteenth century forced them to adapt their lifestyle to new circumstances. Consequently, they included more communal aspects in their way of living, and added an apostolic dimension to their religious life. They became friars along with the emerging orders of mendicants such as the Franciscans, Dominicans, and Augustinians.

The apostolic orientation of Carmelite life demanded serious theological study to prepare clerical friars for ministry. By the end of the thirteenth century, the friars had entered the great university movement begun earlier in the century and established houses of study near the great educational centers of Europe. The intellectual life of the order flourished. Carmelites were numbered among the renowned theologians, spiritual writers, and humanists of the fourteenth and fifteenth centuries.

Later developments However, the great activity and academic life of the friars, together with the negative effects of the Black Plague, the Hundred Years War, and the Western schism, led to a decline in the observance of the Rule. This produced many attempts during the fourteenth and fifteenth centuries to restore balance between the contemplative and active aspects of the Carmelite life and to recapture the original spirit of those first hermits on Mount Carmel.

An important development of the order began in 1450. Pope Nicholas V signed a bull that permitted pious women to come under the protection of the Order of the Blessed Virgin Mary of Mount Carmel. Under the guidance of Blessed John Soreth, the general of the order, and Blessed Frances of Amboise, the Carmelite nuns blossomed and flourished throughout Europe. Their cloistered life dedicated to interior prayer and the public worship of God revitalized and deeply enriched the spirit of Carmel.

Teresa of Jesus

Teresa of Jesus, born Teresa de Ahumada y Cepeda in 1515, joined one of those convents in Avila, Spain—the Carmelite convent of the Incarnation—in 1535. She entered when she was twenty years old, and lived there for twenty-seven years. Those years were marked both by periods of mystical graces received in contemplative prayer and by inner conflict. For many years, Teresa resisted God's call to deeper fidelity.

Teresa's conversion When Teresa was thirty-nine years old, a profound conversion transformed her life. One day in prayer, she discovered the liberating love of the humanity of Jesus Christ, which freed her from the attachments that for almost twenty years had prevented her from giving herself more completely to God. As she grew freer, Teresa realized that contemplative prayer held the key to healing and transformation in her life.

Teresa's conversion profoundly shaped her understanding of interior prayer. In her autobiography, she defined prayer as "an intimate sharing between friends."[1] To pray is to enter into a loving relationship with Jesus Christ, who lives in the depths of our hearts. The more Teresa opened herself to God's love through contemplative prayer, the more she experienced herself as loved by God—not just once, but many times, and at ever deeper levels of her being. This loving relationship healed her brokenness and cleansed her of the attachments and sinful patterns that had earlier prevented her from centering her life completely on God. Teresa thus came to see relationship as the essence of prayer. She discovered that prayer is a loving relationship that transforms us because love alone heals and purifies the human person.

Teresa did not relegate interior prayer only to formal periods of solitude. She understood prayer as a way of life. Prayer and life go hand in hand. We are in relationship with God, not only when we are on our knees, but in every aspect of our lives. For this reason, Teresa emphasized the importance of constant growth in virtue as a foundation and expression of our relationship with God. She particularly stressed the virtues of love of neighbor, humility, and detachment. She knew from her own experience that mutual love and respect, truthfulness, and interior freedom are necessary for contemplative living and are also fruits of its increase in our lives.

Encountering Jesus For Teresa, the experience of God was also an encounter with Jesus Christ. Her earliest method of prayer was to strive to remain present to Jesus Christ living within her.[2] As her relationship with Christ deepened, the risen Lord revealed himself powerfully to her as a faithful friend and companion in life. He introduced her into the mystery of the Trinity.

As a result, Teresa stressed the importance of the humanity of Jesus Christ in our relationship with God. In and through Jesus Christ, we learn who God is and what it means to be fully human. As our model and faithful friend, Jesus leads us to an ever-deepening experience of our triune God. Throughout her writings Teresa taught her readers to "look at" Christ—within themselves, in the gospels, in the Eucharist, and in one another.[3]

Finally, Teresa's prayer became increasingly interior and dynamic.

As her contemplative life deepened, Teresa became more and more conscious of God's presence within her. In *The Interior Castle,* she wrote that the "soul is like a castle made entirely out of a diamond or of very clear crystal, in which there are many rooms."[4] At the very center of this castle dwells God, who imparts to us life, beauty, and dignity. Prayer is the doorway through which we enter this castle. The contemplative life is an interior journey into the very depths of our being where we meet our loving God. As our journey inward deepens, we become more conscious of God's dynamic presence within us and of our own life being rooted in Christ.

The Teresian reform Inspired by the primitive ideals of the first hermits on Mount Carmel and responding to the religious upheaval caused by the Reformation, Teresa began a reform convent of Carmelite nuns at San Jose in Avila in 1562. Her ideal in establishing this community was to gather a small group of women who would live as good friends of Christ and good friends of one another, all occupied in unceasing prayer for the good of the church. Five years later, Teresa set out to establish other reformed communities throughout Spain.

In 1567, while making her second foundation of nuns in Medina del Campo, Teresa met a young Carmelite friar named John of St. Matthias. Before their encounter, John had been discerning his desire for a life of deeper solitude and prayer. Teresa persuaded him to join her reform. In 1568, John and another friar, with Teresa's assistance, established the first monastery of men in the Teresian reform. At this time he changed his name to John of the Cross.

The friars shared Teresa's vision and charisma. They dedicated themselves to a life of contemplative prayer and public worship of God. However, unlike the nuns, who lived an enclosed religious life, the friars engaged in pastoral ministry. They preached in local parishes, taught catechism, heard confessions, and became renowned as spiritual directors. Their life of interior prayer, combined with public ministry, disposed them for a rich experience of God and of human nature that enabled them to assist others seeking a deeper relationship with God through prayer. John of the Cross, whose writings and example we follow in this book, became such a spiritual guide.

John of the Cross

John was born of a poor family in 1542 in Fontiveros, Spain.[5] He entered the Carmelite friars in 1563 in Medina del Campo and was ordained in 1567.

Our divine vocation Writing out of his profound experience of God and human nature, John addressed his major works to the pastoral need for better spiritual guidance for his contemporaries. He showed them a way of purifying and healing their hearts.

In his ministry as confessor and spiritual director, John met many people whom God was inviting to deeper contemplative prayer, but who felt confused and dismayed by their own interior poverty and darkness. Few spiritual directors seemed equipped to understand and discern the purifying movements of the Spirit in contemplative prayer. John desired to enlighten and encourage both spiritual people and their directors.

The starting point for understanding John's spiritual teaching is our divine vocation to "union with God through love." He taught that God longs to be in relationship with us, that we are made out of love and for love. By our very creation, God has destined us to participate fully through grace in the divine life of love and to love other persons and our world with God's own mind and heart.

Our human condition However, a profound disorder exists in our relationships with God, others, and the world. Despite our best efforts, we find it difficult to love as God created us to love. Our human nature has been wounded by original sin, our past sinful choices, and our personal history with all the factors that make up our personality. We need healing and purification.

Our disordered relationships are seen in how easily we become enslaved by inordinate desires and attachments. We tend to pour out ourselves into created reality that will never fully satisfy us. We futilely seek peace and satisfaction of heart in material possessions, food, honors, unhealthy relationships, and even spiritual consolations in prayer. Our inability to love properly is present whenever self-gratification motivates our relationships with God, others, and creation. When we pray, help others, and fulfill our daily tasks solely for our own pleasure, we make our own egos the center of attention.

Sin and inordinate desires wound us so profoundly that we cannot heal ourselves. Only God's love can penetrate the deepest recesses of the human heart to purify its selfish desires and disordered relationships. In *The Ascent of Mount Carmel* and *The Dark Night,* John analyzed the human condition and gave us a path toward healing. He taught that contemplation, which he described as a secret and peaceful inflow of God's love in the soul, heals the human heart of these disordered relationships. Contemplation is the fire of God's love that heals, purifies, and transforms our hearts, recreating them to reflect the image of God for whom we were created.[6]

Contemplation: a path of purification John's symbol for this process of healing and purification is the dark night of sense and spirit. This night is both active and passive. In the active part, we undertake to purify ourselves out of love for God; in the passive part, God's love purifies, heals, and transforms us. Although we may experience the dark night as an absence of God or a time of painful self-knowledge and crisis, John believed that the dark night signals the dawn of new life, and is God's loving concern to restore and heal human nature.

The path of purification, John also taught, means following Jesus Christ. In *The Ascent of Mount Carmel,* John placed before us the life and death of Jesus as the model of the path of purification.[7] Jesus lived a life of total dedication to his Father and of self-giving love for others that called for a total surrender of false securities and self-gratification. His death on the cross summed up his life of self-emptying love. Jesus performed his greatest work of salvation when he was most empty and poor on the cross. Following Jesus implies a life of loving dedication to God and the surrender of our attachments and selfishness in order to love more freely. It means becoming empty of self for the love of God and others in imitation of Jesus Christ.

Finally, John taught that the journey toward union with God means living the theological virtues of faith, hope, and love. These virtues both unite us to God and purify us; they are the way to union with God. God infuses the virtues into us and through them we enter into communication with God. Faith, hope, and love purify us by empty-ing the intellect, memory, and will of all that is not God. For John, the theological virtues are more than truths we assent to or actions we perform; they make possible our loving, interpersonal relationship with God that purifies our souls.

Subsequent Carmelite History

The Teresian reform officially became an order separate from the Carmelites of the Ancient Observance in 1593. Known as *Discalced* (because they went barefoot or wore only sandals) Carmelite friars and nuns, the order spread rapidly throughout Europe.

Even in Teresa's lifetime, mission efforts, which continue in this day, began in Africa. In 1790, Teresa's "daughters" (religious sisters follow-ing her reform) came to the United States and made the first founda-tion of Discalced Carmelite nuns in Port Tobacco, Maryland. From 1209 to the present, Carmelites from both branches of the order have witnessed by their lives of prayer and apostolic zeal to the transform-ing power of prayer and the presence of the living God in our world. Among them are some of Christianity's great spiritual teachers.

Some Carmelite saints One example is Mary Magdalen de Pazzi in sixteenth-century Florence. From an early age, God graced Mary Magdalen with a profound insight into God's love for each individual and God's fidelity to us even in the midst of great interior darkness. She was known as an "angel of charity" because of her ardent love for God and others.

The seventeenth-century French lay brother, Brother Lawrence of the Resurrection, is widely known among Protestants and Catholics for his practice of the presence of God. This humble brother served his community as cook and sandal-maker, and found God just as much among the pots and pans of his kitchen as when on his knees in chapel.[8]

His French Carmelite "sister," Elizabeth of the Trinity, announced a similar message in the twentieth century. Elizabeth based her spiritual life on the simple but profound truth that our triune God dwells within the deepest recesses of our hearts. We possess all riches within us, and need only allow the divine life within us to grow.

Another great French spiritual teacher of Carmel is Therese of Lisieux.[9] Therese lived a hidden life of prayer and sacrifice, yet she is recognized as the patroness of missions and as a genius of the spiritual life for her simple and refreshing Gospel message. Many people who experience their interior poverty and brokenness find an authentic path of transformation in her "little way" of confident surrender to God's merciful love.

Two martyrs Two great twentieth-century prophets of the Carmelite tradition of prayer are Blessed Titus Brandsma and Blessed Teresa Benedicta of the Cross (Edith Stein). Titus surrendered his life to God in 1942 in the Nazi death camp of Dachau, and Teresa Benedicta sacrificed hers the same year in Auschwitz. In imitation of Jesus Christ, both offered their lives freely for the salvation of a world stigmatized by hatred and violence. They proclaimed by their sacrificial lives the liberating and purifying effect of contemplation in a person's life. Titus and Teresa Benedicta stand among many of Carmel's prophets who, for nearly eight centuries, have prophesied that contemplative prayer is a path of self-emptying love that can heal and transform our personal and collective lives.

DC

✠ PART II

MEDITATION INSTRUCTIONS
AND GUIDANCE IN PRACTICE

✣ 4 ✣

Instructions for Insight Practice:
Preparation, Breath, Body, Thinking

THIS AND the following chapter give explicit instructions on how to practice insight meditation. Learning insight practice is simplest when you consolidate work with each aspect of it before going on to the next. We recommend spending some time—at least a week of daily practice—working with each instruction before adding later ones. Thirty minutes of practice a day is an excellent beginning.

Preparation

Our first considerations are proper posture and the *primary object*. Proper posture greatly helps practice. Our primary object is "home base" for our attention while meditating.

Establishing posture Insight practice is best done sitting in a firm and unmoving posture. You may sit in a straight chair, or cross-legged on a firm cushion on the floor, or kneel on a *seiza* (sitting or prayer) bench. Putting a mat or folded blanket underneath you cushions legs and knees. Initially, while still establishing basic practice, you might occasionally move to adjust an uncomfortable posture. Eventually you should sit as still as possible.

Sitting in a good posture, with a relatively straight spine, helps prevent stress on muscles. Holding your back straight is easiest when your hipbones are higher than your knee bones. If using a cushion, sit near the front edge so that all your buttocks, but none of your upper legs, are on the cushion. The simplest cross-legged posture is Burmese style. Bend the knee of one leg and draw the heel in as close to your groin as you can. Bend the other knee, and pull that leg in as close to the first one as possible. Both knees and ankles should rest on the floor. You can help leg muscles loosen for this by practicing sitting outside of formal meditation time—such as while watching television or talking with friends or family.

Sitting benches throw your back into a good alignment, but ankles often are stiff at the beginning. This discomfort lessens in time. If you meditate sitting in a chair, do not lean against the back. A chair that slopes slightly toward the front is most helpful. Putting one-half to one inch blocks under the back legs of a chair, or obtaining a firm foam wedge for the seat of the chair, helps produce this slope. Both feet should rest firmly on the ground, one to two feet apart.

Your shoulders should be over the hipbones, and your earlobes in line with your shoulders. It helps to tuck your chin slightly and make the back of the top of your head the highest body point. Once seated, adjust the curve in your spine to a comfortable position by drawing your navel forward or pushing it backward. You can also try lifting your chest up and forward. Check to be sure that your shoulders are hanging loosely, and are not hunched up around your neck. Place your hands however feels comfortable; some people cup them together and others rest them on their legs.

When correctly seated, your bones will simply stack themselves on top of each other. Eventually, this will enable you to hold an erect posture with very little strain or effort. Until posture is well established, check at the beginning of each sitting to be sure that you are not tightly holding your body in place and that your shoulders hang loosely.

Don't expect to have perfect posture immediately! Play around with it until it feels right. Erect posture is important, not for any "magical" reasons, but simply because it helps to minimize strain on the body.

Choosing the primary object We choose a primary object, an experience we begin practice by attending to, and to which we return when nothing else is drawing attention. We usually use the breath since it is almost always easily found. Going back to the breath at regular intervals deepens concentration as a foundation for awareness practice. It also gives us a focus for attention when there are no other experiences to watch.

Identify where you experience your breath most easily. Sitting with your eyes closed, pay attention to the flow of the breath. Try to discern in which of three places you feel the sensations of breathing most clearly. Check where the upper lip meets the nostrils, the rising and falling of the chest, and the rising and falling of the diaphragm or belly.[1] Try to let go of any preconceived ideas about where it is best to feel the breath, and just look to your own direct experience. If no place stands out more clearly than the others, see if your mind more comfortably gravitates to one place. Once you have chosen a place, use it regularly unless you and a teacher decide that you need to change it.[2]

Instruction 1: Breath Awareness

If you have worked with the breath in any other form of meditation practice, please set that aside. How we work with breath in this practice prepares us for the rest of the practice. Using other breathing practices will compete with mindfulness practice; you will likely "ping-pong" between practices and not really be doing either practice.

Beginning practice Sitting comfortably erect, become aware of where you have chosen to watch the breath. Hold awareness there without moving it around, and feel all of the sensations of the breath at that place. Put all your awareness on the sensations of the breath at the place where you are watching until the inhalation ends.

As soon as you notice that an inhalation is starting, acknowledge this awareness by "noting"—softly whispering in your mind—"in." If you are watching at the chest or diaphragm, you may note "rising" if you prefer. Such *mental noting* is an important tool in this practice. It lets you know that you are attending to your experience.

When you become aware that an exhalation is starting, softly note "out" or "falling." Put all your awareness on the sensations of the breath at your place until the exhalation ends. Continue in this way to experience inhalations and exhalations of the breath. Try to note the very beginning of awareness of each inhalation and exhalation. However, do not anticipate the start of the breath; that would make the note a command to your body to breathe.

The note should be a very soft mental whisper, using no more than five percent of available energy. Make it loud enough to help hold you on target, but not so loud as to draw attention away from the sensations. You may make a short note at the beginning of the breath, stretch it out across the whole breath, or choose something in between. Do whatever most helps you stay focused.

Be in very close touch with all the sensations of the breath where you are observing. Do not look down at the sensations from your head, or at some image you make of them. Put your awareness "inside" the sensations themselves, where the nerve endings are. Make no attempt to control the breath in any way; let it flow just as it does by itself. Smooth, bumpy, long, short, even, irregular—all are okay. Do not "grasp" at the sensations; they come by themselves when you are attentive.

When you are not with the breath When you become aware that attention has wandered from the breath, acknowledge the experience to which you are attending by softly noting it with a descriptive word—"thinking", "hearing," and so on—to acknowledge awareness of where attention went. Then gently bring attention back to the breath. Getting lost in thought is the most common early experience; it says nothing about your ability to do this practice. So long as you return to the breath as soon as you become aware of wandering, you are doing the practice correctly.

If discomfort keeps drawing awareness from the breath, first try to note it and return to the breath. If you still feel the need, you may gently adjust posture to reduce it. Also note any other sensation or emotion that draws your attention, then return to the breath. Eventually all these other experiences will not be treated as wandering from the task; they become part of the practice after you have learned how to work with them.

If there is a pause between breaths, move awareness to feeling your whole body sitting. Note "sitting," and feel your body sitting until the next breath starts. If the pause is long, add awareness of a place where part of your body is touching something. This may be buttocks on seat, hand on leg, or any other place you can feel a touch sensation. Note "touching," and feel its sensations. If the pause is very long, go back and forth between "sitting" and "touching" until the breath starts again. Never try to make pauses in the breath occur.

Some general instructions Sometimes working with the breath is very difficult, such as when you have a head cold. You may then want to use "sitting-touching" as the primary object, holding awareness on each for about the length of an in- or out-breath.

To begin practice well, it helps to build some concentration and become comfortable working with breath awareness before adding other steps. Spend at least half a dozen hours working with the breath before tackling the next instruction.

Instruction 2: Working with Body Sensations

This section teaches you how to work with body experiences. Body sensations fall into three main types: temperature changes, feelings of movement, and touch sensations.

Temperature changes When you meditate, you might become aware that your body feels cooler or warmer. Sometimes a particular part of your body might feel like it is burning or freezing. When such awareness stays on the fringe of attention, remain centered on the breath.

However, if temperature draws your attention from the breath, immediately focus fully on that sensation. Note it with a descriptive word, such as "coolness," "burning," "warm," or "freezing." Do not try to hold onto breath awareness also; you are no longer there. Put all your attention inside the feeling of temperature.

If the experience ends, go back to the breath. If attention wanders to something else, note it, then return to the breath. If the awareness of temperature continues, repeat the note about every five or ten seconds—often enough to hold attention firmly, but not so often as to distract you from feeling the sensation. After a minute or so, go back to the breath. If the same awareness again draws attention, work with it again. So long as it keeps drawing attention, you can work with it. Remember, though, to take regular "breathers" back to the sensations created by the breath—to go back frequently to the primary object.

Movement sensations Sometimes your body might feel like it is moving. When such sensation is strong enough to draw attention away from the breath, sink awareness into it. Immediately note it with an appropriate word, such as "floating," "swaying," "vibrating," or "bouncing." Put full attention inside the movement sensation. Do not try to recapture the breath or check to see if your body actually is moving. If you experience moving, it is "real" for the practice, and you work with it.

Repeat the noting as explained above for temperature changes. Also follow those instructions on returning to the breath. When working with movement, add an intention to still the body when returning to the breath. Otherwise, if actual movement is occurring, it will almost certainly again claim attention. We want it to be possible for another experience to surface. However, do work with movement whenever it draws your attention.

Touch sensations Touch sensations can be of many kinds. In initial practice, most of them are unpleasant. We are so accustomed to quickly tuning out uncomfortable body sensations, or making minor adjustments to eliminate them, that we do not really know how our bodies feel most of the time. When we sit attentively, these discomforts come into awareness. This initial unpleasantness will lessen.

As soon as you become aware that a body sensation has become strong enough to draw attention from the breath, sink awareness into the experience, noting it with an appropriate descriptive word. Some examples are "itching," "cramping," and "tingling." You can use generic words like "sensing" or "touching" if a more descriptive word does not easily come to mind. Follow the instructions above on repeating the note and on returning to the breath.

If a touch sensation is particularly intense, you may return to the breath more frequently to rest your mind. You can also place the sensation along the edges of awareness for a while, and deliberately focus attention on the breath. Never try to push the sensation away, or to pretend that it is not there. Sometimes making the area of sensation being watched either larger or smaller makes it easier to stay with the sensation.[3]

Other considerations Once we start work with body sensations, we try to sit as still as possible so that we do not cut off experiences. When you begin a sitting, make the silent resolve "May I not move without knowing it." This will help you see urges to move before you are in motion. Eventually, doing so will become habitual.

Try not to move on your first impulse to move—or on subsequent ones; see if you are willing to settle back and be with the experience a little longer. However, this practice is to be done very gently. Do not over-control, tense up, or otherwise fight an experience. When your willingness becomes "thin," make whatever adjustment is needed, go back to the breath, and begin again. Willingness will gradually grow, and you will also notice that petty environmental discomforts bother you less. Your body is not harmed if your legs "fall asleep"; that and itching are very common experiences.

Gerunds, words that end in "ing," are the best words for noting because they capture the sense of an ongoing process. However, do not look hard for just the right word to note meditation experiences. Over time, a vocabulary will automatically build to note different kinds of experiences.

Work with body sensations for at least half a dozen hours of practice before adding another instruction. This will give you a solid grounding in doing the practice.

Instruction 3: Working with Thinking

You have undoubtedly noticed that sensations can continue while you focus mindful awareness on them. Thinking is different; to keep a train of thought going, we usually must get lost in it. Once we turn the bright spotlight of awareness onto thinking, it evaporates like mist.[4]

Escaping the present moment With thought, we "create" alternative worlds to inhabit, instead of living in the actual reality of here-and-now experience. We make imaginary fantasy worlds when we talk to our-selves about what is happening or write mental stories about it. Thoughts seduce us, and we often want to continue living in their world. When we do, we are no longer meditating.

We escape from the present moment into thought in three basic ways. First, we might try to hold onto the past. When we get caught up in memories, or replay past experiences, we are doing this. We can-not experience the past directly; it is not happening now. When we try to hold onto it, we are only re-creating it in the imaginary world of thought.

Sometimes we try to make the future present now—again, an impossible endeavor. We can only create thoughts about the future, and then live in this unreal world of our own making. We do that when we get caught up in planning, rehearsing, or anticipating.

Sometimes we simply just push away the present moment or dis-tance ourselves from it. We might judge experiences or ourselves, complain mentally about what is happening, or stage a drama with self as the star. We also might analyze what is happening, or keep a running commentary going on in the mind.

There is nothing wrong with thoughts coming. Thought is perfectly natural, and we cannot stop it by trying. Some insights and other important information might come in the form of thought. However, we do not want to get lost in thought since that closes down medita-tion. It stops the very process that brings us important understanding.

Managing thinking Every meditator spends time lost in thought. Sometimes we can see thoughts come and go without following off after them, but at the beginning we are more likely to get lost in them. Do not be dismayed by this; it will improve with practice. Just persist-ently note "thinking" as soon as you become aware of it, and then return to the breath. A major problem is our reluctance to leave thought. You need to be careful not to let greed for thoughts draw you away from meditation practice.

Remember that thoughts die when awareness is focused on them; eventually you will clearly see how thought dissipates. Whenever an experience ends, we return to the breath, so immediately return to the breath after noting thought. If you wait to see what will happen instead of returning to the breath when you become aware of thinking, another thought will come quickly. Pretty soon you will be lost in thinking again.

We can refine work with thought by noting the kind of thinking we do. This is not the content of thought—their object or "story line," but just the type of thought. You can use such notes as "remembering," "planning," "self-dramatizing," "complaining," and so on. This helps us see where we spend most of our time running away—into the past or future, or just pushing away the present. We realize this without thinking about it; it comes from just doing the noting.

Become fully comfortable practicing all the instructions given so far before moving on. Instructions continue in the following chapter.

MJM

✳ 5 ✳

Instructions for Insight Practice: Other Senses, Mind-States, Points of Freedom, Walking

T HIS CHAPTER completes the basic meditation instructions. It gets us to the heart of how meditation removes impediments to our freedom.

Instruction 4: Working With the Other Senses

In awareness practice, we note and attend to our own experiences only. When the body is cramping, tingling, or itching, that this is our experience. However, the various kinds of seeing, hearing, smelling, and tasting that we experience are only simple experiences of these senses. The bird is chirping, the car is roaring, and so on. These experiences are the bird's and car's, not yours; your experience is just hearing.

This makes work with these other four senses—seeing, hearing, smelling, and tasting—easy compared to body sensations. We have only one note for each of them: "seeing," "hearing," "smelling," or "tasting."[1] Use the guidelines given for body sensations for attending to these experiences, noting them, and going back to the breath.

Some people get a lot of visual imagery as soon as they close their eyes to meditate. Others are flooded with sound. Still other people may practice for years and seldom experience such things. There is no right or wrong way. Work with the practice as it happens for you.

Sometimes we have repetitious experiences. Someone may be running a lawn mower, and attention keeps going to the sound. Or, some kind of visual imagery may occur repetitively. In such instances, note and work with the experience the first few times it draws attention. Then "invite" it to rest around the edges of awareness as background, and go to the breath to allow other experiences to surface. This is rather how we look at a painting; much in a painting is background, as we focus on one object at a time. However, if an experience again draws you away from the breath, work with it again.

Do not ask if what you see, hear, smell, or taste is "real." If you experience it, it is "real" for the practice. Do not worry about whether your mind is creating experiences or not. It does this every night when you dream. Meditation is just one other situation that can cause this to happen.[2]

Instruction 5: Working with Mind-States

Mind-states include emotions, states of awareness, sets, moods, and some mental "housekeeping" functions. We are most easily aware of strong mind-states like anger, sleepiness, fear, or joy.

Understanding mind-states To easily understand mind-states, think of them as a dye or tint in your mind. This coloring of the mind affects everything else you experience. A mind-state is like colored glasses you wear; you see everything else through it. When you are angry, anger tints everything else you experience. When intense joy is present, even difficult circumstances or events are not a problem because joy colors them. Sleepiness puts a haze and heaviness on everything.

In conditioned reality (explained in Chapter 2), mind-states are always present. Some are very subtle, and attention is not likely to be drawn to them. At the end of a very peaceful day, you might realize that the whole day was colored by this state of peacefulness. Usually you won't be aware of this unless you stop to reflect on it. The mind-state is the blueness, peacefulness, restlessness, jitteriness, and so on that we experience. It is different from the thoughts about those states that they usually draw.

All mind-states have associated body states. Some are very obvious. Sadness brings tightening and heaviness in your chest and choking in your throat. If you are about to cry, you feel stinging in your eyes. When you actually do cry, there are heaving, shaking, and sobbing movements. With sleepiness, you have heaviness in your eyelids and sinking feelings. Anger often brings heat and tense muscles. The body states connected to very subtle mind-states might be difficult to feel. Instructions on working with mind-states in meditation follow shortly.

Emotional management In meditation practice, we handle emotions differently than we do in our everyday lives. In our everyday lives, we usually do one of two unhelpful things with strong emotions.

Sometimes, when we feel one coming, we do everything we can to avoid it. We call a friend to talk on the phone, escape into watching whatever happens to be on television, go out looking for something to do—or reach for our favorite addiction. We can hold off the bad feeling for a while. But two hours, two days, or two weeks later, it returns. We have not solved anything because we have not dealt with it.

A second unfruitful strategy is the opposite of this. We get completely lost, and "drown" in the mind-state. We lose all perspective, and start feeding the mind-state with thoughts that intensify it. We might grind around on resentments, calling to mind all the shoddy things that someone did to us. We might think of everything that could go wrong tomorrow when we interview for a job we really want, and get lost in anxiety. We might feed sadness with self-pity or melodrama, talking to ourselves about our woes or sorrows. Some people go on crying jags, trying to "cry it all out."

It can be terribly tempting to think that, if you just really dissolve into such mind-states, you can resolve them. Instead, this tends to simply strengthen them. The more you ruminate on a hurt feeling, for example, the more deeply it ingrains itself in your mind. You give it a tighter hold on you.

Working with mind-states When we work with mind-states in awareness practice, we fully experience them, not pushing them away. But we also do not get lost in our emotions or feed them with thinking. We avoid both these errors that do not work well for us in our ordinary everyday experience. This meditative way of experiencing mind-states allows them to be healed.

When a mind-state draws attention from your primary object, fully sink awareness into the mind-state, not trying to hold onto the breath also. As soon as you notice the mind-state, note it with an appropriate word such as "sadness," "sleepiness," "anger," "fear," and so on.

Do not look through your body for physical experiences that go with the mind-state, but do sit with openness to be aware of what is happening in your body. If a body experience draws your attention, note it with an appropriately descriptive word. Work with it like all other body experiences.

You can go back and forth between noting the mental and bodily sides of a mind-state, as different experiences related to it occur. You should be noting something at least every five to ten seconds. So long as you are noting, you are not lost in the experience. You are both experiencing and observing at the same time.

Be very alert to catch thought when working with mind-states. As soon as a thought comes, see it clearly, note "thinking," and return immediately to the breath. Thoughts associated with a mind-state invite it to stay around and grow stronger. You do not want to chase the mind-state away, but you also do not want to do anything to encourage it to stay or intensify.

After working with a mind-state for a minute or so, take a breather back to the breath. If another experience draws your attention, work with it. If the same mind-state draws you again, stay with it again for a while. You can spend most of the sitting on the same mind-state if it keeps drawing you, but remember to take breaks to the sensations of the breath. This keeps concentration strong and allows other experiences to draw attention.

Build your awareness practice carefully. Work with mind-states added to your practice for at least half a dozen hours before adding the next instruction.

Instruction 6: Working with Our Points of Freedom

Feeling-tone and intention are two special mind-states. They are very important in insight meditation practice because they are mark places where we can get free of conditioned reactions; they are our *points of freedom.* Careful attentiveness to feeling-tone helps keep us from getting lost in unwholesome mind-states. Working with intention gives us space to be able to say "no" to unhelpful behavior.

Feeling-tone Everything we experience has a feeling-tone—a degree of pleasantness, unpleasantness, or neutrality. Pleasantness, or anticipating pleasantness, draws out greed—such as lust, avarice, gluttony, and so on. Unpleasantness, or anticipating unpleasantness, draws out aversion—such as anger, sadness, fear, anxiety, and so on. When feeling-tone is neutral, the experience does not grip us strongly and we may "space out;" we become inattentive, bored, or sleepy. This puts us in delusion, ignorance of the true nature of what is happening.

Ordinarily, we are not aware of feeling-tone until it precipitates us into one of the unwholesome mind-states. Paying careful attention to feeling-tone shows us that our conditioned emotional reactions can become a choice. We can get free of the mind-states that so often keep us in mental turmoil.

We work with feeling-tone like any other mind-state. Do not search your mind looking for it, but sit with openness to be aware of it. At times, it will arise in the mind as a dominant experience. Intensely pleasant or unpleasant feeling-tone is the easiest to see; neutrality is usually not seen until practice is rather advanced.

When feeling-tone draws your attention, sink full awareness into its pleasantness, unpleasantness, or neutrality. Note it as "pleasant," "unpleasant," or "neutral." If associated body experiences come into awareness, work with them also.

When you are experiencing a lot of greed or aversion, becoming aware of feeling-tone is very helpful. This also helps you work with intense sensations. Eventually you will see that mind-state reactions to our experiences are voluntary, and also that even intense feeling-tone will finally dim and change without your doing anything.

Awareness of feeling-tone is helpful in everyday life, too. When emotions come up, try to see to what pleasantness or unpleasantness you are reacting. You should be able to see that the problem is not really that unpleasant other person or this delicious ice cream, but simply that you are reacting to feeling-tone. Such awareness greatly moderates unhelpful reactions to life events.

Intention An intention forms before every action we take. Sometimes we are clearly aware of it as an intention, but sometimes it feels only like some impulse or urge arising in us.[3] Once an intention becomes strong enough, action follows automatically; we are past being able to decide about it.

We can trust our intentions or impulses to act only when we know our minds to be free of unwholesome reactivity. Only then can situations draw an appropriate response from us. When we become clearly aware of intentions, we can change our mind about unhelpful ones by countering them with a contrary intention before they propel us into action. This helps free us from committing wrong actions.

When you feel an impulse to move while meditating, be aware that this is an intention and note it as "intending." Careful noting of intention often helps us counter it with a contrary intention, and we can remain unmoving. Watching intention also shows us that, without our doing anything at all about them, intentions will eventually go away. This teaches us that all urges will end whether we act on them or not.

If you make a voluntary movement, be sure to note the initiating intention. Also note the actions of scratching, lifting, or turning—whatever your movements—while paying attention to the sensations you are creating while moving.

Becoming aware of intentions in daily life is very helpful. Whenever you react strongly to any experience, intentions are apt to arise. By being prepared for them, you can accept them without being drawn into unthinking action. Work with feeling-tone and intention ends the basic instructions for formal sitting practice.

The chain of behavior For all of our behavior, we can trace five important components. First, there is the impact of an experience. Second is its feeling-tone, which comes simultaneously with the experience.[4] If we are not very alert, reactivity to it—the mind-states arising from the pleasantness, unpleasantness, or neutrality of feeling-tone—might then come. When a mind-state becomes sufficiently intense, it gives rise to an intention to act upon the greed, aversion, or delusion that has arisen. When an intention becomes strong enough, it propels us into action, the final step.

So, we have a chain of "Experience/Feeling-tone———➤Reactive Mind-states———➤Intentions———➤Overt behavior." The major point of freedom from suffering negative emotions is between feeling-tone and reactive mind-states, and that from inappropriate behavior is between intentions and overt behavior.

Each of these five parts is, in itself, another experience that triggers its own chain. So, our experience in everyday life is a complex network of many simultaneous chains from experience to action. Meditation practice slows down our experience enough so that we can actually see all these parts. Working with them in practice then carries over to everyday life.

Instruction 7: Walking Practice

During retreats, walking practice is important to balance energy. Combined with sitting, it makes a complete meditation practice. Off retreat, we are usually energized by other activities, but some people still find walking very helpful. When your mind is especially scattered, some walking practice before sitting may gather it in, so that you are really grounded when you sit. Some people also like to do walking practice just for its own sake. Outside of formal practice, awareness of walking while moving around during the day helps keeps us balanced and mindful.

Basics of walking To do formal walking practice, choose a path ten to twenty steps in length. You walk back and forth along this path. By just going back and forth, you pretty quickly realize you are not going anywhere, and settle down to pay attention simply to the walking itself. Hold your hands however you wish, in front or in back of your body, but do not keep changing them around, as that distracts you. Cast your eyes on the ground about two to four feet ahead; do not look around.

Divide the walking period into three parts at different walking speeds. At the beginning, take about one-third of the walking period for each part. Later you will see that sometimes you need more of the brisk movement for energy, and at other times walking quite slowly for most of the period feels appropriate.

First, walk at near-normal pace. Pay attention to the sensations in the moving leg. You will probably feel only the pressure of putting your foot down. Do not actually look at your leg, but sink awareness into feeling the sensations that walking creates in it. As you walk, note "left, right" to acknowledge your awareness of which leg is moving. (You may note "stepping, stepping" if you have left-right confusion.)

When you reach the end of the path, stop. Note "standing," and feel your whole body standing. Closing your eyes briefly and/or running attention up or down your body sometimes helps. Then turn around. As soon as you start the turn, note "turning," and feel the movement of your body turning. Then go back over the path noting each step and feeling the sensations in the moving leg.

For the second part, go more slowly. For each step, note both "lifting" and "placing." Try to feel how the sensations of lifting differ from those of placing. Keep attention on the sensations in the moving leg. Each time you reach the end of the path, note "standing" and "turning" as described above.

More refined attention For the third part of walking practice, you may go as slowly as you can while still maintaining balance.[5] Note four parts to each step: "lifting," "moving," "placing," and "shifting." After shifting weight, bring attention to the back leg and begin another step. This walking looks peculiar, since it is not how we ordinarily walk. Both feet will be flat on the floor during the shifting. You should fully complete one step before beginning the next. Stand and turn at the end of the path as described above.

If you have trouble with balance, taking smaller steps will help. You may also walk alongside a wall, and balance against it, if necessary.

If attention goes to other things while walking, let them be "background" awareness, and hold your attention on the sensations in the moving leg. Do not note other things while walking. If they keep drawing attention, stop walking to note and attend to them briefly. Then bring attention back to your leg, and again begin walking.

If you want to refine walking practice, add working with intention. You can observe and note the intention before turning, and before beginning to walk each length. During very slow walking, you might want to note the intention before each lifting movement. Do not note intentions in the middle parts of a step.

In Conclusion

This ends the insight meditation instructions. These instructions given are for beginners. As our practice matures, the basic method remains the same; however, we make some adjustments on how long we watch any given experience, moving attention among experiences, and noting. Seek guidance from a teacher when your practice begins to ripen or if you have questions.[6]

MJM

✢ 6 ✢

Establishing Your Meditation Practice

T HIS CHAPTER helps you get started. It summarizes the instructions given, describes major issues in starting practice, and offers some reflections on the process.

Getting Launched

This practice is most easily learned in a retreat taught by a competent teacher, since guidance is immediately available. The second easiest way is in a class, with instructions given over a six- to eight-week period. However, you can get a good start from the written materials in this book. If working only from written materials, do not try to do too much at once. Introduce the practice gradually so you can consolidate learning at every step.[1]

General practice summary The basic insight practice is quite simple in theory. However, developing concentration and awareness takes commitment. We start with a primary object, usually the breath, to establish concentration. We attend to all other experiences with mindfulness, according to a simple method.

1) Become aware of the dominant event occurring in your body or mind.

2) Acknowledge and anchor this awareness by descriptively "naming" the experience at the very first awareness of it. Make a soft little whisper in the mind called mental noting.

3) Observe all that happens within the experience until it ends, resting full attention in it in a receptive manner.

4) Maintain a soft, gentle, persistent willingness. Do not try to make any experience come, stay, or be a particular way; do not try to prevent or push away any experience.[2]

Insight meditation for beginners Since Christians usually begin meditating with a "thinking" or discursive practice, we are sometimes asked whether they may safely start with a non-discursive practice like insight meditation. Can they dispense with the classic Christian model of starting with discursive meditation and moving to non-discursive or contemplative prayer when the signs indicate that the time is right?

John of the Cross advised beginners to practice discursive meditation to deepen their knowledge and love of Jesus Christ. Delight in this new knowledge and love reinforces their commitment to follow Christ, especially in hard times. John maintained that leaving discursive meditation before we are established in this knowledge and love can be detrimental.

Yet many Christians report never being able to pray discursively; from the very beginning of their spiritual journey they have practiced non-discursive meditation.[3] As their meditation has deepened, their knowledge and love of God has also grown.

The Buddhist practice this book teaches is a suitable non-discursive method for Christian beginners. We start insight practice with a stable posture, focus on the present moment's experience, and a receptive attitude. Then meditation practice unfolds through the normal developmental stages that lead eventually to enlightenment.

We maintain that Christians can begin interior prayer with such non-discursive meditation, provided their knowledge and love of God is nourished in other ways—such as liturgical worship or *lectio divina* ("divine reading"). When knowledge and love of God deepen through other sources, discursive meditation is not necessary. Also, simply doing the meditation practice, making oneself fully open to God's purifying action, is itself an act of love for God.

Some people are drawn to discursive meditation in the beginning and profit from it greatly. Yet eventually they must let go of it when they are called to deeper, more contemplative prayer. Be guided by your own individual needs.

Hindrances to Practice

Traditionally, Buddhists name five problems that make early meditation practice difficult. They can derail us if we do not deal with them
vigorously. The most important remedy is to be acutely aware when
these hindrances are present. Making them objects of observation
defuses their power and can prevent our becoming caught up in them.

Greed Greed covers several Christian capital sins—avarice, lust,
and gluttony. Clinging to what is pleasant or appealing can even keep
us from starting spiritual practice. Although this hindrance literally
refers to sense pleasures, greed has many faces. A Buddhist text men-
tions "attachments to family, property, business, and friends."[4] Greed
quickly and easily draws us to its objects, and can be subtle and hard
to recognize.

Greed invades meditation practice. Getting lost in trains of thought
shows greed is at work. We are amazingly attached to thought, and
often do not want to relinquish it to meditate. Sometimes we want to
get lost in emotions—even unpleasant ones like sadness, as well as
compelling ones like lust. We might enjoy dramatizing ourselves in
self-pity or self-blame. We might even justify wallowing in so-called
spiritual emotions, and claim that encouraging such feelings is good.
This is particularly seductive, but we are no longer meditating when
we get lost in such entanglements.

Sometimes we try to make a particular experience happen. We also
want to sink into pleasant meditation experiences and get lost in them.
Accordingly, Teresa of Avila said some people "seem afraid to stir, fearing they might lose the least little bit of their delight and devotion; this
shows how little they understand the path."[5] Foggy, unclear absorption—into which devotional engrossment can easily slip—feels very
good, but we are no longer meditating when we lose sharp mental
clarity.

Some people are not satisfied with a practice as classically taught.
They want to tinker with it, suiting it to their own liking. They sometimes refuse to relinquish incompatible practices—such as a sacred
word—when learning insight practice. On retreats, some cling to

activities—like exercise or devotions—that are good in other set-tings, but are distractions incompatible with the retreat.

Aversion Just as greed wants to hold onto something, aversion wants to push away an object or experience. It covers the capital sins of anger and envy, and includes other emotions like fear, guilt, sadness, anxiety, impatience, and resentment.

When unpleasant things happen, aversion often follows. We might get irritated with any available object that we can find to blame. Alter-natively, some become dejected and want to give up. Sometimes we get mixtures of many feelings. We need to acknowledge them, and realize that situations do not create anger, sadness, or fear. They merely show us the tendencies our hearts are already harboring.

Fear can potently affect spiritual practice. We are afraid to really throw ourselves into practice because of what might happen. We fear physical or emotional pain, and pull back. Some people spend an entire retreat worrying about the food served or whether they are getting sufficient rest.

So long as we are unwilling to be with what is unwanted, our prac-tice cannot progress. Reminding ourselves why we are meditating can help us stay on track.[6]

Sloth and torpor Sloth and torpor clearly correspond to the cap-ital sin of sloth. Sloth characterizes a lethargic and inert mind. When it is strong, we feel unable to arouse enough energy to help ourselves. Sleepiness and boredom are two of its major manifestations.

Sometimes sleepiness occurs in practice because the mind is used only to sleeping when it is still; it has not learned to be simultaneously alert and quiet. It says, "Nothing's happening, so it must be time to sleep."[7] Sometimes we get sleepy when we want to avoid something in our practice. Sleep is an excellent escape from an unwanted situation, and can destroy a meditation sitting if we let it.

To manage sleepiness, try sitting with open but unfocused eyes to let in light. Doing brisk walking, washing face and eyes with cold water, and pulling the earlobes up and down vigorously until they are hot also help. As a last resort, meditate standing up. While it can be done, falling asleep while standing is difficult.[8]

Boredom comes from lax attention. John of the Cross realized that it could be an escape, commenting that some people "become bored when asked to do something unpleasant."[9] We best handle boredom by bringing attention closer to the meditation object and carefully holding it there.

General sluggishness might indicate a genuine need for rest. However, moving the body vigorously for a while often rebuilds sagging energy. You might have noticed that a brief, fast walk in the late afternoon refreshes you enough to continue with a day's tasks.

Anxiety and restlessness The hindrance of anxiety and restlessness can manifest in either body or mind. It sometimes takes the form of obsessive thinking.

Teresa of Avila caught its mental flavor; she described some minds as scattered like restless, wild horses no one can stop. They run all over and never settle down.[10] The mind is too excited and active when restlessness occurs. Accustomed to being very active when it is alert, it is unable to stay both still and alert. It says, "Nothing's going on, so it's time to stir up some excitement."

Brisk walking can burn off excess energy. During a restless meditation sitting, giving the mind a little space often helps. Open to awareness of all the sound around—remembering to note "hearing"—for a few minutes.

A common form of anxiety is guilty ruminating, repeatedly replaying past mistakes in our minds, and then feeling bad about ourselves. When guilt is about admitted and abandoned past actions, it is best simply to acknowledge the feeling, not feed it with thought, and return to meditating. If we feel guilty about bad behavior we have stopped doing, but haven't admitted to anyone, confession often helps. Guilt about bad conduct not yet given up calls for very firm resolutions and seeking whatever assistance we might need with self-management.

We might also obsess over plans for the future or worry about other people. It helps to remember that obsessing does not accomplish anything positive, and that a thought about another person is not that person. Obsessive thinking and body restlessness can also be ways we avoid meditating.

Doubt The most deadly hindrance is doubt, which can completely close down practice. Doubt attacks anything we can find as a target—the practice, the teacher, the teachings, our own ability or suitability, the time or place, and so on. Doubt exhausts us, leaving us indecisive and unable to settle on what to do. It leads some of us to flit about among various practices.

Doubt is sneaky. We might start doubting as an excuse to stop meditating when we find it difficult. When we let doubt trick us this way, we are likely to go looking for an easier way not requiring effort—a "magic bullet" or "instant salvation."

To keep doubt from closing down practice, a time-limited commitment to practice helps. When doubt occurs, we simply remind ourselves to continue our daily sitting until the time is up. On retreat, we recall that we committed to the retreat and stay to the end.

Obviously, we do not continue to invest ourselves in every option we explore. However, we do not give a practice sufficient opportunity to show what it can do for us unless we make some commitment to it. A time-limited commitment also holds for how long we stay with a new practice to give it time to show us benefits.

Other Common Issues in Practice

Wandering mind happens frequently in early practice. Developing an obedient mind is not easy, so we must not become discouraged. We simply bring the mind back to the practice whenever it gets lost.

Another issue is the discomfort of seeing much that had been hidden from awareness. Meditation experiences of both body and mind are sometimes very painful. Patience and surrendered willingness are antidotes for both problems.

Meditators are sometimes tempted to get lost in analyzing their experiences. Some also want to wallow in mental contents that have fascinated them. Yielding to such temptations derails practice.

Once practice is fairly well developed, other problems are more likely. *Sinking mind* sometimes happens—most easily if we abandon the tool of noting. Once we feel "grounded," letting go of this tool is tempting. The mind then easily goes into a fuzzy, comfortable, amorphous state that lacks the sharp, clear awareness needed for meditation. Teresa of Avila was well aware of this problem, and warned against it. She concluded, "This foolishness is nothing but wasting time. Such people feel nothing through their senses nor do they feel anything about God."[11]

Because this state feels so good, we enjoy sinking into it; however, it is not meditation, and greed for it is a potent barrier to meditation. The cure is to commit to noting vigorously until the mind is so captivated by the object that it becomes absolutely impossible to fall into sinking mind. For persistent sinking mind, making the primary object more difficult helps.[12]

Awareness practice is meant to deal with our unfinished business, so frightening and overwhelming unconscious mental contents might come into awareness. Holding fast to noting protects us from getting lost in such content, but still allows us to experience it fully for healing.

Maintaining the Commitment

Most important for establishing and maintaining practice is the daily sitting. Insight meditation enlivens our prayer life only to the extent that we meditate regularly. The Carmelite and many Buddhist traditions agree that we must meditate daily to fully experience the fruits of meditation.[13]

Daily meditation The standard sitting in our insight meditation tradition is 45 to 60 minutes long. The more time we can practice, the better. Realistically, most find that at least one half-hour daily is possible in even the most demanding daily schedule. However, if you are not willing to invest that much time, make a commitment to sit daily for however long you are willing to sit. Sit daily whether you feel like it or not, and do not shorten your time, or you will miss valuable learning experiences.

People often ask about the best time to sit. This varies from person to person. Many people find attention less sharp soon after eating or late in the day, but this does not bother some. Most important is to have a regular time in your schedule for practice. If you try to "work it in" whenever you can, it will very soon get "worked out."

Many people make sitting part of their morning "getting up" routine. Other common times are before eating lunch or right after getting home from work before starting any other task—email, answer machine, cooking, or speaking to others. Some like to sit at night, but this holds the danger of lowered levels of energy and of finding other tasks to do until it is too late to sit. Some also find it too stimulating to meditate before sleep.

Gradually meditation becomes as routine a part of your day as brushing your teeth and combing your hair. As you see benefits in your life from practice, you will become willing to sit for longer periods. You will realize that meditation makes time for itself. The time it saves us in emotional turmoil, unfocused attention, and sluggish energy more than makes up for the time it takes. Many people need less sleep when meditating regularly.

We recommend making a minimum six-month commitment to practice regularly. By then you should see some benefits. It might not become your preferred spiritual practice, but unless you give it a chance to show what it can do, you will never know how much it might help.

Practice is greatly enhanced if you take odd minutes during the day to call yourself back to mindful awareness. You could use some act that you do frequently during the day—such as reaching for something— as a signal to be mindful. You might choose to do some routine activity—such as washing dishes, walking to the office, or brushing teeth—with very careful mindfulness. Buddhist monk Thich Nhat Hanh uses bell sounds as a call to mindfulness.[14] A chiming clock also works well for this.

Protecting the practice Protecting the practice means keeping ourselves motivated to work at it. There are some time-honored ways to protect practice. You might reflect on the beauty of a saintly life, or the merits of a meditator you admire. You can offer a short dedicatory prayer, or remind yourself of the high goal of spiritual practice. You might do loving-kindness practice.[15] If negative images move you, reflect on the shortness of life or the ugliness of a disordered heart.

A special protection is an act of surrender. It expresses willingness to be with all meditation experiences as an offered healing. Surrender opens us to accept the needed purgation that practice effects in us. It helps us maintain a soft gentleness that does not grasp after or push away any experience.

Many Buddhists begin meditation practice with "May I be surrendered to the Dhamma." Dhamma, in this context, is analogous to the Holy Spirit.[16] You may want to begin your sittings with an act of surrender to the healing and sanctifying power of the Holy Spirit.

Sharing merit Merit is whatever makes us "shine within." We are all aware of the inner glow that comes from feeling good about what we have done. Sharing merit can be seen as a way of praying that all beings enjoy that feeling. All acts of virtue, piety, goodness, spiritual practice, and the like, create merit. We can share it with any other being, living or dead.

Some people share merit after each meditation sitting. This "sweetens" practice and dedicates it to the good of others. Sharing merit is, itself, a meritorious action that increases merit. So the more we "bankrupt" ourselves for others, the richer in merit we become. Accumulating merit is not an ideal motive, however!

To share merit, use a simple formula like this: "May the fruits of my (generosity, virtue, spiritual practice) be for the good of (my mother, 'Jane Doe,' all beings everywhere)." Simply name the meritorious action and the person(s) with whom you wish to share. Merit can be shared with any being or group of beings you choose.

MJM/KC

✛ 7 ✛

Getting Guidance in Practice

THIS CHAPTER describes aids to practice that are easily available, discusses getting and working with a teacher, and makes some further suggestions for guidance. We open with a few fears some people express.

Concerns That are Not Problems

Sometimes meditators are concerned about things that are not real problems. Much of this worry has no factual basis, once we understand more fully what is happening.

Self-manipulation We are not isolated "parts"—spirit, mind, emotions, body—in how we function; we work as an integrated unit. What affects any part of our being affects all of our being. Whether we choose to do it consciously or not, we are continually effecting changes in different parts of our being

Some people fear they are simply manipulating their minds in meditation practice. Using psychological methods to assist the aims of prayer has a time-honored place in spiritual traditions. We do not seek these psychological changes for their own sake, but to make us "ripe" to receive grace.

Creating desired experiences A related concern is that we might be "creating" experiences that we want to have. Most meditators are sufficiently committed to truth that they need not concern themselves with this. People who meditate to create particular experiences quickly find that meditation does not work that way.

Our practice is simply a tool to help us be surrendered and listening. We cannot force any result, but we can do everything possible to prepare the ground for spiritual unfolding. When we practice in a surrendered fashion, we receive whatever experiences—desirable or unpleasant—come to us.

Getting in over one's head Some people fear that they will get to places in meditation that they cannot handle. Some people who have carelessly gone on "meditation binges"—such as practicing long hours without adequate rest, nutrition, or guidance—have sometimes gotten themselves in trouble. Faulty method can also be a problem.

If we practice carefully and moderately, following the method taught, we are protected. The wisdom that guides the practice "gates" experiences according to our ability to manage them. Using this psychologically sound method, which has proven itself over 2500 years, is safe.

People do sometimes feel that they should "back off" some in practice, fearing that they are getting in "too deep." Sometimes such a feeling needs to be honored, especially by those with a psychiatric history; most often it is simply resistance. You can explore this situation with a teacher to arrive at the best decision.

Suggestions for Continuing Practice

Appendix II offers information on some aids that will help you maintain a practice. Here are a few more points to consider.

The method is reliable Once learned, this practice is safe to do on your own if you meditate no more than several hours a day. To practice intensively for many hours a day, you should be under the guidance of a teacher; intensive practice can bring up very powerful experiences that might be emotionally unsettling.

The main thing the teacher will do, however, is remind you to use the method carefully, as it was taught to you. This method has proven itself over time. Using it faithfully and consistently brings the results it promises. Since it is not "broken," do not "fix" it. If you alter vital parts of it, you may waste time or get lost in upsetting experiences. The method both allows the purifying healing to occur and protects us while it is being done.

The second major thing a teacher offers is reassurance. If you remember to use the method, you need not worry about what happens in your practice. Various experiences that you do not understand might come, and some of them might even be frightening. You will be fine if you stick to the protective method. We need not understand everything that happens when we meditate, although most often we eventually get insight into important earlier experiences.

Asking for help During difficult times, a teacher's help can make practice smoother and more effective. This is particularly true during the rugged periods, those meditation stages that correspond to the "dark nights" of John of the Cross.[1] Prior to such times, you might also have methodological questions that need answers.

If you feel you need help at any time, for any reason, you should ask for it. Be prepared to describe what happens in your sitting practice in some detail so that the teacher can diagnose your situation. You might have fallen into faulty method or need elaboration of a technique; sometimes all you need is just to be encouraged toward patient persistence.

Choosing a teacher Exercise some care in choosing a teacher for either a retreat or continuing guidance. Most Eastern meditation methods have been refined over millennia by practitioners who took their work very seriously. The methods are quite powerful, and have sound psychologies behind them. You want a teacher sufficiently knowledgeable and experienced in work with the method to guide your practice.

Customarily, people start teaching Eastern techniques when their own teacher feels they are ready. The potential teacher's personal practice should have ripened to a certain point, and he or she should also have sufficient conceptual understanding of the practice. Unfortunately, not everybody who offers to teach is truly prepared to do so. Some teach far too soon; some even teach without having been under the regular guidance of a teacher themselves. Some think being a spiritual director or having sat a few retreats qualifies them.

Ask potential teachers several key questions. Find out if they have a teacher with whom they practice regularly. Ask how their teacher feels about their teaching. Find out if they have someone to whom they can refer people who need guidance beyond their competence to give. Notice carefully how answers to these questions are managed. Also observe whether teachers live as you expect people committed to spiritual work to live.

See how the teacher handles money and power relationships. Run in the opposite direction at any hint of sexual or financial abuse of students. Nobody should get rich selling spiritual teachings; wealth should be a red flag. Traditionally, teachers do not ask for money for themselves for spiritual teachings. However, they can charge to cover travel expenses to lead a retreat, the cost of students' room and board, and incidental expenses incurred in putting on a retreat.[2]

Look also to see if the focus is on the teachings or the person of the teacher. Good teachers do use examples from their own lives and practice in their teaching; how they do so is the issue. When a teacher is nearly worshipped, or expects to be excessively revered by students, this is a warning signal. Sound teachers discourage any attempt to make themselves special.

Good teachers may be well spoken of by others, but this alone is not a sufficient criterion. Some people are good at appearing to have more to offer than they actually do, and some good teachers lack social "sparkle."

Does the teacher promise you impossible things, such as instant enlightenment or special powers? The only thing you can safely be promised is hard work and progress in proportion to that work. The focus should not be on enhancing the ego, but on becoming selfless. If a teacher encourages much talk about interesting experiences, this probably supports egoism. Beware also a teacher who promises progress without pointing out the need for a firm moral base.

Working with a teacher Teachers can be a great help in spiritual practice. One who teaches a method need not be the only teacher you have.[3] Other teachers can also help you integrate spiritual living into your life as a whole. Here are some guidelines to help you profit most from work with any teacher.

After choosing the teacher very carefully, adopt an obedient spirit regarding guidance. The teacher might not always be right, and we should not be blind to striking error. However, often we most need to hear what we most dislike hearing. If we discard what is not agreeable to us, we are wasting both the teacher's and our own time. Keeping several teachers on tap to have one who yields to our whims in different situations is self-defeating.

Be completely honest. Sometimes what must be discussed with a teacher is uncomfortable, but this can be the cutting edge of growth. If we protect ego when meeting with a spiritual teacher, we cannot expect to dissolve egocentricity. This does not mean that the teacher must know every trivial detail of your life; wanting that can in itself be egoism. However, anything relevant to your working together should be shared.

Having a truth-teller in your life is a great blessing. The Buddha said:

> If you see wise ones who see your faults and reprove you, it would be good, not bad, to be with them and regard them as revealers of treasures. Let the wise advise, let them instruct, let them dissuade you from what is wrong. They are loved by the good and hated by the worldly.[4]

Be grateful for what you are given. Many people lack opportunities for spiritual practice and guidance. Appreciate this real gift. Accept the limits of the teaching relationship. Do not expect the spiritual teacher to function as a parent, therapist, or best friend.

Bringing Wisdom into Daily Life

No matter what practice we do, how many teachers we consult, or whatever acts of surrender we make, our lives must reflect our commitment. We must willingly work on those areas of life and person where we need improvement. We cannot expect God or the teacher to make magic for us. All of life must be lived in a way compatible with spiritual aspiration.

Clear comprehension A very important activity is practicing clear comprehension or wise consideration in all our actions. This means bringing great clarity to all our daily activities. When we practice wise consideration, we consult our own wisdom about the conduct of our lives.

We need first to be clear about what we want to accomplish, so that we choose appropriate actions. We need to see an action for what it is without interpretation, which could always be faulty. We discern whether the act is beneficial or not. In all our choices, we try to bring meditative wisdom into daily life. This deepens our sitting practice, but also builds the habit of mindfulness in all of life.

Being mindful with clear comprehension is a powerful way to "pray always" and practice presence to God. Mindfully tending our experiences of body and mind is being lovingly attentive to the moment we are now being given to live. Doing so, we accept the healing work of the Holy Spirit in our life experiences.

Enriching other prayer life To enliven your entire prayer life, we recommend meditation immediately before reading sacred Scripture or celebrating Eucharist. This prepares your heart to hear God's word in new ways, and sets the stage for new insight into the deeper meanings of the words and symbols you celebrate in worship.

Dr. Herbert Benson's research recommends sitting quietly and comfortably, without discursive reflection, and paying attention to your breathing just before religious exercises. This frees your brain to form new neural connections that physiologically mediate new meaning and insight.[5] Meditation literally prepares you physiologically to get the most benefit from spiritual reading and liturgical worship.

Christian insight meditation thus aims to enrich rather than replace other forms of Christian prayer. Often, however, to make time for meditation, people discontinue some other prayers or devotions that might have become merely habitual. They then discover a deepening in their remaining prayer, especially liturgy, sacred reading, and the practice of the presence of God. They find "a pearl of great price"[6] that gives new life to their desire to pray always.

Consulting the teacher within Most importantly, rely on the divinity within whether you invoke it as the Holy Spirit or the essence of Dhamma, the force within our hearts drawing us to greater purity and virtue.[7] Put your spiritual practice and daily life in surrender to the purifying and sanctifying action of the Holy Spirit. When we are surrendered to this inner divinity, we have a teacher who never fails us.

Meditation practice shows us when we are continuing to try to control the outcome of all that happens in our lives, closing our hearts to our neighbors, fearing failure, and not managing our selfish impulses. Then we recognize that our hearts are still far from pure and that transformation takes some time. We become more aware of our absolute need for God's love to heal and transform us. We reaffirm our need for the guidance of the Holy Spirit in our lives. Such understanding is a common fruit of Christian insight practice.

Guidance the Practice Gives Us

Christian insight meditation helps us to grow in the purity of heart, poverty of spirit, and emptiness of self that dispose us for God's work in our lives. Its fruits guide us to fuller Christian living.

Contemplative emptying Christian insight meditation is particularly valuable for those whose prayer is going beyond discursive or thinking prayer, and is entering the state of contemplation.[8] The practice helps them maintain the non-discursive, passive, surrendered, loving attention in God's presence that John recommended for those who are beyond the stage of beginners. We are guided into contemplative prayer by simply watching the breath and gently noting all that comes into awareness, neither consciously pushing away nor clinging to any arising phenomenon.

Moreover, readiness to accept passively everything that comes into consciousness disposes us to receive into awareness all the unresolved conflicts, hurts, and grief hidden in our unconscious minds. One recovering alcoholic said, "This practice brings up everything I drank to get away from."

Any effort to sustain and to derive satisfaction from discursive reflection would prevent these phenomena from becoming conscious. In insight meditation, this self-knowledge is revealed to us. We receive it passively into awareness, like a painful but lovingly bestowed gift of God, to be clearly seen, felt, and healed. The meditation method protects us and prevents our becoming overwhelmed by it.[9]

Praying always Jesus taught us "to pray continually."[10] Over the centuries Christians have responded to his challenge in various ways that express the total human person as a body/spirit, social/private being. Christian insight meditation, like any other contemplative practice, intends to strengthen our entire prayer life and help us to live always in communion with God.

Christian insight meditation guides us into praying always. Accepting with full attentiveness, moment to moment, the experience that we are given to live in each moment is prayer. When we receive all these experiences as from the hand of God, we are praying always. We are living our lives in the presence of God.

Longing for God The experience of silence and solitude that comes with faithful insight practice also strengthens our longing for God and our desire to hear God's Word awakening, as if from sleep, in the depths of our beings. This attitude of loving attention to God grows, not only during formal mental prayer, but throughout the entire day. It heightens our readiness to perceive God communicating with us through all creation and in all the events of our daily life, and guides us into living more spiritually.

Finally, in insight meditation we see sensations, thoughts, emotions, moods, feelings, pain, terror, and delight come into consciousness; these are noted and then pass out of consciousness. Observing closely this constant flow of phenomena deepens our appreciation of the truth expressed in the famous saying of Teresa of Avila: "All things pass away. God alone suffices." We are thus guided into abandoning our desires for less than God.

A Closing Thought

Let us look at spiritual life as many spiritual giants have portrayed it. At the beginning, the work is mostly ours. We must do our part or nothing else will happen. In the middle, increasing purity is both God's and our work together. In the end, God will do it all. Twentieth-century Vedantic mystic Sri Aurobindo added that, in the very, very end, we realize it was God all along.

Over time, we become increasingly sensitive to the wisdom and guidance communicated to us in our practice. However, we must have done all that we can do earlier, and must have made ourselves completely docile to God's action. We can do no more important thing with our lives.

MJM/KC

✦ 8 ✦

The Course of Practice

M EDITATION PRACTICE follows a predictable course of development for most people. It goes through alternating periods of discomfort and ease. This chapter compares Christian stages of contemplative prayer with Buddhist levels of insight absorption.[1]

Early Practice and Absorption

Successful meditation requires that we are trying to live morally and develop good habits. Establishing our practice can take some time as we accustom body and mind to the new enterprise. This task can be somewhat difficult since we must persevere before we see pronounced benefits. We also have to deal with the hindrances discussed in chapter 6.

Teresa of Avila described the task of early meditation practice as like hauling buckets of water to irrigate a garden.[2] Hauling bucket after bucket—repeatedly placing attention on the meditation object—dominates experience. We must do this continually to keep attention on the object. Before absorption begins, we frequently abandon the task, and our attention stays focused on its object for only fleeting minutes before wandering off. Sometimes it feels like we cannot even find the bucket!

With practice, mental stability becomes increasingly pronounced. Our efforts finally reach what Christians call *active recollection* and Buddhists name *access concentration*. These states indicate having a sufficient stability of mind, developed by our own efforts, to stay on the meditation object for some time. It protects us from the hindrances to practice.

Even deeper mental stability or concentration—the absorptions—makes Buddhist practice feel more like it happens in us than as something we do. Christians experience deeper prayer the same way. John considered this a sign of the gift of contemplation. Absorption deepens as we faithfully practice; it has five major levels.[3]

First Level of Absorption;
Prayer of Simplicity or Passive Recollection

When we can easily stay with the object for some time, we have reached the first level of absorption. Although our attention stays on the object, small amounts of thought—focused only on the object of practice—can occur. Our thought processes function normally, which accounts for the difficulty some people initially have in seeing this state as different from ordinary mental functioning.[4] A common means of discernment is greater ease in practice. Initially this is weak and sporadic, but it gradually deepens.

With the first absorption, Teresa's task of "hauling buckets" becomes much easier, we feel well established in the routine, and remain with the task. We keep reaching for that bucket over and again with greatly decreased effort. Buddhist texts refer to a feeling of mental seclusion here; distracting experiences no longer yank us about. However, when we are still new to absorption, we easily fall out of it.

For Christians, this is the flickering start of the receptive passivity of contemplation—the move from Active Recollection to the Prayer of Simplicity.[5] The will feels captivated by the meditation object, which draws us to itself. We can reach the first level of absorption doing lectio divina and other discursive practices since some thinking is still possible.[6]

Second Level of Absorption; Prayer of Quiet

After some time, during which we practice both virtue and meditation, a second stage emerges. John named it *the passive dark night of sense,* and Buddhists call it *early insight*. This paradoxical time gives us both great happiness and great suffering.

Understanding the second absorption The second absorption is like using Teresa's water wheel to water the garden; once we have the system running, we do not have to keep starting it, but just keep it going. We still have to do some work—keep being attentive to the object. However, since attention stays on the object, we have only to hold it there and not keep placing it.

With the second absorption, the greater ease in prayer becomes clearly apparent. John spoke of the reduced effort here.[7] This stage's Prayer of Quiet clearly establishes Christian contemplation. It feels very quiet in relation to the "noisy" thinking of previous practice. Meditative experience strongly draws us, and we would like to spend long hours in it.

While some surface distractions might come, the object still holds us "underneath" them. In insight meditation, we dwell "within" the object, experiencing it from "inside." Buddhists explain that ordinary mental processes break down into more finely grained perception; we start seeing processes and not things. A clear image and some conceptual understanding of the object can still be present.

Since the intellect is also captivated here, and cannot do ordinary imaging and thinking, discursive thought does not occur. However, some forms of prayer use a word or repetitive phrase as the object.[8] A prayer like the rosary can reach this level. It is often easily reached with loving-kindness (metta) practice and methods like the Jesus prayer.

Sensory experiences Meditators sometimes see when there is no visual stimulus, hear without an auditory stimulus, and so on. Many situations can make such things happen. We hallucinate every night when we dream, and have sensory experiences in intense isolation—such as desert mirages. Sometimes bodily illness creates sensations.[9] Meditation is just one of many causes of such events. Although this stage is its most common time, some people hallucinate even earlier in meditation practice.[10]

Auditory experiences in meditation often begin with a sound like surf. We can also hear very loud bells and chimes, and even human voices. Visual experiences can be of lights, colors, geometrical symbols, faces, scenes, and so on. Meditators sometimes feel like something is touching or pulling them, and some smell peculiar odors and/or taste unusual tastes.

The body also can feel greatly distorted. Body parts might feel like they are in the wrong place. Some parts might feel ballooned out or grotesquely large, while others feel flattened out or squashed. Deepening concentration causes such distortions.

Although hallucinations should not alarm us, we also should not seek them. Visionary experiences do not signify holiness, and most meditators do not experience them. John repeatedly urged us to place no importance on such occurrences, but to stay "in dark faith—the means toward union."[11]

Outcomes This time of passive purification involves real suffering.[12] We begin to see our own interior unpleasantness in finer detail, and may experience intense remorse. Buddhist meditators start clearly seeing the three characteristics of created or conditioned reality described in chapter 2: its ultimate unsatisfactoriness, momentariness, and essencelessness.[13]

These insights usually come with some grief. It often seems as if all we had learned were falling apart on us, and we might feel a strong sense of personal helplessness. The Buddhist disappearance of the sense of an active "I" corresponds to John's saying that meditators feel that they can no longer meditate as they had before. Self is no longer in charge as it once was.

John taught that this purification stabilizes us in infused contemplation, which is "received" rather than done. Similarly, insight practice becomes "automatic;" we no longer need to work hard at meditating, but simply attend to the interior work being done in ourselves.

John summarized some benefits of this development: "We get four benefits from this night: the delight of peace, habitually remembering and caring about God, cleanliness and purity of soul, and the practice of virtue."[14] Both traditions agree that this rugged period greatly intensifies faith. It brings considerably increased energy for and commitment to spiritual practice.

Third Level of Absorption; Prayer of Simple Union

Those who persevere during this passive purification next have tremendous ease in practice. The third absorption corresponds to the Christian illuminative way with its Prayer of Simple Union, which can hold even the senses captive. It is like Teresa's watering the garden with a stream. The stream flows by itself without any effort on our part, just as the meditation object "grasps" and "holds" our attention. We adopt the attitude of an Eastern aphorism; "Don't push the river; it flows by itself."

Understanding the third absorption John called this the *stage of proficients* because considerable purification of mind has already taken place. He said, "Without the work of discursion, we easily come to very serene, loving contemplation and spiritual delight."[15] Insight meditation proceeds with similar effortlessness, peace, and delight. Buddhists call it *arising and passing away* because of the ease with which we see experiences come and go.

This very delightful level of absorption is characterized by strong joy, "sweetness," and high energy. There may be pauses in the breath or peculiar patterns of breathing. Intense raptness and ecstatic awareness can occur. We might feel grasped or held by God, as raptness dominates here.

Distraction is virtually impossible. Attention easily follows the rapid flow of experiences, and is so captivated that it might become impossible to move it to even a very exciting thought. At other times, we rest in great tranquility and stillness. Awareness of time, space, and self might be lost in focusing on the object with total attention—hence "simple union" with it.

Many forms of traditional Christian prayer are too "busy" for this level; loving-kindness practice and the rosary can reach it. Simple mantras like the Jesus Prayer easily carry us this far. In such practice, meditators sometimes become unable to repeat the word or words upon which they are concentrating. In insight meditation, we might become temporarily incapable of noting experiences. When we can no longer say the words, it can feel like concentration is lessening.

However, this occurs because the mind has gone beyond any capacity for words.

Raptness A wide range of body sensations associated with rapt attention sometimes happen. They come from having strong concentration and an interested focus on the object of meditation practice. Intense sensations or very strong energies might charge through the body—even move us physically. Raptness also comes as intense heaviness, or as feeling pushed or pulled strongly in one direction. Various powers and energies may activate, like the *kundalini* experience of yoga. It can feel like undergoing an exorcism.

Some raptness is extremely pleasurable and other intensely painful. Sometimes pleasure and discomfort occur simultaneously. Teresa spoke of a paradoxical mixture of pain and great sweetness. "Since this pain is so sweet and delightful, we never think we can have enough of it."[16]

John was concerned about sensual movements that sometimes occur spontaneously during spiritual practice.[17] When raptness is very intense, prolonged waves of orgasmic-like sensations can flood the body with intense bliss. Skin can become so sensitive that even a faint breeze across the cheek can trigger waves of delightful body sensations. Eastern traditions that have studied such phenomena for millennia explain that, although all our vital energy is connected, these experiences are spiritual rather than sexual ones.

Involuntary movement can occur. Teresa wrote, "Some persons say they experience a tightening in the chest and even external bodily movements that they cannot restrain."[18] The force of such movements can even bounce a person off the meditation seat. We might feel like we are levitating. "Resisting was impossible; it carried off my soul and my head without my being able to prevent it—and sometimes my whole body until it was lifted off the ground."[19]

Meditators prone to intense raptness need guidance from a competent teacher who understands such experiences. They need to learn not cling to them or encourage them, but also not try to push them away, all the while staying balanced in mind.

Dangers If raptness is improperly managed, we might come to overvalue it. We can easily become greedy for striking experiences—often very subtly so—and impede further spiritual progress. John held that the weakness of human nature causes the bodily manifestations of raptness: "Our sensory nature is too weak to receive vigorous spiritual communications. Because they impact us there, we can suffer infirmities, injuries, and digestive problems that fatigue us."[20]

Both traditions have outlined other dangers for this period. We readily become attached to the delights of spiritual practice, and might develop intense and subtle greediness. Buddhists refer to ten *corruptions of insight*—wonderful experiences, in themselves good and joyful, but which we appropriate to ourselves with vanity and greed. John said, "Illusions and deceptions grow so much in some people that they might not return to practicing authentic spirituality."[21]

Christian practitioners eventually realize that the task is not complete; "until we are completely purified spiritually, we seldom have so much peaceful prayer that it hides our remaining deeply-rooted disorder. We keep feeling that something is lacking or remains to be done."[22] Buddhist meditators come to a similar decision: "The brilliant light and the other things I experience are not the Path. Delight in them is merely a corruption of insight. I must go on with the work."[23]

Fourth Level of Absorption; Prayer of Betrothal

Practice enters a second intense passive purgation when we willingly embrace the remaining work. Then follows the most harrowing and terrifying stage of practice. Buddhists call this period *advanced insight,* and John called it *the passive dark night of spirit.* It is the time of the Prayer of Betrothal.

This absorption is like Teresa's rainfall that waters the garden. The mind becomes truly saturated with the meditation object, so that nothing else appears to exist. Attention is totally captivated by the object, seen more as a subtle essence than as a gross object; this can make it difficult to see.

Paradoxical experience The most intense raptness with its ecstatic joy ceases. It yields to the subtle satisfaction of feeling like we are coming home. Although this can be an anguished time, still poise and equanimity characterize it. Practice here is quite often very paradoxical, combining great suffering with great peace.

We now deal with issues related to the human condition itself, beyond the purely personal. Anguish, terror, hopelessness, powerlessness, terrible aloneness, disgust at self and life, the apparent vanishing of motivation for spiritual work, loss of meaning, purposelessness, felt loss of value, feelings of being doomed or beyond any satisfaction of any kind—there is virtually no end to the possible dismal states we might experience.

John beautifully described this: "the intellect dark, the will arid, the memory empty, and the emotions intensely afflicted and anguished. We feel empty, poor, and deprived of all natural support, consolation, and understanding."[24] Both traditions realize this is truly a time when we have absolutely nothing to hold onto. We also realize that nothing but God—or Nibbana—gives true satisfaction.

In Buddhist terms, this stage purges deeply rooted subtle tendencies that can arise in our minds with sufficient provocation. John spoke of rooting out the residual effects of personal and original sin. This deepest purification gets at the root causes of human misery and moral failure. That "our sufferings at this time cannot be exaggerated"[25] holds true in both traditions.

Yearning Next comes an intense desire for deliverance that ushers in the fifth absorption. A Buddhist master wrote, "Even if we direct thought to the happiest sort of life and existence, or to the most pleasant and desirable objects, the mind will not delight in them, will find no satisfaction."[26] John said that we "impatiently desire and long for God. The lover's desire to have and unite with the Beloved is so ardent that even the slightest delay feels long, annoying, and tiresome."[27] "The touch of divine love and fire dry up the spirit and ignite our longings to slake our thirst for this love."[28] We repeatedly turn our longings over in our minds and pine for God continually. "God's absence usually causes such intense suffering and pain when we are nearing our goal that we would die if the Lord did not provide."[29]

Fifth Level of Absorption; Prayer of Marriage

This fifth level of absorption is John's *unitive way,* the most interior mansions of Teresa's "interior castle," and the Prayer of Marriage. The fully ripened single-mindedness here is like the high stage of prayer that Teresa described as feeling like she was caught up in a cloud.[30] The mind is totally immersed in and penetrated by the meditation object.

At the fifth level of absorption, awareness of time, space, and self does not occur. All that we "see" is the meditation object; we have completely "disappeared" into the object. Even happiness fades, and all that remains is the one-pointed focus on the object with great stillness and balance of mind. Nothing is able to disturb the underlying calm of mind. The breath may cease for periods of time.

John said, "We do not find satisfaction in anything or understand anything in particular, but remain in emptiness and darkness embracing all things with great preparedness."[31] "In true love, we receive anything that comes from the Beloved—prosperity, adversity, even chastisement—with the same evenness of soul, since we see them as God's will."[32]

Spiritual fruition can come here. From this balanced state of mind, remaining unmoved by whatever might befall us, we can "see God" or "touch" Nibbana. We may have spent years in terrible purgation, even years in balanced equanimity, before this happens. The experience is unstable at first, with regular "falls" back into both equanimity and harrowing purgation. Over time, the loving knowledge becomes more stable and, with further purification, it is deeper and more intense.

Both traditions say that eventually all craving extinguishes. "Those who are not greedy for things rejoice in them all as though possessing them all. Those who see them with a possessive mind lose all the delight in them. Cares do not molest the detached."[33]

MJM

✠ PART III

THREE LEVELS OF PURIFICATION:
JOHN OF THE CROSS AND
THERAVADAN BUDDHISM
COMPARED

✛ 9 ✛

John of the Cross on Purity of Conduct: Purification of Disordered Appetites

"**C**LEANNESS OF HEART," wrote John of the Cross, commenting on the beatitude Jesus proclaimed, "is nothing less than God's love and grace." Jesus called the pure of heart blessed because "love possesses them, and happiness comes only from love."[1]

Love and Grace: The Christian Path of Purification

Christian love is our response to God who has first loved us unconditionally in the life, death, and resurrection of Jesus Christ. In practice, it demands continual conversion of mind and heart to imitate Jesus in all our actions. It requires interior emptying of our spirit through faith to allow Jesus to awaken within us. It means openness to receive God's gracious self-communication that ultimately heals our sinfulness, transforms us in Jesus, and finally establishes us in the eternal blessedness of the Trinity.

Conversion of life for union with God The path of Christian purification demands conversion of life, interior emptying, and openness to God's revelation. This parallels the three Buddhist levels of purification—conduct, mental contents, and the heart—leading to Nibbana, the only unconditioned and unchanging Reality. Motivated by Christian faith and love, and enlightened by Buddhist teaching and practice, Christians who embrace the path of purification discover Jesus as they have never known him before. They follow him more faithfully in their daily lives, experience his awakening within their hearts, and are gradually transformed into his life of wisdom and compassion.

The goal of Christian life is perfect union with God through love. As a spiritual guide, John wanted to help us realize this union as quickly as possible. He understood union with God to mean simply a union of our wills with God's will. This "union of likeness" is begotten in mutual love. We have come to it when the human and divine wills are in complete harmony with each other.[2] Guiding persons to this union quickly does not involve providing a secret or magic formula, but rather pointing out the most direct path possible.

Union of wills To imagine this union of wills, think of the sun coming through a window. When the window is dirty, distinguishing the sunlight from the window is easy. The smudges on the window reveal clearly that the window and the sun are two separate entities. However, when you wash the window perfectly clean and remove all the smudges, distinguishing the sunlight from the window is virtually impossible. Although they remain separate, the two appear to have become one. If you have ever walked smack into a perfectly cleaned glass door leading to a sun deck, you know from experience that the window seems to have disappeared, leaving only the sunlight.

Using this analogy, John taught that although we always remain distinct from God, we can be so united with God's will that we appear in all our actions to be God. We become "God by participation,"[3] filled with the light of God's wisdom and the warmth of divine compassion. For this union, we must first be purified of everything that prevents its happening. Like the smudges on the window that must be wiped away before the window "becomes" the sun, so we must be purified of sin and its effects before we can be completely transformed into the life of God.

Levels of Purification

To achieve this union of transformation, we must be purified, John taught, through mortification, faith, and contemplation. Each prepares a different level of our personality. Mortification purifies "sense," the area of our lives centered in sensory experiences as we relate to objects in the visible world around us. Faith purges "spirit," the dimension of our lives that enables us to know, to love, and to relate to that which transcends the visible universe. Finally, contemplation, God's self-communication to us in knowledge and love, purifies us to our depths of everything that prevents total transformation in God.

The levels of purification This purification is a collaborative work between God and ourselves. We do what we can through mortification and faith to purify sense and spirit; God purifies our entire persons through contemplation. We cannot achieve union with God by mortification and faith alone, but God does not purify us with divine loving knowledge unless we dispose ourselves in sense and spirit to receive this gift.

These three levels of purification are not consecutive, as though mortification precedes faith, and faith must be perfect before contemplation begins. They occur simultaneously, although one form of purgation may predominate at different stages of the journey.

For example, beginners concentrate mostly on mortification, although saying "no" to disordered desires is always part of the spiritual journey no matter how far advanced we are. Contemplation, God's self-communication, or the "secret, peaceful, and loving inflow of God"[4] into the soul, is the main purification of persons advanced in the spiritual journey. However, it is never absent, even as we begin to walk the spiritual path. And, obviously for Christians, faith, together with hope and love, must be present at every stage of the journey, although these virtues are expressed or experienced differently at different stages along the way.

A *lifelong task* Preparation for union with God is thus a lifelong process. In John's opinion, relatively few are so purified in this life that their wills are completely one with God's like the perfectly clear window is one with the light of the sun. Nonetheless, it is possible through God's grace and human effort. Mary of Nazareth is a perfect example of one so united, as are other acknowledged saints like Francis of Assisi, Teresa of Avila, and perhaps millions of others of whom John was unaware.

Regardless of the level of holiness attained in this life, we cannot be totally united with God through love until our purification is complete. If not finished in this world, then it continues hereafter—possibly in the death process itself or in the vision of the risen Jesus. No matter how and when it happens, we will not be completely united with and transformed in God until our hearts are totally purified through mortification, faith, and contemplation.

Disordered Appetites: Obstacle to Divine Union

We begin describing each level of purification in more detail, starting with the senses and the mortification of disordered appetites. What today we call desire, John called appetite.

Objects of appetite Appetite or desire is needed for human survival, growth, and development. It moves us to unite with objects that promote human life. We would probably not eat unless we had an appetite for food and enjoyed the pleasure it gives us; the human race would likely end if men and women stopped desiring one another and the physical pleasure their union produces.

Every desire for union with an object is implicitly a desire for union with God, the ultimate fulfillment of both the individual person and the entire human family. And it is through a lifetime of ordered relationships with objects—persons, places, things, ideas, and memories—that we come finally to union with God.

History demonstrates, however, that many do not seek their personal fulfillment in God, but instead choose objects of desire as their ultimate goal in life. They habitually choose to sate themselves with the pleasure objects give them—or money, or power, or reputation, or countless other things. When this happens, their appetites have become disordered. They are no longer directed to union with God. Until these disordered appetites are righted, union with God through love is impossible.

Jesus said, "People cannot serve two masters: they will either hate the one and love the other, or they will be devoted to the one and despise the other. You cannot serve both God and money."[5] In the same vein, John reasoned, "Two contrary things cannot coexist in the same subject."[6] Disordered desires for created things drive the Spirit of God from us; we cannot have both God and creatures as the ultimate end of our longings and desires. John explained, "We have only one will, and if we encumber or preoccupy it with anything, we will not have the freedom, solitude, and purity needed for divine transformation."[7]

Damage appetites cause Not only do disordered appetites preclude union with God through love, they also damage our personality. Every choice we make affects us. Just as acts of virtue bring us mildness, peace, comfort, light, purity, and strength, so acting out disordered desires torments, fatigues, wearies, blinds, and weakens us.[8] As a result, we become fragmented and dysfunctional.

We can observe this in our own behavior when we are driven by desire for something, even something as insignificant as a cigarette. The desire quickly takes control of us, enslaves us to a cylinder of paper three inches long packed with tobacco, and leaves us no peace until it is satisfied. Appetites "are like restless little children who are hard to please, always whining to their mother for something, and never satisfied."[9]

On a larger scale, the morning paper and the nightly news describe the damage done every day to persons, families, nations, and the international community by disordered desires for power, wealth, security, fame, and pleasure. The more we follow disordered desires, the more seriously we damage our personalities, ending in disruption of our fundamental relationships. John observed, "It is sad to think about the condition of the poor people who are full of disordered appetites. They are unhappy with themselves, cold toward other people, and sluggish and slothful in the things of God!"[10]

Small attachments Yet even slightly disordered appetites—"a small attachment we never really want to conquer, for example, to a person, clothing, a book or a bedroom, or to the way food is prepared, or to frivolous conversations, or wanting small satisfactions like tasting, knowing, and hearing things, and so on"[11]—can seriously damage us by being an obstacle to spiritual progress and transformation in God. John illustrated this with the analogy of a bird tied to the ground with a thin thread. The thread may be easier to break than a heavy rope, but the bird cannot fly free until it is finally broken. Neither are we free for perfect union with God in love, as long as we are bound by disordered desires.

Thus, every disordered desire, however small, has the potential power to remove God's grace from us and to destroy our personalities. Thus, all who seek union with God must make purification of these appetites a priority. We must mortify—literally, put to death—our disordered desire for sensory pleasure produced by created objects. John reminded spiritual masters that their chief concern with their disciples is to "immediately attack every disordered appetite. Guides should make people remain empty of what they want to set them free from so much misery."[12]

Counsels for Purifying Sense

John told us how to repair disordered desires. He gave specific counsels for centering our appetites, affections, and desires primarily on God. His advice is essential for beginners in the spiritual life, but remains valid for the entire journey.

The first counsel The first counsel is to "habitually desire to imitate Christ in everything you do by bringing your life into conformity with his. Study his life to understand how to imitate him and how to behave as he would in all situations."[13]

Jesus is God's perfect self-communication to us. To act in all things as Jesus would is to act in union with God's will. This is especially true in mortifying our disordered appetites for sensory pleasure. Jesus' "meat and food" was to do his Father's will.[14] When our love of Jesus inspires us to seek God's will in everything, especially in things that provide pleasure to our senses, we bring order to our sensory desires.

John gave an example:

> If you have a chance to hear interesting things that are not concerned with the service and glory of God, do not seek this pleasure or want to hear these things. Do so with all the other

senses to the extent that you can properly avoid such satisfaction.[15]

This practice purifies and empties the will of disordered desires for sensory pleasure and brings great spiritual progress in a short time.

The second counsel John's second counsel is aimed at establishing harmony and tranquility in our emotions. Like desires, emotions—joy, hope, fear, and sorrow—strongly affect our sensory life. He wrote:

> Endeavor to always be inclined not to the most delightful, but to the most distasteful; not to wanting anything, but to wanting nothing. Do not seek the best of worldly things, but the worst, and, for Christ, desire to come to complete nakedness, emptiness, and poverty in everything in the world.[16]

Practicing this counsel delivers us from our natural tendency to cling to pleasant experiences and avoid unpleasant ones. Personally, it frees us to pursue truth and goodness, even when the price in self-denial is high. Socially and politically, it challenges power and progress as public priorities in favor of goals that benefit the real needs of people. Ultimately, this counsel centers our emotions in God. It helps us to rejoice "only in what is purely for God's honor and glory," hope for nothing else, feel sorrow only for what diminishes that glory, and fear only God.[17]

The third counsel John's third counsel regards concupiscence—the desires of the flesh and eyes, and the pride of life addressed in the evangelist John's first epistle.[18] "Try not to over-value yourself, and want everybody else also to treat you that way."[19]

This hard saying, like those of Jesus, strikes at the disordered relationship we establish with our own selves. It seeks to establish an attitude of personal non-attachment that breaks over-dependency on persons, places, and things to satisfy our emotional needs. The counsel attempts to free us from attachment to our own egos and selves so that we may seek God's kingdom first.[20]

John described his final set of counsels for disciplining desire as instructions for journeying to union with God. They are, in part, as follows:

> To reach satisfaction in all, desire satisfaction in nothing. To possess all, desire to possess nothing. When you delay with anything, you stop rushing toward the All. And when you do possess the All, possess it without wanting anything. Because if you want to have anything else, your treasure in God is not purely your all.[21]

John's words here recall the gospel paradox that is found in nearly all mystical literature: to have all we must give up all. God alone is the center of our lives, the sole purpose for our existence. No thing can replace God in our lives. We must not delay with anything, but seek God from the very first movements of our hearts.

Therapy of Desire

John's counsels amount to a therapy of desire. They all focus on desire: "desire to imitate Christ," "try always to incline yourself not to the easiest, but to the most difficult," "try to act without attachment to yourself," and "to find satisfaction in all, desire satisfaction in nothing."

Motive of love The motive for working on our desires is love for Jesus Christ, who exemplifies total fidelity to God's will—even to dying naked on the cross, empty of all material possessions and deprived of every sensory pleasure. Imitating Jesus' total self-emptying on the cross purifies sensory life, inspires virtuous behavior, and leads us securely toward total transformation in God. Overcoming our repugnance to these counsels, and practicing them faithfully with order and discretion, eventually heals our beings and bestows interior peace, tranquility, delight, and consolation.

In this therapy, John intended, not the destruction of desire, but its transformation.[22] He attempted to help us become "recollected in one appetite alone, the desire for God."[23] In practice this means "wanting to perfectly fulfill God's law and to carry Christ's cross."[24] Imitating

Jesus in everything is to become our one constant desire—*un ordinario apetito.*[25]

Transformation of desire The mortification of disordered appetite thus means transforming our undisciplined desires for sensory pleasure into a focused desire for God alone so that longing for God, rather than the pleasure provided by created things, motivates all our behavior. This single desire for God purifies all of sensory life. It gradually transforms our disordered appetites for sensory pleasure into seeking "another, better love." Our pleasure now becomes following Jesus "with the anguished yearning of love."[26] Our main concern is translating these longings into virtuous behavior that reflects the Gospel.

Purification of the senses means putting to death—mortifying—our desires for pleasures that arise from any other source than our longing for God. More purgation still remains before we are fully transformed in God: faith must purify our spirit, contemplation our total beings. But before describing these further purifications, let us see what parallels may be found in Buddhism to John's teaching on the mortification of appetites.

KC

✦ 10 ✦

Teachings of the Buddha on Purity of Conduct: The Gift of Morality

THE BUDDHA said that walking a spiritual path requires us first to consider conduct. Right speech, right actions, and right livelihood are the morality steps of the Buddha's noble eight-fold path. Meditation practice greatly sharpens self-examination in these areas, and can radically change how we look at what we do. When we harmonize conduct, we enjoy freedom from the suffering harmful behavior causes.

Morality for Our Dark Side

The early Buddhist scriptures have a word for our dark side—*kilesa*. These problem-causing attitudes, feelings, and reactions make us unhappy when we experience them, and can lead to inharmonious actions that harm others. Kilesa is commonly translated "defilement," referring to the impurity of such states. A truer translation is "torment of the mind."

The harm in cravings The translation of kilesa as "torment of the mind" describes the Buddhist understanding that cravings torture us. The *Dhammapada,* a collection of aphorisms attributed to the Buddha, teaches: "Fools in their mischief do not see the suffering their deeds bring to themselves as certainly as fire brings pain."[1]

Kilesas trap us in endless rounds of suffering, and the more intense they are, the greater the torment. "Those wrapped up in craving become terrified like trapped hares. Long they come to sorrow again and again."² Cravings give us no rest; even if we satisfy them, desires again spring up and cause more thirst. This constant buffeting by desire is one way in which Buddhists say that earthly life is ultimately unsatisfactory.

Allowing desires to prevail increases delusion. "Fools are their own enemies doing evil deeds the fruit of which are bitter. For a while an evil deed tastes sweet as honey but when it ripens the fool comes to grief."³ Craving blinds us. The more we allow it to reign, the more it co-opts our understanding into justifying and supporting it. We see things only as desire colors them, and can seriously deceive ourselves.

Finally, cravings make practicing virtue more difficult. The *Dhammapada* teaches, "Like a vine strangling a tree, those who are corrupt do to themselves what enemies would wish for them. It is easy to do things that are not beneficial to yourself but it is very hard to do those things that are good and beneficial to yourself."⁴

The importance of sila When the Buddha was asked for spiritual guidance, he put establishing morality first. "Be perfect in conduct and manner, and seeing fear in the slightest fault, train by undertaking the training precepts."⁵ The morality path steps, called *sila* (*see'*-lah), are the necessary basis for the other parts of the path. Sila is our starting place in the task of overcoming kilesas, of freeing ourselves from the grip of desires. Nibbana—the "home" toward which Buddhist practice aims—is sometimes defined as putting out the fires of desire.

The behaviors we choose all bend our character ever so slightly in one direction or another.⁶ "Just this once won't count" is not true. The *Dhammapada* teaches: "Do not make light of evil. A jug fills drop by drop even if gathered little by little. So the fool becomes full of evil."⁷

The training in sila involves self-restraint. We abstain from unskillful acts that cause suffering, and cultivate skillful action. Moral conduct brings peace and harmony to our minds, relationships, and society. It protects our dealings with others, prepares our minds for meditation practice, and frees us from guilt, shame, and remorse.⁸

Right Livelihood

Traditionally, right livelihood deals with how we earn a living. In the Buddha's time, this determined almost all the rest of your lifestyle. Today, people engaged in the same livelihood choose many different lifestyles. Since lifestyle sets the framework in which our entire lives unfold, we now need to understand right livelihood more broadly.

Work The work we do is a very important part of total lifestyle. Buddhist teachings prohibit work that causes suffering or harms others. Dealing in five objects is considered unskillful: weapons, living beings, meat, intoxicants, and poisons. So also is any wrong conduct in earning a living; this includes acts like cheating, usury, deception, flattery, harassment, and bribes. We are not to use "low worldly knowledge;" we do not offer people what is useless, induce desires in them for our own gain, or use coercive advertising. Finally, we are to respect all persons and objects involved in our work.

We are to choose work that we see as good or necessary to do. Work chosen only for extrinsic reasons—such as ease, money, convenience, or privileges—does not provide a satisfying basis for life. Vietnamese Buddhist monk Thich Nhat Hanh, nominated for the Nobel Peace Prize by Dr. Martin Luther King, Jr., developed conduct guidelines for contemporary people. He said, "Do not live with a vocation that is harmful to humans and nature. Do not invest in companies that deprive others of their chance to live. Select a vocation which helps realize your ideal of compassion."[9]

Lifestyle Besides work, many other activities determine lifestyle. Avoiding actions with destructive potential is most important. A life laced with intoxicants, luxury, ambition, stinginess, and overindulgence in pleasures leads to trouble. These things can cause illness, and predispose us to heedlessness, restlessness, dullness, and unkindness.

Nhat Hanh also spoke to this. "Do not accumulate wealth while millions are hungry. Do not take as the aim of your life fame, profit, wealth or sensual pleasure. Live simply and share time, energy and material resources with those who are in need."[10] Nhat Hanh's precepts clearly touch issues that we could avoid by narrowly focusing on morality as defined in simpler times. He forces us to be accountable in often uncomfortable, but clearly necessary, ways if we honestly try to live appropriately in today's world.

You can test your lifestyle's rightness for one committed to spiritual living. Ask where it falls on such dimensions as luxury versus temperance, stinginess versus generosity, ambition and competition versus cooperation, and moderation versus indulgence. When we bring a bare simplicity to how we live, we establish ourselves in right livelihood. We develop living patterns that dispose us to virtue rather than problem-causing speech and behavior.

Right speech

We often overlook how very important speech is. Outer speech can cause considerable harm and suffering, but inner speech precedes all outward behavior. Intentions form in the mind before any action takes place. Building habits of right speech with other people helps our minds develop right inner speech. The Buddha named four important considerations in speech.[11]

Lying Truthfulness is the first right speech. Something that is not true simply should not be said. Lying brings suffering to both the liar and the person lied to. It destroys trust, creates a "tangled web" to defend, and finally causes delusion when we believe our own lies. Non-lying is commitment to what is real; we choose fact over desire-fueled fantasy when we resolve not to lie. To truly follow the Buddha's path to satisfaction, we must always monitor speech for truthfulness.

When we avoid deliberate lies, we start seeing many ways that we shade the truth without realizing it until afterward. Then we begin catching ourselves in the act of these small exaggerations, self-justifications, and self-glamorizing. I have not yet sat a long vipassana retreat in which I did not tell the teacher such an inadvertent lie. A helpful practice for this, when I catch myself doing it, is to confess the lie and tell the truth.

We also start seeing how we lie to ourselves to avoid the discomfort of recognizing our true motives, attitudes, and expectations. If we think we are really truthful, seeing all these tendencies in ourselves can be very painful. However, it would be a rare person in whom they are not present.

Slander or tale-bearing The second wrong speech is causing dissension or separation among people. Slander or tale-bearing is often fueled by envy, resentment, or self-seeking. It disrupts relatedness and destroys unity. Creating a rift in the spiritual community is one of the more serious moral failures in Buddhist thought. Nhat Hanh singled out this issue: "Do not utter words that can create discord and cause the community to break. Make every effort to reconcile and resolve all conflict, however small."[12] Opposed to slander is speech that promotes good feeling, friendship, and harmony among people.

Harsh speech The third wrong speech is unnecessarily harsh speech. This usually occurs in intense emotion, and is less serious than premeditated slander. However, it springs from anger and aversion, and creates unhappiness. "Do not speak harsh words for they will rebound on you. Angry words hurt."[13]

Our antidote is patience, tolerating unpleasant situations without lashing out. When we have an issue to resolve with someone, we are first to get our emotions under control, and then approach the situation in a problem-solving—not blaming—manner.

Idle speech The fourth wrong speech is idle speech, speech that is untimely or not useful. This guideline does not rule out affectionate talk between intimates, polite conversation with acquaintances, or speech needed to get work done. Much talk at offices, parties, and nightclubs, however, is idle speech. One Buddhist teacher said that quitting talking about other people eliminated over ninety percent of his speech.

The teachings list thirty-two categories of unprofitable speech.[14] They give us an almost humorous way to examine how much we speak idly. The list names speech about rulers, criminals, government employees, armies, dangers, battles, food, drink, clothing, dwellings, adornments, perfumes, relatives, vehicles, villages, towns, cities (sports teams, maybe?), provinces, the opposite sex, heroes, streets, baths, relations who have died, this and that, the origin of the world, the origin of the ocean, views about eternity, views about annihilation, worldly loss, worldly gain, self-indulgence, and self-mortification. Is there much left to talk about?

Other considerations In thinking about right speech, we should also think about listening. Do we listen to slander or idly spend hours watching television or reading junk fiction? Do we turn to an iPod or stereo to fill the environment with distracting and useless noise? Spending an evening alone without any speech, music, radio, television, or reading is an interesting experiment.

Nhat Hanh also emphasized the importance of speaking when speech is needed. This precept reads:

> Do not say untruthful things for the sake of personal interest or to impress people. Do not utter words that cause division and hatred. Do not spread news that you do not know to be certain. Do not criticize or condemn things that you are not sure of. Always speak truthfully and constructively. Have the courage to speak out about situations of injustice, even when doing so may threaten your own safety. [15]

Right Action

Right action means to avoid three types of behavior: killing, stealing, and sexual misconduct. Such actions create an enormous amount of suffering.

Killing Taking the life of any sensate being is prohibited; this includes even insects, those beings that crunch if we step on them or that whir around our heads. Deliberate harming—such as assault, torture, or maiming—is also prohibited. Thich Nhat Hanh's rendering reads, "Do not kill. Do not let others kill. Find whatever means possible to protect life and to prevent war." [16]

Working with this path step requires carefully assessing our attitudes on many life issues. In the controversies that rage over some— such as abortion, right to die, and stem cells—others often seem forgotten. These include war, civil rights, health care, and basic life necessities like food and shelter for the needy. We cannot forget these in developing reverence for life.

Taking what is not given The second wrong action is taking what is not given—interesting wording that says more than merely not stealing. It suggests that we should not borrow anything without permission, nor assume the right to use anything unless clearly meant for us. What havoc following this simple practice would eliminate from family life in many homes! No one would ever have to wonder who borrowed the missing scissors or what happened to the tape that disappeared from the desk.

This guideline also prompts us to consider failing to give to others what should be given to them. Nhat Hanh's advice reads: "Possess nothing that should belong to others. Respect the property of others, but prevent others from enriching themselves from human suffering or the suffering of other beings."[17]

If other people need things we own, how much of what we are not actively using is it right for us to possess? Do not material goods properly belong to those who need them, rather than those able to accumulate more than they can use? If a year goes by without her wearing an article of clothing, one woman I know says it no longer belongs to her. She gives it away where it will be used.

Sexual misconduct Buddhist texts list two main forms of sexual misconduct. The first is adultery—breaking a sexual commitment or being sexual with someone in commitment to another. The second is sexual activity with inappropriate other persons.[18] This includes close family members, people vowed to celibacy, and vulnerable people unable to give free consent, like children or prisoners. To these we need to add mentally or emotionally impaired people and those over whom we exercise power, such as employees, students, and clients.

Sexual misconduct is broadly defined as using sexuality in a way that harms oneself or any other being. Much is implied in this; it certainly rules out all manipulation, force, deceit, trickery, or irresponsibility in sexual behavior. It should rule out the social problems of unwanted pregnancies and sexually transmitted disease.

Nhat Hanh looked at sexual conduct very broadly.

Do not mistreat your body. Learn to handle it with respect. Do not look on your body as only an instrument. Preserve vital energies (sexual, breath, spirit) for the realization of the Way. Sexual expression should not happen without love and commitment. In sexual relationships, be aware of future suffering that may be caused. To preserve the happiness of others, respect the rights and commitments of others. Be fully aware of the responsibility of bringing new lives into the world. Meditate on the world into which you are bringing new beings.[19]

Precepts

These path steps of right speech, right action, and right livelihood are the training in morality. We freely train ourselves to avoid unskillful actions. We recognize that our choices affect not only ourselves, but also all beings and all things. The ripples created by dropping a small pebble into a large pond may be subtle, but they become increasingly wider until they affect the entire pond.

These training guidelines of sila are formalized in five precepts that all Buddhists are to observe. Others who do Theravadan Buddhist practice usually undertake the precepts before beginning a retreat or other intensive meditation practice, for the duration of the retreat. The precepts are not commandments, but guidelines that indicate which actions create suffering and should be avoided. They are helpful to anyone wanting to cleanse his or her heart.

The first precept is not to kill. On retreat, this sometimes becomes a "befriend a bug" exercise. You can remove insects from your territory if you don't want to live with them, but you do not kill them.[20]

The second precept is not to take what is not given to you.

The third precept of avoiding sexual misconduct has a special meaning for intensive spiritual practice; meditators on retreat are fully celibate, even regarding solitary sexual acts.

The fourth precept against wrong speech also has a special retreat meaning—observing the "noble silence." Those on retreat speak only at designated times, such as with the teacher or when a real need must be tended.

The fifth precept is to refrain from intoxicants or mind-altering substances. This precept keeps the mind clear enough to be conscientious about the other precepts. Prescription medicines needed for health may always be taken. Caffeine is allowed—probably because it seldom has harmful effects and it keeps meditators more alert for practice.

We undertake these trainings to serve both others and ourselves. From the wisdom of the *Dhammapada*: "Whoever destroys life, who speaks untruth, who in this world takes that which not given, who commits adultery, who are addicted to intoxicating drink are ones who, even in this world, dig up their own roots."[21]

If you have ever been with someone whose integrity seems absolutely unshakeable, you know the comfort and security you felt. We seek to become that kind of being. The happiness we find in this is far more deeply satisfying than what any unskillful behavior we have renounced could give us. "From craving springs grief. From craving springs fear. For those who transcend craving's bonds there is no grief, no fear."[22]

MJM

✠ 11 ✠

John of the Cross on Purity of Mind: Purification of Intellect, Memory, and Will

"To begin journeying to God," wrote John of the Cross in an early chapter of *The Ascent of Mount Carmel,* "your heart must be burning with the fire of divine love and cleansed of wanting any created thing."[1] Chapter 9 explained how mortifying our disordered desires for created things prepares us at the level of sense. This chapter describes how faith purifies us at the level of spirit. Chapter 13 shows how contemplation—the fire of divine love—burns, illumines, purges, heals, and transforms our hearts, uniting us with God in the Trinitarian life of love.

The Journey to Who We Are

In seeking union with God, we seek to become fully who we already are. John maintained that all human beings, even the world's greatest sinners, are united with God. Without God's creative power sustaining us from moment to moment, we would cease to exist. In this "substantial union," God is fully present in the very substance of our beings sustaining us in existence.

Coming to union Our purpose in life is to journey from this unconscious substantial union, which always exists even though we are unaware of it, to a fully conscious "union of likeness." This union comes about only through love, when "God's will and ours are in complete agreement, so that nothing in either is repugnant to the other." When we rid ourselves of what is repugnant and not conformed to God's will, we are "transformed in God through love."[2] We "become" God through participation in God. Like Balaam, the Hebrew Bible sooth-sayer, we "hear what God says, know what the Most High knows, and see what the Almighty sees."[3]

To arrive at this conscious union of likeness with God, we must do more than purify sensory life through mortification of disordered desire; we must also purify our spirit through faith. John called faith a "certain and obscure habit of soul" that enables us to believe divinely revealed truths that exceed natural human understanding.[4] Accepting God's self-revelation purifies our spirit and prepares us to eventually see God who alone "is the substance and basis of faith."[5] Faith leads us to God. John taught that we can know God only obscurely in this life; however, in the "next life," we will see God clearly, directly, and face-to-face.

Purification by faith, hope, and love Our "spirit" permits us to know and love others and to be in personal communion with God. This communion is possible because our powers of intellect, memory, and will enable us to know and love and to receive God's self-revelation to us. Faith, together with hope and love, purges these spiritual powers for union with God. Faith purifies intellect, hope purifies memory, and love purifies will.

This spiritual purification is not an arbitrary exercise; God's very being demands it. Ultimately, God is transcendent, totally inconceiv-able and unimaginable, and completely beyond human experience. No human thought, understanding, image, feeling, or emotion is able to apprehend or "capture" God. Faith, hope, and love purify our attach-ment to inadequate concepts, images, and emotional experiences of God so that our spirit is free to be united with incomprehensible good-ness and to receive all of God's self-communication to us. Until this purification is complete, we are not fully transformed in God, no mat-ter how profound our thoughts of God, compelling our imaginings, or emotionally intense our religious experiences.

Besides preparing us for transformation in God, purifying our spirit in faith, hope, and love also heals our personalities where the effects of sin present in our relationships with others have damaged them.

Faith, for example, can free us from a distorted image of God as a puni-
tive parent that keeps us imprisoned in neurotic fear and guilt. Hope
can release us from painful memories that bind us emotionally to negative experiences of the past and lead us to childish reactions to present problems. By choosing to love God first in everything, love can
heal dysfunctional human relationships. "I never got it right with my
wife and kids," reported one recovering alcoholic, "until I started getting it right with God."

Counsels for Purifying Spirit

To help us purify our spirit, John offered detailed advice for working
with thoughts, memories, images, and emotions so that they do not
become obstacles on the journey toward union with God. We might
call his advice "active faith" because it stresses what we do to prepare
our spirit for God; in a later section on contemplation, we speak of
"passive faith," or accepting what God does in us to prepare us for divine
union.

Knowing by not-knowing John taught that, because God transcends human knowledge, we are never to rest completely in our present understanding of God as though we have intellectually "caught" or
comprehended God. God is always more than our present concept of
God. We must always remain open to receive God's further self-
revelation until we see God face-to-face in eternity.

"We must go to God," John wrote, "by not understanding rather
than by understanding, and we must exchange what changes and what
we can know for the unchanging and incomprehensible."[6] Our present knowledge of God that comes through nature, revelation, and contemplation might be perfectly true, but is always incomplete.
Attachment to this incomplete knowledge can become an obstacle to
receiving what God wants to further reveal to us.

"I just don't know any more," a contemplative nun of many years
once told me. "I always thought I knew who God was, but the longer
I live and the more I pray, the more I realize God is completely different than anything I ever imagined." She was discovering the truth of

John's words that we "must walk the path knowing God by what God is not rather than through what God is."[7] She was experiencing the "exchange" of the comprehensible for the incomprehensible. Clinging to her earlier understanding of God would only slow her spiritual progress.

Non-attachment in memory Surprisingly, the counsel of non-attachment holds even for special hidden knowledge that we receive passively from God. Attachment to these special communications delays our journey to God, and can create harmful attitudes like pride and self-satisfaction. John explained:

> We need always and very carefully to reject this knowledge, and should want to come to God by unknowing. What God wants to accomplish through these passive communications will remain impressed upon us without our needing to make any effort. We reject this knowledge to guard against error.[8]

Similarly, John gave a "general rule of conduct"[9] for purifying the memory. Because intellect and memory are closely associated in human knowing, the method is nearly identical to that for purifying the intellect. He taught:

> As often as distinct ideas, forms, and images come to us, we should not rest in them but immediately turn to God with loving affection, emptying ourselves of everything we remember. We should not think or look on these things any longer than is needed to understand and satisfy our obligations, if they refer to these. We should consider these ideas without getting attached to them or wanting to enjoy them, lest they leave effects in us. We are not required to stop recalling and thinking about what we have to do and know since we will not be harmed if we are not attached to holding onto such thoughts.[10]

Aware that this counsel might strike some as iconoclastic, John insisted that he was not minimizing holy images, whether exterior ones like sacred icons or interior ones held in our memory; rather, he was "explaining the difference between these images and God." He continued his defense:

> Images will help us toward union with God only as long as we pay no more attention to them than is needed for this love, and that we allow ourselves to soar—when God bestows the favor—from the painted image to the living God, letting go of every created thing.[11]

Centering will on God Finally, John taught us how to purify the will, the spiritual faculty that enables us to love. The will invests all the energies of the soul—intelligence, memory, desires, feelings, and emotions—in what we love. We purify the will when, in response to God's unconditional love for us, we continually choose to center our lives in God rather than in other persons, wealth, status, individual talents, charismatic gifts, religious experiences, or whatever else may attract us.

John stated his guiding principle for purifying the will when discussing the emotion of joy: "We should rejoice only in what gives honor and glory to God."[12] He then applied this principle to purifying the will of its attachment to temporal goods such as money, position, power, influence, and family.

> At the first pull toward joy regarding things, we ought to curb it, and remember this principle: Nothing is worthy of our joy except serving God and bringing about God's honor and glory in all things. We should seek only this when we use things, turning away from vanity and concern for our own delight and consolation.[13]

Paradoxically, this non-attachment heightens rather than destroys appreciation for, and sensitivity to, creation. We experience a "spiritual joy, a hundred times greater" from continually lifting our minds and hearts to God in the presence of breathtaking beauty, stirring music, delightful fragrances, delicious food, delicate touches and whatever else delights our senses. "If we do not conquer the joy of appetite, we will not come to the serenity of habitual joy in God through God's works and all creation. Only the pure of heart find joyful, pleasant, chaste, pure, spiritual, glad, and loving knowledge of God in all things."[14]

In summary Such acts of faith, hope, and love purify our spirit for union with God. They create within us an attitude of non-attachment to our concepts, memories, images, feelings, and emotions—especially those that pertain to God. This attitude of non-attachment frees our spirit to respond to God's movements in our lives that lead us to divine union. We train ourselves to be continually mindful of the *first movements* of our intellect, memory, and will.[15] We learn to quietly center these movements in God while interacting with the persons and events of our lives. We open our lives completely to God.

Jesus Christ: Faith's Object, Model, and Reward

Christian faith is, above all, an interpersonal relationship with God. We understand faith's purification of our spirit better when we see Jesus Christ as faith's object, model, and reward.

What we ask of God John of the Cross imagined that were we to ask God for personal favors like private visions or revelations to help us on our way to divine union, God could respond in these words.

> I have already told you everything in my Word, my Son, and I have no other word, so what answer or revelation can I give you now that would surpass this? Keep your eyes on him alone because I have spoken and revealed all in him, and there you will find more than you could ever want or ask for. Hear him because I have no more faith to reveal or truths to show.[16]

We discover more than we ask for or desire in Jesus because he is an incomprehensible mystery, always more than our deepest understanding of him. Yet he is also our way to union with God through love.

His example teaches us how to purify sense and spirit. He models the death to self that is necessary for our lives to be transformed in God.

Imitating Jesus John insisted:

> We make progress only by imitating Christ, who is the Way, the Truth, and the Life [John 14:6]. Thus, I do not think that any spirituality that seeks sweetness and ease and runs from imitating Christ is worthwhile. Christ is the way, and this way is a death to our natural selves in both the sensory and spiritual parts of our beings.[17]

From his own meditation on the gospels, John pictured Jesus dead on the cross as totally naked, emotionally abandoned, and completely empty in both sense and spirit. Yet, in that moment, Jesus wrought his greatest work, "the reconciliation and union of the human race with God through grace." In the cross, "truly spiritual" people come gradually to understand the "way (which is Christ) that leads to union with God." We see that "our union with God and the greatness of anything we do will be measured by our death to self for God in the sensory and spiritual parts of our beings."[18]

Letting go John concluded:

> When we are reduced to nothing, the highest degree of humility, our spiritual union with God will be completed. Our journey does not consist of consolation, delight, and spiritual feelings, but of the living death of the cross, sensory and spiritual, exterior and interior.[19]

Letting go of disordered attachments to objects of sense and spirit is our "living death of the cross." Yet, in this non-attachment, we discover a new presence of Christ within us. John illustrated this with an episode from Jesus' risen life.[20]

> He who bodily entered his disciples' room while the doors were closed and gave them peace, without their knowing how

this was possible, will enter our souls spiritually without our knowing how or using any effort of our own, once we have closed the doors of intellect, memory, and will to all other objects.[21]

We purify our spirit through non-attachment to concepts, memories, images, feelings, and emotions. Then Jesus Christ, faith's reward, awakens in the depth of our souls, removes our fears, fills us with peace, and draws us into deeper love. As our love for Jesus within us deepens, we feel more keenly the fire of his love purifying us and transforming us in wisdom and compassion.

Faith: A Dark Journey

The journey to union with God in love is thus a dark journey because we travel always in purifying faith. We know God, not solely by the light of natural reason or various religious experiences, but primarily by accepting God's self-revelation. The journey is dark also because we voluntarily undertake to purify and empty sense and spirit of every disordered attachment that hinders God's purifying and transforming self-communication. This effort toward total self-emptying is our loving response to a God whose infinite love for us was expressed in Jesus' self-emptying death on the cross.

Yet, in dark faith and emptiness we also discover the Spirit of the risen Lord present within us guiding our lives, leading us to divine union. In this union,

> God's Spirit makes us know what we must know and ignore what we must ignore, remember what ought be remembered and forget what ought be forgotten, and makes us love what we ought to love, and keeps us from loving whatever is not of God.

In this union, the first movements and operations of all our human faculties become divine, "since they are transformed into divine being."[22]

To be "transformed in divine being" is to become fully who we already are: persons united with God. The journey from an unconscious "substantial union" to a conscious "union of likeness" based on love requires that we continually purify our spirit through active faith, hope, and love. It demands, further, a faith completely open to receive God's purifying and transforming love in contemplation.

Before describing this contemplation, we first look at the Buddhist teaching on the purification of mental contents and the training of the mind.

KC

✳ 12 ✳

Teachings of the Buddha on Purity of Mind:
Purification of Mental Contents,
Training the Mind

THE MEDITATION steps of the Buddhist path of spiritual practice involve training the mind to be docile, purifying its contents. This brings a much subtler happiness than sense delights or mental excitement; once it is deeply tasted, desire for grosser pleasures wanes. The steps on the noble eightfold path to this satisfaction are right effort, right mindfulness, and right concentration.

The meditation instructions tell us how to work with these steps in sitting and walking practice. To be spiritually committed, we must also live these disciplines daily. Life itself becomes a meditative work of training and cleansing the mind.

Right Concentration

What we concentrate on, where we rest our attention, is the food we give our minds. It "becomes" our minds, just as the food we give our bodies becomes our bodies. One meditator said that her mind continually replayed scenes from soap operas for the first three weeks of a three-month retreat.

Our culture considers it entertaining to watch stories full of brutality, violence, lust, and greed. We cannot control what gets aired on the media, but we can choose what we invite into our own minds. Theravadan Buddhists recommend three traditional types of concentration objects: neutral ones, objects of suffering, and beautiful mind-states.

Neutral objects Over our days, we often let our minds spin out, running wild through unimportant or even unwholesome ideas. Any time we start feeling scattered, we can check in with the breath for grounding. Before I started concentrating on the sensations created by walking while going to my university office, I usually spent that time in idle or disturbing thoughts that started my day poorly.

We can use routine bodily movements for concentration practice—like brushing teeth, scrubbing in the shower, washing dishes, stirring a pan, or sweeping a floor. If this does not sound "spiritual" to you, reflect that it means openhandedly embracing life moment to moment, fully living this moment you have been given to live. This is an attitude of deep spiritual surrender.

Unpleasantness and suffering The second group of concentration objects—suffering ones—is not appealing to our modern mentality. Yet it helps to realize that life is not without limit, that someday we will die, and that passing pleasures do not give lasting satisfaction.

A psychotherapist friend kept a small skull on his desk for perspective.[1] People had very interesting reactions to it; some tried hard not to see it, some shoved it out of sight, and some even asked him to remove it. Very few showed a fully appropriate reaction, accepting its presence without aversion.

Daily life provides many objects of suffering upon which to concentrate. If we really paid attention to any newscast, tears of compassion might come. However, we usually block awareness of such suffering. How interesting that people become intensely engrossed in fictional suffering in TV dramas, and yet cannot attend to the very real suffering going on around them!

Thich Nhat Hanh considered being open to suffering very important. He wrote:

> Do not avoid contact with suffering or close your eyes before suffering. Do not lose awareness of the existence of suffering in the life of the world. Find ways to be with those who are suffering by all means, including personal contact and visits, images, sound. By such means, awaken yourself and others to the reality of suffering in the world.[2]

Beautiful states The final concentration objects are inspiring and beautiful ones. These include virtues, devotional objects, and the *brahmaviharas* (heavenly mind-states), which describe appropriate attitudes toward other people. One way to concentrate on such attitudes is to practice meditation on them, which Buddhists do as an adjunct to insight meditation.[3] You can also help train yourself to wish others well by doing so mentally throughout your day.

The first heavenly mind-state is loving-kindness, universal friendliness and good will toward all beings with no exception. This includes the underprivileged and powerless of any society, next-door neighbors, and also people halfway around the world. It includes the elderly, the ill, pets, and insects. It also includes those who wield power. The Buddha told his monks to extend loving-kindness to beings who were making trouble for them. It does not matter whether we find another being appealing or not; we are to treat all with the same loving-kindness.

The Buddha explained the wisdom of such good will: "In this world hate never yet dispelled hate. Only love dispels hate. This is the law eternal."[4] A habit of loving-kindness can save us when we are pulled toward feeling ill will. The fruits of this practice will be seen in such caring actions as generosity and service.

The second heavenly mind-state is compassion, the right attitude toward beings who are suffering. Simply doing awareness practice, being with and exploring our own suffering, draws out compassion. As we realize the suffering in our own beings and in all beings, we can be with the suffering of the whole. We feel with those who suffer, and want to relieve the suffering we see.

Along with wisdom, compassion is one of the great "wings" of the Buddha's teachings. Compassion is very different from pity or from anger over suffering. In pity we condescend, setting ourselves apart from the sufferer. Anger dulls the ability to see clearly the sheer fact of suffering; it makes compassionately entering into it impossible.

Sympathetic joy is taking delight in the good that others enjoy. This difficult heavenly mind-state directly opposes envy and jealousy. Although human nature does not easily rejoice when someone else has advantages, even the smallest taste of sympathetic joy is an extremely beautiful feeling.

The fourth heavenly mind-state is equanimity.[5] We can wish others all the loving-kindness, compassion, and sympathetic joy in the world, but our wishes alone will not bring them happiness. These wishes are effective only as others can receive such blessings, and that depends upon what they choose. With equanimity, we develop the peace of accepting this fact.

Right Mindfulness

Thich Nhat Hanh taught how to bridge the gap between concentration and mindfulness: "Do not lose yourself in dispersion and in your surroundings. Learn to practice breathing to regain composure of body and mind, to practice mindfulness and to develop concentration and understanding."[6]

All the world's great spiritual traditions agree that seekers should always be mindful, should know what is going on. How can we remember to be mindful at all times? The Buddha helped us by naming four foundations of mindfulness. If we check these regularly, we become more and more mindful.

Four foundations of mindfulness Mindfulness of the body means noticing changes that occur in the body. On entering a new situation, be aware of its odors, sounds, and sights—and of the body's reactions to these. Is there tightening or relaxing? Is there a new sensation somewhere? Such experiences tell us how we are reacting to the situation, and can prevent poor management. We ought also to become aware of how the body feels during particular actions, such as eating and speaking. We can learn the effects on the body of particular entertainments.

Mindfulness of the behaviors we choose is of the greatest importance.[7] From the *Dhammapada*: "Those who earnestly practice mindfulness of the body will know what they are doing. They will not do that which should not be done. They will do that which should be done."[8]

The second foundation of mindfulness is feeling-tone, the hedonic quality that accompanies all experiences, ranging from very unpleasant through neutral to very pleasant. Our stronger pleasant or unpleasant experiences most often trigger our problem reactions—such as greed, anger, or fear. Awareness of feeling-tone gives us an edge in self-management.[9]

A third major area of mindfulness is mind itself and the "colorations" on it of our different moods, sets, emotions, and states of consciousness. The Buddha said to know when the mind is with or without greed, aversion, and delusion. Unwatched, these states get us into the most trouble. If we can see an emotion as it starts to develop, we can deal with it before it propels us into problem behavior.

The fourth area of mindfulness is the objects of experience. This includes all sense objects, the mind-states that work for our benefit or loss, and underlying truths like impermanence and unsatisfactoriness.

Insight practice requires that we focus attention on these basic realities. The mind, however, is very much in the habit of paying attention to its own creations—the stories we write in our minds about our experiences. These mental creations make up *conventional reality*.

Conventional realities Concepts, from which we form opinions and beliefs, and with which we create all aspects of culture, are socially agreed upon conventions. These conventional realities are not basically "real" like the four foundations of mindfulness are. They endure only as long as human minds hold them in existence. They "die" when people stop attending to them.

Concepts are a potent problem in spiritual practice because we seldom realize that our thoughts about something are not the reality itself. My thought about a banana is not a banana, and if I spend all my time thinking about bananas, I will never directly enjoy a banana. Similarly, my thought about God is not God. Truth can be fully grasped only in experience, not conceptually.

Zen Buddhist exponent Alan Watts explained our imprisonment in concepts: "If you try to capture running water in a bucket, it is clear that you do not understand it and that you will always be disappointed, for in the bucket the water does not run. To 'have' running water you must let go of it and let it run. The same is true of life and of God."[10]

He also said that settling for concepts or images about God is like going into a restaurant when we are hungry and eating the menu.[11]

Our persistent patterns of thoughts, the tapes we play and replay for ourselves, are our own creations, our versions of experience edited by our needs and wishes. Thinking them when we are meditating closes down our practice. Living in conceptual understandings can block direct awareness of important truths.

We accept many notions without examining them. Doing so can make it impossible to experience directly what is true. Truth cannot enter a full or closed mind. This understanding underlies the Buddha's teachings on faith.

The Buddha on faith The Buddha was very practical, and he realized that attachment to ideas is a serious problem in spiritual work. He said not to believe anything that anyone tells you, no matter on what authority, including what he himself said. If a spiritual teaching attracts you, try it out. See what you get from its practice, what fruits it bears in your life. Jesus also told us to assess value by observing fruits. If they are good, then a teaching is worth following. If not, it should be discarded. We must verify in our own experience what we adopt. We should never affirm what we have not tested; suspending judgment is the appropriate response to all untried teachings.[12]

Westerners often consider faith a matter of conceptual beliefs, and think that strong faith means feeling certain about these opinions. Alan Watts wryly said that belief sucks the thumb that points to truth, instead of following in the direction it indicates. Belief insists that reality is as we say it is, while faith is full openness to truth. "Belief clings, but faith lets go."[13] Faith is always open to truth, whatever it may be. The more beliefs or opinions we have, the more we insist that particular concepts are truth, the less we have the openness that faith demands.

Buddhists see faith as willingness to invest in spiritual practice, as confidence in value seen, not as opinions held. Jesus also taught that mere "lip service" is not enough. Faith increasingly develops by being confirmed over and again in the fruits of practice. Buddhist saints come to invincible faith that keeps them completely true to what they have realized.[14]

Right Effort

Right effort has four parts. We prevent unwholesome mind-states from arising, and remove unwholesomeness that is present. We encourage wholesome mind-states to arise, and retain wholesomeness that is present.

Prevention We want to prevent mind-states rooted in greed, aversion, or delusion. A major practice for this, sense restraint, does not mean withdrawal from experiences. If we are mindful of experiences and their feeling-tone, we are protected from being overcome by greed or aversion. If we are open to sensory events without mindfulness, they easily draw us into negativity. In the untrained mind, appealing objects draw out greed—the whole point of advertising. Unappealing objects elicit some form of aversion: anger, fear, or sadness.

We have proper sense restraint when we can see sensory experiences as simple, passing phenomena, without getting caught up in such notions as "my experience" or "my pleasure or pain." Lack of mindfulness is the problem, not having experiences. However, it helps to choose experiences wisely, for we all remain vulnerable until we reach a very high level of understanding.

Removing In order to abandon a persistent unwholesome state, we can directly "confront" the unwholesome attitude as we do in meditation. When carefully explored and examined, it loses its strength to move us, and simply becomes an object of study. A friend, prone to depressions, decided to stare depression in the face until it left her. Although she is not a meditator, this solid method worked; the depression lifted in days rather than the usual weeks.

The Buddha also encouraged us to cultivate the opposite of unwholesome attitudes. When we obsess about feeling unjustly treated, anger arises. When we feel deprived, resentment or sadness follows. When we cultivate opposite attitudes, such as gratitude and surrender, unwholesome mind-states drop off. Thich Nhat Hanh recommended this method:

> Do not maintain anger or hatred. As soon as anger and hatred arise, practice the meditation on compassion in order to deeply understand the persons who have caused anger and hatred. Learn to look at other beings with the eyes of compassion.[15]

Sometimes this proves too hard. Then we can develop inner revulsion to the negativity with two wholesome mind-states. Moral sensitivity *(hiri)* shrinks from unwholesomeness as degrading and unworthy. Moral conscientiousness *(ottappa)* dreads doing anything that causes harm, so pulls away from unwholesome attitudes. We must be careful not to fall into self-hatred: we develop revulsion to the unwholesome mind-state, not to ourselves.

When I found myself frequently drawn into ugly gossip about a colleague, my teacher suggested a vow against such speech. I feared that I could not keep the vow, but he explained that it would make me more sensitive to "invitations" to backbiting before I was already into it. I would then more easily catch myself before the fact, rather than after. I broke the vow a few times, but promptly retook it. Eventually, seeing the ugliness of such speech released me from wanting to be part of the office group sharing it.

If cultivating revulsion fails, a fourth method is deliberately diverting attention to something else. A possibly apocryphal story tells that one meditator, bothered with sleepiness in practice, aroused feelings of lust to get rid of it—and, of course, he wound up with more trouble than he had in the beginning. Thus we must carefully choose the object for this, so that we do not jump from the frying pan into the fire.

The fifth method to get rid of unwholesome mind states, deliberate and vigorous suppression of the unwholesome attitude, is drastic. Scriptural texts say to screw up your face and bite your tongue to force the attitude away.[16] Such tactics should be used only if we are becoming overwhelmed by a mind-state—such as intense anger on which we might presently act—and all else has failed. Persistent problematic emotions might call for psychotherapy or other treatment.

Many people feel they must openly express anger or depression to get rid of them, while the opposite is actually true. The more we act on such states, the more we strengthen them. It is important to recognize when they are present, not denying their existence, but absolutely not necessary to act upon them.

Developing Two meditation methods develop wholesome mental states. Concentrative meditation focuses attention on the attitude we want to increase, such as loving-kindness. Our insight practice, which cultivates wisdom, brings with it beautiful and appropriate mind-states.

We can also develop wholesome states through daily choices. People tend to bring ideas and attitudes into line with behavior, so we can "prime the pump" by doing things that encourage wholesome states. For example, we can deliberately cultivate attitudes the Buddha called "great good fortune." These include reverence, a heart grateful for what it has received, and the humility of being "teachable" and learning from others. Simply doing actions that reflect such attitudes—"going through the motions"—encourages the corresponding attitudes to arise.

We can also choose experiences that bring wholesome attitudes. Being willing to see suffering makes occasions for compassion. Seeing good in others arouses loving-kindness. We can change habits of focusing on what is wrong about others to noticing what is right.

Maintaining Acting on wholesome mental states makes them habitual so that they will come more frequently and stay longer. Some Buddhists cultivate generosity by vowing to act on every serious thought of giving something. If we become aware when such wholesome states arise, and fully encourage them, we develop a mind increasingly filled with them.

In Summary

To purify mental contents, we have right effort, right mindfulness, and right concentration. In formal meditation practice, they train and purify the mind, making it receptive for wisdom. In everyday life, we can continue the effort.

MJM

✣13✣

John of the Cross on Purity of Heart: Contemplative Purification

AFTER THE PURIFICATION of sense and spirit through mortification and faith, we still need further purification before we are united with and transformed in God through love. This is the purification of our entire beings through contemplation. Why is more purification necessary? What obstacles to union with God still remain?

John of the Cross maintained that our desires for sensory pleasure are so strong and pervasive, and our self-love so deep and subtle, that we are incapable of purifying them by our own efforts alone. Only God can cleanse us of every obstacle to divine union. God does this in the deep states of contemplation, which is God's intimate self-revelation and self-gift to us in love. Contemplation is divine loving knowledge that illumines and purifies our entire being. As fire transforms a log into itself, so God's self-communication purifies our hearts, heals all our wounds, and transforms us into the divine life of Trinitarian love.

The Pleasure Principle and Unconscious Motivation

Using the seven capital sins, John described how the pleasure principle motivates beginners on the spiritual journey. Even though their conversion to the spiritual path is real and their desire to love and serve God is genuine, problems remain. Subtle forms of spiritual pride, avarice, lust, gluttony, envy, anger, and sloth continue to inspire their behavior, especially their religious exercises.

Purification of motive Some undertake meditation and other spiritual exercises primarily because they give them a feeling of well-being; others involve themselves in social causes to express their unrecognized anger with authority. Even those who have progressed into higher stages of prayer continually discover that their conscious self-sacrifice for others is often motivated by previously unnoticed needs for acceptance and approval. They eventually recognize that unconscious needs move them, but feel helpless—despite continual prayer and mortification—to discover and purify their real motives and change their behavior. The deep roots of their disorder are hidden from their eyes.

Through contemplation, God purifies our persistent desire for sensory pleasure and the barriers to divine union alive in our unconscious minds. John described contemplation as "an inflow of God into our souls that purges us of habitual ignorance and imperfections, natural and spiritual." Infused contemplation, which is God's own "loving wisdom," secretly and painfully teaches us "the perfection of love." By illuminating and purifying all our motives, contemplation prepares us "for union with God through love."[1]

God's self-revelation Contemplation is God's most intimate self-revelation to us. Nature reveals God's beauty, majesty, and power. Scripture and tradition reveal God as a Trinity of Persons, as incarnate in Jesus Christ. In contemplation, God communicates with us as a personal friend. For John, Jesus—the total, complete, final self-revelation of God—was "a brother, companion, master, ransom, and reward."[2] Jesus was the bridegroom of his soul for whom John felt "love's anguished yearning." John imagined Jesus as sleeping "on my flowering breast that I kept solely for him alone."[3]

John believed that he was able to reach "the sweet and delightful life of love with God" because of "the strength and warmth he got from loving this bridegroom in obscure contemplation."[4] God's self-communication in contemplation is like the mutual self-revelation of human lovers in the growth and expressions of their love.

Prayer

We open ourselves to receive God's self-communication through prayer, which is a conscious centering of our minds and hearts in God, concerned to please God alone.[5] Prayer ordinarily develops through two major stages. It begins with discursive meditation and, usually after a relatively short time, passes on to contemplation. Prayerful reflection or discursive meditation is our work for God; contemplation is God's work in us.

Two stages Discursive meditation is a prayer for beginners on the spiritual journey. It relies heavily on sense and imagination to bring sensory delight and emotional involvement in the object of meditation. From this sensory and emotional experience comes pleasure in the idea of God and courage for serving God. By contrast, contemplation, the prayer of those more advanced along the spiritual journey, is centered in the spirit—a quiet receiving of God's loving knowledge in intellect, memory, and will.

Discursive meditation prepares us for contemplation; contemplation brings us to union with God in love, a state of being in which prayer becomes a continuous act of love. However, before contemplation begins, we must first be purified of the subtle self-seeking that often motivates our discursive meditation and religious exercises.

Discursive meditation "Beginners' practice," John wrote, "is to meditate using discursive reflection with the imagination."[6] Meditation for John was primarily a discursive practice. Using memory and imagination, we form mental images. With our reasoning, we reflect upon these images and other religious concepts, and draw out implications for our daily lives. Examples of images John suggested for discursive meditation are "picturing Christ crucified, at the pillar, or in some other scene; or imagining God seated on a throne with resplendent majesty; or considering and imagining glory as a beautiful light, and so on."[7]

Involving our feelings and emotions in these images and concepts usually inspires fervent acts of love for God and resolutions to serve God faithfully. This discursive practice brings us "some knowledge and love of God."⁸ The delight and satisfaction arising from meditation enables us to disengage our desires from the attractions of the world and center them in God, preparing ourselves for God's self-communication in contemplation.

Dryness Discursive meditation as a way of praying usually ends when we experience, sometimes suddenly after months of delightful communing with God, psychological and spiritual dryness. This dryness involves a loss of pleasure in the things of God and of the world, together with a sudden inability to meditate discursively, although our longing for union with God remains. The dryness occurs because God is beginning to communicate more directly to our spirit, and less through our senses and imagination. Consequently, our sensory life begins to feel like a desert as God speaks more immediately to our spirit. "God wants to lead us to more spiritual, interior, and invisible graces by taking away the gratification discursive meditation gives us."⁹

Contemplative Purification

If we choose to continue prayer in the midst of this emotional desert, our primary motive now becomes our faith and love for God rather than the pleasure prayer gives us. Dryness has purified our pleasure principle.

Transition When loss of pleasure, increased longing for God, and inability to meditate discursively occur simultaneously, we know that God has begun to "wean us and place us in the state of contemplation."¹⁰ John counsels a complete change in the way we pray here. We no longer need to reflect discursively on Gospel episodes or religious images, or to derive emotional delight and satisfaction during our periods of prayer.

Such discursive activity now becomes "an obstacle in the path of God, the principal agent who secretly and quietly inserts loving wisdom and knowledge in the soul, without our doing any particular thing." Instead, John advised meditators to "stay only with loving advertence [attentiveness] to God, without doing any specific thing. We should conduct ourselves passively without making any effort except the simple loving awareness, as if opening our eyes with loving attention."[11]

In this quiet, passive, loving attention to God, we make the transition from meditative or discursive prayer to contemplative prayer. Our challenge in prayer now is to be still before God in the depths of our beings with our minds and hearts—intellect, memory, and will—totally open to receive God's self-communication in divine, loving knowledge.

For years, our prayer may remain simple, quiet, peaceful, and spiritually energizing, even in the midst of external activities and pressures. Nevertheless, despite this abiding peace, our spirits are still not yet fully purified. In fact, the longer we pray contemplatively, the more conscious we become of our need for God to purge the deep roots of our self-love, roots that we have become increasingly aware of, but feel helpless to purify on our own.

Loving knowledge God eventually responds to our desire for purification with a more intense self-communication to us. We may experience this communication interiorly as general, non-specific loving knowledge—light and heat together, like a fire. In the light of this knowledge, our awareness of God as Incomprehensible Goodness increases. Consciousness of the risen Lord's loving presence within us grows steadily.

At the same time, we also see ourselves more clearly. In the light of God's love for us, we become vividly aware of the self-seeking in even our most altruistic activity. We wonder if we love God at all. Worse still, as we observe our incessant self-seeking, we wonder if even the all-good God can possibly love one so self-centered as ourselves. On the one hand, our longing for God deepens as we become more aware of the divine goodness; on the other, we fear never being worthy of God because of all the unhealed disorder we see in ourselves.

The growing awareness of God's love, the pain caused by our own self-knowledge, and the fear of losing God now begin to cause us psychological highs and lows. At times, we are deeply consoled and confident that God could never abandon us, only shortly afterward to be cast down into helpless feelings of unworthiness and fear that God could never love us.

At other times, we feel lost at sea. We could never return to our former ways of living, yet we wonder if God could possibly ever receive us. The thought of the future fills us with dread. In these emotional ups and downs, God finally purges us of our deepest attachment to ourselves, heals our souls, and transforms us in the divine life of love.

Purification and healing We are purified, healed, and transformed in this emotional upheaval precisely because our "spiritual eye" gives us a very clear picture of ourselves. "Our sufferings at this time cannot be exaggerated; they are just a little less than those of purgatory." Through this interior suffering, however, God "heals our souls of their many infirmities, bringing them to health. All our infirmities are brought to light and are set before our eyes to be felt and healed."[12]

Nothing remains hidden; the fears, delusions, compulsions, projections, and jealousies that subtly motivate our behavior are finally revealed to us. We recognize that for years we have been unconsciously working to establish our own illusory self rather than the kingdom of God. We are deeply embarrassed and ashamed to see all our inner workings; yet, we also trust that this painful awareness is healing us so that in everything we can live and act for God's honor and glory alone.

As this healing of our self-love nears completion, the emotional ups and downs lessen, a sign that the contemplative purification is nearly over. The "state of perfection," in which we are united with and transformed in God, is at hand. This state consists in the perfect love of God and complete non-attachment to self. Because this state demands knowledge of both God and self, we have necessarily been tried in both. Alternately we have been consoled in God's love and humbled by what we have discovered about ourselves. Finally, "the ascent and descent stop when we acquire perfect habits. Our souls will then have reached God and united themselves with God."[13] We are no longer drawn to any inappropriate thought or behavior.

Transformation in Divine Loving Wisdom

In his *Spiritual Canticle* and *The Living Flame of Love,* John described the loving union of the human person and God with rich imagery and vivid detail. From the viewpoint of human purification, this union of love is primarily a union of the human and divine wills. Thus, we experience transformation in God as a complete reformation of our motives. We are now moved to act, not by the satisfaction or dissatisfaction we find in persons, things, and events, but by the Holy Spirit.

John depicted Mary of Nazareth as the perfect exemplar of a transformed human being because "she was always moved by the Holy Spirit."[14] He wrote, "Perfected souls, like true daughters of God, are moved in all things by the Spirit of God, as the apostle Paul taught when he said that those moved by the Spirit of God are children of God."[15] Their intellect is God's intellect, their memory is God's memory, their will is God's will, and their delight is God's delight. Although they always remain uniquely themselves without their substance ever becoming God's substance, they "become God through participation in God."[16]

Continually inspired by the Holy Spirit, the living flame of divine love, persons transformed in God are moved only by love. Everything they do is an "exercise of love." In loving God alone, they also love all beings unconditionally and unselfishly. They expend all their energies serving God and others.

They have lost interest in satisfying themselves or pleasing others out of mere human respect. The persistent demands of their egos to live an autonomous life apart from God's will have ceased. Their soul is in peace, like a "house at rest,"[17] no longer disturbed by conflicting desires and emotions.

They experience their breathing as one with the breath of God. John explained, "The Holy Spirit sublimely elevates our souls and makes them able to breathe in God the same breathing of love that the Father breathes in the Son and the Son in the Father."[18]

In prayer, such individuals have passed beyond all methods and simply enjoy communion with God in faith and love. They continually seek more solitude to deepen their "attentiveness to God and the continual practice of love in God."[19] They are convinced that deepening this communion with God is their best way of serving God's people. They believe that "a little of this pure love is more precious to God and our souls, and more beneficial to the community—even though it seems we are doing nothing—than anything else we might do all put together."[20]

John of the Cross: A Transformed Personality

When John exclaimed poetically that the night of purgative contemplation "has united the Lover with the beloved, transforming the beloved in the Lover,"[21] it is hard to miss the autobiographical character of his words. Indeed, John exemplifies a human personality transformed in God's love.

Serving others People generally think of John as a man who removed himself from the stressful burdens of daily life to revel in extraordinary aesthetic and mystical experiences. While he always longed for deeper solitude, he in fact spent his adult years in nearly continuous administrative and educational service to his Carmelite brothers and sisters, and in providing sacramental ministry and spiritual guidance to numerous people. He wrote poetry and spiritual treaties only as he could find time in his busy schedule.

That such activity did not prevent his transformation in wisdom and compassion is perhaps best illustrated by an incident near the end of his young life. A Carmelite nun had written to him decrying the shameful plot of one of his Carmelite brothers to drive him from the order. In response, John wrote back:

> Do not let what is happening to me, daughter, cause you any grief, because it does not cause me any. People do not do these things, but God, who knows what is suitable for us and arranges things for our good. Think only that God ordains all, and where there is no love, put love, and you will draw out love.[22]

With divine wisdom, he interpreted events through the eyes of God; with divine compassion, he responded to people with the nonviolent heart of Jesus Christ. The words John used to describe people always moved by the Holy Spirit aptly apply to himself: "It seems to them that the entire universe is a sea of love in which they are engulfed. Conscious of the living center of love within themselves, they cannot catch sight of the boundaries of this love."[23]

Our purification ends in this state of union and transformation. It has come about, finally, because of God's self-communication to us and our own passive or receptive faith. In contrast to the active faith of chapter 11, passive faith is our openness to accept all that God desires to accomplish in us. Contemplation is thus not limited to times of formal prayer, but becomes the experience of life itself. We recognize God purifying, healing, and transforming us in every event of our lives.

A Final Thought

John of the Cross taught that "here on earth, only love cleanses and illumines us."[24] God's total self-giving in Jesus Christ initiated this love; our total self-emptying of sense and spirit responds to this love. As we continually surrender ourselves to God through faith, mortification, and prayer, God's self-communication to us becomes more intense, transforming us gradually into divine being.

If we are faithful to God, God is faithful to us. John wrote:

> Were you to eliminate these sensory and spiritual impediments, living in pure nakedness and poverty of spirit, your soul in its simplicity and purity would then be immediately transformed into simple and pure Wisdom, the Son of God. As soon as natural things are driven out of an enamored soul, the divine are naturally and supernaturally infused since nature cannot tolerate a void.[25]

Let us now turn to the realization of wisdom and compassion in the Buddhist tradition.

KC

✢ 14 ✢

Teachings of the Buddha on Purity of Heart: Wisdom, the Goal of Realization

ONCE OUR MINDS can remain still and contented, then the highest happiness can develop—the satisfaction of wisdom. Wisdom ripens fully only when behavior and mental contents are rightly ordered. The path's wisdom steps are right understanding and right intention or motivation. Right understanding is the fruit of formal meditation practice and of spiritually earnest living in everyday life. From right understanding comes right motivation, making us saintly presences in the world.

Barriers to Wisdom

Even when conduct and mental contents are relatively pure, subtle impediments remain. These are mostly not conscious, and rest on strongly conditioned tendencies of the heart.

Clinging to opinions The Buddha said that clinging to opinions can keep us locked in the bondage of ignorance, making it difficult or impossible to see truth. Thich Nhat Hanh has a solidly Buddhist concern about dogmatism. His very first precept is: "Do not be idolatrous about or bound to any doctrine, theory, or ideology, even Buddhist ones. All systems of thought are guiding means; they are not absolute truth."[1]

We seldom realize that we often "worship" words because we confuse concepts with that to which they point. We get very attached to comfortable understandings of ourselves, reality, others—even God.

Holding onto favorite understandings often makes us feel very secure, but this "safety" rests on shifting sand, not firm reality.

Many consider clinging to opinions virtuous, and fail to see the folly of it. We consider it great strength when nothing can change our minds. From Thich Nhat Hanh: "Do not think the knowledge you presently possess is changeless, absolute truth. Avoid being narrow-minded and bound to present views. Learn and practice non-attachment from views to be open to receive others' viewpoints."[2]

Nhat Hanh pushed us even farther: "Do not force others, including children, by any means whatsoever, to adopt your views, whether by authority, threat, money, propaganda or even education."[3] He continued, urging us to help others renounce fanaticism and narrowness through compassionate dialogue. I recall an old cartoon in which a crusader sits high on a big white horse, holding his spear at the throat of an Arab man spread-eagled on the ground. The caption reads: "Suddenly I'm very interested in this Christianity of yours. Tell me more."[4]

Clinging to opinions blinds us into not seeing clearly, and has led some people to do much evil in the guise of good. Opinions might make us feel like we understand, but can work against spiritual growth. As we understand more, we need to revise our beliefs. When we willingly relinquish old opinions that have outlived their usefulness, we increasingly open to truth.

Underlying assumptions The assumptions we hold are another problem. We often do not even know what these are, because they stay unconscious until we ferret them out. We unthinkingly accept much as true about the world, others, and ourselves. These presuppositions powerfully condition our behavior, so our choices reveal what we assume and expect. Since underlying assumptions often directly oppose what we know consciously, it requires some work to understand them.

For example, in spite of knowing that it leaves me feeling groggy, unmotivated, and out of sorts, sometimes I still reach for the second bowl of ice cream. People who use food unskillfully unconsciously accept overeating as a good choice; it must meet a deeply felt need. Perhaps we want to fill ourselves with something good to ward off guilt, or we might want a greater buffer between the outside world and ourselves. Understanding how we irrationally act against ourselves is part of being purified.

Similarly, how we react to changes in fortune tells us what is binding us, what we assume we absolutely need. The Buddhist tradition describes four pairs of alterations in fortune: pain or pleasure, praise or blame, gain or loss, and companionship or isolation. If any alteration causes grief, that is a sign of attachment. Such attachments imprison us, and keep us trying to hold on to what cannot be secured. "The wind does not shake a rock. Praise and blame do not falter the wise."[5]

Because assumptions are deeply entrenched and unconscious, they are a harder task than conscious opinions. Meditation practice helps by baring much that we hide from ourselves. It can reveal an assumption's origin, most frequently in early life. Getting rid of these hidden, harmful tendencies of the heart breaks subtle chains that bind us.

Understanding the darker forces in our minds is a bridge to right motivation. Opinions and assumptions not only obscure our seeing of truth, but also are strong motivational forces.

Seeing motivations Let us now do some diagnostic work on motives. Without such self-understanding, spiritual endeavor will not bear fruit. To what do our minds turn when not engaged in other activities? What do we spin out into?

Do we think of power, prestige, material gain, being loved, ambition, pleasures, or ease? Does the mind go to some specific addiction—a particular substance, person, or activity? Do our minds mentally dwell in the past or future, or distance us from the present by analysis, complaint, or spacing out? If we carefully watch in our sitting meditation and daily life, seeing where the mind goes will show us the strong motivational forces in our lives.

Behind these conscious preoccupations are tendencies to misuse experiences, relationships, and possessions. Any obsessive bent of mind almost always results in abuse. Not even spiritual aspirations are free of this. Do we sanctify as "spiritual yearnings" other motives like self-importance, control, or gain? Thich Nhat Hanh is sensitive to this:

> Do not use the Buddhist community for personal gain, or transform your community into a political party. A religious community, however, should take a clear stand against oppression and injustice and should strive to change the situation without engaging in partisan conflicts.[6]

We are also motivated to defend ourselves against raw self-knowledge. Defense mechanisms are subtle, self-protecting, mental maneuvers. We tell ourselves these little lies somewhat unconsciously. Every time we justify ourselves, defensiveness is at work. Whenever we insist on our own rightness, force others to see something our way, or try to control what happens, defensiveness is present. We need great honesty and humility to unmask ourselves, to see the self-protective motives that keep us from more appropriate ones.

Right Understanding

Right understanding means clear-seeing, seeing reality as it truly is, without the blinders of desires, aversions, or delusions. It is seeing the truth of things unclouded by any smoke screens that self-sense throws up in self-protection. Life itself teaches us these truths at one level, just as we may intellectually comprehend them even more superficially.

Faithful and careful awareness practice brings increasingly deeper, clearer seeing—seeing that can radically purify our hearts. What Buddhists call *insight knowledge comes* from deepening meditation practice. This is not conceptual knowledge or even simple lived awareness of these truths experienced in our lives. In meditation, understanding comes by deep, direct seeing that produces life-changing learning.[7]

Body and mind The first insight knowledge is of mental and physical reality. It means clearly understanding physical realities, such as sensations we call painful or the sound when a bell is struck. It also means understanding mental phenomena—consciousness and mind-states; for example, just what is a thought, or what is anger or fear? We also clearly distinguish physical from mental phenomena. We become able to distinguish among different types of mental experience. Initially, many people have trouble seeing the difference between an emotion and thought about the emotion.

Cause and effect A second insight knowledge is cause and effect. We see how pleasantness of feeling-tone easily leads to greed if we are not alert, how unpleasantness draws out aversion, and how we become bored and inattentive when feeling-tone is neutral. Clear awareness of feeling-tone can keep us from moving into greed, aversion, or delusion.

We also see how intentions precede each action. Awareness of intentions lets us cancel those that are not appropriate. If we fail to see intentions, they impel unskillful action whenever an unwholesome mind-state gets sufficiently strong. Feeling-tone and intention mark crucial points of freedom once we clearly see cause and effect regarding them.

Knowledge of cause and effect goes even deeper. We see multiple cause-effect relationships in our choices, understanding how they condition future options and situations. We realize that each choice to indulge a habit, obsession, compulsion, or addiction tilts the balance making it easier to so choose the next time. We see how each "no" to unwholesomeness makes saying "no" again easier. We realize that nothing is free; everything counts and has its consequences.[8]

We see the absolute interconnection of all of us in and with all of nature! I have frequently commented that "the Mystical Body of the Christ" was just beautiful words to me until I had direct experience of our connectedness in Buddhist practice.

Insight practice shows how our choices affect not only all beings, including ourselves, but all matter also. As a people, we are becoming painfully aware of how habits of waste affect our environment. In practice, we see even more subtle connections that attest to everything's being part of one cosmic process. We become attentive to the effects of all our choices. We see these truths by faithfully paying full attention to the physical and mental experiences that draw awareness to themselves.

The three characteristics Another insight knowledge reveals the nature of conditioned reality, of all realities subject to cause and effect. A rugged period of practice teaches us to see clearly the three universal characteristics that mark everything except Nibbana.

We see for ourselves the truth of suffering in all lives. Irrefutable meditation experiences also show the fleeting nature of phenomena, how things come into existence simply to pass out again. We comprehend what the Buddha meant by no-self, understanding how—since only Nibbana is unchanging—all lived realities are truly only processes with a beginning and end.

This time in practice is often very unpleasant; however, it purges attachments, develops patience and compassion, and finally leads to a holy life. These insights leave us greatly humbled and deeply committed to spiritual practice. Our meditation becomes self-propelling with sharp, clear, and penetrating understanding.

Knowing the path In the following delightfully easy period of practice, we are in great danger of attachment to pleasant meditation experiences. Eventually, deepening knowledge brings sure seeing of the right path of practice. We realize that we do not practice for comfort or pleasure, but for purgation. We understand that purifying conduct and mind is the only way out of the human dilemma—that no magic, hard wishing, or other maneuver does the job. This greatly lessens attachment to pleasantness, and prepares us for the even more rugged purgation that follows.

Advanced insight In advanced insight, we radically experience the three characteristics. We see clearly that all is change; even consciousness itself dies with each experience and is reborn with the next. Although "things" and experiences look solid and continuous, they are only rapidly changing processes. Everything is simultaneously being born and dying.

We deeply realize that what is never stationary, never lasting, can never be lastingly satisfying. The suffering in even pleasant experience becomes very apparent. All pleasures end; all favorite cups eventually break.[9] All relationships come to parting—by death, if not before.[10]

However beautiful, delightful, inspiring, or joy-filled an experience, it ends and therefore brings no lasting satisfaction.

We clearly see that nothing has any unchanging fixedness we can consider a permanent, enduring entity. We recognize how what we call our selves are simply interlocking processes that have come together because of conditions, and will eventually come apart. All is process, the constant interchange of processes within processes within processes. Often these realizations come with stark feelings of aloneness, impotence, vulnerability, and lack. The purgation is rigorous and intense.

A great yearning for liberation that consumes all of one's being eventually comes. Next follows the deeply balanced equanimity of complete surrender; we accept any and all occurrences equally. This balanced state of mind is "near" Nibbana. Buddhists say that we have the wisdom of knowledge and vision of the way at this point.

Fruition Advanced insight culminates in "touching" Nibbana, being "in" the one Reality not subject to the fluctuations, insecurity, and suffering of human life. Nibbana—the unconditioned, the unchanging, the unborn, the undying, the permanent, peace, rest, haven, home—is beyond any earthly joy, delight, or stillness. Thing-ness and flux cease; faith has been perfected, and we now know by direct experience. This is the highest wisdom, analogous to John's loving knowledge of God.[11]

Right Motivation

Clearly seeing, coming to wisdom or spiritual fruition, affects how we live in the world. "The good, wise, and righteous—for the sake of self, for the sake of others—do not use unjust means to seek success."[12] There are three traditional right motives or intentions: renunciation, loving-kindness, and compassionate nonviolence. These counter greed, self-centeredness, and cruelty.

Renunciation Practicing renunciation is not suppression or heavy-handed self-control, but a willing letting-go; this does not mean it is easy to do. The Buddha understood our struggles. "Renunciation is difficult. It is difficult to delight in it."[13]

Understanding that we must relinquish what is harmful is easy, needing only simple common sense. Precepts help by giving us guidelines.

Next we let go of things that easily lead to harming. Buddhist monks and nuns take additional precepts to practice this. They fast from midday until dawn, give up frivolous entertainment, and refrain from adorning their persons. They avoid unnecessary ease of posture, and some do not handle money. This parallels the notion of Christian monastic vows of poverty, chastity, and obedience, which are designed to break attachments to possessions, pleasure, relationships, and one's own will.

A third level of renunciation—refraining from things that draw attention from what is important—is very difficult. In meditation practice, we give up thinking, looking around, and unnecessary activity that might disturb concentration. In daily life, we must ruthlessly surrender whatever distracts us from our spiritual purpose. These small attachments can be very difficult to see and, when we do see them, we find it easy to justify them.[14]

The final relinquishment—of separate self-sense and the suffering that goes with it—is the fruit of spiritual practice.[15] When we deeply understand suffering, impermanence, no-self, and the effects of actions, we want this final relinquishment. We cannot make the transforming touch of Nibbana or God happen, but we can prepare for it. We can live according to the eightfold noble path: being moral, purifying mental contents, and cultivating wisdom and radical purity of heart.

Loving-kindness Chapter 12 discussed loving-kindness, the second correct motivation. It must not be only a nice feeling to enjoy, but needs to be translated into action. Harmonious behavior and attitudes support loving-kindness. Looking for good in others makes loving-kindness habitual.

The practice can easily be brought into daily life. Some people have developed the habit of sending blessings to whomever might be in some kind of trouble every time they hear an emergency vehicle siren—even when it is just a police car chasing a speeder. When waiting in line or caught in a traffic snarl, realizing that the other people around you are as trapped as you are can open your heart to sending them blessings of loving-kindness.

Harmlessness The third right mind-set, harmlessness and compassion, flows from loving-kindness and from understanding suffering and the effects of choices. As spiritual practice ripens, so does compassion. Practicing renunciation and mindfulness in daily life helps it develop. We shrink from inflicting hurt, and feel great compassion for those who do harm, knowing they are making great suffering for themselves. Wisdom and compassion, the two great wings of Buddhism, mutually feed each other.

One beautiful example of compassionate understanding is that of a British hostage, who was held in the Middle East for a long time, then released in 1990. When asked if he wanted revenge, he said no, for he would not maim himself with such motives. In contrast, a 1991-released American hostage felt his captors should be chained for twenty years, the cumulative amount of time he and fellow captives were chained. Which hostage is now truly free?

Virtues Buddhist teachings list ten virtues—called *paramis*—that the Buddha perfected and which each spiritual practitioner must develop.[16] They make right intention more concrete for us. First is generosity, exactly the opposite of clinging or grasping—the major cause of suffering.

We have already discussed the next four. Morality is the necessary basis for further purification, and renunciation is the deepening, progressive letting-go that constitutes spiritual work. Wisdom, fully right understanding, finally liberates us. Diligence appears in more Buddhist lists of necessary qualities than any other.

Sixth is patience. Truthfulness is the seventh. Eighth is resolution, the ability to stick with our practice. We have also discussed the ninth virtue of loving-kindness and the tenth of equanimity. With these virtues, our "touching" Nibbana becomes a consecrated life.

MJM

⊹ 15 ⊹

John of the Cross and the Buddha on
Purification of Our Beings:
Integrative Summary

T HE TEACHINGS of John of the Cross and the Buddha on the
purification of our beings reveal some striking similarities.
These have important implications for spiritual practice at all
three levels of purification.

Purification of Conduct

First of all, both John and the Buddha share a common understanding
and experience of the dark side of human nature. John wrote of disordered appetites that torment, weaken, blind, and defile us. The
Buddha spoke of cravings—"torments of the mind"—that have the
same effects.

Human darkness Both John and the Buddha agree that our inordinate cravings for sensual pleasure create suffering and disharmony
in our relationships on all levels: personal, societal, universal, and cosmic. A quick perusal of the daily newspaper or a few minutes listening to the evening news on the television verifies the havoc and pain
born in our personal and collective lives from our attachments to such
things as alcohol, material possessions, codependent relationships,
power, and prestige. According to the Buddha and John, we need liberation from disordered desires that prevent us from experiencing the
fullness of life for which we were created.

Unity of meditation and life Their teaching on our need for purification of conduct and disordered appetites points to a second, related similarity. As all mystics of the major world religions, John and the Buddha emphasized that meditation and life go hand in hand; they form a unity. We cannot pray seriously and at the same time malign our sisters and brothers or engage in self-destructive behavior. The meditative life calls for total dedication to God and service to others expressed in concrete behavior. Therefore, spiritual practice demands conscious ordering of our moral conduct; this requires serious discipline in the way we relate to God, others, and the world around us. John referred to this discipline as mortification of the appetites. Buddhism speaks of it as renunciation.

Spiritual discipline Herein lies another similarity between John and the Buddha. Both offered counsels and guidelines that serve as a concrete, spiritual discipline to uproot selfishness and to bring about peace and harmony in both our relationships and our selves.

John placed the person and life of Jesus Christ at the center of his counsels. "Habitually desire to imitate Jesus Christ in all you do by bringing your life into conformity with his."[1] Any reformation of behavior or discipline that we undertake to purify our beings is born from a personal relationship of love with Jesus Christ and rooted in imitation of his life.

Furthermore, John offered some maxims with a method for mortifying disordered desires and establishing tranquility and harmony in our emotional life. "Try always to be inclined not to the easiest, but the most difficult; not to the most delightful, but the most distasteful."[2] Although John's advice seems a bit abstract at a first reading, deeper reflection on his life and a broader understanding of his doctrine reveal that he challenged us to actively work toward uprooting selfish attitudes and behavior patterns that are contrary to Gospel values. The way we live out these counsels depends upon the uniqueness of our personality and our life situation.

Spiritual practice and healing Buddhism also offers a well-tried morality path. This path presents concrete precepts that, if taken seriously and integrated into daily life, provide a tangible discipline for interior transformation and peaceful and harmonious relationships.

Right livelihood, right speech, and right action offer clear guidelines to cultivate simplicity of life and selfless, loving relationships. For anyone who might feel puzzled by some of John's abstract maxims and wonder how to apply them in daily life, the five precepts of Buddhist morality contain a sound and practical method of entering into the self-emptying process about which John wrote in his counsels.

Finally, through insight meditation we become aware of the inordinate desires and attachments that create so much suffering in our personal and collective lives. We see clearly the torments of our minds and hearts. In the depths of silent meditation, God's healing light shines in the darkest corners of our hearts and exposes and heals our addictions and disordered relationships. In clear and simple awareness, the possibility exists for God's love to heal and purify our conduct.

Purification of Mind

Throughout this book we discuss our need for purification and healing. As we work our way through the various levels of purification, we may lose sight of its purpose. Why undergo such self-knowledge and growth? Why expend so much energy on spiritual practice?

John would reply: because we were created for happiness and wholeness. The Buddha said he taught only one thing: suffering and the end of suffering. The purification of mental contents explained in previous chapters has as its purpose our happiness and fulfillment.

Our goals of love, wisdom, and happiness The writings of John reveal a profound concern for us as beings created to love and be loved. According to him, our purpose in life is to journey from an unconscious "substantial union" with God to a conscious "union of likeness" whereby we love God, others, and creation with God's very own love. We were created to participate in God's life. Conscious, loving awareness of our union with God and sharing this love with others bring us abiding spiritual peace, joy, and health, even in the midst of suffering.

The Buddha said we are in an unaware state of enslavement to cravings that create suffering and cloud clear seeing into the impermanent and unsatisfactory nature of life. He understood our vocation in life as a movement to a state of ever-deepening insight into the true nature of reality. Wisdom and compassion—Buddhism's two great wings—are born from this insight. They bestow upon us the blessings of interior freedom, happiness, serenity, and loving-kindness toward all beings.

Training for wisdom and love Even though God created us for love and happiness, we find these difficult to attain. We carry inside us a whole world of damaged images and inadequate concepts of God; painful memories of past hurts; and powerful emotions such as anger, lust, jealousy, and fear. They lurk deep within our psyches, and prevent us from enjoying the joy, peace, and love for which God created us and constantly offers us. John and the Buddha knew that so much unhappiness and suffering continue in our lives because we live unaware of this inner world and its influence in our personal and collective lives.

For this reason, they challenged us to train our minds and hearts for wisdom and love. They taught us the interior discipline of non-attachment to knowledge, memories, images, emotions, concepts, beliefs, ideas, and unwholesome mind-states that keep us from discovering truth. They offered us spiritual practices to help us empty ourselves of the mental contents that distort our vision of reality, and prevent us from becoming who we are.

The theological virtues For John of the Cross, the theological virtues of faith, hope, and love purify and heal our spirit. Through an active and living faith in God who transcends all concepts and images, we can surrender our inadequate and neurotic images of God. We can rest secure in the mystery of our incomprehensible God whom we trust loves us unconditionally and sustains us even in our brokenness and dark moments.

Past memories can imprison us emotionally and keep us from living whole, healthy, and mature lives. The virtue of hope empowers us to let go of our painful, paralyzing memories. Hope helps us see God's hand in all life's circumstances—painful as well as joyful—and enables us to surrender the past to the merciful love of God.

John's doctrine on the purification of the will teaches us to become mindful of our deepest emotions and interior movements. Through conscious acts of loving, we mindfully choose to center our lives in God rather than to invest our emotions and energies in persons, wealth, status, and power in ways that fragment us.

To embrace the theological life of faith, hope, and love is to enter into the dying and rising of Jesus Christ. This path of discipleship requires an ever-deepening awareness of the interior movements of our minds and hearts so that we can let go of those concepts, images, emotions, and memories that prevent us from living in close communion with God, others, and the world around us.

Concentration, mindfulness, and effort We find a similar path in Buddhism. Right concentration, right mindfulness, and right effort are spiritual disciplines that purify the mind and heart. Right concentration keeps us rooted in reality and helps us to focus our minds on what is wholesome, truly compassionate, and loving. In holding the mind steadily on wholesome contents, right concentration purifies memory—an outcome that we need, according to John.

Right mindfulness trains us to become aware of what is going on around and within us. So many problems and much suffering arise because we live unaware of what we are feeling, thinking, and doing. Unmindful that we are angry, we might lash out at others before we can stop ourselves. A history of broken relationships might stem from deep unconscious feelings of insecurity that drive us to control others. Right mindfulness purifies the intellect by keeping us aware of our inner world, and keeping us from investing energy needlessly in thoughts, concepts, and ideas.

Furthermore, the Buddha taught right effort as a means of determination and perseverance on the path. Becoming an enlightened person demands commitment and diligence. Right effort demands cultivating wholesome thoughts and letting go of unwholesome ones such as anger, greed, and jealousy. The Buddha's teaching on right effort resonates with Jesus' saying "It is not those who say to me, 'Lord, Lord' who will enter the kingdom of heaven, but those who do the will of my Father in heaven."[3] Right effort also corresponds to

John's task of purifying the will of interior movements contrary to the honor and glory of God.

If practiced daily, the Buddhist disciplines of right effort, right concentration, and right mindfulness plunges us into the process of dying to what brings suffering and unhappiness to our lives, and rising to what bestows peace, love, and serenity. Like the theological virtues of faith, hope, and love, they encompass a whole way of life and illustrate that meditation is more than an exercise we do once or twice daily. Rather, meditation is a way of being, a path of transformation.

The value of insight meditation Finally, the teachings of the Buddha and John point to the value of insight meditation. This practice offers us a door to enter our interior world of images, concepts, emotions, and memories. It teaches us how to be with these mind-states helpfully. Just as we see more clearly in a pool of water when it is calm and still, so in interior silence we begin to perceive the movements of our hearts and minds. As we grow in awareness of all that fuels our lives and motivates us, we journey steadily toward the happiness, peace, and love for which God created us.

Purification of Heart

John and the Buddha agreed that spiritual practice demands serious and concrete discipline. The two previous sections of this chapter showed how they taught us specific ways to purify ourselves in mind and behavior. John strongly emphasized self-emptying in the transformation process, and the Buddha taught that we must realize the emptiness of "self."

The need for deep healing John taught that purification of the heart ultimately lies beyond our human capacity. It is gift to which we open ourselves with sincere spiritual practice. To begin with, both John and the Buddha were profoundly aware of the extent of our sinfulness and brokenness, our suffering. They held that the pleasure principle has sunk deep roots within us. It unconsciously and pervasively motivates much of what we do, even our most religious actions.

John described how it appears in such forms as spiritual pride, avarice, lust, gluttony, envy, anger, and sloth. It disguises itself in consoling prayer experiences to which we become attached, or in acts of service to others fueled by unrecognized needs for acceptance and approval.

The Buddha was also aware of the strongly conditioned tendencies of our hearts. They manifest themselves when we tenaciously cling to our opinions, ideas, and theories, and remain closed to other ways of thinking. Subtle forms of selfishness reveal themselves in self-defensive behavior, unconscious assumptions, and the lust for power, prestige, and ambition.

Because the roots of sinfulness and conditioning lie so deeply hidden within us, we are powerless to heal and purify ourselves. Both John and the Buddha agreed that we need something beyond human effort to illumine our wounded hearts and to transform us.

The healing power of awareness According to John, contemplation enlightens the darkness of our hearts and heals the hidden roots of our inability to love as God created us to love. In contemplation, which John defined as infused loving wisdom of God, we are illumined, purged, and healed; all that obstructs union with God through love is transformed.

Contemplative purification is a deepening process that calls for passivity and surrender to the Holy Spirit. There are periods of emotional highs and lows. There are times of searing, painful self-knowledge followed by deeper peace and interior freedom. Moments of consolation may follow days or months of dryness and interior darkness. Throughout all the peaks and valleys of the transforming process, we need to remain passive, receptive, and open to all that God desires to accomplish within us. We must persevere in prayer and embrace all that God sends us in faith, hope, and love.

For the Buddha, wisdom, the fruit of right understanding, sheds light upon the dark forces of our minds and transforms our hearts. Clear seeing comes from sustained, disciplined awareness practice and sincere spiritual living every day. These practices gradually bestow deeper and sharper insight into the truth of our lives and the nature of reality. Right understanding, however, involves more than just meditative insight into our interior poverty and the nature of reality; clear seeing truly purifies us and uproots strongly conditioned tendencies of the mind and heart.

This path of purification is a dynamic process that requires sustained passivity, surrender, and openness. As insight deepens, we begin to understand the nature of physical and mental reality. We gain insight into how we push away the unpleasant in our lives and cling tenaciously to the pleasant. We become acutely aware of our underlying intentions and motivations, and see how our daily choices affect others and ourselves.

We perceive the truth of suffering, earthly life's unsatisfactoriness, and the fleeting nature of phenomena. Such realizations often come with stark emotional highs and lows, and with feelings of aloneness, vulnerability, and powerlessness. We go through periods of joy, happiness, and freedom as well as times of struggle, suffering, and feeling overwhelmed. Throughout all the stages of deepening insight, a profound transformation, to which we must remain open and surrendered in faith and trust, is taking place.

Transformation, the fruit of purification Both the Buddha and John believed that the fruits of purification make the spiritual journey worthwhile. John wrote of the freedom experienced when we arrive at union with God through love. Liberated from our enslavement to disordered desires and the pleasure principle, we can freely respond to the movement of the Holy Spirit in our lives. Just as fire transforms a log of wood so that the wood possesses the properties and actions of fire, God transforms us so that we share the very properties and actions of God. Love becomes the unifying factor of our lives. In short, we love God, others, and the world with the unconditional, compassionate, and merciful love of God.

Similarly, the Buddha taught that the wisdom born from right understanding profoundly affects how we live in this world. If we closely examine the state of right motivation, what emerges is the description of a person totally dedicated to love. The motives of renunciation, loving-kindness, and nonviolence depict a life completely committed to the ideals of love and compassion.

Renunciation calls for letting go of harming and self-centeredness so that we can love more freely and purely. Loving-kindness, harmlessness, and compassionate nonviolence speak for themselves. They require harmonious and caring behavior and a willingness to forgive in even the most painful, evil, and unjust situations. Truly, to live in such a way is to touch Nibbana—and "taste" peace, rest, and tranquility even in the midst of suffering.

The importance of spiritual practice The doctrines of John and the Buddha on contemplative purification of the heart point once more to the importance of serious meditation practice. We all experience the need for radical purification and our helplessness in healing ourselves. John and the Buddha proclaimed a message of hope to all who long for deeper liberation and transformation. They challenged us to surrender ourselves to God, to the Dhamma, through a life of serious prayer and committed spiritual living.[4]

Insight meditation is a path of purification. It develops clear insight into the true nature of life, especially our wounded self-love. It gives us the freedom that is born of clear seeing. Furthermore, moment-to-moment awareness, being simply with what is in the present moment, teaches us how to remain open, passive, and surrendered to the purifying process. If practiced seriously with an attitude of faith and love, trusting in the merciful love of God, it will bring about the healing and wholeness for which we long and for which God created us.

DC/MJM

✠ PART IV

QUESTIONS CHRISTIANS ASK

✠ 16 ✠

About Prayer, Meditation, Contemplation, and Insight Practice

Sometimes people ask us to define prayer, meditation, and contemplation, and to describe the relationship between them. Unfortunately, we cannot give a short, definitive answer to this question. These words are used so differently both within and across traditions that one common set of definitions for everybody is impossible.

No Set Terminology

Some prefer to use the word "prayer" only when describing communion with a personal God within a religious tradition. They see prayer as an essentially personal communion with God in faith, hope, and love. They limit the term "meditation" to spiritual practice before the Absolute or Unconditioned—sometimes without reference to religion. In this understanding, prayer assumes faith in a personal God, whereas meditation does not.

Also, different traditions use the same word to refer to different practices. Some Christians think of meditation as discursive or step-by-step mental prayer. Buddhist insight meditation is a non-discursive practice that emphasizes relinquishing voluntary thought, imagination, memory, and emotion to pay close attention to immediate experience.

Even within the same religious tradition, spiritual masters use the same word in different ways. In his *Spiritual Exercises,* Ignatius of Loyola presented contemplation as imaginative reflection on scenes from the gospels to arouse fervor for commitment to Jesus. John of the Cross, a fellow Spaniard in Ignatius's time, considered contemplation an inflow of God into the soul.[1]

To avoid confusion, we try to state clearly our understanding of these terms when we use them in the context of Christian insight meditation. This does not imply that ours is the preferred understanding, but it situates insight meditation within Christian prayer life.

Types of Prayer

We see prayer as the general category in which meditation and contemplation are specific types. We can distinguish various types of prayer. One way is between "talking prayer" and "listening prayer." Another is between interior and exterior prayer.

Talking and listening When young, we were taught to "say our prayers," to pray by talking. We praised God, thanked God, apologized to God, and petitioned God for our own and others' needs. Sometimes this prayer was in formal, set words, and sometimes we improvised it, just talking to God about our lives and feelings.

For many Christians, prayer is only reciting formal words in either liturgical celebrations or the rote repetition of memorized prayers. Those with greater intimacy in prayer may "tell God the news" or ask God for assistance. Some such people discount the value of listening prayer, non-discursive meditation, saying that it feels like "doing nothing."

For prayer as Teresa of Avila defined it, as conversation with God, we must listen.[2] Real conversation implies two-way interaction. It is not conversation if we "hog the floor." When faced with one who has more to offer than we do, our greatest profit comes from mostly listening instead of getting in our own words. How much more true this should be of prayer! Mystics have frequently said that listening is much higher prayer. How much better off we are when we become still to hear God!

All forms of classical, non-discursive meditation are prayers of listening, of just making ourselves available to receive. They are usually quite simple, because we do not want to complicate listening prayer. However, meditation is not just making the mind blank. Simplicity is a grace of advanced practice; we cannot force it by trying to make the mind empty. Most of us lack the mental ability only to listen unless we have a "tool" to help us. Different types of meditation use different tools to keep attention sharp and clear while we listen.

Some talking forms of prayer can be meditative; the words become mental anchoring devices that allow us to listen. This is true of some liturgy and private devotions like the rosary and the stations of the cross, which involve repeating similar words. Lectio divina and loving-kindness practice are done meditatively. However, when such methods stir up thinking, which can be thought of as mental speech, we are not practicing listening prayer. Such "thinking" practice is called discursive meditation; John of the Cross understood it this way as well.[3]

Exterior and interior prayer We can consider prayer exterior or interior depending on which aspect of the human person it expresses. Exterior prayer refers to those social, communal, externally expressive forms of communion with God. These include Eucharist, sacraments and liturgical worship, sacred ritual, religious song and dance, popular devotions like the public recitation of the rosary or stations of the cross, pilgrimages and other external ways of praising, thanking, adoring, and petitioning God.

By contrast, interior prayer—or mental prayer, as it is often called—takes place primarily within our minds and hearts. Here we enter privately into the sanctuaries of our own beings to be alone with the Alone present within us. Traditionally, meditation and contemplation are ways of interior prayer. Among Carmelites, meditation usually means all that we do to establish communion with God in interior prayer, whereas contemplation is what God does in us, the inflow of divine loving knowledge into our beings.

Some prayer forms Liturgy is our primary communal prayer, especially the Eucharist and other sacraments. There we pray socially, as a community of faith. We gather together in the risen Lord to remember what he did for us in his life, death, and resurrection. We open ourselves to receive the fruits of his life-giving death. We become incorporated into the Lord's risen body. We are nourished and sustained by his word and the Eucharist. We experience Christ's healing touch restoring us to wholeness. We receive his strength to meet life's challenges and fulfill our social commitments as his disciples.

We find ourselves becoming gradually transformed in Christ as, year after year, we participate in the church's liturgical cycles celebrating his life, death, resurrection, ascension, and the sending of his Spirit. As we repeatedly recall the great events that gave us new life in Christ, we ask the Father to "bring the image of your Son to perfection within us."[4]

Closely associated with liturgy is lectio divina. This prayerful reading of sacred Scripture is itself an ancient and powerful form of contemplative prayer. Meditative reading of the Hebrew Bible and New Testament allows God's word to sink deeply into our hearts, transforming us into Christ, the scripture's fulfillment.

Christian prayer has many popular devotions and private prayers that express our human needs to God. One of the most popular, the way of the cross, allows us to identify the struggles of our own lives with the Lord's suffering and death. The rosary recalls Mary of Nazareth, Jesus' mother and ours, who models faithful Christian discipleship and openness to the Holy Spirit. Beyond these, literally countless public and private prayers and devotions help us to adore, praise, thank, and petition God.

Meditation and Contemplation

Some Christian prayer forms called meditation involve thinking, while classical meditation requires refraining from thinking to focus simple and complete awareness on some meditation object. We call the latter practice "contemplative prayer."

Two types of meditation What people call "meditation" can be either discursive or non-discursive. Discursive meditation involves thinking, reasoning, imagining, remembering, and feeling, as we described earlier.[5] John called this discursive process "meditation" and contrasted it with contemplation, which is more advanced prayer.

Ignatius of Loyola called discursion "contemplation" when he invited us to reflect prayerfully on the mystery of Jesus' incarnation.

Non-discursive meditation, on the other hand, attempts to quiet these mental activities in order to be silent and passive before God, receptive to whatever God chooses to communicate to us. We close down the noise of words in surrendered openness, and stop trying to control things by analyzing or problem solving. The Eastern traditions generally consider meditation a non-discursive process. From now on, we speak of meditation in this classical, Eastern understanding of it as a non-discursive practice; this usage corresponds closely to Western understandings of contemplative prayer.

Non-discursive meditation usually involves four basic elements: a suitable place, a proper posture, a passive attitude, and an object of focus—a sacred word or phrase, a mantra, an icon, the breath, or experiences of body and mind.[6] Such meditation falls into two main types.[7]

Two non-discursive types Concentrative meditation focuses attention upon a single object and excludes everything else; an image, icon, word, sound, the breath, a candle flame—almost any single object will serve.[8] The object differs across traditions, and sometimes at different stages of practice. As soon as we become aware of straying to anything else, we gently bring attention back to the chosen object. We close out everything else, more and more deeply experiencing that one object.

In much Christian contemplative prayer, the object is often some form of Jesus' name that represents the presence of Jesus. A common Eastern object is a deity's "seed" syllable, similarly seen. Concentrative practice aims to transform the meditator into the object of focus. Most Christian contemplative prayer is concentrative meditation.

Unlike concentrative meditation, in uncovering or awareness meditation—the second type—we accept into awareness as much of what happens as possible. The movement is almost exactly the opposite from concentrative meditation; practice will have many different objects. We do not choose our experiences; we let them choose us. We try to be aware with fresh observing of all we experience. Attention is repeatedly drawn to different objects to be noticed: emotions, body sensations, sound, and so on. We become willing to "hear" whatever is being said to us, to be with whatever experience comes. This is not just letting the mind wander, though; very disciplined methods guide such practice. This book teaches one of them.

Non-discursive meditation as contemplative prayer There are various ways of praying contemplatively. When teaching her nuns to pray, Teresa of Jesus reminded them of the old sister who became a great contemplative through faithfully praying her Our Fathers every day. Many different and useful techniques exist to practice both concentrative and awareness meditation. Both can eventually bring loving knowledge of God; they are simply different paths to this goal.

We can consider non-discursive meditation a form of contemplative prayer. Its non-discursive quality and receptive attitude help dispose us to accept the communication of God's loving knowledge. So we call Christian insight meditation contemplative prayer, just as we speak of the Jesus prayer, praying with icons, lectio divina, and Christian meditation as contemplative prayer.

Deepening practice When non-discursive meditation practice deepens, we experience it more as done in us than as something we do ourselves. Buddhists attribute this to the effects of deepened concentration. When prayer becomes so "received," John of the Cross called it contemplation—God's direct self-communication to a person disposed through self-emptying in faith and love to receive this intimate revelation. He said it is not our activity, but God's. It is not our achievement, but a grace freely given to us. It is not something we ourselves do; rather, it is something God does in us. We dispose ourselves in meditation to receive this grace, but we cannot make it happen.

John taught that in contemplation God "fires our souls in the spirit of love"[9] and "supernaturally instructs us in divine wisdom."[10] Contemplation "is knowledge and love together, that is, loving knowledge."[11] Contemplation shares in God's own loving knowledge that purifies and transforms our human knowing and loving so that we know and love as God knows and loves. We receive contemplation by opening ourselves to it, just as we receive sunlight into a room when we open the shutters on the window. The loving knowledge of God communicated to us in contemplation transforms us and unites us with God in love.

Uncovering or Insight Meditation

You might have wondered how watching the breath, body experiences, and mind states (emotions, moods, states of awareness) can truly be called prayerful. Within our conceptual framework, Christian insight meditation is one method of non-discursive meditation, and is contemplative prayer.

Features of insight practice The specific quality of Christian insight meditation as contemplative prayer is its focus on purifying the heart and emptying out self to dispose us to receive God's gift of contemplation. Insight practice disposes us to stay empty before God's action. It helps prepare us for the gift of contemplation by actively purifying sense and spirit through faith, hope, and love.

Insight practice teaches us listening, how to become very still. It guides us in letting go of the noisy busyness of mind-chatter, of craving particular experiences in prayer, and of wanting to be in charge of the conversation with God. It teaches us simply to be there, attentive, and surrendered to the purifying action of the Holy Spirit. It empties us of everything that John said must be emptied out to receive God's self-communication. We become docile and pliable before the Spirit.

A major gift we receive in insight meditation is self-knowledge, which John said is the necessary road to God. We cannot know God if we do not know ourselves. Since we already know what we are comfortable knowing about ourselves, most of the needed self-knowledge is painful. If we faithfully accept it, we see even more deeply; we get into the subtle recesses of our deeply ingrained resistance to purification.

Our experience shows insight meditation to be a particularly potent and direct method of purification for the nakedness of spirit needed for very deep experience of God.[12] Teachers in other traditions have agreed with us.

Along with awareness, insight meditation also develops concentration.

Experiences differ from those of concentrative meditation, but follow the same general progression.[13]

Mental noting and contemplative prayer The soft mental noting that is characteristic of insight meditation fosters the interior non-attachment we need for contemplative prayer to develop. We must remember to hold on to this meditation tool until it becomes impossible to do so.

At times, we might experience profound joy and love for God. Noting these experiences maintains sharp, clear awareness and keeps us from getting lost in these delightful moments. We enjoy them as long as they last, but let go of them when they pass. Noting also enables us to be present to mental and physical pain, aware of its passing nature, and not be overcome by it or turn away from it simply because it is unpleasant.

At times, our absorption can be so deep and powerful that we are unable to continue the mental noting.[14] We seem completely surrendered to God and open to all that God chooses to do in us. We feel deeply touched by God, if only for a short time. We feel powerless to do anything for as long as this touch lasts. But when it passes, we resume noting our experiences. We trust that God's own purpose has been accomplished in this ineffable moment, and continue in the non-attached attitude that is essential for progress in contemplative prayer.

Outcomes of practice Eventually, we become full of the gifts of the Holy Spirit, the virtues Buddhists call paramis.[15] We also begin to see reality as it truly is. Things earthly and heavenly, even God's intimate secrets, are eventually revealed to us. As we more totally empty out, we can be increasingly filled with God.

As we let God work on and in us, we become more purified of the unwholesome inclinations of mind and heart that keep us from God. The more we are willing, the closer we come to the total self-giving that transforms us. John said that very few are willing to be radically surrendered before God, and to stay surrendered when the going gets hard. Insight meditation is a method for staying surrendered.

What is our goal? To become pure receptivity in the conversation with God, to hold nothing in our hearts that is contrary to God's presence.

As we empty out, God "inflows," and God's inflowing empties us out even more. John spoke of this as a transformation that brings a union of likeness with God. When there is only God with all else emptied out, our knowing, our loving, and our total experiencing is that of God. In their substance, our souls cling only to God.

Summary

Both concentrative and awareness methods are prayers of deep listening to God. Both dispose us for contemplation. Most methods of Christian contemplative prayer—such as the Jesus Prayer, the prayer of *The Cloud of Unknowing,* and the desert method that Cassian taught—are technically called concentrative meditation techniques. Such practice gradually transforms a meditator into his or her object of focus.

Insight meditation is awareness practice, which draws up the impurities in the mind and heart to be healed by the Wisdom that guides the practice. It is often less pleasant, but seems to move people more quickly toward their goal. Since John of the Cross encouraged this aim in his work, we recommend awareness practice as a method for his spirituality.

MJM/KC

✠17✠

About Jesus Christ, the Holy Spirit, and the Church

S OME QUESTIONS asked about Christian insight meditation concern Jesus Christ and the Holy Spirit. During insight meditation we do not think about Jesus, imagine him, repeat his sacred name, nor gaze upon the crucifix or a sacred icon. We simply sit quietly, anchored in the breath, open to observe peacefully whatever comes into our awareness, neither avoiding nor clinging to anything. Can doing this really open us to the guidance of the Holy Spirit? Where is Jesus Christ in it?

The Imitation of Christ

As in all Christian contemplative prayer, Jesus is central to Christian insight meditation. However, we relate to Christ in this practice primarily by imitating his death on the cross. Our self-emptying during meditation is our loving response to him who emptied himself for love of us.

Dying to self We experience Jesus' death on the cross and his resurrection from the dead by cultivating non-attachment—not only to delightful objects in the world around us, but especially to the desires, thoughts, memories, feelings, and emotions of our inner world. Through non-attachment we die to the self that our disordered desires, thoughts, imagination, and emotions have created to rise to a new life in Christ, hidden in the substance of our souls.[1]

Jesus demanded such death for Christian discipleship. As we saw earlier, Jesus told us that following him requires willingness to take up the cross and surrender our lives. When we give our lives for Jesus, we save them.[2] In meditation we deliberately stop giving psychic energy to desires, thoughts, feelings, memories, images, and emotions that lead us away from sharing Christ's death and prevent his rising in our lives.

The apostle Paul With Paul we try to imitate Christ who "emptied himself," yet reigns in glory.[3] Imitation demands not merely recalling Christ's death, but actually sharing it. Paul told the Philippians that all he wanted was to reproduce in himself the death of Christ that he might know Christ and the power of his resurrection. In this way, we can hope to take our places in the resurrection.[4] In this spirit, Christian insight meditation pays careful attention not only to delightful interior experiences, but equally so to pain and suffering, acknowledging the call to new life that they contain.

John of the Cross John taught that imitating Christ is the essential way to purify our hearts and prepare them for God's transforming love in contemplation. For John, imitating Christ means primarily imitating his "living death of the cross, sensory and spiritual, and exterior and interior."[5] He observed, "Some people are content with a certain amount of virtue, prayer, and mortification, but never come to the nakedness, poverty, selflessness, or spiritual purity—they are all the same—about which Jesus advised us."[6]

Furthermore, imitating Jesus' death is not limited to overcoming disordered sensory appetites; it is required for the entire journey to union with and transformation in God. "Nothing, nothing, nothing," John wrote on the middle road of his sketch of Mt. Carmel, "and even on the Mount nothing."[7] The "truly devout," John explained, "seek the living image of Christ crucified within themselves, so they are pleased when everything is taken from them and they are left with nothing."[8]

There is never a moment in the spiritual journey when Jesus' total self-emptying on the cross ceases to be the model for Christians seeking union with God in love. No matter where we are along the journey, we sit in meditation before God with clear, sharp, non-attached awareness. We trust that, as we strive to give up every disordered sensory and spiritual attachment, we are becoming transformed in Divine Wisdom, the Son of God. As John assured us, nature does not tolerate a void.[9]

Paschal Mystery

By imitating Jesus' "living death on the cross," we try in Christian insight meditation to enter completely into the paschal mystery—the death and resurrection of Jesus Christ. This, Vatican II taught us, is the heart of Christian life, worship, and spirituality. By doing so, we prepare to proclaim in Eucharist the "Mystery of our Faith—Christ has died, Christ has risen, Christ will come again!"[10]

These words both affirm our faith in the Lord of History and commit us to embrace the dying and rising involved in each day's struggle to free ourselves from everything that keeps us from offering our lives in love and service. "The Son of Man came, not to be served, but to serve and to give his life as a ransom for many."[11]

Devotion to the Holy Spirit Jesus' death on the cross brought the outpouring of his Spirit. "One of the soldiers pierced his side with a lance," observed an eyewitness, "and immediately there came out blood and water."[12] In Christian insight meditation, imitating Jesus' total self-emptying on the cross opens our hearts to receive this outpouring of his Spirit into our lives.

Following his resurrection, Jesus breathed on his disciples and said, "Receive the Holy Spirit."[13] From its very beginnings, Christianity has attached deep spiritual significance to the breath. Our breathing reminds us that God breathed life into us at our creation and constantly sustains us by empowering us to breathe. It recalls especially the outpouring of Jesus' Spirit to renew our lives.

Praying with breath Because of its profound biblical symbolism, Christians have quite naturally incorporated the breath into their prayer. Eastern Christianity's Jesus Prayer coordinates the constant repetition of "Lord Jesus Christ, Son of the Living God, have mercy on me" with each inhalation and exhalation. The final words of John's *The Living Flame of Love* describe the breathing of a person united with and transformed in God as "enkindled in love by the Holy Spirit and filled with unfathomable good and glory in the depths of God."[14]

In Christian insight meditation, sitting quietly with our breathing has sacred significance. It deepens awareness of our "substantial union" with God and our longing for the "union of likeness" in which we are transformed in God through love.[15] It anchors our attention during prayer, symbolizes our openness to receive the Holy Spirit, and—most importantly—aims to illuminate our motivational life under the Spirit's guidance.

Transformation of Motivation

John of the Cross held that the main psychological fruit of transformation in God through contemplation is motivational. When united with God in perfect love, we are no longer moved to seek satisfaction from sensory and spiritual objects as we were in early stages of the spiritual journey; rather, only the Holy Spirit moves us. John referred to Jesus' mother Mary as an example of this. He pointed out that she was never attached to any created thing because she let herself be moved only by the Holy Spirit.[16]

First movements To dispose ourselves to be "always moved by the Holy Spirit," John counseled us to consciously direct our activities to God in their very first movements.[17] For example, as soon as we feel moved to satisfy ourselves with some object, John advised us to direct that movement to the things of God and to seek delight in God. The more aware we become of our first movements toward action, the freer we are to steer these actions toward God's honor and glory. Our increasing awareness and freedom prepares us to be moved in all our actions by the Holy Spirit.

In this transformation process, insight meditation makes us increasingly aware of our first movements. Frequently, we act unaware of the interior movements that lead to external behavior. Previously, when I smoked a pack of cigarettes a day, I was often amazed at how frequently I became aware that I was smoking only when I was snuffing out my cigarette in an ashtray.

I was completely unaware of the first impulse to light up, the movement of my hand for the pack in my shirt pocket, striking the match, the first deep inhaling of smoke, and flicking the ashes into an ashtray and—more often—onto the floor. A whole chain of movements had taken place before I became aware that I was smoking. Without this awareness, I was not free to intervene at some point in this series of events and choose not to smoke.

Freedom with mindfulness The more aware we are of our interior movements, the more freedom we have to choose appropriate responses to the persons and events of our lives.[18] We can act more intentionally and less compulsively. Our behavior becomes more proactive and less reactive.

Mindfulness and awareness—not only in formal prayer, but also in the many activities and interpersonal interactions throughout the day—give us greater freedom to raise the first movements of our minds and hearts to God, and direct our behavior to God's honor and glory. Such mindfulness disposes us to be moved more by the Holy Spirit than by our own unrecognized impulses, feelings, and emotions. We taste more often the fruits of the Spirit—love, joy, peace, patience, kindness, goodness, trustfulness, gentleness, and self-control.[19]

On Church Teachings

Some meditators express concern about the church's position on practices like Christian insight meditation. They heard that the church issued warnings about Eastern practices.

Interfaith sharing The Second Vatican Council articulated the official Roman Catholic respect for the ancient religions of the East and their spiritual practices. It encouraged Catholic religious missionaries to assimilate ascetical and contemplative practices that reveal God's hand at work in ancient cultures before the coming of the Gospel.[20]

Implementing the council's commitment to interfaith dialogue, Pope Paul VI established the Secretariat for Non-Christian Religions, later renamed the Council for Inter-religious Dialogue. He entrusted responsibility for dialogue with monks of Asian religions to the Bene-dictines and Cistercians. They responded enthusiastically, and eventu-ally formed the North American Board for East-West Dialogue.

The Bangkok monastic conference in 1968, where Thomas Merton died, resulted from Paul VI's initiative. Today, inter-religious dialogue includes scholarly discussion, shared prayer, exchange of monastic hospitality, and combined compassionate social action.

Pope John Paul II continued to promote interfaith collaboration. During his pontificate, the work of the Council for Inter-religious Dia-logue increased. On pilgrimage to Asia in 1981, he stated, "The Church of Jesus Christ in this age experiences a profound need to enter into dialogue with [other faiths] so that mutual understanding and collab-oration may grow; so that moral values may be strengthened; so that God may be praised in creation."[21]

1989 Vatican letter In 1989, the Vatican Congregation for the Doc-trine of the Faith issued its "Letter to the Bishops of the Catholic Church on Some Aspects of Christian Meditation."[22] The letter reaffirmed Vatican II's recognition of the value of Eastern spiritual practices for Christian prayer. However, it warned of possible dangers in how we assimilate these practices, such as over-absorption in self or disregard for Jesus as the way to divine union. The letter asserted, as we do in retreats, that union with God is primarily a union of wills, a union of likeness in which our wills are in such complete agreement with God's will that we want nothing contrary to God's will.[23]

The letter also advocated, as we do, a Christian understanding of self-emptying. Thus, non-attachment to desires, sensations, thoughts, images, memories, and emotions is not an end in itself. It is a neces-sary discipline to free us from the interior obstacles—created by attachments to these phenomena—that prevent us from giving our-selves totally to God and others in love and service.

Christian insight meditation directly addresses the major concerns of the Vatican's warning. For example, the letter cautioned against mis-interpreting meditation experiences. It expressed concern about Christians using Eastern methods "to generate spiritual experiences similar to those described in the writings of certain Christian mystics,"[24] or meditators' taking "a feeling of quiet and relaxation, pleasing sensations, perhaps even phenomena of light or warmth for the authentic consolations of the Holy Spirit."[25]

With John of the Cross, we explain that "one act of love is more precious to God than all possible extraordinary experiences."[26] We hold with Joseph Goldstein, a leading American teacher of insight meditation, that "pleasant or painful feelings do not indicate how well your practice is going. The goals we seek through practice are wisdom and compassion, not some permanent tingle."[27] Drawing on the Gospel, Buddhism, and John, we emphasize not pleasant or extraordinary experiences, but interior purification. We insist that purifying the heart is absolutely necessary for seeing God.

The church's position Pope John Paul II perhaps best summarized the church's position on using Eastern meditation practices in Christian prayer. In a 1982 homily honoring Teresa of Avila, which is footnoted in the Vatican's letter, the pontiff stated, "Any method of prayer is valid insofar as it is inspired by Christ and leads to Christ, who is the way, the truth, and the life."[28] It is not the method per se that determines its validity for Christians, but the intention, faith, and love of the person using the method.

Thus, Christians can use insight meditation practice to deepen their personal union with God in love, to enter more fully into Jesus' paschal mystery, and to open themselves completely to the inspirations of the Holy Spirit. This transforms Buddhist vipassana into Christian insight meditation.

Education for Contemplation

Angry and disappointed Catholics, who feel cheated of a precious birthright, have demanded to know why the church has not taught meditation and contemplative prayer as part of its normal religious education. There are probably many explanations.

The church's role One possible reason is the relative youth of the

American church and its history as an immigrant community. The American hierarchy was established a little over two hundred years ago when John Carroll was appointed the first bishop of Baltimore. Since then, the hierarchy's principal concern has been to maintain the church as a visible Christian presence in the United States.

Associated with this was the task of educating millions of Catholic immigrants from Europe. They were taught the basics of Christian doctrine to sustain their faith in the new world, and were given a secular education necessary to take their place in American society. This agenda left little room for contemplative prayer.

By the middle of the last century, however, the American church was quite well established and its members well educated and positioned. Catholics now began to long for a deeper experience of Christian faith. Probably more than anyone else, Thomas Merton awakened Americans to desire a contemplative Christianity. Today, judging from the sheer volume of literature and programs in spirituality, this desire has become a widespread thirst in the church.

In his May 1993 "*Ad Limina*" address to the bishops of Iowa, Kansas, Missouri, and Nebraska, Pope John Paul II pointed to this thirst as a major pastoral challenge for the Church in the United States today.

> In the midst of [America's] spiritual confusion, the Church's pastors should be able to detect an authentic thirst for God and for an intimate personal relationship with him. Pastors must honestly ask whether they have paid sufficient attention to the thirst of the human heart for the true "living water" which only Christ our redeemer can give.[29]

Christian insight meditation The Vatican II documents and the Benedictines' example have guided our efforts to assimilate Buddhism's insight meditation into the Christian contemplative tradition. But why attempt this?

To recall just one benefit, insight meditation enhances the teaching of John of the Cross on self-emptying. Although he explained that emptying sense and spirit disposes us for God's transforming love in contemplation, John provided little concrete methodology for practicing and maintaining this emptiness in prayer.

Insight meditation also emphasizes self-emptying as a condition for the emergence of wisdom and compassion, and it provides a detailed meditation methodology for doing this. Assimilating the insight method of self-emptying into Christian contemplative prayer thus helps those who embrace John's teaching that "evangelical perfection rests on nakedness and emptiness of sense and spirit."[30] It helps us dispose ourselves through self-emptying for God's purifying and unifying love in contemplation.

Christian insight meditation directly addresses "the spiritual renewal of the Church in the United States"[31] called for by the Pope in his talk with the Midwestern bishops. It offers a sound Eastern meditation practice in the context of a reliable Christian prayer tradition. It helps Christians practice daily the moral and spiritual consequences of their religious faith. It disposes them for the ineffable gift of God's purifying and transforming love in contemplation.

Moreover, Christian insight meditation highlights the providential role of John of the Cross as a spiritual guide during this critical stage of church history. He taught an authentic Vatican II spirituality that is thoroughly Christ-centered and leads us unhesitatingly into the mystery of Jesus' death and resurrection. At the same time he was completely Trinitarian. John explained how the Holy Spirit, the living flame of love, transforms our lives into God's. He also detailed for us the practical implications of both the immanence and transcendence of the incomprehensible Godhead. He thus serves as a bridge for dialogue with Eastern religions, offering critical guidance for assimilating practices from these religions that can enhance growth in Christian contemplative life.

Summary

Christian insight meditation is a form of contemplative prayer that satisfies any concern the church has about Eastern methods. It involves imitating Jesus' self-emptying on the cross and disposing ourselves to be moved in all that we do by the Holy Spirit. It has proven that it produces these outcomes. Like every method of Christian prayer, we evaluate it by its fruits.

KC

✢ 18 ✢

About Carmelite Prayer

S OME PEOPLE have asked us if Carmelite saints like John of the
Cross and Teresa of Jesus specifically taught Christian insight
meditation. They want to know its relationship to the Carmelite
tradition of prayer. Although Carmelite authors agree on many essential elements of contemplative prayer, they do not give us one specific
Carmelite method of meditation. They are very free in their approach
to meditation and respect the many ways in which the Holy Spirit leads
us in prayer.

Carmelite teachers of prayer, especially Teresa and John, do not
explicitly describe insight meditation as taught in this book. However,
their teachings on contemplative prayer reveal some remarkable similarities to insight meditation. When approached with an attitude of
faith in God's indwelling presence and an ardent desire to be lovingly
present to God, insight meditation is a practice that integrates much
of what Teresa and John teach about the heart of true prayer. We see
this when we explore their essential teachings on prayer.

Teresa of Jesus (Teresa of Avila)

Teresa defined prayer as "intimate sharing between friends; it means
frequently taking time to be alone with Him who we know loves us."[1]
With utter simplicity, she explained her early method of entering into
this loving relationship with God: "I tried as hard as I could to keep
Jesus Christ, our God and our Lord, present within me; this was my
way of prayer."[2]

Understanding Teresa A first reading of Teresa's way of prayer might make us think that when she prayed she kept within her a mental image of Jesus—such as Jesus dying on the cross, and that this mental picture was the object of her meditation. We might also think that she spent her prayer time pondering the teachings of Jesus or the spiritual life, and from her reflections drew out beautiful thoughts and resolutions to apply to her life. This is an incorrect understanding of Teresa's manner of prayer.

In the same passage where Teresa explained her method of prayer, she admitted that, no matter how hard she tried, she never had any talent for discursive reflection, nor the type of imagination that could picture the humanity of Jesus Christ. A few chapters later in her autobiography, she said that she was unable to represent things with her intellect. She could only think of Christ as he was as man, but she could not picture him within herself despite all she read about his beauty and the many images she saw of him. She compared herself to a blind person or someone in the dark. They speak with a person and know that the person is with them because they believe that he or she is there, although they cannot see the other.[3]

Teresa's way When she wrote that she tried as hard as she could to keep Jesus Christ present within her, Teresa meant that she strove to become conscious of the Spirit of the risen Christ within her heart and to remain there in his presence. She entered prayer with an attitude of deep faith in the presence of Christ and the simple ardent desire to love him and "to be his companion."[4]

To remain interiorly centered on the presence of Christ, Teresa needed an anchor for her wandering mind. Although she mentioned several ways of recollecting herself, such as using a picture of Christ or looking at nature, most often scripture provided her a useful tool for concentration. She might read a passage from the gospels—like Jesus in the Garden of Olives, and place herself in the scene next to Jesus, remaining there at his side trying to console him by her loving presence.[5]

If she read the passage of the Samaritan woman at the well, she herself would become the Samaritan woman longing for the living water

Jesus promised. Far from trying to develop elaborate reflections from the gospel scenes, Teresa read the Scripture texts as a way to focus attention within to the presence of Christ. Once she made contact with Christ, she simply remained quietly and lovingly in his presence. However, as Teresa's mystical life deepened she became conscious of God's presence without any effort on her part. God's presence was more and more revealed to her, and she became more passively quiet.

Teresa's method Teresa's inability to meditate discursively caused her much suffering for many years. When she prayed, her distracted mind ran like noisy machinery. Out of this experience and to help people with the same difficulty, she taught them how to reach the Prayer of Recollection in Chapter 26 of *The Way of Perfection*.⁶ Teresa stated that the Lord gave her this method, and that we make greater progress following it than meditating with the intellect.⁷

Fundamental to this way of prayer is the faith conviction that God dwells in the depths of our hearts. It is there that we seek God. Consider that St. Augustine sought God in many places but found him ultimately within himself. "Do you think it doesn't matter for someone with a wandering mind to understand this truth, and to see that we need not go to heaven to speak with or delight in our eternal Father? All we need do is go into solitude and look at him within ourselves."⁸

Once God's presence is remembered, the next movement is interior. We collect our senses and faculties together and direct our attention within to be with God.⁹ This movement is one of faith and love directed toward a personal encounter with God.

When we enter within ourselves to be with God, what do we do? Teresa directed us to "look at" Christ. She was not telling us to think about him, draw out concepts, or make subtle, intellectual reflections. All she asked was that we "look at" him. For Teresa, to look at Christ is an act of faith and love. It is paying loving attention to the presence of Christ within. It may or may not involve words. What is most essential is to be with Christ.

The heart of Teresian prayer This loving attention to Christ touches the heart of Teresian prayer. In *The Book of Her Foundations*, Teresa taught that our progress in prayer lies not in thinking much, but in loving much.[10] She repeated the same thought in *The Interior Castle*. "The important thing is not to think a lot but to love a lot, and to do whatever best stirs you to love."[11]

Teresa was quite clear, however, that attention to God within might not necessarily be consoling or pleasurable. The silent, loving "look" at Christ may take place in dryness and aridity. We could experience God's presence as absence. We might find it difficult to still our restless minds. The attitude of faith and love we bring to prayer is essential.

Entering within herself to be lovingly attentive to the divine guest dwelling there expresses Teresa's method of prayer most precisely and simply. Love—not thinking—is the essence of prayer. An attitude of faith must also permeate prayer because we often do not experience spiritual consolations when we meditate.

John of the Cross

Because he was primarily interested in teaching the nature of contemplation, John did not give us detailed instructions on how to meditate.[12] Rather, he told us how to empty ourselves to grow in relationship with God, and described the purifying effects of contemplation.

John said very little about discursive meditation. He referred to it only in those texts where he described the prayer of beginners or discussed the movement from meditation—discursive reflection with the intellect and senses—toward a more passive form of contemplative prayer.[13] John understood discursive meditation as a passing, transitory phase. Its main purpose is to gain a deeper knowledge and love of Jesus Christ. It helps beginners on the spiritual path to become more interior. It brings them to a sensible awareness and knowledge of God's love for them that leads to further conversion and detachment.[14]

Emptying for contemplation Although John did not teach us the mechanics of meditation, he offered considerable guidance on how to empty ourselves so we can be filled with God. His major concern was to help us dispose ourselves for the gift of contemplation.

He taught us to disencumber ourselves in prayer and life from activities that impede a loving awareness of God's presence and the purifying action of the Holy Spirit. He believed that God is ever-present, like the sun above us is always ready to communicate its beneficent rays.[15] To receive those rays, we must remove clutter and clear the ground of our hearts of all that obstructs the action of God's Spirit within us. John assured us that, if we did our part to surrender to God's transforming presence, we would experience the liberating love of the Spirit through contemplation.

To surrender to God's gracious presence in contemplative prayer, John believed that we must undergo a conversion in how we naturally commune with God. God is a mystery of love. God is both intimately close to us, yet beyond all we can think, feel, or conceive. God communicates with us in a "supernatural" way that transcends our natural faculties of thinking, loving, feeling, and acting. That is why we can never judge God's presence or absence in our lives by our feelings or whatever beautiful thoughts we might or might not have about God. God communicates with us secretly through "a simple, loving knowledge" that is peaceful, quiet, and serene.[16]

Bases for contemplation Contemplation, which John defined as loving knowledge of God infused within us secretly, quietly, and obscurely, is God's pure gift. We can neither earn it nor attain it through our natural faculties of knowing, loving, or acting. We receive it passively.

We dispose ourselves to receive this gift by communing with God according to God's mode of communing with us—quietly, serenely, and peacefully. We lay aside our natural active modes of being to become receivers rather than givers, and passive rather than active. In prayer, we let go of our desire to do something, to feel God's presence, to make subtle reflections about God, and to control our relationship with God. Instead, John instructed us to become non-doing, passive, and tranquil in God's presence.[17]

When John discussed the movement from discursive meditation to contemplation in *The Ascent of Mount Carmel* and *The Living Flame of Love*, he encouraged a prayer of loving attention. "We should learn to remain in God's presence with loving attention and a tranquil mind, even though we seem to ourselves to be idle."[18] We need to conduct ourselves passively, without efforts of our own other than a simple loving awareness, as if we were "opening our eyes with loving attention."[19]

Disposing the soul We naturally want to be active in our relationship with God and to keep our minds busy chattering and grasping for ideas. Becoming receptive and tranquil in God's presence is difficult. John maintained that pacifying the soul, making it calm and peaceful, inactive and without desire, is no small accomplishment because it is an essential disposition for contemplation.

Remaining in God's presence with loving awareness gradually brings about a divine calm and peace that dispose us for a sublime loving knowledge of God that God infuses within us. Our Lord asks of us through the prophet David: "Learn to be empty of all things—interiorly and exteriorly—and you will see that I am God."[20] The prayer of loving attention implies such self-emptying.[21]

It invites us to surrender our cravings for self-gratifying experiences, lay aside our compulsive thinking, and just remain in God's presence in peace and quiet with simple, loving advertence to God. When we do so, God will not fail to communicate with us, silently and secretly. That would be less possible than it would be "for the sun not to shine on clear and uncluttered ground."[22]

Insight Meditation

Our examination of Teresa and John's ways of prayer reveals several similarities between the Carmelite tradition of prayer and insight meditation. When approached with faith in God's indwelling presence and a desire to be lovingly attentive to God, insight practice can help us integrate some of their essential and fundamental teachings on contemplative prayer.

Loving presence to God First of all, in both Teresa and John, the essence of contemplative prayer is being in loving presence to God— not thinking. Although Teresa encouraged using scripture or a picture of Christ to aid concentration and to make us aware of Christ's presence, her way of prayer is essentially being in loving presence to Christ who dwells within us.

We find the same teaching in John's discussion of the prayer of loving attentiveness. He emphasized the importance of learning to remain in God's presence with simple, loving advertence. This pacifies our hearts, which, John emphasized, is a major accomplishment because it allows God—the principal author of prayer—to infuse divine loving knowledge into our lives.[23]

Insight meditation develops an ever-deepening awareness. As a contemplative practice, it teaches us to recollect ourselves and to direct attention to the present moment where alone we find God. Remaining in the present moment with clear and simple awareness quiets and calms the mind and heart, thus creating a listening, empty, and receptive space for God's creative action in our lives.

Awareness of first movements Self-knowledge is an important gift of Carmelite prayer. In insight meditation, as we attend to all that we experience—body sensations, thoughts, memories, feelings, emotions, desires, intentions—we gradually become aware of the first movements that can lead us to action. We recognize, for example, a feeling of pleasantness or unpleasantness or neutrality associated with the memory of a particular person. A pleasant feeling draws out of us a mind-state such as delight or longing; fear or anger arises from an unpleasant feeling; boredom or indifference comes from a neutral feeling.

We see that out of such mind-states an intention forms to perform an action. Angered by the unpleasant feeling associated with the memory of a painful encounter with some person in the past, we begin planning an act of retaliation for the next time we see the person. As we become aware of and note this chain of events within ourselves, we increasingly come to the self-knowledge that John said is needed to know God, and begin to experience freedom.

As we are increasingly aware of the first movements of which John spoke—such as the feeling of unpleasantness at the memory of this person—we gradually recognize that we need not let them lead to indulging in unwholesome mind-states (in this case, anger). We can choose to react with compassion. Anger over past events need not move us to act negatively in the future. We can choose to act cooperatively and compassionately.

Being in the present moment   One particularly important Carmelite prayer is the "practice of the presence of God," a phrase associated with Brother Lawrence of the Resurrection, a seventeenth-century French Carmelite lay brother. In this prayer, we try simply to be aware of God's presence in every moment of our day, in every activity and occupation. We look for God nowhere else than in this present moment, regardless of what we are doing.

Brother Lawrence said he found God, not only in formal prayer in church, but especially among the pots and pans in the monastery kitchen where for years he prepared his brothers' meals. Lawrence considered it "a big mistake to think that the time for mental prayer should be different from any other time. We must be just as closely united with God during our activities as we are during times of prayer."[24]

Self-emptying   Another similarity between Carmelite prayer and insight practice concerns the self-emptying process. We refer primarily to John's teaching that we must become empty in order to be filled with God. "God does not fit into an occupied heart."[25]

We must do our part to free our hearts and minds from inadequate and distorted ideas and concepts about the incomprehensible God, from desires for self-gratification in prayer, and from activities that prevent the peaceful inflow of God's loving presence into our hearts. We must learn to become passive, inactive, tranquil, and lovingly attentive to God's presence. This requires letting go of our natural activities of knowing, loving, and feeling to allow God's purifying love to awaken and transform us.

Insight meditation as a path of purification is a powerful means to bring about the emptiness about which John wrote. It directs us to silence our chattering minds, to surrender our craving for sensible satisfaction, and to rest from our compulsive need to do something in prayer.

Insight practice teaches us to become receptive and empty in God's presence. We learn to let go of obsessive thinking and ideas (holy as they may be) and of emotional states (delightful as they may feel). By surrendering to this moment's experience with bare and simple attention we become disposed for the gift of contemplation.

DC/KC

+ 19 +

About Christian Grace
and the Buddhist Dhamma

W HEN I PRESENTED a conference paper comparing meditation development in John of the Cross and Buddhism,[1] a
commentator agreed that there is great correspondence.
He then added that an irreconcilable difference between the traditions
exists: the important of grace to Christians. Many others also ask about
the role of grace in Buddhist practice.

Grace and Meditation

In meditation, we open ourselves to grace when we stay present with
a sound method. "A method is generally requisite for mental
purification and mastery that one may become a vessel for grace."[2]

Experiencing grace On my first insight meditation retreat, my
teacher had emphasized that we have to walk our own road, nobody
will do the work for us, and we must apply ourselves to practice to
purify consciousness for enlightenment. At one point, I told him that
my experience differed from this teaching. Because experience is para-
mount in this Buddhist tradition, he asked me to explain. I said, "I have
never felt more carried in my entire life." Smiling, he said, "Oh, yes,
once you start to experience the unfolding of the Dhamma, they are
both true."[3]

Grace and method Christians see grace as God's help freely given
to us without our meriting it. Although Buddhists do not use the term
"grace," this example shows that they also experience it. What we call

such experiences is not important. What matters is that we recognize the "grace" in them and cooperate with it.

Eastern traditions do not believe that method itself produces transformation. However, sound meditation methods help us truly surrender so that we can receive transformation; surrender in meditation draws down help to accomplish what we cannot. "The discipline of practice is inevitable to make us grasp the importance of letting go. But the final state is accomplished only by grace in response to our total abandonment."[4]

Dhammoja, *Word, and Spirit*

The term Dhamma is very rich. Literally, it means "support." It translates as Truth, Reality, eternal law, the teachings, the practice, the path, the basis of all realities, the underlying pattern of realities, the phenomena of the present moment, that which supports and upholds us, that which underlies all that is real, that which leads us home, and so on. Although Buddhist teachings consider Dhamma an impersonal notion, its similarities to both Word and Holy Spirit in Christianity are obvious.

Essence of Dhamma Dhammoja, the essence of Dhamma, is the accumulated force of purity in our hearts from the virtues called paramis. All Buddhists try to acquire these virtues, though no one else achieves them as fully as a Buddha does. When we listen to Dhammoja, we grow in such virtue. To the extent that we follow its impulses, we continue to grow spiritually and to strengthen its effects in our lives. The more virtuous and intent on spiritual living that we become, the stronger Dhammoja becomes and the more insistently it pushes us to even more growth.

Just as Jesus said, "I am the Way, the Truth, and the Life," the Buddha said, "When you see me, you see the Dhamma; when you see the Dhamma, you see me."[5] Each identified himself with the Truth and the way to Truth. As the Holy Spirit carries on Jesus' work of sanctification, the Dhammoja, the essence of Dhamma, impels us to continue in the spiritual work the Buddha taught.

The Way and the Spirit Experientially, Dhammoja is analogous to the Christian indwelling Holy Spirit. The Spirit's guidance fosters development of the fruits of the Holy Spirit, virtues like the paramis that increase our purity of heart and make us increasingly docile to the Spirit.

John of the Cross wrote, "So far as we are rid of sensory desires and appetites, we obtain freedom of spirit in which we acquire the fruits of the Holy Spirit."[6] By listening to the guidance of the Holy Spirit and corresponding with the Spirit's graces, we grow in holiness and in the life of the Spirit. John taught that, when "we are loving God and simultaneously experiencing the love with humility and reverence, this indicates that the Holy Spirit is working within us."[7]

Parami and fruit Buddhist teachings say that liberating meditation instruction comes when we have sufficiently developed the paramis. Then we can meditate to speed up purification of the heart. Whenever a group gathers to learn the practice, each person has earned the right to be there. So, the paramis are a precondition for certain spiritual gifts to come to us, a sign that we have made some progress on the path, and a continuing task for us.

After warning the Galatians against various bad behaviors, the apostle Paul said, "Those who practice such things will not inherit the kingdom of God."[8] He listed the signs that the Spirit is leading us, calling them "the fruits of the Spirit." The fruits are prerequisites for life in the Spirit, a sign that we are in the Spirit, and a challenge for further docility to the prompting of the Spirit—an understanding clearly like the role of the Buddhist paramis and Dhammoja.

The fruits of the Spirit are variously translated, and different numbers of them are given. Here is one listing, with some alternate translations: love or charity, joy, peace, patience or long-suffering, kindness or gentleness, goodness, faithfulness or faith, humility or meekness, longanimity or forbearance, and self-control or temperance. The paramis are generosity or giving, morality, renunciation, wisdom, effort or diligence, patience, truthfulness, resolution or resolve, loving-kindness, and equanimity.[9] The similarities between the paramis and the fruits of the Spirit are readily apparent.

Paramis and Fruits in Comparison

We now look more closely at the paramis and fruits—the signs of grace at work in us. They prove to be alternate terms for the same qualities of soul.

Generosity and charity Buddhists consider generosity extremely important because it is exactly the opposite of clinging or grasping—a major root of suffering. Generosity is open-handedness toward others, rather than holding on to what we have. Buddhist teachings say that we should practice generosity to make all beings happy, without judging them as worthy or not. Generosity is not just for those we approve of or like.

The Buddha named generosity the most important virtue for beginning practitioners to develop, and one that we continue to refine across the course of spiritual growth. He said that if we truly understood the power of giving, we would not let a single meal go by without sharing.

Christian charity similarly must be made effective in action. John urged, "Do not refuse anything you have, even though you might need it."[10] He poetically described a spirit ripe with giving love. "A trait of valiant souls, generous spirits, and unselfish hearts is how they give rather than receive—even to giving themselves."[11]

Morality and goodness Morality is the basis of all spiritual practice. Choosing to refrain from action known to inflict harm on others or oneself is a bare minimum needed for beginning spiritual aspirants. The five basic precepts of Buddhist morality and the Judeo-Christian Ten Commandments are similar, as are the moral restraints prescribed by all time-proven spiritualities.[12]

The Christian fruit of goodness corresponds to Buddhist morality. John praised moral people: "Blessed are they who set aside their own pleasure and inclinations to consult reason and justice before acting."[13]

Renunciation and temperance Renunciation corresponds to Christian temperance. It requires letting go of even what is lawful, to learn how to say "no" to ourselves, so that we can do so when needed. Buddhists practice renunciation to bring morality to full perfection so that they become completely harmless to all beings. The same idea is behind Christian "mortification," renunciation to kill potentially troublesome tendencies.

Most spiritual teachers give renunciation a key importance in spiritual life. John said, "Even though you do many good deeds, if you do not deny your will and submit yourself, setting aside anxiety about yourself and your own affairs, you will not progress."[14] He pointed out a mistake some make: "They think denying themselves in worldly matters is sufficient without annihilation and purification regarding spiritual matters."[15] Giving up sensory pleasures is not sufficient; we must also take care not to become attached to spiritual delights or to particular practices as well.

Patience and long-suffering Patience connotes willingness to be worked on. Just as we sometimes become patients of professional people, in meditation we make ourselves the Holy Spirit's patients. When we are patient—willing to be worked on—we accept without complaint the work done. John taught, "If we are more patient in suffering and more able to go without satisfaction, this shows that we are more skilled in virtue."[16]

Patience includes tolerance regarding others' faults. Both the Buddhist and Christian traditions emphasize that the work done on us is often dealt by environmental inconveniences, annoyances caused by other people, and such human circumstances as illness and aging. When we accept such unpleasantness as fodder for our spiritual work, we become the seed fallen on good ground that will "bring forth fruit with patience."[17]

Truthfulness and humility Truthfulness includes, but goes beyond, the morality of not telling lies. Our total being is to become truth; that is, we are to be in accordance with the true reality of things. Buddhist truthfulness also means that, once we have given our word on something, we will not go back on it. Others can rely on us to bring to full reality whatever we say we will.

Truthfulness includes being in touch with unpleasant truths about our beings that are more comfortable not to see. We very easily slip into what psychologists call the "defense mechanisms," subtle lies we

tell ourselves so we can feel good about ourselves.[18] Spiritual practitioners cannot let such pride win. Christians have thus equated
humility with truth. Humility is simply recognizing the truth of our
beings.

In John's teachings, understanding ourselves plays a very important
role; "self-knowledge is the first requirement of advancing to the
knowledge of God."[19] He said of passive purgation, "The main benefit
this dry and dark contemplation brings is knowledge of ourselves and
our own misery, which we had not yet seen. We consider ourselves to
be nothing, and find no satisfaction in self because we see that by ourselves we cannot do anything."[20]

Resolution and faithfulness Buddhist resolution refers to a stick-
to-it attitude, especially when faced with difficulty, as does the Christian fruit of faithfulness. We need to remain constant in spiritual work
when it is not to our liking as faithfully as we do when it is pleasant.
We avoid many needed growth experiences if we take a vacation from
spiritual work when we just don't feel like doing it.

John captured well the flavor of this. "Never give up your practices
because they do not satisfy and delight you. Nor should you perform
them just because they are satisfying or delightful. Otherwise, you will
not be able to be constant and conquer your weaknesses."[21]

Loving-kindness and gentleness Buddhist loving-kindness corresponds to the fruit of kindness or gentleness. It wishes others well
universally, not differently regarding different persons. This unshak-
able kindness makes us helpful to all with its soft and caring quality.[22]

John tersely suggested some practices for developing this gentle, kind
attitude toward others. "Do not complain about anyone."[23] "Never listen to talk about others' weaknesses."[24] "Do not refuse work even if you
think that you cannot do it. Let everyone find you compassionate."[25]

Acting with simple good manners is part of our practice. A curt
or overly abrupt attitude does not foster gentle friendliness; dealing
with others mildly is helpful. We also need to avoid greed and pos-
sessiveness in relationships. Out of consideration for others, we
sometimes have to refrain from doing innocent things that we want
to do.

Equanimity and peace The root of the Buddhist word for "equanimity" means essentially "there-in-the-middleness." Equanimity means not letting our experiences pull us out of serenity and balance. Keeping our senses under control and maintaining a meditative attitude greatly aids us in developing equanimity. Living lightly, with few needs, also helps. We cannot have peace and balance when we are continually hankering for something.

The Spirit's fruit of peace describes the mind in equanimity. When we are peaceful, we have an underlying satisfaction that remains undisturbed by any alterations of circumstances or by any conditions we might encounter. We also do not expect anything in return for whatever we do for others, nor do we try to control or manage the lives of others.

John had a prescription for practicing this: "Be satisfied with emptiness to reach the highest tranquility and peace of spirit."[26] He agreed with the Buddhist tenet that high equanimity signifies great advancement: "Those who have truly mastered all things are not gleeful when they are satisfying, or sad when they lack savor."[27]

Diligence and forbearance Diligence, effort, or energy appears in more Buddhist lists of necessary attributes than any other quality. It mobilizes us to do the necessary work at any given time. The Spirit's fruit of forbearance also captures the vigor, valor, and wholeheartedness of proper effort.

Spiritual work requires heroic, valorous endeavor. John said, "Reflect on the need for holy rigor in our quest for perfection."[28] However, we need to maintain a proper balance in our endeavor, avoiding excess as well as laxness.

Part of diligence is being teachable. We must put in our own effort, but also recognize when we need help from more knowledgeable persons. Listening to those who are wiser, better informed, kinder, or holier than we are can greatly support our efforts. Choosing to be around diligent people helps; this is one way a sitting group helps us.[29]

John said that our efforts are met with help. "God does not want us to be lazy and fearful. To avoid this God helps us so that with a little diligence we can grow in every virtue."[30] We do our part and make our best effort. Then we find ourselves met with the help we need.

Wisdom and joy One parami is left: wisdom. Although wisdom is not a fruit of the Holy Spirit, the remaining fruit of joy well corresponds to Buddhist wisdom. In Buddhist thought, wisdom or fully right understanding, seeing things as they truly are, finally liberates us from suffering and brings us true joy.

John saw an intimate connection between purification, wisdom, and joy. "The purest suffering brings the purest and most intimate knowing, and this produces the purest and highest joy because we know from further within."[31] He also taught, "Wisdom comes from love, silence, and mortification."[32] "Contemplation infuses both love and wisdom in each of us according to our capacity and need. It illumines us, and purges us of ignorance."[33] Meditation practice thus brings us the grace of the highest spiritual wisdom and joy.

John said "love and wisdom"—a close correspondence to the two wings of Buddhism: wisdom and compassion. Buddhist thought holds that wisdom, or insight knowledge, purges us of mental torments—of which ignorance is the main one. It helps us understand what is beneficial and what causes harm, with intuitive knowing that is effective in action. Deeply knowing our own suffering brings compassion for suffering others.

John made another congruent point: "Contemplation is secret wisdom, hidden from the workings of intellect and our other faculties."[34] Both traditions emphasize that they are not speaking of something that comes from thinking or studying, but which is the outcome of the purification of our beings through spiritual practice.

Beyond Concepts

We end with a reminder of our need not to become trapped in concepts or explanatory ideas. When we focus too much on words and ideas, we might lose sight of the experiences from which they came, and become unable to recognize experiences that are not packaged with a familiar concept. Here is another true story of Buddhist "grace."

"Conviction of sin" A "born-again" Christian told me that Jesus Christ had given him the grace of convicting him of sin in his heart.

When I asked him just what he had experienced, he could only repeat, "Jesus Christ convicted me of sin in my heart." I shared an experience I had on an insight meditation retreat.

The man sitting in front of me seemed to be struggling for he kept shifting position and moving around. An odd sort of delight arose in me, and then the memory came that earlier this man had annoyed me. In a flash, I realized that I was enjoying the suffering of someone who had previously caused me discomfort. This was followed by hot, searing pain in my chest, disgust with myself, judging myself to be vindictive, deep revulsion to so being, feeling trapped by such a reaction, desire to be freed from this emotional snare, burning of my cheeks, a sense of shame, intense remorseful sorrow, and silent tears running down my cheeks.

I asked the "born-again" man if his conviction of sin in his heart had been anything like my experience. He was genuinely confused, and said that he was talking about a religious experience, and I was talking about feelings that came in a pagan practice. He could not see that our experiences were probably very similar; he saw only his interpretation and not what he had experienced. These experiences brought both of us the grace of deeper knowledge of disorder in our beings—whatever concepts we use to describe them.

Summary

Our work of developing the paramis or the fruits of the Spirit opens us to the grace of further growth. We are encouraged and led on by the indwelling Holy Spirit, by the force of accumulated merit that is Dhammoja, the essence of Dhamma. We often find ourselves carried, find the work being done in us by a power far beyond the effort we have made. This is what Christians call grace.

MJM

✠ 20 ✠

About Karma, Rebirth, and Purgatory

Most Westerners are confused about the complex and subtle Eastern teaching about *karma*.[1] Some wonder if it means unalterable fate. Others want to know if there is a parallel Christian teaching.

The word karma itself simply means "action." The "law of karma" refers to the effects of chosen actions as they later bear fruit—that is, moral cause and effect. This teaching is similar to Christian notions of sin and its effects, and some teachings about rebirth can be seen as akin to the Christian doctrine of purgatory.

Jesus, Karma, and Rebirth

Jesus spoke much about the effects of moral choices. His teaching on judgment according to our charity is a teaching on karma.[2] In a lengthy discourse on how all sin comes to light and needs to be accounted for, Jesus said, "I tell you solemnly, you will not get out till you have paid the last penny."[3] Elsewhere, he suggested that forgiveness of sin after death is possible. He said that sin can be forgiven, but that the sin against the Holy Spirit "will not be forgiven either in this world or in the next."[4]

In one striking scriptural story, the disciples asked Jesus if a man was born blind because of the man's personal sin or that of his parents.[5] Jesus didn't say that such thinking is erroneous, but explained that this case had another reason.

The apostle Paul said all our works will be made manifest and tried. Those who fail the test can still be saved, but "it will be as one who has gone through fire."[6] Church teachings that purgation comes with suffering lay the basis for later doctrines on purgatory, another Christian teaching on karma.

Karmic Effects in Buddhism

Buddhist teachings emphasize volition in the law of karma. All actions begin with a mental act of volition.

Creating karmic effects Volition determines the karmic effects of actions. For example, Buddhists are not to intentionally take the life of any sensate being. However, if you accidentally step on an ant and kill it, no karmic effect occurs. For karma to accumulate, you must choose to kill the ant.

We are responsible for all volitional actions, even those we did not realize were harmful; all ignorance is culpable. Buddhists consider a harmful act even more blameworthy when done without knowing that it is wrong. "I didn't know" doubly convicts us—first of the unskillful behavior, and secondly of ignorance. "There is a taint worse than all others. Ignorance is the greatest taint."[7]

When we are ignorant of creating harm, rectifying our conduct is more difficult. When we do something we know is out of bounds, we can more easily choose otherwise in the future. We are also less likely to do it wholeheartedly; something in us pulls back at least a little. Wholehearted engagement in an action creates a greater force in its effects.

Nature of karmic effects Karmic effects are not simple to understand. The Buddha said that trying to figure it out could drive you crazy. However, popular notions of karma are far too simplistic—such as believing that being blind in this life must mean that you blinded someone in a past life. Such one-to-one effects are not how karma works.

We can most easily understand karma by how we understand other laws of cause and effect. Each moment sets up the conditions of the next moment. Such understanding supports all our science in the laws that govern matter, life, and mind.[8] The law of karma works the same way. Each moment of intentional action conditions or sets up the next moment in a chain of causes and effects governing choices. Each moment of choice creates effects that produce the kind of mind and world we have in the next moment.

Sometimes we see immediate and obvious external effects of our choices. If you don't study for an exam, your grade reflects the reality you have chosen to create. If you treat another person cruelly, you might lose a valuable relationship. If you lie, other people stop trusting you. If you steal, you could even do time in prison.

We sometimes get by without obvious external consequences, but every volitional choice always affects the mind. Every choice bends our inclination ever so slightly in one direction or the other—thus choices form character. Whenever we surrender to a discordant impulse, it becomes easier to surrender the next time. Each helpful "no" to unwholesome whims makes it easier to say "no" again. Choices always have this consequence.

How we handle choices conditions the next moment in the mind. Inch by inch, we "grow" ourselves in some direction. We can trace the development of both good and bad habits of choice over our lifetime. If we are insightful enough, we can also see how these choices made the life we have. They determine the realities we create for ourselves. The saying "what goes around comes around" catches popular belief in this principle. Karmic effects come from the type of mind we have developed. "Mind is the forerunner of reality."[9]

Choices are not the only conditions determining our fate; other laws of cause and effect also operate, but choices make considerable input. If nothing else, they strongly affect the attitude we take toward our lives and what happens to us. This, in turn, is a major cause of how much satisfaction we have in life.

Our place of freedom The Buddha's teachings on conditioning are very similar to contemporary behavioral psychology. However, they differ in one radically important respect: the Buddha taught that we could break the chain of conditioning and free ourselves. He clearly explained how we can come to make better choices.

Our conditioning, the habits we have formed, keeps us attached to wrong choices. The major point of freedom lies in the link between feeling-tone and our reaction to it.[10] Our task is to be with pleasant-ness without grasping, with unpleasantness without pushing it away or striking out at it, and to stay fully attentive to neutral experience. Being highly aware of and willing to experience feeling-tone can eventually break our conditioned reactions to it.

Similarly, John of the Cross said we need to catch the first move-ments within ourselves, for which we are not responsible, to keep bad behavior for which we are responsible from occurring.[11] Being able to see first movements or feeling-tone is a fruit of spiritual work, espe-cially meditation practice.

Karma and Rebirth

In Buddhist teachings, the effect of choices is not confined to one life-time. We sometimes see effects of our choices in this life, and some fruits of choices can ripen in a later life.

Karma and beings Just as the body's matter decays according to governing laws, consciousness continues on after death according to its laws. The last moment in one life conditions the first moment of consciousness in the next. The ongoing process of consciousness bears with it our karmic effects, all our volitional habits of mind.

However, there is a subtlety here. The process of consciousness con-tinues, but not all of what we call "me" does.[12] The material part gets recycled. Some previous embodiment of your consciousness deter-mined the heredity and circumstances of your present being. You inher-ited the karma that another being created and, after you die, "your" process of consciousness will be reborn as part of another being—the heir of the mind you have created. Referring to "my karma" is a short way of saying all of this.

Such an understanding leaves no room to blame anyone for his or her heredity, circumstances, and weaknesses—physical, mental, or moral. We inherited it all. However, it does define our work for this life. Hopefully, we will pass on a better inheritance than that we received to the beings reborn from the minds we create.

Karma and judgment The circumstances of rebirth depend upon the state of consciousness at death, which will reflect how we have lived. This includes choices in the immediately previous life, but circumstances might also favor the ripening of karmic seeds from former lives as well. The conditions of rebirth are not specific actions, but the quality of mind developed.

Every choice we make is like planting a seed. Not all seeds ripen; other conditions are also necessary. However, if we want a peach, we better plant peach seeds and not acorns! The seeds we have planted affect the quality of mind at death, and this determines the conditions of the next birth. That quality of mind has been building for many lifetimes. We cannot point to one occasion or simply one lifetime as the sole basis conditioning the next rebirth.

In other words, the state of a mind at the time of death determines the fate in which it will next find itself. This is very similar to the Christian idea of a judgment at death that determines what next happens— heaven for the completely pure, some kind of additional purgative experiences for those reasonably pure but not entirely so, and hell for those basically impure.

No realm of being in the Buddhist cosmology is permanent. Their inhabitants, though, experience some heavens and hells as eternal, and the life span in some is very long. Similarly, John taught, "Those in purgatory greatly doubt whether their afflictions will ever end."[13]

Karmic effects in rebirth Certain choices create weighty karma that always manifests. Enlightenment comes from doing a lot of spiritual practice. Even the lowest level enlightenment experience produces a mind that can never create a lower-than-human realm for rebirth. So partially enlightened beings will always be reborn as human or higher. Since enlightenment is a touch of Nibbana, this is similar to saying that those who have had experiential knowledge of God will never again be able to turn their backs completely on God.

Killing one's parent or a fully enlightened person produces conditions of mind that inevitably next create a hell realm. This particular hell is a very long-lasting one. Nobody casts any beings into hell; hells come from a type of mind that creates hell experience. People who do not have weighty karma usually die as they have lived. The type of mind they have habitually cultivated will likely form their dying moment and create the situation in which consciousness takes rebirth.

The elaborate Buddhist cosmology describes a wide range of both suffering and happy realms. The Christian poet Dante's abyss of hell and mountain of purgatory describe levels of purgation that are similar to the Buddhist suffering realms of existence; he also described levels of paradise.[14]

Buddhists believe in helping dying people draw out positive mental characteristics. They may read scriptures to them, chant, or remind them of their virtue. This helps them die in a wholesome state—a goal similar to that of offering Christian sacraments to a dying person. However, dramatic transformations at death are rare in both traditions.

Christian Teachings on Purgation

Many Christians and Buddhists hold that those who die less than completely pure must undergo further purifying experiences. Buddhists explain this as rebirth, and many in the early Christian church also endorsed this belief. The validity of the church council that declared it a wrong belief has been questioned.[15] Christian teachings now posit purgatory as the means for continued purgation.

Purgatory The Christian teaching on purgatory evolved over time, greatly influenced by images from the ancient world and the early church fathers.[16] Some early Christians urged prayer for the dead that they be released from their sins and come to happiness. Jewish writings of the same period contain similar notions. Such sayings have continued across the Christian tradition. For example, the eighth-century Venerable Bede urged us to suffer for the dead. Other spiritual traditions have also said such things for millennia.

Some early Christian fathers and saints, including Pope Gregory the Great, had visions showing that the dead expiated their sins here on earth where they had done the sinning.[17] Later Christian apologists—Bonaventure, Albert the Great, and Thomas Aquinas—said the place of purgatory is indeterminate, but that there must be various locations.[18]

The notion that the dead have impurities needing purgation early established itself firmly in the church's belief, yet no doctrine on purgatory was formally declared for some time. It remained just a condition for being purified, so that one might come to God. It was not until the second Council of Lyons in the late twelfth century that purgatory was truly "born" and became a special "place."[19]

Purgatory birth   Some people find it disturbing that Buddhist thought looks to many lifetimes before reaching the final goal. However, this is not so different from Christian teachings on purgatory. Purgatory is some state or place where purifying still needed after this lifetime occurs. Clearly, it could be seen as another lifetime—or possibly a series of lifetimes—between this lifetime and finally coming to know God fully. Where purgatory may take place is not at all clearly defined, and mystics have referred to life on earth as purgatory.

Purgatory could itself be described as a place of rebirth—a place where we reappear in another form of existence. This benign "doing time" offers additional opportunities for purifying experience. The purpose of purgatory is a "penal sentence" caused by impediments to "coming home." John said, "Unpurified souls must suffer in the next life to reach union with God."[20]

Across Christian history, many brilliant minds and honored mystics have held that the purgative process could be seen as a series of "rebirths" or states of experience. We can draw nearer and nearer to God over them, according to our spiritual work and our willingness to be purified, accepting suffering that John likened to that of purgatory.[21]

The basic teaching   The basic ideas that shaped understandings of purgation are simple and universal. They assert that most of us die unfit to "go home" to the Ultimate Reality, and that existence benignly gives us a chance beyond this lifetime to prepare ourselves. From this simple belief, found across numerous spiritual traditions, various stories developed about how such purgation might occur. These doctrinal formulations are secondary to the intuitive understanding that purification is both necessary and possible.

People not only believe that most of the dead need more purification, but also that we can help them with it. Buddhists practice sharing merit.[22] Merit makes one "shine within," and is "acquired" through various acts of piety, virtue, and spiritual practice. The living can share their merit with any being, including those who have already died. The similarity to praying for the souls in purgatory or offering the fruits of good acts for them is striking. We can also send loving-kindness to those who have died.[23]

Purgatory in this life Buddhist teachings state that, from all the possible realms into which beings are reborn, the human one is best for purgative work. It has just the right mixture of pleasure and pain—not too little pain as the heavens, not too little pleasure as the lower realms. The suffering motivates us, but does not overwhelm us. Christian saints and mystics who spoke of purgatory on earth told us that we could choose to do now what we will have to do eventually.

We each have tasks for this life, based on the karma inherited. However, the most obvious "dis-ease" in our being might not be the root task. A sexually promiscuous person may more need to learn not to fear real intimacy than to control sexual energies. A habitual liar may need to learn trust. Someone who compulsively steals may need to deal with deep feelings of deprivation and insecurity. Someone who drinks excessively may need to recognize unfulfilled spiritual yearnings. A murderer may need to learn compassion for herself. Insight practice eventually shows us our tasks underlying the more immediately obvious ones.

We also learn that when we truly know our own minds, we know all minds. We all contain the seeds of all possibilities—mental remnants hidden deep within. As Thich Nhat Hahn beautifully put it: I am both the young girl who drowns herself after being raped by a sea pirate, and that sea pirate who is not yet sensitive. I am the con artist and his victim. I am the dragonfly and she who crushes it.[24]

Conclusions

The Christian and Theravadan Buddhist traditions teach that, if life ends without sufficient purity to "die into" God or Nibbana, we must have more purifying experiences to make this possible. They also agree that those living on earth can help with the purification of those who have already died.

To understand these teachings, we must distinguish between religious mythology and underlying truths. Many spiritual traditions affirm the basic ideas presented here. The stories that the various traditions composed, elaborating how it works, show differences shaped by culture, politics, and other conditions. That is the nature of religious mythology, which is secondary to experience. We must act on the basic truths underlying the stories to come to freedom.

These teachings on karma, rebirth, purgatory, and purification show us our need to get free of impediments that make us continue to suffer, and free of rebirth or purgatory. They teach us how spiritually hungry hearts can eventually find rest and satisfaction. They offer the possibility of finally being purged of clinging to anything other than God.

MJM

✛ 21 ✛

About Buddhist No-Self and the Christian Soul

N O EASTERN TEACHINGS confuse Christians, including many who attend our retreats, more than those of abandoning self, no-self and emptiness, and letting go of ego. Some misinterpret these Buddhist teachings as referring to regressing to an infant's state of mind, without a defined sense of one's own being. Others conclude that abandoning ego means acting only on impulse. Some believe the teachings mean that we will have only a vast "nothing" at the end of our lives.

Some Teachings on No-Self

Teachings on no-self form the very heart of the contemplative quest. They are the core teaching of many who claim intimate knowledge of the Highest Good.

Contemplative no-self teachings From Tibetan Buddhist master, Kalu Rinpoche:

> We live in illusion and the appearance of things.
> There is a Reality. We are that Reality.
> When you realize this, you see that you are nothing,
> And, being nothing, you are everything. That is all.[1]

John of the Cross tersely echoed:

> To come to being all, desire to be nothing.
> To become what you are not
> You must go in a way in which you are not.[2]

As another Buddhist teacher put it: "Big self, big problem. No self, no problem." These teachings mean something quite radical. We truly must relinquish separate self-sense. No-self does not mean that beings and things do not exist, but that nothing stands independently of everything else, and nothing has a fixed, unchanging core. John's teaching on "the substance of the soul" well mirrors Buddhist understanding.

Christians sometimes balk at the notion of "no unchanging soul." For spiritual practice to make sense, whatever of us can experience God must be in process. Were "soul" fixed and unchanging, knowledge and love of God could not increase. Were it completely isolated and unconnected, it could never be fulfilled with the Last Supper prayer of Jesus that we participate in the life of the Trinity.[3]

Some other Western positions Philosopher Sartre said, "Hell is other people." Sartre, though wrong, is close to right. Hell is seeing other people as Other. Hell is seeing oneself as some thing separate and distinct from everyone and everything else. So long as we are full of self, there is no room for God. John reminded us that "an occupied heart" leaves no space for God.[4]

Psychologist Carl Rogers said that "self" is a bunch of perceptions I have about what I call "I" or "me." Because it is not a thing, but a process, it continually changes. If we look at the perceptions that make up "I" or "me" in any given instant, they seem to depict a lasting thing. We think the concept "I," and then see the processes called "I" as an enduring, unchanging thing. But then in an instant, it changes. What I considered "me" a second ago is now different. Rogers even said that self-sense is only a hypothesis we make for meeting life.[5]

So, for Rogers, self is a collection of ideas about rapidly changing processes called "I" or "me." Its incessant changes are most easily seen in deep meditation practice. Such ongoing change is one truth our practice shows us.

Creating Concepts

The Buddha understood as psychologist Rogers did about the self-concept. Buddhist teachings on concepts and impermanence help us understand this more clearly.

Solidifying experience Many experiences are like ones that happened before, so we form concepts about them, calling them that "thing." Forming a concept congeals experience, making it look solid and unchanging. When I say "tree," an experience of light and color and shape and movement is turned into a fixed, unchanging "thing." But we know that is not true; various experiences called "tree" differ from each other. Even one particular "tree" is never exactly the same from instant to instant. The same is true of us. When all the processes of body and mind are found together in a being, we have what we call a person—not a thing, but a collection of processes.

What we call sea is continually shifting movement of drops of water, which are themselves chemical interactions of hydrogen and oxygen. Similarly, what we call a symphony is a succession of sounds—notes of music—each one rising, lingering, dying. Where is the "thing" we call a symphony? And what we call a sunset is moments of shifting movement and patterns of light and shadow and color. Can you hold the "thing" called sunset?

We must not try to capture the running water of real experience in the bucket of concepts.[6] Getting stuck in notions impedes being in touch with direct, immediate experience. Clinging to concepts about God and self are most dangerous for spiritual growth. Our aim is not concepts about God—the "back" of God—but God's "face."[7]

Flux and the process nature of reality The Buddha's teaching on impermanence says that everything is in constant flux. Even the most solid-appearing mountain is always eroding in some places and adding bulk in others; its vegetation also continually shifts and changes. Nothing in earthly experience ever stays the same.

That is certainly also true of "me." Part of what I called "me" this morning went down the drain when I showered and dead skin cells flaked off. What I called cereal this morning is now becoming "me."

Biologists say that no cell in the body lasts beyond seven years. As cells divide, their contents are replaced using the protein building blocks we have eaten, according to the genetic code in the body's cells. But mistakes occur; we call them aging. The reproducibility of cells increasingly falters until finally what is reproduced can no longer sustain life. Then the material process I call "me" ceases—unless an accident or illness gets there first.

As with the tree, the sea, and the sunset, so it is with us. Not only bodies, but also everything else we might call "me" is in constant flux: emotions, thoughts, and imaginings. Even memories change, for we continually rearrange how we recall the past.

The Buddha on Self

As Rogers said directly, the Buddha also taught: we are each a process, made up of sets of interlocking processes—not some static, fixed thing. We will later see that, for John, the substance of the soul is also not a "thing," but simply a capacity for experience of God.

Processes "When [the Buddha] refers to 'self,' he is talking about an idea we hold of an unchanging essence to whom experience is happening. *Anatta* (no-self) means understanding that experience does not refer back to anyone."[8] It just happens. The classical *Visuddhi Magga* says, "Phenomena alone flow on—cause and component their condition."[9]

Seeing the process nature of our beings and the deep connection of all being helps us understand selflessness. It eventually comes down to our contingency—a teaching mirrored in Christian thought. Nothing has any fixed, unchanging nature that can be considered a permanently enduring "thing." Everything is a process. "All phenomena come and go of their own accord, responding to their own natural laws. Their occurrence is beyond our control."[10] We come to see that all that exists is the constant interchange of processes within processes within processes.

Not me, not mine Buddhist scriptures also point out that what we cannot control is not ours. The body would not cause affliction if we could command how we want it to be. "But because body is non-self, the body leads to affliction, and we cannot say of body, 'Let my body be thus; let my body not be thus.'"[11] Their conclusion is the same about all the other processes that make up our beings. We cannot control them; we do not "own" them.

As well as our not being able to command the processes we call "me," they are also impermanent and unsatisfactory. Scriptures ask, "What do you think, is body permanent or impermanent?" "Is what is impermanent suffering or happiness?" "Is what is impermanent, suffering, and subject to change fit to be considered mine, my self?"[12] Their conclusion about all aspects of our beings is again their process nature: that we lack any unchanging core we can point to as a permanent, fixed self.

Some people fear that accepting this teaching means annihilation. "Body and mind will not disappear, what disappears is the urge and the reaching out and the affirmation of the importance and supremacy of this particular person, called 'me.'"[13] Relinquishing this brings deep serenity. The *Dhammapada* advises: "Cut off your attachment to self. Cultivate the path of peace."[14]

John of the Cross on the Substance of the Soul

Both the Buddha and psychologist Rogers clearly saw the fictional character of the idea of self. John's teaching on the substance of the soul suggests that he, too, saw it similarly.

The substance of the soul Christians understand "soul" in various ways. Most consider it some kind of airy, ethereal "thing." However seen, notions of soul often bend us to view it as fixed and unchanging.

John distinguished between substance or lasting reality and qualities or characteristics that pass. He recognized the passing nature of bodies, emotions, thoughts—even what we call personality, which is merely a combination of memories, thoughts, reactions, and emotions. John called what is left when we peel away all that is not lasting the "substance of the soul." He referred to it "as our heart *(seno)*"[15]— or deepest being. Theravadan Buddhists also symbolize our deepest center as located in the heart.[16]

John saw the substance of the soul as a capacity to experience God beyond the limits of the reasoning mind. "We are no longer satisfied with knowing and communicating with only the 'back' of God."[17] God's "back" is second-hand knowledge—ideas and images about God. "We can be satisfied only with God's face, which is an essential communication of divinity to our souls."[18]

In this life, we can grasp this communication only "in the substance of the soul."[19] When we go beyond all of us that does not last, only this capacity to experience God is left. At our core, we are each an "emptiness" waiting to be filled with God.

Soul experience We experience God differently according to our state of soul. While the residue of original and personal sin remains, contemplative knowledge of God is painful. John said of unpurified souls: "In the substance of the soul they suffer abandonment, great poverty, dryness, cold, and sometimes heat. They find no relief in anything, and no thought can console them."[20] Purification necessarily involves suffering; because we cling to them, relinquishing our attachments is painful.

After purification, our experience changes. John wrote, "You are no longer heavy and overwhelming to the substance of my soul but rather its glory, delight, and fullness."[21] The "touch of God gives intense satisfaction and enjoyment to the substance of the soul,"[22] "rejoicing it with floods of God's delight, divine contact, and substantial union."[23] "Usually these touches are exceptionally sublime and delightful experiences of God."[24]

Experiencing God as becoming God As dross is removed, "we are transformed in God and drink of God in our substance."[25] All that remains in the end is our knowing God—"becoming" God. "So great is this union that even though they remain different in substance, in their glory and appearance our souls seem to be God, and God seems not different from our souls."[26]

A purified soul ceases to be a "thing" standing apart and separate. It is interpenetrated with the loving knowledge of God, just as a burning log is not separate and apart from fire.[27] Separate self, separate log of wood, cease. As John's "Dark Night" poem puts it, "all things ceased." When there is no separate "thing-ness," all that is left is God. The greatest power of the substance of the soul is fully experiencing this "all that is left" after thing-ness ceases.

John did not say that individual personality or ego becomes divine. It ceases to stand out as separate, truly ceases to literally "ex-ist"— stand apart or be away from. We no longer create from passing phenomena the sense of a separate, distinct self to whose fortunes we are attached. The substance of the soul, knowing all that there is to know, "becomes" the object of its loving knowledge just as the mind "becomes" all the objects of its thought.

The center of the soul The substance of the soul is transformed into God at different depths. "The soul's center is God. When we have reached God with all the capacity of our being and the strength of our functioning and inclinations, we have come to our final and deepest center in God."[28] Then only God is known, so only God is. The knowing/loving substance of the soul completely "becomes" the object of its knowing/loving—God.

Again—self or ego does not become divine. The only enduring aspect of our beings—the substance of the soul, the capacity for loving knowledge of God—becomes completely full of such loving knowledge. In our deepest depths, any reference to the passing phenomena we call self—or to other passing phenomena, such as God-concepts—is impossible. Before we reach that deepest point, where all else yields to God, we can be interpenetrated with loving knowledge of God to different depths in our center.

Deeply Understanding No-Self

To understand no-self fully, we must look beyond our own beings. We are also not "separate," for the processes that define each of us interact with many other processes.

Inter-relatedness When the Buddha said that there are no fixed essences, he meant that nothing exists that is not a continually changing process, always affected by other processes with which it interacts and the larger cosmic process of which it is part. This includes "I" or "me."

In the exchange of solid matter, of fluids, of gasses—the very air we breathe in and expel—continual interchange with encompassing environmental processes occurs. The "sacraments" of the kitchen and the bathroom celebrate the constant recycling of matter among all that is in the universe. The taking in of what matter we need, and giving back of what is no longer helpful to us, are sacred signs of our oneness.

There is also more within us than we think. We are each an ecosystem, host to a multitude of smaller existences. Our eyelids and eyebrows house hundreds of microorganisms. We could more honestly say that the friendly bacteria in our digestive tracts digest our food, rather than our doing it. And biologist Lewis Thomas said that each of our cells contains little critters that power them, without whom "we would not move a muscle, drum a finger, think a thought."[29] Where or what is the "I" or "me" in all this?

Scientists who study chaos, apparently random chance occurrences in the universe, say that close looking shows that everything is interrelated. Nothing can really be called an accident. Everything is caused—the Buddha would say conditioned—by all the ongoing processes that affect it. These scientists describe "the butterfly effect," how a butterfly fluttering its wings in Hong Kong in January affects weather patterns in America the next summer.[30] Truly, as the poet John Donne said, not one of us is an island; we are all connected.

In a very real way, we are our experiences. If we focus our attention on a solidified understanding of bodily or mental processes as self, we are that—and we experience the hell of isolation. We can focus attention on the larger cosmic process in which the processes making up self are embedded. Then we can experience the Mystical Body of the Christ or the unfolding of the Dhamma—the Christ or Buddha nature in all that is. Finally, if we focus on God or Nibbana, we "are" that by participation.

Our final end   John taught that, when completely pure, the substance of the soul rests in loving knowledge of God. These pure ones do not die of diseases or age; "their soul is wrested from them only by some impetus and meeting with love that tears through this veil."[31] They "die into" God's love.

Buddhist teachings say that when purification is complete, and we are at the end of our last lifetime, consciousness fixes on Nibbana at the time of death. Then "dying into" Nibbana is all that there is.

How similar these teachings are! We have in the final end the substance of the soul knowing God, or the knowing consciousness fixed on Nibbana. Our capacity for experiencing is full of only the Ultimate, in which all else is found. Any other "thing" we called "me" or "I" is unimportant, and goes back to the dust or the energy from which it was drawn.

What do these teachings tell us? That most of what we concern ourselves with as "me" is simply a passing phenomenon that we cannot finally hold on to anyway. That what the "I" or "me" ultimately comes to is knowing, touching, dwelling in, or tasting that which is really Real and indestructible. That we come to this only when we are utterly pure of heart, and that a major obstacle to this purity is clinging to that pitiful cluster of processes that I call "me."

Summary and Conclusions

Often we try to fill the deep void and hunger in ourselves with something other than God, especially with the trappings of self. However, our "capacity is deep because the object of this capacity—God—is profound and infinite. Therefore, our capacity is infinite, our thirst is infinite, and our hunger is also deep and infinite."[32]

When we stop focusing on "self," we can see the only true and enduring Real. In that's being all there is when "all things cease," when we have thus become no "thing," we will become everything. We end with a quote that also appeared in our opening chapter. "A grain of wheat remains a solitary grain unless it falls into the ground and dies; but if it dies, it bears a rich harvest."[33]

MJM

Appendix I

Developing the Silence and Awareness Retreat and Christian Insight Meditation

THE INSPIRATION to integrate Buddhist insight meditation with Carmelite prayer first came in the summer of 1986. I (Mary Jo Meadow) was on leave from Mankato State University (now Minnesota State University, Mankato), where I was professor of psychology and director of the religious studies program. I had devoted the 1985–86 academic year to a spiritual pilgrimage, exploring programs of spiritual practice throughout the United States.

I began my year by making a three-month Buddhist vipassana retreat at the Insight Meditation Society in Barre, Massachusetts from mid-September to mid-December. For the concluding experience of my year in June, I attended the Carmelite Forum's summer seminar in Carmelite Spirituality in Notre Dame, Indiana, where my friend and colleague Kevin Culligan, O.C.D., was lecturing.

Exploring Similarities

At that time, I had meditated and also studied John of the Cross for over thirty years. I was convinced that vipassana meditation, which I had practiced daily since my retreat, was highly congruent with the teachings of John. Especially striking was their common emphasis on purification and self-emptying as essential ascetical practices. I felt that vipassana had much to offer Christian prayer.

During the Carmelite seminar, I explained insight meditation to Kevin, and asked his reaction to my impressions. When he also saw the similarities, we began to discuss ways to explore them further. We were both licensed clinical psychologists and active members of Division 36, Psychologists Interested in Religious Issues, of the American Psychological Association (APA). In previous years, we had collaborated on presenting symposia and programs in psychology of religion and mysticism at annual APA conventions.

We agreed that a logical first step would be to test this insight with colleagues at the next APA convention. We titled our presentation "Similarities between Carmelite Spirituality and Buddhist Meditation: A Psychological Analysis." Kevin presented six areas of similarity between Buddhism and Carmelite spirituality: both are developmental, produce radical change within individuals, emphasize interiority, have social consequences, demand personal discipline, and involve passive purification. I then described similarities between development in vipassana meditation and the stages of spiritual growth outlined by John of the Cross.[1] The psychologists we addressed responded positively enough to encourage us to pursue our insights further.

We proposed a paper that described the similarities in spiritual development between John and Theravadan Buddhism for the international Buddhist-Christian conference scheduled for August 1987, in Berkeley. I read our paper to about seventy-five interfaith scholars and other persons interested in the spiritual practices of Buddhism and Christianity.

Again the response was positive, prompting us to revise our paper and submit it for publication in *The Journal of Transpersonal Psychology*. Our coauthored "Congruent Spiritual Paths: Christian Carmelite and Theravadan Buddhist Vipassana" appeared in the 1987 volume of the journal.[2]

Silence and Awareness Retreats

Up to this time, we had been publicly comparing Buddhist meditation and Christian prayer only in theory. I was continuing to sit insight meditation, and also believed that these similarities are true in practice. I felt that insight meditation can lead us toward the emptiness in sense and spirit that John of the Cross maintained is a necessary disposition for union with God.

We later learned that, in a retreat with contemplative women in May 1968, Thomas Merton had offered a similar opinion while discussing a book by Heinrich Dumoulin, a German-Japanese Jesuit. He said that "Zen is nothing but John of the Cross without the Christian theology. As far as the psychological aspect is concerned, that is, the complete emptying of self, it's the same thing and the same approach."[3]

Planning the retreat To test such conclusions, we planned a Christian retreat based on three assumptions. First, although it originates in Theravadan Buddhism, insight meditation does not require belief in any religious tenets; it is essentially a spiritual practice available to all persons of all religions. Second, Christians can use insight meditation as an effective means of deepening their faith and love in Christ Jesus. And third, insight meditation helps Christians embrace fully Jesus' total emptying of self in sense and spirit on the cross, which John of the Cross maintains is the door to transformation of our lives in God through love.

The retreat itself was to be similar to those offered at the Insight Meditation Society, but within a Christian framework. We knew that Christian Zen retreats were offered throughout the United States,[4] but were unaware of any that taught Theravadan insight meditation within a Christian framework, and specifically within the context of John's Carmelite spirituality.[5]

With the Carmelite Forum's summer seminar not scheduled for 1989, we planned an eight-day retreat that year to be held during the Forum's usual last two weeks of June. We invited Fr. Daniel Chowning, O.C.D., and Fr. Anthony Haglof, O.C.D., two of Kevin's Carmelite confreres who had experience with insight meditation, to join us in leading the retreat.

The launched retreat Finally, on June 25, 1989, sixty-six persons from both coasts, the Caribbean, and throughout the Midwest and Canada gathered in Minnesota for the first retreat: "Silence and Awareness: A Retreat Experience in Christian-Buddhist Meditation." Kevin and I again offered the retreat the following year. In 1991, 1992, and

1993, Kevin, Daniel, and I planned and directed the retreat for thirty to thirty-five participants each year.

From 1989 to 1993, 170 persons made the retreat, some of them several times. To accommodate growing and wide-spread interest, Resources for Ecumenical Spirituality, the non-profit corporation I founded in 1987 to study interfaith spirituality, began in 1994 to offer two additional Silence and Awareness retreats each year in different locations around the United States. Since that time, the retreat has also been offered a number of times each in Canada, Australia, and Scotland. It is now impossible to number how many people have attended the retreat.

Retreat schedule A sample daily retreat schedule, somewhat less rigorous but based on the vipassana retreats at Insight Meditation Society in Barre, Massachusetts, is as follows:

6:30 A.M.	rising
7:00 A.M.	Eucharist
7:45 A.M.	breakfast
8:45 A.M.	sitting meditation and instruction
10:00 A.M.	walking meditation
11:00 A.M.	sitting meditation
11:45 A.M.	walking meditation or questions and answers
12:30 P.M.	lunch, optional walking meditation
2:15 P.M.	sitting meditation
3:00 P.M.	walking meditation
3:45 P.M.	sitting meditation and instruction
4:45 P.M.	walking meditation
5:15 P.M.	loving-kindness practice
6:00 P.M.	supper, optional walking meditation
7:30 P.M.	retreat conference
8:30 P.M.	walking meditation
9:15 P.M.	sitting meditation
10:00 P.M.	further practice or rest

Interior and exterior silence is maintained throughout the retreat. Such silence excludes eye contact, reading, writing, journaling, listening to tapes, and any unnecessary speech, all of which dissipate meditative energy.

Whenever possible breakfasts and lunches are vegetarian, emphasizing whole foods with balanced proteins. Supper might include a light animal protein. Sugar and "heavy" food are used sparingly, as they hinder meditation with energy fluctuations and turgidity.

Other retreat activities Those who wish to celebrate the sacrament of Reconciliation with one of the priests ordinarily do so during individual interview time. Mass is offered very quietly. A brief homily follows the gospel reading; the liturgy of the Eucharist emphasizes the liturgical words and gestures, and there is an extended period of silence after communion. The Sunday Eucharist that concludes the retreat, however, is celebrated with song and full active participation.

Time is provided each day for either individual or group interviews with retreat team members. These focus on issues related to doing the meditation practice, rather than upon personal problem solving, discernment, decision-making, or theoretical issues.

Throughout, the retreat emphasizes interior and exterior silence, concentrated awareness of all our experiences of body and mind, and deepening the spirit of prayer in meditation practice. The purpose is to help those attending to become empty of roles, voluntary experiences, and other trappings of ordinary daily life so that they may be more available to God and the purifying love of the Holy Spirit.

Foundations of the Retreat

In planning these retreats, we (Kevin, Daniel, and I) pursued two goals. We wanted to offer a traditionally Christian retreat and to teach the insight meditation practice in all its integrity so that those attending the retreat can learn the entire practice within eight days.

Across-traditions precursors Inspiring our planning was the example of men and women from other religious orders—notably the Benedictines and Jesuits—who, in the spirit of the Second Vatican

Council, integrated Eastern meditation practices into Christian prayer. We felt strongly that Carmelites, with their long tradition of contemplative prayer, should also respond to this challenge.

We also believed that we were involved in an ancient process in which the Christian faith community takes from the cultures in which it lives those human achievements that help to deepen the understanding and practice of its Christian faith. In the thirteenth century, Thomas Aquinas drew upon the revival of Aristotelian philosophy to better understand and explain Christian beliefs. In the twentieth century, the church enhanced its pastoral care with new understandings of person and community from contemporary psychology and sociology.

Enriching Christian life We were convinced that meditation practices developed over many centuries in the East could enrich Christian life, especially contemplative prayer. On these premises, we planned a retreat that included Eucharist and the sacrament of Reconciliation. We scheduled retreat conferences explaining the relationship of insight meditation practice to the deepening of Christian faith, hope, and love—the central challenge in Christian spirituality, according to John of the Cross.

Within this Christian context, the entire insight meditation practice—both sitting and walking—is taught in a classical, unadulterated manner with the focus primarily upon learning the practice. Discussion of its relationship with Christian faith occurs primarily in the daily conferences. Times are also scheduled when those attending can ask their own questions about theory and integration.

Outcomes from the Retreat

Most participants have responded very favorably to the retreat. However, not everyone has found it personally helpful.

Concerns Some think there is too little explicit reference to Jesus Christ, too much Buddhist teaching; too little emphasis on Eucharist, Christian prayer, and Carmelite spirituality, too much emphasis on learning the practice of insight meditation; or too much of John's asceticism, too little of his mysticism. Others believe that the retreat leaders should make more explicit efforts to integrate the meditation practice into Christian faith. Some wanted more of a seminar than a retreat.

One participant wanted more help from the team to manage the more difficult moments of the retreat when we feel exposed, vulnerable, and without masks or defenses. Another reported that the retreat's intensity precipitated a three-month clinical depression upon returning home, and advised the team to be more careful in screening applicants.

Positive results It is, of course, extremely difficult to directly measure progress in the stated goals of the retreat—such inner states as purity of heart, emptiness of self, and openness for God. However, most who attend report that the retreat brought them such benefits as a deepened self-awareness, mindfulness, inner stillness, and interior peace; more discipline in prayer; a stronger desire for God alone; a realization of the need for purification to grow spiritually; reassurance of the compatibility of Buddhist meditation with Christian prayer; healing of memories and emotions; and help with managing persistent physical pain more gracefully.

Many express gratitude for being given assistance with prayer that they have found nowhere else. A number of them also have adopted insight meditation as their principal form of contemplative prayer. Many of these have regularly attended the retreat, some almost annually.

Developing Christian Insight Meditation

We named our teaching of insight practice within the context of the spirituality of John of the Cross "Christian insight meditation." This title avoids the awkwardness most Americans find in pronouncing the Pali word "vipassana;" it also distinguishes the practice from other current approaches to contemplative practice such as Christian Zen and John Main's Christian meditation.[6]

Assisted by evaluations from those attending the retreat, we worked to improve the theory and practice of Christian insight meditation, making slight alterations in the retreat schedule. This included adding an optional communal Reconciliation service during the last full day of the retreat.

After several years experience with the Silence and Awareness retreat, we became convinced of its helpfulness in spiritual living. We concluded that vipassana, the meditation practice of Theravadan Buddhism, contributes positively to Christian contemplative life. Over the years, we have seen this proven in the lives of many attending the retreat.

KC/MJM

Appendix II

Resource Aids for Practicing Insight Meditation

AWARENESS PRACTICE can easily be done without much additional help except at critical periods. However, some aids are available that greatly support practice.

Retreats

Insight meditators are advised to sit a week-long retreat at least annually. If you do only weekend retreats, try to do two or more a year. Retreats deepen practice by offering an opportunity for continuous, mindful, concentrated awareness. Being free of other concerns allows the mind to penetrate experience more deeply. Because attention is not dispersed, concentrated focus comes more rapidly.

Our sponsor, Resources for Ecumenical Spirituality (RES), holds Silence and Awareness retreats regularly, teaching awareness practice as a method for the spirituality of John of the Cross. To get on the mailing list, write to RES, PO Box 85, Forest Lake MN 55025-0085 or email resecum@msn.com.

Various Buddhist settings offer awareness retreats. Sitting insight practice with Buddhist teachers can be a very good experience for Christians. Although they do not include Christian practices, many fine teachers lead them. One special place is Insight Meditation Society, 1230 Pleasant Street, Barre MA 01005; they will put you on their mailing list on request. Other retreats are available around the country, and can be found online. One good resource for locating retreats is *Inquiring Mind* newspaper.

Sitting Groups

To maintain regular practice, a sitting group greatly helps. Meditating regularly with other people committed to practice supports and nurtures your meditation practice. Sitting group meetings usually start with a 30 to 60 minute meditation sitting. After that, members sometimes simply disperse. However, most groups have other activities. Some socialize, some study together, and some have a teacher who offers material. The members decide what their group does. Groups work best when they are flexible about attendance.

Sitting groups meet as frequently as their members want. One RES group meets twice weekly; some meditators come every meeting, some once a week, and some only occasionally. Another meets only monthly. For information on our sitting groups, contact RES at resecum@msn.com; PO Box 85, Forest Lake MN 55025; or (651) 464-7489. We can supply some information on other sitting groups also.

You can start a sitting group if there is not one near you. Its members do not all have to do the same practice, so long as you sit in silent meditation together. Your study could be of general spiritual teachings.

Published Materials

Inquiring Mind is a twice-yearly publication of the vipassana community that offers articles on various forms of awareness practice. It lists both retreats offered worldwide that are led by approved teachers and also sitting groups in various locations. They will send it to anyone who asks, but request a donation toward covering costs from those who can afford it. Contact them at PO Box 9999, North Berkeley Station, Berkeley CA 94709.

Credence Cassettes in Kansas City published the 1991 Silence and Awareness retreat. It has since been purchased by Credence Communications, PO Box 30433, Kansas City MO 64112; (816) 454-1500.

Listening to recorded instructions and to lectures exploring the teaching of John of the Cross in the light of awareness practice can help those not sitting with a teacher.

RES also offers recordings of previous Silence and Awareness retreat talks to those who support its ministry with membership. Membership in RES is available for a minimum donation of US$25 annually. Members can purchase audio copies of talks at previous Silence and Awareness retreats for $5 each with a minimum purchase of five recordings. Some in print and discontinued books by RES members are also available at a discount. Contact RES at the address given above.

Tapes and CDs from other teachers in the Buddhist community are also available. Insight Meditation Society teachers offer them through Dharma Seed Library, Box 66, Wendell Depot MA 01380.

Reading other books on practice is helpful, too. Some resources for reading materials were given in the notes of Chapter 2 of this book. See the bibliography also. For additional, detailed self-help guidance, see the forthcoming book by Mary Jo Meadow, *Practicing Insight Meditation: Guidance from Buddhist Writings and John of the Cross*.

RES as a Resource

We cannot teach meditation by phone, mail, or email. However, RES remains willing to help anyone who has practiced insight meditation with us. An email address is maintained just for that purpose. It is reshelp@msn.com. A letter sent to the RES address given above will also be answered. If you prefer telephone consultation, making an appointment is best to ensure teacher availability. Please understand that RES must return some calls collect. Routine ongoing guidance is also available for serious meditators who want it. For business, including retreat inquiries and registration, use resecum@msn.com.

MJM

Notes

Preface

1. Kevin Culligan, Mary Jo Meadow, and Daniel Chowning, *Purifying the Heart:Buddhist Insight Practice for Christians* (New York: Crossroad Publishing, 1994). Much of the content of this preface is drawn from the first edition's preface, written by my co-author Kevin Culligan.

2. Matthew 13:45–46.

3. Appendix I describes the retreat and traces its development.

4. References to John's work are made to the work and section in it as given in Kavanaugh and Rodriguez, *The Collected Works of St. John of the Cross,* rev. ed., trans. by Kieran Kavanaugh and Otilio Rodriguez (Washington, D.C.: Institute of Carmelite Studies, 1991) since most American readers are most familiar with that translation. The works are referenced in the notes as follows: *Ascent* for *The Ascent of Mount Carmel, Night* for *The Dark Night, Sayings* for *The Sayings of Light and Love, Canticle* for *The Spiritual Canticle,* and *Flame* for *The Living Flame of Love.* The names of all works are those given by Kavanaugh and Rodriguez; in some instances, other translations name them differently. Names of minor works are cited in the text by full name. We gratefully acknowledge permission from ICS Publications, granted at the time of the first edition of this work, to reprint some material from this book.

5. References to Teresa's work are also made to the work and section in it as given in the Kavanaugh and Rodriguez translations of her works (Washington, D.C.: Institute of Carmelite Studies). The works are referenced in the notes as follows: *Life* for *The Book of Her Life, Castle* for *The Interior Castle, Testimonies* for *Spiritual Testimonies, Way* for *The Way of Perfection, Song* for *Meditations on the Song of Songs, Foundations* for *The Book of Her Foundations.* The names of all works are those given by Kavanaugh and Rodriguez; in some instances, other translations name them differently. Names of minor works are cited in the text by full name.

6. Declaration on the Relationship of the Church to Non-Christian Religions *[Nostra Aetate],* no. 2.

7. Decree on the Church's Missionary Activity *[Ad Gentes],* no. 18.

8. See chapter 19 for a discussion of the Holy Spirit in relation to the Buddhist Dhamma.

9. Christian scripture quotations not translated directly by the authors from original sources are taken from the following translations: Donald Senior, Mary Ann Getty,

Carroll Stuhlmueller, and John J. Collins, eds., *The New American Bible* in *The Catholic Study Bible* (New York: Oxford University Press, 1990); Alexander Jones, General Editor, *The Jerusalem Bible* (Garden City, N.Y.: Doubleday & Co., 1966); Alfred Marshall, *The Revised Standard Version* in *The R. S.V. Interlinear Greek-English New Testament* (Grand Rapids, Mich.: Zondervan Publishing House, 1968).

10. Mary Jo Meadow, *Gentling the Heart: Buddhist Loving-Kindness Practice for Christians* (New York: Crossroad, 1994) is now out of print. It is available from RES, PO Box 85, Forest Lake MN 55025. Inquire at that address or resecum@msn.com. The book might eventually go into revision for republication.

11. One of these translations is Kavanaugh and Rodriguez, cited in note 4. Many older readers might be most familiar with the translation by E. Allison Peers. Sheed and Ward published these in the mid-twentieth century; the Doubleday Image series in paperback followed this publication. The Spanish edition, the one many American Carmelites prefer, is compiled by Maximiliano Herraiz, *San Juan De La Cruz: Obras Completas,* segunda edicion (Salamanca, Spain: Ediciones Sigueme, 1992).

CHAPTER 1, PURITY OF HEART: THE TEACHING AND EXAMPLE OF JESUS

1. Matthew 5:8.
2. Geoffrey W. Bromiley, *Theological Dictionary of the New Testament,* abridged in one volume (Grand Rapids, Mich.: William B. Eerdmans Publishing Company, 1985), 416.
3. Matthew 15:10–11; Mark 7:14–16.
4. Matthew 15:12–20; Mark 7:17–23.
5. Gotama the Buddha, *Dhammapada,* 165. The Dhammapada, a collection of aphorisms of the Buddha, is available in many editions. To facilitate finding references in any edition, we cite by aphorism number. We primarily follow an unpublished translation by the late Bill Hamilton, a long-time insight meditation practitioner and teacher. Chapter 10 has some additional quotes from the Dhammapada that speak of purity and impurity.
6. *Ibid.,* 281.
7. 1 John 3:2–3.
8. Matthew 5:3–10.
9. *Dhammapada,* 290.
10. John 2:25.
11. Matthew 8:5–15; Mark 6:5–6.
12. Mark 8:34–38.
13. John 12:24.
14. Philippians 2:5–11.
15. *Ibid.,* 3:10–11.
16. Romans 5:5.
17. *Ibid.,* 8:26–30.
18. 1 Corinthians 6:9–11.

19. Galatians 5:16–26. Chapter 19 further discusses the fruits of the Holy Spirit in re- lation to Buddhist virtue.
20. Mark 4:30–32.
21. Psalm 51:12.
22. *Dhammapada,* 236.
23. *Ibid.,* 282.
24. Understanding that John did not mean that ego or personality becomes God is im- portant. Chapters 13 and 21 explain this teaching in more detail.
25. Matthew 7:21.
26. 1 John 3:2–3.
27. John 3:8.
28. Matthew 6:34.

Chapter 2, The Buddhist Tradition of Insight Meditation

1. The famed bookmark of Teresa of Avila closely mirrors Buddhist teachings on im- permanence. It says to let nothing agitate or disturb us because all things pass, and only God can satisfy us. Chapter 7 contains its text.
2. Chapter 21, on no-self and soul, discusses this issue more completely.
3. Chapter 20 discusses issues related to this teaching.
4. "*Chabbisodhana Sutta*: The Sixfold Purity," *Majjhima Nikaya* iii.29–37. Sutta 112, in Bhikkhu Nanamoli and Bhikkhu Bodhi, trans., *The Middle Length Discourses of the Buddha: A New Translation of the Majjhima Nikaya* (Boston: Wisdom Publications, 1995), 903–8. See also *Udana* 1.10. This basic teaching appears in many places in various forms.
5. Gotama the Buddha, *Dhammapada,* 372.
6. For a good translation, with commentary, see Nyanaponika Thera, *The Heart of Buddhist Meditation: A Handbook of Mental Training Based on the Buddhist Way of Mind- fulness* (London: Rider Press, 1962).
7. Some of these scriptures can be obtained from Wisdom Publications, which has commissioned an entirely new translation in more user-friendly English. The Pali Text Society has also published others of these scriptures. Some of these can be ob- tained from Vihara Book Service in Washington, D.C.
8. Buddhaghosa, *The Path of Purification (Visuddhi Magga),* translated from the Pali by Bhikkhu Nyanamoli (Kandy, Sri Lanka: Buddhist Publication Society, 1979). Peter Feldmeier, a priest who was with us for several retreats, has written *Christianity Looks East: Comparing the Spiritualities of John of the Cross and Buddhaghosa* (New York/Mahwah, N.J.: Paulist Press, 2006). I mention this book with reservations since Peter draws some conclusions with which I strongly disagree, and which I think would be moderated by further practice of insight meditation.
9. Available works can be obtained through the Buddhist Publication Society, Sri Lanka, and the Vihara Book Service, Washington, D.C. I highly recommend a book by a foremost disciple of his: Venerable Sayadaw U Pandita, *In This Very Life: The Lib- eration Teachings of the Buddha* (Boston: Wisdom Publications, 1992).

10. Insight Meditation Society, 1230 Pleasant Street, Barre MA 01005 or www.dharma.org. You can write to get on their mailing list.

11. *The Experience of Insight: A Simple and Direct Guide to Buddhist Meditation*, 1983; *Seeking the Heart of Wisdom: The Path of Insight Meditation, 1987*; and *Insight Meditation: The Path to Freedom*, 1993, were all published by Shambhala Press, Boston. More recently (2002), HarperCollins published his *One Dharma*.

12. RES (Resources for Ecumenical Spirituality), PO Box 85, Forest Lake MN 55025-0085, resecum@msn.com, 651-464-7489. You can get on the mailing list by writing with your request. Appendix I explains in more detail the origins and early history of Christian insight meditation.

13. Buddhist outreach regularly brings this practice into prisons and jails with proven benefits, such as lower rates of recidivism in practitioners. It is used in chemical dependency treatment in Asia. Chapter 13 describes some spiritual benefits of such contemplative practice as seen by John of the Cross.

14. *Dhammapada*, 289.

15. This can be found, among the other Beatitudes, in Matthew 5:3–10.

Chapter 3, The Carmelite Tradition of Prayer

1. Teresa's classic definition of prayer is: "For mental prayer in my opinion is nothing else than an intimate sharing between friends; it means taking time frequently to be alone with him who we know loves us." *Life*, 8,5.

2. Teresa explained her early method of prayer as an effort to keep herself in the presence of Jesus Christ. "I tried as hard as I could to keep Jesus Christ, our God and Lord, present within me, and that was my way of prayer." *Life*, 4,7. Teresa's method of prayer was not a discursive reflective one, but rather a psychological effort through faith and love to keep herself present to Christ living within her. She confessed in this same chapter and paragraph that she found difficulty with discursive meditation. Her way of prayer was simply to keep herself present through faith and love to the reality of Christ's presence within her.

3. In Chapter 26 of *The Way of Perfection*, Teresa explained her method of prayer. It offered a solution for those who, like herself, found difficulty with discursive meditation. It involves a recollecting of one's senses and directing one's attention lovingly within oneself to the Presence, the reality of God within. Teresa explained to her readers that she was not asking them to think about Christ, but to "look at him." To "look at" Christ means to remain present to the reality of Christ within our hearts. To "look at" Christ is an act of faith and love and does not necessarily mean imaging Christ with the imagination.

4. *Castle*, 1,1,1.

5. Actually, historians are uncertain about the exact date of John's birth. The closest date they come to is 1542. See *God Speaks in the Night: The Life, Times, and Teaching of St. John of the Cross* (Washington, D.C.: ICS Publications, 1991).

6. *Night I*, 10,6. In *The Living Flame of Love*, John uses the image of fire as a symbol of God's purifying love at work in contemplation.

7. *Ascent I,* 13; *Ascent II,* 7.
8. Chapter 18 further discusses Brother Lawrence.
9. Along with John of the Cross and Teresa of Avila, Therese has been named a doctor of the church, a rare honor that certifies an individual's teachings are considered worthy.

CHAPTER 4, INSTRUCTIONS FOR INSIGHT PRACTICE: PREPARATION, BREATH, BODY, THINKING

1. If you have an illness or other condition that regularly draws attention to one of these areas, it would not be a good one to choose as your primary object. The sensations of the breath might get confused with other sensations.
2. Sometimes illness or other body conditions make a place we have been using less suitable. If you believe this to be the case, discuss it with a teacher who can guide you. It is best also not to initially choose a sensitive area of your body as the primary object.
3. Chapter 6 further discusses painful sensation. For more detailed information on managing practice, see the forthcoming book by Mary Jo Meadow, *Practicing Insight Meditation: Guidance from Buddhist Writings and John of the Cross.*
4. See chapter 12 for a further discussion of the nature of thought as conventional reality. See chapter 11 to understand how John of the Cross considered thought a problem in spiritual practice.

CHAPTER 5, INSTRUCTIONS FOR INSIGHT PRACTICE: OTHER SENSES, MIND-STATES, POINTS OF FREEDOM, WALKING

1. My daughter Rebecca Bradshaw, an IMS teacher who sometimes teaches with us, likes to say, "Of course, if you are actually sitting there chirping, then you can note 'chirping.'"
2. Meditators sometimes worry if they might be "losing it" when this happens because they know that in certain kinds of mental illness people see and hear things that are not really there. The mentally ill believe such perceptions to be factual; meditators see them as a meditation phenomenon. Chapter 8 further discusses this issue.
3. You now have a name for those impulses to move that we advised you to monitor when you started watching body experiences. A more refined method for working with them follows.
4. Awareness of the type of experience we are having also comes simultaneously with the experience. Buddhists call it "perception." Your mental noting acknowledges your perception of the kind of experience you are having.
5. If you try to move slowly, you will probably lose your balance. If you pay careful attention to each part of the step, that will slow you down. The more meticulous your attention, the more slowly you will move.

6. Chapter 7 discusses getting guidance. For full details on practice and its management, see the forthcoming book by Mary Jo Meadow, *Practicing Insight Meditation: Guidance from Buddhist Writings and John of the Cross.*

CHAPTER 6, ESTABLISHING YOUR MEDITATION PRACTICE

1. If you decide to make awareness meditation part of your life, other aids like retreats help support practice. Appendix II offers a number of such aids.
2. We offer this summary because it shows how simple the practice is conceptually. The full instructions are given in the previous two chapters, and they should guide your practice.
3. Teresa of Avila was one of these people. See chapters 3 and 18.
4. U Pandita, *In This Very Life: The Liberation Teachings of the Buddha* (Boston: Wisdom Publications, 1992), 64. This listing of hindrances comes from the fifth-century *Visuddhi Magga,* a comprehensive text on Buddhist meditation. John of the Cross referred to these objects as temporal goods, and discussed the problems they can create in *Ascent III,* 18,1.
5. *Castle,* 5,3,11.
6. John delineated four passions of the soul—joy, hope, fear, and sadness. When wrongly directed, they become the problems of greed and aversion. We feel joy when we possess a good; clung to, it is greed. Greed-based hope can arise when expecting a good. Fear comes when we anticipate something unpleasant. When actually faced with an undesirable experience, aversive sadness arises. See *Ascent III,* 16,2. John is obviously not referring here to spiritual joy or to the virtue of hope. The unruly passions are desire-based phenomena, although we can have desires for acceptable as well as bad things.
7. I believe I initially heard this way of putting it, as well as the corresponding one for restlessness discussed later, from Joseph Goldstein.
8. Some Buddhist practitioners are familiar with U Pandita's eye drops as a method for staying awake. Those who have used them swear they must be pure pepper sauce. They are quite effective!
9. *Night I,* 7,4. What Kavanaugh and Rodriquez translate as "boring," Peers translates as "irksome."
10. *Way,* 19,2.
11. *Castle,* 4,3,11. She also discussed this in various other places.
12. Use a four-part primary object, alternating awareness of breath with awareness of sitting and touching. The object is then in-breath, out-breath, sitting (for the length of the in-breath), and touching (for the length of the out-breath). Do not stop breathing when noting "sitting" and "touching," but just direct your attention to awareness of sitting and touching as chapter 4 discussed.
13. Should you miss one or more days, do not give up. You can always begin again no matter how lax you have been.
14. The following unit discusses some of Thich Nhat Hanh's teachings in more detail.

15. Chapters 12 and 19 further discuss loving–kindness. To learn the practice, see Mary Jo Meadow, *Gentling the Heart: Buddhist Loving-Kindness Practice for Christians* (New York: Crossroad Publishing, 1994). To obtain a copy, see note 10 in the preface.

16. This very rich word has many meanings—including the way, the path, Truth, Reality, realities, the practice, that which supports and upholds us, and the underlying and supporting pattern of all that is. Chapter 19 further discusses Dhamma as a guiding force. Similarities to Christian understandings of both the *Logos* (Word) and the Holy Spirit are obvious.

Chapter 7, Getting Guidance in Practice

1. The following chapter sketches these stages of practice.
2. They do, of course, accept free-will donations. Some depend upon them for their livelihood.
3. India makes an interesting distinction between the teacher who guides your general spiritual life and one who teaches you a method. You usually stay with the former, a *diksha* guru, for life. You might have several of the latter, *shiksha* gurus.
4. Gotama the Buddha, *Dhammapada,* 76–77.
5. Herbert Benson (with William Proctor), *Your Maximum Mind* (New York: Avon Books, 1989), 24–47, 189–212.
6. Matthew 13:45–46.
7. Chapter 19 further discusses the Holy Spirit and Dhammoja.
8. Chapter 13 discusses this transition more fully.
9. The method is one of the great gifts of insight meditation. Some people meditate in self-developed or "loose" methods of practice that allow unconscious material to surface, but lack a method for dealing with it in a healing way. Some have "shipwrecked" in their attempts, and others have strengthened the hold this material has on them by dealing with it inappropriately.
10. Luke 18:1.

Chapter 8, The Course of Practice

1. In the section on right understanding, chapter 14 discusses the insight knowledge that arises at each of these stages.
2. *Life,* 11,7.
3. The Buddhist scriptures used a four-stage model, which we followed in the earlier edition of this book. However, the five-stage model, which is used in the Buddhist *Abhidhamma,* corresponds much more closely to Christian teachings on prayer. Since one can argue for either usage, we have adopted the five-stage model for this revision. Our first and second are the first in the four-stage model, our third is the second, our fourth the third, and our fifth the fourth.
4. Teresa was one of these. Initially she did not separate out the Prayer of Simplicity or Passive Recollection from the following Prayer of Quiet.

5. Some authors call this the Prayer of Simplicity, and others call it the Prayer of Recollection. We have put in the word "passive" in the section heading to distinguish it from the earlier-occurring Active Recollection.

6. Lectio divina is structured so that, ideally, it goes from being discursive to becoming non-discursive as we drop thinking to "rest" wordlessly in what we were reading.

7. See *Ascent II,* 14,2,4.

8. This is the case in concentrative meditation where we focus on a chosen object.

9. Teresa of Avila complained of a cacophony of noise in her head, and probably suffered from an inner ear disorder called tinnitis. See *Castle,* 4,1,10.

10. What psychologists call hallucinations, religions tend to call visions and locutions. John and Teresa considered them "supernatural" phenomena because they knew of no natural cause for them. Knowing that hallucinations occur in some mental illness, sometimes meditators fear they are losing their minds. Mentally disordered persons usually believe that the sensory events have physical reality, while meditators tend to realize that they are meditation phenomena.

11. *Ascent II,* chapters 19 and 20. This is why John put no importance on visionary experience, which is most common at this relatively early stage of practice.

12. Chapter 13 discusses signs of this transition given by John of the Cross. Buddhists also have indicators on which they rely, but which are not usually publicly discussed.

13. Chapter 2 briefly described these characteristics of earthly life, chapter 14 further discusses them, and chapter 21 focuses on no-self or essencelessness.

14. *Night I,* 13,6.

15. *Night II,* 1,1.

16. *Way,* 19,9.

17. See *Night I,* 4. The most common translations of John's work call these "impure" movements. John used the Spanish word *sensual,* which is somewhat less weighted. He did, however, seem to consider them disordered movements.

18. *Castle,* 4,2,1.

19. Teresa of Avila, *Life,* 20,4.

20. *Night II,* 1,2.

21. *Ibid.,* 2,3.

22. *Ibid.,* 7,6.

23. Mahasi Sayadaw, *The Progress of Insight: A Treatise on Buddhist Satipatthana Meditation* (Kandy, Sri Lanka: Buddhist Publication Society, 1985), 16.

24. *Night II,* 3,3; 9,4.

25. *Flame,* 1,21

26. Mahasi Sayadaw, *op. cit.,* 20.

27. *Night II,* 19,5.

28. *Ibid.,* 11,5.

29. *Canticle,* 1,22.

30. *Life,* 20,2.

31. *Night II,* 8,5.

32. *Canticle,* 11,10.
33. *Ascent III,* 20,3.

CHAPTER 9, JOHN OF THE CROSS ON PURITY OF CONDUCT: PURIFICATION OF DISORDERED APPETITES

1. *Night II,* 12,1.
2. *Ascent II,* 5,3. Chapter 11 contains the text of this teaching.
3. *Ibid.,* 5,7.
4. *Night I,* 10,6.
5. Matthew 6:24.
6. *Ascent I,* 4,2.
7. *Ibid.,* 11,6.
8. *Ibid.,* 12,5.
9. *Ibid.,* 6,6.
10. *Ibid.,* 10,4.
11. *Ibid.,* 11,4.
12. *Ibid.,* 12,6.
13. *Ibid.,* 13,3.
14. John 4:34.
15. *Ascent I,* 13,4.
16. *Ibid.,* 13,6.
17. *Ascent III,* 16,2.
18. 1 John 2:16.
19. John of the Cross, *Ascent I,* 13,9. John's original Spanish in this third counsel uses the phrase *en su desprecio,* which Kavanaugh and Rodriguez translate as "contempt for yourself." It could just as well be translated as "lower the price on yourself," "discount yourself," or "do not value yourself too highly." We interpret this phrase more as non-attachment to self rather than contempt for self. Self-contempt, at least in our current English usage, connotes a pathological condition arising from negative conditioning in childhood and adolescence. We do not believe John intended by this counsel to reinforce this negative attitude toward the self. At the same time, he very much wanted us to act, speak, and think without inordinate attachment to ourselves and to desire that others do so also.
20. Matthew 6:33.
21. *Ascent I,* 13,11–12.
22. For a discussion of transformation of desire in John of the Cross, see Constance FitzGerald, O.C.D., *Spiritual Canticle as the Story of Human Desire: Its Development, Education, Purification, and Transformation,* four cassette audiotapes (Canfield, Ohio: Alba House Communications).
23. *Ascent I,* 10,1.
24. *Ibid.,* 5,8.
25. *Ibid.,* 13,3.
26. *Ibid.,* 14,2.

CHAPTER 10, TEACHINGS OF THE BUDDHA
ON PURITY OF CONDUCT: THE GIFT OF MORALITY

1. Gotama the Buddha, *Dhammapada,* 136. See chapter 1, note 5, for an explanation of how we cite the Dhammapada.
2. *Ibid.,* 342.
3. *Ibid.,* 66, 69.
4. *Ibid.,* 162–3. Notice the similarity of the harms in cravings cited by Buddhist teachings to what John of the Cross said of disordered appetites. See *Ascent I,* 12,5.
5. "*Ganakamoggallana Sutta*: To Ganaka Moggallana," *Majjhima Nikaya,* iii.2. *Sutta* 107.3, in Bhikkhu Nanamoli and Bhikkhu Bodhi, trans., *The Middle Length Discourses of the Buddha: A New Translation of the Majjhima Nikaya* (Boston: Wisdom Publications, 1995), 874.
6. For a further discussion of this, see chapter 20.
7. *Dhammapada,* 121.
8. Morality as gift is discussed in *Anguttara Nikaya,* iv.246.
9. Thich Nhat Hanh, *Interbeing: Commentaries on the Tiep Hien Precepts* (Berkeley, Calif.: Parallax Press, 1987), 51.
10. *Ibid.,* 37.
11. These are given in various places, including "*Saleyyaka Sutta*: The Brahmins of Sala," *Majjhima Nikaya* i, 41.9. In Bhikkhu Nanamoli and Bhikkhu Bodhi. trans., *The Middle Length Discourses of the Buddha: A New Translation of the Majjhima Nikaya* (Boston: Wisdom Publications, 1995), 380–381.
12. Thich Nhat Hanh, *op. cit.,* 45.
13. *Dhammapada,* 133.
14. See "*Udumbarika-sihanada Sutta*: The Great Lion's Roar to the Udumbarikans," *Digha Nikaya,* iii.36–37. *Sutta* 25.2, in Maurice Walshe, trans., *Thus Have I Heard, The Long Discourses of the Buddha (A New Translation of the Digha Nikaya)* (London: Wisdom Publications, 1987), 385.
15. Thich Nhat Hanh, *op. cit.,* 47.
16. *Ibid.,* 54.
17. *Ibid.,* 56.
18. Buddhist teachings make no mention of homosexual behavior as forbidden; this is a debated issue among contemporary Buddhists. Many gay and lesbian people have found Buddhism and Buddhist openness to discussion of such issues appealing.
19. Thich Nhat Hanh, *op. cit.,* 57.
20. I have drawn only one objection when inviting retreat attenders to take the precepts. An elderly nun indignantly said, "Jesus never said that we can't kill bugs."
21. *Dhammapada,* 246–7.
22. *Ibid.,* 216.

CHAPTER 11, JOHN OF THE CROSS ON PURITY OF MIND: PURIFICATION OF INTELLECT, MEMORY, AND WILL

1. *Ascent I,* 2,2.
2. *Ascent II,* 5,3.
3. Numbers 24:2–17.
4. *Ascent II,* 3,1. John went on to emphasize that this is not a matter of the intellect or reason. See chapter 12 for the Buddha's views on faith, and chapter 12, note 14 for the editor's understanding of John's stance on faith.
5. John of the Cross, *Canticle,* 1,10.
6. *Ascent II,* 5,3.
7. *Ibid.,* 2,3.
8. *Ascent II,* 26,18.
9. *Ascent III,* 15, chapter title.
10. *Ibid.,* 15,1.
11. *Ibid.,* 15,2.
12. *Ibid.,* 17,2.
13. *Ibid.,* 20,3.
14. *Ibid.,* 26,5–6.
15. See chapters 17 and 18 for a more complete discussion of John's notion of first movements.
16. *Ascent II,* 22,5.
17. *Ibid.,* 7,8–9.
18. *Ibid.,* 7,11.
19. *Ibid.*
20. John 20:19–29.
21. *Ascent III,* 3,6.
22. *Ibid.,* 2,9.

CHAPTER 12, TEACHINGS OF THE BUDDHA ON PURITY OF MIND: PURIFICATION OF MENTAL CONTENTS, TRAINING THE MIND

1. This was the late William Schofield of the University of Minnesota—deeply valued teacher, mentor, and friend.
2. Thich Nhat Hanh, *Interbeing: Commentaries on the Tiep Hien Precepts* (Berkeley, Calif.: Parallax Press, 1987), 34.
3. If you want to learn *brahmavihara* practice in greater depth, see Mary Jo Meadow, *Gentling the Heart: Buddhist Loving-Kindness Practice for Christians* (New York: Crossroad Publishing, 1994). To obtain a copy, see note 10 in the preface.
4. Gotama the Buddha, *Dhammapada,* 5.
5. See chapter 19 for more information on equanimity.
6. Nhat Hanh, *op. cit.,* 42.
7. See the discussion of clear comprehension in chapter 7.
8. *Dhammapada,* 293.

9. Notice the similarity of feeling-tone to John's first movements discussed in chapters 11, 17, and 18.

10. AlanWatts, *The Wisdom of Insecurity* (NewYork: Pantheon Books, 1951); cited from 1968 paperback edition, 24.

11. I regret being unable to find the location of this citation.

12. The Buddha often told us not to believe anything we have not personally experienced. One popular accounting of this is in the Sermon to the Kalamas. It can be found in *In the Buddha's Words,* Bhikkhu Bodhi, ed. (Boston: Wisdom Publications, 2005), 88–91.

13. Watts, *loc. cit.*

14. I believe that John held similar opinions about faith. He often said that we must relinquish our notions about God—ideas, concepts, and beliefs—to go to God in dark faith, our only guide. In his *Dark Night* poem, he states that the only guide is that light burning in our hearts. So I see John saying, as Buddhists do, that faith is primarily a motivational—not a cognitive—concept; it is that confident setting out to attain that for which our hearts yearn. For more on faith—Buddhist and Christian—see Mary Jo Meadow, *Through a Glass Darkly: A Spiritual Psychology of Faith* (NewYork: Crossroad, 1996). This out-of-print book can be ordered through RES, PO Box 85, Forest Lake MN 55025-0085.You may inquire at resecum@msn.com.

15. Nhat Hanh, *op. cit.,* 39.

16. When I first heard this, I thought of Therese of Lisieux, clinging to a stair railing to keep herself from greedily going in to chat with her sister, who was Mother Superior in her convent. See Therese of Lisieux, *Story of a Soul: The Autobiography of St. Therese of Lisieux,* trans. John Clarke O.C.D. (Washington, D.C.: Institute of Carmelite Studies, 1975), 237.

CHAPTER 13, JOHN OF THE CROSS ON PURITY OF HEART: CONTEMPLATIVE PURIFICATION

1. *Night II,* 5,1.

2. *Ascent II,* 22,5.

3. *Ascent,* poem, stanzas 1,6.

4. *Night I,* explanation, 1–2.

5. See *Ascent III,* 35,7; 36,1–3; 37,2; 43,2; 44,1–4.

6. *Flame,* 3,32.

7. *Ascent II,* 12,3.

8. *Ibid.,* 14,2.

9. *Ibid.,* 12,6.

10. *Flame,* 3,32.

11. *Ibid.,* 3,33.

12. John of the Cross, *Flame,* 1,20–21.

13. John of the Cross, *Night II,* 18,3–4.
14. *Ascent III,* 2,10.
15. *Ascent III,* 2,16; the embedded scripture is Romans 8:14.
16. John of the Cross, *Flame,* 2,34.
17. John of the Cross, *Ascent,* poem, stanzas 1,2.
18. *Canticle,* 39,3.
19. *Ibid.,* 29,1.
20. *Ibid.,* 29,2.
21. *Ascent,* poem, stanza 5.
22. *Letters,* #26.
23. *Flame,* 2,10.
24. *Night II,* 12,1.
25. *Ascent II,* 15,4.

CHAPTER 14, TEACHINGS OF THE BUDDHA ON PURITY OF HEART: WISDOM, THE GOAL OF REALIZATION

1. Thich Nhat Hanh, *Interbeing: Commentaries on the Tiep Hien Precepts* (Berkeley, Calif.: Parallax Press, 1987), 27.
2. *Ibid.,* 30.
3. *Ibid.,* 32.
4. This appeared in a very early issue of *The National Catholic Reporter* newspaper. Clearly, in today's world it has more poignancy than when the first edition of this book appeared.
5. Gotama the Buddha, *Dhammapada,* 81.
6. Nhat Hanh, *op. cit.,* 49.
7. Insight knowledge unfolds across the stages of practice that chapter 8 described.
8. Chapter 20 further explores the consequences of behavior.
9. When asked to state the teachings simply, the late Thai master Ajahn Chah said, "Enjoy your favorite cup as if it were already broken."
10. The late John Brantner of the University of Minnesota, a beloved friend, mentor, and colleague, opened his seminars for divorced and bereaved persons with these words.
11. Chapter 21 discusses how coming to Nibbana relates to knowing God.
12. *Dhammapada,* 84.
13. *Ibid.,* 302.
14. For a list of some small attachments from John of the Cross, see the section on small attachments in chapter 9.
15. Chapter 21 further delves into this teaching as found in both Buddhism and the writings of John of the Cross.
16. Chapter 19 describes each of these virtues in more detail.

CHAPTER 15, JOHN OF THE CROSS AND THE BUDDHA ON PURIFICATION OF OUR BEINGS: INTEGRATIVE SUMMARY

1. *Ascent I,* 12,3.
2. *Ibid.,* 13,6.
3. Matthew 7:21.
4. Chapter 19 further explores the Buddhist notion of Dhamma.

CHAPTER 16, ABOUT PRAYER, MEDITATION, CONTEMPLATION, AND INSIGHT PRACTICE

1. In Ignatius see, for example, the five "contemplations" on Jesus' incarnation and nativity during the first day of the second week in the *Spiritual Exercises,* nos. 101–31, in George Ganss, S.J., ed., *Ignatius of Loyola: The Spiritual Exercises and Selected Works,* Classics of Western Spirituality (Mahwah, N.J.: Paulist Press, 1991), 148–53; see also discussions of the terminology, 61–63, 402 (no. 56). In John of the Cross, see *Night I,* 10,6 and 12,4; *Night II,* 5,1; *Canticle,* 13,10; and *Flame,* 3,49.
2. See *Life,* 8,5.
3. *Ascent II,* chapters 12–15.
4. Preface of Lent, I.
5. Chapter 13 discussed discursive meditation. We consider it only briefly here.
6. Herbert Benson, *The Relaxation Response* (New York: William Morrow, 1975), 78–98.
7. Some people have mixed the two types to produce a hybrid form. This began with the Maharishi when the Beatles found him. He determined to modify classical Hindu meditation so that, in his opinion, Westerners would be able to do it. Transcendental Meditation (TM) was the result. The classical Hindu tradition has little respect for TM because it frequently abandons a "concrete" object—necessary until practice is quite advanced—for what it calls "resting in the Absolute." Christian centering prayer, though done for a different motive, uses the basic TM method of holding only loose attention to a tangible meditation object.
8. For a more detailed treatment of concentrative meditation practice, both management of problems and course of development, see Mary Jo Meadow, *Gentling the Heart: Buddhist Loving-Kindness Practice for Christians* (New York: Crossroad Publishing, 1994). To obtain a copy, see note 10 in the preface.
9. *Night I,* 10,6.
10. *Ibid.,* 12,4.
11. *Flame,* 3,32.
12. John of the Cross opened his *Ascent of Mount Carmel* by indicating that he was writing for the seriously committed who are willing to do what it takes to reach the necessary nakedness of spirit for union with God. While not always the most pleasant practice, insight practice is a "fast track" that satisfies John's aim.
13. Chapter 8 described the course of practice and chapter 14 explained the insight knowledge that unfolds over the stages of practice.

14. We are not referring here to a disinclination, which can be a sign of a sluggish mind, but to actual inability. Genuine inability to note cannot be expected before the time of the Christian Prayer of Simple Union or Buddhist arising and passing away.

15. Several chapters have referred to the fruits and the paramis. Chapter 19 explains them more fully.

CHAPTER 17, ABOUT JESUS CHRIST, THE HOLY SPIRIT, AND THE CHURCH

1. Chapter 21 explores John's notion of the substance of the soul.

2. This teaching, cited in chapter 1, is from Mark 8:34–38.

3. Philippians 2:5ff.

4. This text from Philippians 3:10–11 is cited in chapter 1.

5. *Ascent II,* 7,11.

6. *Ibid.,* 7,5. John's scriptural reference is to Mark 8:34–35.

7. See the "Sketch of Mount Carmel" in *The Collected Works of St. John of the Cross,* rev. ed., trans. Kieran Kavanaugh, O.C.D., and Otilio Rodriguez, O.C.D. (Washington, D.C.: ICS Publications, 1991), 110–11.

8. *Ascent III,* 35,5.

9. *Ascent II,* 15,4. Chapter 13 contains the text of John's teaching.

10. This is one of several affirmations of faith that are spoken during the Eucharistic celebration.

11. Mark 10:45.

12. John 19:34–35.

13. John 20:22.

14. *Flame,* 4,17.

15. *Ascent II,* 5,3.

16. *Ascent III,* 2,10.

17. This is analogous to awareness of feeling-tone in Buddhist teachings. See chapter 5.

18. Chapters 4 and 5, which taught the method of practice, explained these inner movements.

19. Galatians 5:22. Chapter 19 discusses the fruits in relation to the Buddhist virtues called paramis.

20. *Nostra Aetate,* no. 2; *Ad Gentes,* no. 18. See the preface for some of the text of these documents.

21. Pope John Paul II, "A Message of Hope to the Asian People," *Origins,* March 12, 1981, 611. Quoted in James A. Wiseman, "Christian Monastics and Interreligious Dialogue," *Cistercian Studies* 27 (1992): 258.

22. Vatican Congregation for the Doctrine of the Faith, "Some Aspects of Christian Meditation," *Origins,* December 28, 1989, 492–98. Probably not coincidentally, the letter was signed by then Cardinal Ratzinger (now Pope Benedict XVI) on October 15, the feast of Teresa of Avila, and released December 14, the feast of John of

the Cross. Perhaps this quietly recommends these two Carmelite doctors of the church in the field of spirituality as teachers of authentic Christian meditation.

23. *Ascent II,* 5,3. Chapter 11 contains the text of this teaching. See also *Ascent I,* 11,2 and *Ascent II,* 5,3.

24. Vatican Congregation for the Doctrine of the Faith, no. 12.

25. *Ibid.,* no. 28.

26. *Ascent II,* 22,19.

27. Joseph Goldstein, *Insight Meditation:The Practice of Freedom* (Boston: Shambhala Publications, 1993), 47.

28. *Origins,* December 28, 1989, 497, no. 12; also, *ActaApostolicae Sedis,* 75 (March 1983): 256, and *Origins,* November 11, 1982, 359.

29. Pope John Paul II, "Beyond New Age Ideas: Spiritual Renewal," *Origins,* June 10, 1993, 59.

30. *Flame,* 3,47.

31. Pope John Paul II, "Beyond New Age Ideas: Spiritual Renewal," no. 5.

CHAPTER 18, ABOUT CARMELITE PRAYER

1. *Life,* 8,5.

2. *Ibid.,* 4,7.

3. *Ibid.,* 9,6.

4. *Ibid.,* 9,4. See also Jesus Castellano's enlightening discussion of Teresa's understanding of representing Christ in prayer in "*Teresa de Jesus nos ensefia a orar*," in Tomas Alvarez and Jesus Castellano, *Teresa de Jesus ensetianos a orar* (Burgos: Editorial Monte Carmelo, 1982), 125–26.

5. *Life,* 9,4.

6. Chapter 8 discussed this and the other stages of Christian contemplative prayer.

7. *Way,* 29,7.

8. *Ibid.,* 28,2.

9. *Ibid.,* 28,4.

10. *Foundations,* 5,2.

11. *Castle,* 4,1,7.

12. Recall that, for John, meditation was a discursive activity. When prayer became non-discursive, he held that contemplation had begun.

13. For instance, John speaks of meditation in the following texts: *Ascent II,* 15,4–5; *Night I,* 1,1; and *Flame,* 3,32ff. This is not a complete list of his texts on meditation.

14. *Ascent II,* 14,2.

15. *Flame,* 3,47.

16. *Ibid.,* 3,34.

17. *Ibid.,* 3,29ff.

18. *Ascent II,* 15,5.

19. *Flame,* 3,33.

20. *Ascent II,* 15,5.

21. If we carefully follow John's discussion of the three blind guides in the third stanza of *The Living Flame of Love,* where he wrote about the prayer of loving attention, we find that the prayer he suggested involves a process of self-emptying so that we may be receptive and disposed for the gift of contemplation. See *Flame,* 3, 28–67.

22. *Flame,* 3,46.

23. In a fine study of John of the Cross, the Carmelite author Guido Stinissen maintains that the prayer of loving attention that John favors resembles *"la meditation profonde"* (meditation in depth, an emptying form of meditation). Stinissen maintains that those who practice Zen and other forms of depth meditation do not have to pass through the classical phase of movement from working with the intellect. What is needed for those who practice depth meditation is a deepening of faith so that their prayer does not become a vague religious sentiment, but rather a true personal encounter with God. See Guido Stinissen, *Decouvre-moi ta presence: recontres avec Saint Jean de la Croix* (Paris: Editions du Cerf, 1989).

24. Brother Lawrence of the Resurrection, *Writings and Conversations on the Practice of the Presence of God,* ed. Conrad De Meester, trans. Salvatore Sciurba (Washington, D.C.: ICS Publications, 1994), 98.

25. *Flame,* 3,48.

CHAPTER 19, ABOUT CHRISTIAN GRACE AND BUDDHIST DHAMMA

1. This talk was later published as Mary Jo Meadow and Kevin Culligan, "Congruent Spiritual Paths: Christian Carmelite and Theravadan Buddhist *Vipassana," Journal of Transpersonal Psychology* 19 (1987): 181–196.

2. Usharbudh Arya, *Yoga-Sutras of Patanjali with the Exposition of Vyasa: A Translation and Commentary.* Volume 1: *Samadhi-pada* (Honesdale, Pa.: Himalayan Publishers, 1986), 243.

3. The teacher was Joseph Goldstein.

4. Swami Siddheswarananda, *Hindu Thought and Carmelite Mysticism* (Delhi, India: Motilal Banarsidass Publishers, 1998), 112.

5. *"Khandhasamyutta*: Connected Discourses on the Aggregates," *Samyutta Nikaya* iii.120. *Sutta* III.22.87, in Bhikkhu Bodhi, trans., *The Connected Discourses of the Buddha: A New Translation of the Samyutta Nikaya* (Boston: Wisdom Publications, 2000), 939. Since Dhamma is clearly a Buddhist "God-concept," the Buddha's statement could be taken as a claim to divinity. However, unlike the followers of Jesus, the early followers of the Buddha did not so interpret. Some Mahayana Buddhists consider the Buddha divine.

6. *Night I,* 13,11.

7. *Ascent II,* 29,11.

8. Galatians 5:21.

9. This is the Theravadan Buddhist list. In some other Buddhists traditions, the paramis (called *paramitas*) are given as six.

10. *Sayings,* #152

11. *Ibid., #*137.
12. Chapter 10 outlined basic Buddhist morality.
13. *Sayings, #*45.
14. *Ibid., #*72.
15. *Ascent II, 7,5.*
16. *Sayings, #*120.
17. Luke 8:15.
18. These are usually lies about our motive or intentions. Examples: "I only told her for her own good." "It must be okay since everybody is doing it." "I wasn't angry." "He needed to be brought down a peg or two."
19. *Canticle, 4,1.*
20. *Night I, 12,2.*
21. *Counsels, #*16.
22. Chapter 12 has somewhat more discussion of loving-kindness. If you want to learn a practice for developing loving-kindness, see Mary Jo Meadow, *Gentling the Heart: Buddhist Loving-Kindness Practice for Christians* (New York: Crossroad Publishing, 1994). To obtain a copy, see note 10 in the preface.
23. *Sayings, #*148.
24. *Ibid., #*147.
25. *Ibid., #*149.
26. *Ibid., #*54.
27. *Ibid., #*51.
28. *Ibid., #*85.
29. Appendix II explains sitting groups.
30. *Letters, #*17.
31. *Canticle, 36,12.*
32. *Sayings, #*109.
33. *Night II, 12,2.*
34. *Ibid., 17,2.*

CHAPTER 20, ABOUT KARMA, REBIRTH, AND PURGATORY

1. I have used the Pali language—the language of the early Buddhist scriptures—for Buddhist terms in the rest of this book. In this chapter, I use the better-known Sanskrit "karma" rather than the Pali *kamma*.
2. Matthew 25:31–46.
3. Matthew 5:26. The entire presentation runs from Matthew 25:32 to Matthew 25:46. See also Luke 12:59.
4. Matthew 12:31–32.
5. John 9:1–3.
6. 1 Corinthians 3:15.
7. Gotama the Buddha, *Dhammapada,* 243.

8. 2500 years ago, the Buddha spoke of laws governing matter, life forms, and mind. A fifth law of cause and effect is about the dispensation of the Buddhas. This is an analog to the notion of God's plan of salvation.

9. *Dhammapada,* 1, the opening verse of this collection of the Buddha's aphorisms.

10. Chapter 5 explained feeling-tone and how to work with it in meditation practice.

11. Chapters 17 and 18 discussed the notion of first movements in the teachings of John of the Cross.

12. Chapter 21 takes up the related matter of Buddhist no-self teachings.

13. *Night II,* 7,7.

14. Dante's *Divine Comedy* is readily available in many formats. Each of its sections— *Inferno, Purgatorio,* and *Paradiso*—can be purchased separately.

15. The pope did not convene the council, and was later forced to ratify it.

16. Jacques LeGoff. *The Birth of Purgatory,* translated by Arthur Goldhammer (Chicago: University of Chicago Press, 1984). See chapter 1 for "ancient imaginings," and chapter 2 for church fathers. See especially pages 61–85 on Augustine, whom LeGoff considered the principal "father" of purgatory.

17. F.X. Schouppe, *Purgatory: Explained by the Lives and Legends of the Saints* (Rockford, Ill.: Tan Books, 1986), 26–27; LeGoff, *op. cit.,* 94.

18. LeGoff, *op. cit.,* chapter 2.

19. LeGoff, *op. cit.,* 3,4. Naming purgatory a place over which the church had control gave the church a wide range of new powers over the lives of people. Purgatory became a major tool both of social control and of combating heresies—opinions that churchmen in power did not like. Eventually, this teaching led to the scandal of selling indulgences that split the Western church.

20. *Flame,* 2,25. John was obviously not endorsing belief in rebirth, but it is interesting that he referred to it as "the next life."

21. *Flame,* 1,24.

22. Chapter 6 gave the method for practicing sharing merit.

23. While formal practice does not allow this, it can be done informally. This notion is discussed briefly in Mary Jo Meadow, *Gentling the Heart: Buddhist Loving-Kindness Practice for Christians* (New York: Crossroad Publishing, 1994). To obtain a copy, see note 10 in the preface.

24. The poem by Thich Nhat Hanh from which these words come is found in many of his published works.

Chapter 21, About Buddhist No-Self and Christian Soul

1. I found this widely quoted saying by Kalu Rinpoche posted in a stairwell at Insight Meditation Society in Barre, MA.

2. *Ascent I,* 13,11.

3. See John 17:20–23.

4. *Flame,* 3,48.

5. Carl R. Rogers, *Client-centered Therapy: Its Current Practice, Implication and Theory* (Boston: Houghton Mifflin, 1951), 191.

6. See chapter 12 for the exact quote from Alan Watts, *The Wisdom of Insecurity* (New York: Pantheon Books, 1951).

7. John of the Cross, *Canticle,* 19,4.

8. Joseph Goldstein, *Insight Meditation: The Practice of Freedom* (Boston: Shambhala, 1993), 93.

9. Buddhaghosa, *The Path of Purification (Visuddhimagga),* 4th ed., trans. from the Pali by Bhikkhu Nyanamoli (Kandy, Sri Lanka: Buddhist Publication Society, 1979), XIX, 20.

10. Sayadaw U Pandita, *In This Very Life: The Liberation Teachings of the Buddha* (Boston: Wisdom Publications, 1992), 194.

11. "Khandhasamyutta: Connected Discourses on the Aggregates (The Characteristic of Non-self)," *Samyutta Nikaya* iii [66] 59 (7). In Bhikkhu Bodhi, trans., *The Connected Discourses of the Buddha: A New Translation of the Samyutta Nikaya* (Boston: Wisdom Publications, 2000), 900.

12. *Ibid.,* [67].

13. Ayya Khema, *All Of Us: Beset by Birth, Decay and Death* (Dodanduwa, Sri Lanka: Parappuduwa Nuns Island, 1987), 29.

14. #285.

15. *Flame,* 4,10.

16. Interestingly, recent reports on heart transplant patients lend much credibility to this idea. A number reported taking on different personality characteristics, which were later confirmed as having characterized their organ donor.

17. *Canticle,* 19,4.

18. *Ibid.*

19. *Ascent II,* 24,4.

20. *Flame,* 1,20.

21. *Ibid.,* 1,26.

22. *Canticle,* 14–15,14.

23. *Flame,* 1,17.

24. *Ascent II,* 32,3.

25. *Canticle,* 26,5.

26. *Ibid.,* 31,1.

27. *Night II,* 10,1.

28. *Flame,* 1,12.

29. Lewis Thomas, *The Lives of a Cell: Notes of a Biology Watcher* (New York: Penguin, 1974), 4.

30. James Bleick, *Chaos: Making a New Science* (New York: Penguin, 1987), 20–23.

31. *Flame,* 1,30.

32. *Flame,* 3,22.

33. John 12:24.

Appendix I, Developing the Silence and Awareness Retreat and Christian Insight Meditation

1. Chapter 8 contains much of this material on stages of practice, as well as some new material.

2. Mary Jo Meadow and Kevin Culligan, "Congruent Spiritual Paths: Christian Carmelite and Theravadan Buddhist *Vipassana*," *Journal of Transpersonal Psychology* 19 (1987): 181–96.

3. Thomas Merton, *The Springs of Contemplation: A Retreat at the Abbey of Gethsemani,* ed. Jane Marie Richardson (New York: Farrar, Straus, Giroux, 1992), 177. This citation from Merton was brought to our attention several years into leading the Silence and Awareness retreats. For a similar affirmation, see note 23 in chapter 18.

4. For a description in word and picture of a Christian Zen retreat, see Hugo M. Enomiya-Lassalle, *The Practice of Zen Meditation,* comp. and ed. Roland Ropers and Bogdan Snela, trans. Michelle Bromley (San Francisco: Aquarian Press, 1990). The very helpful works of American Jesuit Robert E. Kennedy, a Zen master, also discuss Zen practice in Christian context.

5. Subsequently, we discovered that the late Denys Rackley, a Carthusian monk with extensive training in vipassana, had been offering insight meditation in three- and ten-day Christian retreats since 1982. His work is described in two articles in the Boston Globe: "A Carthusian Monk Reflects on Prayer and John Lennon," by James L. Franklin, January 14, 1983, and "An Eye on Eternity: A Priest Goes East in Search of His Soul," by Richard Higgins, December 17, 1990. In his retreats, Fr. Rackley presented vipassana in the context of selected New Testament themes that he explained in light of the meditation.

6. Chapter 15 discussed some distinctions among types of contemplative prayer.

Bibliography

Abbott, Walter M., ed. *The Documents of Vatican II*. New York: America Press, 1966.

Anguttara Nikaya: Discourses of the Buddha. Nyanaponika Thera (trans.). Kandy, Sri Lanka: Buddhist Publication Society Wheel #155–158, 1970.

Anguttara Nikaya: Discourses of the Buddha. Nyanaponika Thera (trans.). Kandy, Sri Lanka: Buddhist Publication Society Wheel #208–211, 1975.

Barnes, Michael. "Theological Trends: The Buddhist-Christian Dialogue." *The Way* (England) 30 (1990): 55–64.

Benson, Herbert. *The Relaxation Response*. New York: William Morrow, 1975.

———. *Your Maximum Mind*. With William Proctor. New York: Avon Books, 1989.

Bromiley, Geoffrey W. *Theological Dictionary of the New Testament*. Abridged in one volume. Grand Rapids, Mich.: William B. Eerdmans Publishing Co., 1985.

Buddhaghosa. *The Path of Purification (Visuddhi Magga)*. Bhikkhu Nyanamoli (trans.). Kandy, Sri Lanka: Buddhist Publication Society, 1979.

Castellano, Jesus. "Teresa de Jesus nos ensfia a orar." In Tomas Alvarez and Jesus Castellano, *Teresa de Jesus ensitianos a orar*. Burgos: Editorial Monte Carmelo, 1982.

Chowning, Daniel, Kevin Culligan, and Mary Jo Meadow. *Silence and Awareness: A Retreat Experience in Christian-Buddhist Meditation*. Twelve cassette audiotapes. Kansas City, Mo.: Credence Communications.

Culligan, Kevin, and Mary Jo Meadow. *Nobody Walks Alone: Spiritual Guidance in the Carmelite Tradition*. Audiocassette program. Kansas City, Mo.: Credence Communications.

Dhammapada, The. Available in and cited from various translations and editions. Our translation relied most heavily on an unpublished manuscript of the late Bill Hamilton. One readily available translation is that of Juan Mascaro. New York: Penguin Books, 1973. Working from more than one translation helps in discerning the meaning of these aphorisms.

Dhiga Nikaya. Maurice Walshe (trans.). *Thus Have I Heard: The Long Discourses of the Buddha (A New Translation of the Digha Nikaya)*. London: Wisdom Publications, 1987.

Enomiya-Lassalle, Hugo M. *The Practice of Zen Meditation*. Comp. and ed. Roland Ropers and Bogdan Snela. Michelle Bromley (trans.). San Francisco: The Aquarian Press, 1990.

Farrelly, John. "Notes on Mysticism in Today's World." *Spirituality Today* 43 (1991): 104–18.

FitzGerald, Constance. *Spiritual Canticle as the Story of Human Desire: Its Development, Education, Purification, and Transformation*. Four cassette audiotapes. Canfield, Ohio: Alba House Communications.

Franklin, James L. "A Carthusian Reflects on Prayer and John Lennon." *Boston Globe,* January 14, 1983.

Freeman, Laurence. "Meditation." In *The New Dictionary of Catholic Spirituality*. Ed. Michael Downey. A Michael Glazier Book. Collegeville, Minn.: Liturgical Press, 1993. 648–51.

Goldstein, Joseph. *The Experience of Insight: A Simple and Direct Guide to Buddhist Meditation*. Boston: Shambhala Publications, 1987.

————. *Insight Meditation: The Practice of Freedom*. Boston: Shambhala Publications, 1993.

Goldstein, Joseph, and Jack Kornfield. *Seeking the Heart of Wisdom: The Path of Insight Meditation*. Boston: Shambhala Publications, 1987.

Higgins, Richard. "An Eye on Eternity: A Priest Goes East in Search of His Soul." *Boston Globe,* December 17, 1990.

Ignatius of Loyola. *The Spiritual Exercises and Selected Works*. Ed. George Ganss. Classics of Western Spirituality. Mahwah, N.J.: Paulist Press, 1991.

John of the Cross, St. *The Collected Works*. Rev. ed. Kieran Kavanaugh and Otilio Rodriguez (trans.). Washington, D.C.: ICS Publications, 1991.

John Paul II, Pope. "A Message of Hope to the Asian People." *Origins,* March 12, 1981, 611.

————. "Teresa of Avila: God's Vagabond." *Origins,* November 11, 1982, 358–60.

————. "Beyond New Age Ideas: Spiritual Renewal." *Origins,* June 10, 1993, 59–61.

Kennedy, Robert E. *Zen Spirit, Christian Spirit: The Place of Zen in Christian Life*. New York: Continuum, 1999.

Lawrence of the Resurrection, Brother. *Writings and Conversations on the Practice of the Presence of God*. Critical Edition by Conrad De Meester. Salvatore Sciurba (trans.). Washington, D.C.: ICS Publications, 1994.

LeShan, Lawrence. *How to Meditate: A Guide to Self-Discovery*. New York: Bantam Books, 1975.

Mahasi Sayadaw. *Practical Insight Meditation: Basic and Progressive Stages*. Kandy: Sri Lanka, Buddhist Publication Society, 1971.

————. *Progress of Insight: A Treatise on Buddhist Satipatthana Meditation*. Kandy, Sri Lanka: Buddhist Publication Society, 1985.

Majjhima Nikaya. Bhikkhu Nanamoli and Bhikkhu Bodhi (trans.). *The Middle Length Discourses of the Buddha: A New Translation of the Majjhima Nikaya*. Boston: Wisdom Publications, 1995.

Meadow, Mary Jo. *Gentling the Heart: Buddhist Loving-Kindness Practice for Christians*. New York: Crossroad, 1994. See note 10 in the preface.

————. *Through a Glass Darkly: A Spiritual Psychology of Faith*. New York: Crossroad, 1996. See note 14 in chapter 12.

Meadow, Mary Jo, and Kevin Culligan. "Congruent Spiritual Paths: Christian Carmelite and Theravadan Buddhist *Vipassana*." *Journal of Transpersonal Psychology* 19 (1987): 181–96.

Merton, Thomas. *The Springs of Contemplation: A Retreat at the Abbey of Gethsemani.* Ed. Jane Marie Richardson. New York: Farrar, Straus, Giroux, 1992.

Nhat Hanh, Thich. *Interbeing: Commentaries on the Tiep Hien Precepts.* Berkeley, Calif.: Parallax Press, 1987.

Nyanaponika, Thera. *The Heart of Buddhist Meditation: A Handbook of Mental Training Based on the Buddhist Way of Mindfulness.* London: Rider Press, 1962.

O'Hanlon, Daniel J. "Integration of Spiritual Practices: A Western Christian Looks East." *Journal of Transpersonal Psychology* 13 (1981): 91–112.

Rahula, Walpola. *What the Buddha Taught.* Rev. ed. New York: Grove Weidenfeld, 1974.

Ruiz, Federico, et al. *God Speaks in the Night: The Life, Times, and Teaching of St. John of the Cross.* Kieran Kavanaugh (trans.). Washington, D.C.: ICS Publications, 1991.

Samyutta Nikaya. Bhikkhu Bodhi (trans.). *The Connected Discourses of the Buddha: A New Translation of the Samyutta Nikaya.* Boston: Wisdom Publications, 2000.

Sayadaw U Pandita. *In This Very Life: The Liberation Teachings of the Buddha.* Boston: Wisdom Publications, 1992.

———. *On The Path to Freedom: A Mind of Wise Discernment and Openness.* Selangor, Malaysia: Buddhist Wisdom Centre, 1995.

Stinissen, Guido. *Decouvre-moi to presence: recontres avec Saint Jean de la Croix.* Paris: Editions du Cerf, 1989.

Swami Siddheswarananda. *Hindu Thought and Carmelite Mysticism.* Delhi, India: Motilal Banarsidass Publishers, 1998.

Teasdale, Wayne. "Interreligious Dialogue since Vatican II: The Monastic-Contemplative Dimension." *Spirituality Today* 43 (1991): 119–33.

Teresa of Avila, St. *The Collected Works.* Kieran Kavanaugh and Otilio Rodriguez (trans.). 3 vols. Washington, D.C.: ICS Publications, 1976–1985.

Vatican Congregation for the Doctrine of the Faith. "Letter to the Bishops of the Catholic Church on Some Aspects of Christian Meditation." *Origins,* December 28, 1989, 492–98.

Watts, Alan. *The Wisdom of Insecurity.* New York: Pantheon Books, 1951; paperback ed., 1968.

Wiseman, James A. "Christian Monastics and Interreligious Dialogue." *Cistercian Studies* 27 (1992): 257–71.

Index

About Wisdom

WISDOM PUBLICATIONS, a nonprofit publisher, is dedicated to making available works exploring Buddhism and East-West themes for the benefit of all.

To learn more about Wisdom, or to browse books online, visit our website at www.wisdompubs.org.

You may request a copy of our catalog online or by writing to this address:

Wisdom Publications
199 Elm Street
Somerville, Massachusetts 02144 USA
Telephone: 617-776-7416 • Fax: 617-776-7841
Email: info@wisdompubs.org • www.wisdompubs.org

The Wisdom Trust

As a nonprofit publisher, Wisdom is dedicated to the publication of books for the benefit of all sentient beings and dependent upon the kindness and generosity of sponsors in order to do so. If you would like to make a donation to Wisdom, you may do so through our website or our Somerville office. If you would like to help sponsor the publication of a book, please write or email us at the address above.

Thank you.

Wisdom is a nonprofit, charitable 501(c)(3) organization affiliated with the Foundation for the Preservation of the Mahayana Tradition (FPMT).